**"I told you," he said, his voice suddenly low.
"Give me the verse and you're free."**

Harry loomed over her, heating the air between them. She
wanted to spit at him, to simply laugh and walk away. But
inexplicably, caught like cornered prey, her body suddenly
remembered. It wouldn't move; wouldn't fight. It began to
soften, to open, to *want,* and she hadn't wanted in so long
she'd forgotten the feel of it.

Somehow she must have betrayed her momentary weakness, because suddenly he was smiling like a wolf.

"On the other hand," he murmured, leaning even closer,
too close, only small inches away, "maybe you want me to
find it myself. Shall I look for it? Should I strip you myself until I can see every inch of milky white skin? Should
I search you, slipping my hands under your breasts to make
sure you haven't tucked it inside, where it would be warm
and damp?"

She couldn't breathe. She couldn't tell if it was fury, fear,
or arousal. She couldn't breathe because he was taking the
last of her air. She couldn't think because he was too close.

"I could do it," he whispered, his mouth next to her ear.
"All I'd have to do is kiss you, right here behind your ear.
You'd let me do anything, then. Wouldn't you, Kate?"

Praise for Eileen Dreyer's

Never a Gentleman

"Exquisite characterization; flashes of dry, lively wit; marvelous villains; and a dark, compelling plot that unfolds in tantalizing ways."

—*Library Journal*

"A pure joy to read! Dreyer displays her phenomenal sense of atmosphere in an emotionally powerful and beautifully rendered love story...the consummate storyteller makes the conventional unconventional. Combining beautifully crafted, engaging characters with an intriguing mystery adds depth."

—*RT Book Reviews*

"As always, Ms. Dreyer has written an engrossing story which will entice the reader into the world of the Regency...If you loved *Barely a Lady*, you won't want to miss the second book of the series."

—FreshFiction.com

"Superb...an intoxicating read. If not having the first book stops you from reading this one, get the first one. The next book promises to be just as exciting and sexy as this one, so just go and buy all of them. You won't want to miss out!"

—TheRomanceReadersConnection.com

"Another winner...will have readers experiencing the entire gamut of emotions and turning the last page with a sigh of satisfaction...Fans of historical romance won't want to miss this one. *Never a Gentleman* is now on my keeper shelf next to *Barely a Lady*, and I'm saving a spot for ALWAYS A TEMPTRESS... Those Drake's Rakes know how to sweep a lady off her feet, so start reading this series and get swept away."

—TheRomanceDish.com

"An enjoyable Regency romantic suspense with twists and spins... fast-paced with a solid mystery subplot to enhance the romance."

—GenreGoRoundReviews.blogspot.com

"Eileen Dreyer writes fascinating characters who are real and not Regency cut-outs... Grace is an admirable heroine, strong and loving, and her slow blossoming... is one of the best features of the book."

—LikesBooks.com

"The story was great, the emotions were incredible and kept me reading to discover who the traitor was."

—NovelReaction.com

"Nice cameos by several beloved characters from the previous novel... A delightful look at the society... during this period of England's history."

—NightOwlRomance.com

Barely a Lady

One of *Publishers Weekly*'s Best Books of 2010
A Top Ten *Booklist* Romance of the Year
One of *Library Journal*'s Best Five Romances of the Year

"Five hearts! Ms. Dreyer definitely knows how to write one passionate and drama-filled story!...A book that keeps you madly flipping through the pages, desperate to know what is going to happen next...Fans of the genre will fall in love with it."

—AJourneyofBooks.halfzero.net

"A beautiful story [with] an amazing supporting cast of characters...a wonderful start to a new series."

—TheFictionEnthusiast.blogspot.com

"Plenty of danger and intrigue...*Barely a Lady* will surely be a hit with romance fans."

—TheThriftyThings.blogspot.com

Also by Eileen Dreyer

Never a Gentleman
Barely a Lady

Always A
Temptress

Eileen Dreyer

FOREVER

NEW YORK BOSTON

Copyright © 2011 by Eileen Dreyer
Excerpt from *Barely a Lady* © 2010 by Eileen Dreyer

Forever
Hachette Book Group
237 Park Avenue
New York, NY 10017
www.HachetteBookGroup.com

Forever is an imprint of Grand Central Publishing.
The Forever name and logo are trademarks of Hachette Book Group, Inc.

The publisher is not responsible for websites (or their content) that are not owned by the publisher.

Printed in the United States of America

First Edition: October 2011

10 9 8 7 6 5 4 3 2 1

To E. Lawrence Helm Jr. Aka: Larry, Stink, Dad, Coach, the Singer with the Band, 1921–2011; the man by whom I gauge all other romance heroes. I miss you, Daddy.

Acknowledgments

First and foremost, to all my librarian friends, who have so consistently supported and encouraged me. Especially John Charles, Kristen Ramsdell, Bette-Lee Fox, Joanne Hamilton-Selway, Mary Kay Fosse, and the best research librarian on the planet, the Dowager Duchess of Little Rock, Sally Hawkes.

To everyone who helped make the research for this book fun, with special apologies to Lieutenant John Nurgood of the 52nd Light Infantry, who actually did lead the Forlorn Hope up the breach in the walls of Ciudad Rodrigo. He, too, survived, though badly wounded. For his bravery, Wellington awarded him the sword of the French commandant of Ciudad Rodrigo.

To the usual suspects: The Divas, the Convocation group, the Beau Monde for Regency trivia above and beyond the call of *Jeopardy!*, and Jan and Judy and all the crew at Wired Coffee, my deadline home. To my family at Jane Rotrosen: Andrea Cirillo and Christina Hogrebe. My family at Grand Central: Amy Pierpont, Lauren Plude, Samantha Kelly, Anna Balasi, Brianne Beers, Jillian Sanders, the amazing Claire Brown, who gives me the most luscious covers, and Isabel Stein, who always cleans up my continuity.

To my real family. You're the only ones who can make me miss a deadline. I love you all madly. And to Rick, who has been sharing this ride for thirty-seven years. I love you most of all.

Always A Temptress

Prologue

September 1815
Dorsetshire, England

Whoever said that no good deed goes unpunished must have been well acquainted with Katie Hilliard. No, Major Sir Harry Lidge corrected himself as he trudged into Oak Grove Manor's Grand Salon to see her holding court by the front window. Not Hilliard. It was Seaton now. Lady Catherine Anne Hilliard Seaton, Dowager Duchess of Murther. But make no mistake about it. The dowager wasn't the good deed. She was the punishment.

It had been the good deed that had brought Harry to Oak Grove in the first place. Well, he amended, considering the other occupants of the ornate gold-and-white room: part good deed, part official business, neither of which he was up to right now.

Not that he wasn't happy to attend his friend Jack's wedding. He was. He was even glad to spend time with the other members of Drake's Rakes, who had gathered for the week-long celebration. Not only were they all excellent fellows, they were some of the best minds available to pit against a band of traitors intent on toppling the government.

Which was the official part of the visit. Marcus Belden, Earl of Drake, the leader of their group, had decided that Jack's wedding was the perfect cover for a strategy meeting. Unfortunately, the gathering had also drawn an unexpected guest. The Surgeon, the most feared assassin in Europe, had made an appearance on the estate, just about the time someone tried to murder Harry's friend Grace Hilliard.

Harry was just returning from a fruitless search for the man with Grace's husband, Diccan, and Jack Wyndham, Earl of Gracechurch. At any other time, Harry would have been impatient to get back out and search. He would have demanded the men retreat to Gracechurch's den so they could rehash what they knew about the threat to both the Crown and his friends, preferably over cigars and whisky. But all he could think of today was that come what may, as soon as the wedding was over, he was going the hell home.

As if hearing Harry's thoughts, Kate turned to watch him lead the other men into the room. "There you all are," she caroled, busy trying to wrest a silver flask from the smiling Lord Drake. "Marcus won't give my back my flask. I expect you to rally to my cause."

Alongside Harry, Diccan Hilliard chuckled. "One thing I can say for you, cuz," he greeted her. "You always have your priorities in hand." Dropping a kiss on Kate's cheek, he walked by to join Grace on the gold settee.

Kate's priorities being herself, Harry thought sourly, stopping in the doorway. They had an assassin on the loose, Grace was still recovering from being poisoned, and here was Kate, brangling over a whisky flask.

"But every girl should have her own flask," she was saying, her sensual green eyes glinting with mischief as she turned back to her victim.

The leader of their merry little band, Marcus, was suavely blond, elegant to a fault, and stood a full foot taller and at least five stone heavier than Kate. Harry knew that banty cock stance of Kate's, though: hand on hip, head back, breasts thrust forward. Marcus might as well hand the flask over now. She was going to harass him until she got it back.

"I'll get you a new one," Marcus assured her, keeping the flask just out of her reach. "Besides, the portrait inside is wasted on you. Let me ogle it." Leaning close, he flashed a slow grin. "Since you won't let me ogle you."

She laughed, slapping his arm. "Don't be a nodcock. There is no comparison. And the inscription! 'Is not the fruit sweet, my first love?' Really." She wrinkled her pretty nose. "If that truly is Minette in that painting, her fruit was plucked so long ago, it's surely long since rotted."

Harry wanted to spank Kate for her thoughtlessness. Both Jack and Diccan looked away, their wives equally uncomfortable. The woman depicted in the flask's miniature had been mistress to both men, and betrayed each.

"Oh, I don't know, Kate, " Harry couldn't help muttering. "If you could tell how long ago a woman lost her...freshness by a portrait, yours would look like a pox victim. Instead, as any man in London can tell you, it looks quite...perky."

If he'd expected her to be upset, he was disappointed. Instead, she laughed, clapping her hands. "Have you seen it, Harry? Tell us everything."

"Is Kate really painted naked?" Grace asked, looking more worried than Kate.

"As the day she was born."

"Someone was naked," Kate corrected him. "But it

wasn't me. I would love to see what the artist thinks I look like, though. Is it really hanging in a gaming hell?"

"You're saying it's a hoax," Harry challenged.

She quirked a wry eyebrow. "Disappointed, Harry?"

"Skeptical."

Her smile grew suggestive. "Too bad you'll never know for sure."

Harry had to admit that the painting hadn't conveyed that certain something that set Kate apart. A Pocket Venus with gleaming chestnut hair and cat-green eyes, she had a body that even clothed would have had the pope reconsidering his vow of celibacy. She was, in fact, every erotic fantasy a man could have, and she knew it.

Harry wasn't even within ten feet of her, and his body was reacting: his blood thickened and slowed; the pulses throbbed heavy in his throat. His cock twitched impatiently, and his muscles tautened, anticipating the lunge into sex. On the other hand, when he'd stood among the crowds in McMurphy's staring up at the lush peaches-and-cream tones of the lounging Kate Seaton, he'd felt nothing more than irritation.

"We need to get them to take that travesty down," Grace urged Kate, her plain face pursed in distress. "You don't want to upset your brother."

Kate's smile was oddly gentle. "My brother was born upset, Grace. One more surprise isn't going to overload his heart. Besides. I had nothing to do with it."

Harry decided that now wasn't the time to call her a liar.

"It's too bad, really," Kate mused on. "My siblings seem to have missed out on the famous Hilliard charm, which has left them all unforgivably judgmental. I choose to believe it is an aberrancy, since, of course, I am the epitome of charm. As, oddly, are all of my nieces and nephews. When they can escape their parents, they are quite good company. It's quite a puzzle."

Suddenly she flashed a bright smile. "But enough about me. What did you find?"

Evidently the discussion about the painting was over.

Jack's fiancée, Olivia, turned to him. "The Surgeon?"

Harry could hear the sharp worry Olivia tried to mask. She, too, had suffered at the assassin's hands. It was impossible to miss the ropy red scar that stretched from her neck to her hairline from the Surgeon's knife.

Jack kissed her. "I'm sure he's scarpered. I still have the men out looking, though."

She smiled, but her eyes were strained. "Then we don't know why he was here."

"He was here to try and hurt Diccan," Grace said, plucking at her sleeves. Considering the fact that she was still a sickly pale green from the poison that had almost killed her, Harry thought her generous. But then, Grace had always saved her concern for others, and Diccan had been implicated and arrested for the poisoning. Only his status and Harry's supervision were keeping him out of gaol.

"I'm not in the least injured," Diccan assured her with a kiss. "All they managed to do was make me even more determined to find that bedamned poem and use it to take down the Lions."

Drake shook his head. "Still say it's a bloody stupid name for a bunch of traitors."

"It may be stupid," Jack said, "but they've been one step ahead of us until now. We need to find out what they mean to do before they manage to kill Wellington."

Still standing by the window, Kate huffed. "They're planning to install themselves on the throne."

"They plan to put Princess Charlotte on the throne," Marcus corrected, "and rule through her. Personally I'd almost let them do it, just to see how quickly she confounds them. I don't think our heir apparent is as malleable as they believe."

"Well," Jack said, abruptly standing. "For the moment, there is nothing we can do. Guards are posted, Whitehall has been notified, and we have a wedding to enjoy." Reaching down, he took Olivia's hand. "My love, why don't we check on the children?"

From the answering smile on Olivia's face, his words were obviously some personal code. Taking his hand, she followed him out of the room, her only farewell a quick wiggle of her fingers.

"Excellent idea," Diccan agreed, bending over to pick up his still-ailing wife. "Come along, Grace. I'm taking you upstairs where you'll be safe till we find him."

And that quickly, the parlor emptied out, leaving Harry behind with Kate. "You'd better hurry," he couldn't help taunting her. "You're letting Drake escape."

Flashing a siren's smile, she stepped up so close that her breasts almost brushed his waistcoat. "No, I'm not," she assured him, fluttering her eyelashes up at him. "Because Drake doesn't want to escape."

Harry struggled mightily, but he couldn't evade the seductive pull of her scent, exotic flowers and vanilla. Her body. The purr of her voice. He was no more immune to her now than he had been ten years ago.

She *tsked*. "Too bad, Harry," she said, running a finger up his Rifleman green uniform tunic. "You had your chance. And nobody gets more than one."

"Believe me," Harry assured her through gritted teeth. "Once was quite enough."

Her smile fixed in place, she swung out the door in a swirl of peacock blue. Harry remained where he was, his posture parade-ground rigid until the moment he heard her heels clatter up the great staircase. Then, with a soft groan, he slumped onto one of the settees and dropped his head in his hands. Damn it. He didn't have the stamina for her.

He probably shouldn't have come to Oak Grove at all. He was too tired to think and too worn to be patient. It had been three months since Quatre Bras. The shrapnel he'd taken under his ribs still bedeviled him, and nightmares kept him from sleeping. Add Kate to the mix, and it was a short trip to fury.

He should go upstairs and lie down. He wouldn't sleep. But maybe he could just lie back and stare up at the cherubs that cavorted on his ceiling for a while, clear his head of Kate and assassins and the past ten years. Maybe he could spend a little time contemplating what he planned to do now that he was selling his commission.

That almost got a smile out of him. His mother was back home, waiting to feed him into insensibility. He had nieces and nephews he hadn't even met yet. He deserved a few months of lounging around the house before setting off again, for once free of responsibility and schedule and command. From now on the only things he planned to be accountable for were his sketchbook, his protractor, and his boots. Let somebody else sort out the world.

He didn't know how long he'd been sitting there fantasizing about his future when he heard it—a quick, echoing crack. His first muzzy thought was, *I know that sound*. His second was to run. It still took him half a dozen heartbeats to connect the two.

"Bloody hell," he suddenly snapped and jumped up. Pain shot through his side, and he clamped his arm to his ribs.

Of course he knew the sound. It was a gunshot, somewhere in the house. Adrenaline coursed sluggishly through him as he thundered down the corridor toward the grand staircase. As always happened in action, time seemed to stretch out like taffy. He noticed that the sun poured through the front windows, lighting the dust motes into tumbling fireflies. He could smell the faint whiff of beeswax and lemon, and his boots slid on the highly polished marble floor. He heard shouts, more clattering feet.

He'd just reached the first stair when new sounds intruded. Shattering glass. A scream. And then, somewhere outside, the sickening sound of thuds.

Oh, hell. Without much of a thought, he spun around and headed out the front door instead.

The activity had come from the far side of the building. He ran across the lawn as if voltigeurs were on his heels. When he turned the corner, he looked up, then down. Halfway down the house a white window sash dangled against the brick, shattered and swaying. The glass was gone, shards of it still spinning slowly toward the ground. Below, the boxwoods were crushed, two bodies flung over them like old laundry.

Harry ran for the one he recognized. "Diccan? Diccan!"

Diccan had been struggling to get up. At the sound of Harry's voice, he slumped back onto the ground and lay there panting. It took only one look at the other body to know it was dead. Bloody froth stained his face, his eyes were fixed and opaque, and there was a jagged branch sticking straight out of his chest. Recognition dawned and Harry gasped. The body was none other than the Surgeon himself. Dead.

But that would wait. Dropping to his knees, he quickly assessed his friend's injuries. Scrapes, a couple of lumps, and an oddly twisted forearm. Damn lucky, considering.

"You going to live, old man?" he asked.

Diccan offered a wry smile. "'Fraid so. Surgeon's come a cropper."

Harry shook his head. "Too bad."

He could hear more people stampeding through the house. Diccan must have heard it, too, because suddenly he looked frantic. Grabbing Harry's sleeve, he tried to pull himself up. "Harry. I think Kate is in danger."

For a second, he froze. "Kate? God's sake, why?"

"Something the Surgeon said. 'The whore has the verse.' Minette isn't the only one who's called a whore. At least not by some people I know."

Harry swore he stopped breathing. "She's involved in all this?"

"I think so."

"Then she's definitely in danger," Harry said, unable to forget Kate's self-satisfied smile. "If she's a traitor, I'll kill her myself."

Chapter 1

Three days later

If there was one thing that showed Kate Seaton's life up for what it was, it was a wedding. Kate loved weddings, especially if good friends were involved. She loved the flowers, the thumping organ music, and the sloppy sentiment that brought handkerchiefs out to be waved like white flags of surrender. She especially loved the smiles. Everyone should smile at weddings. Everyone should have a wedding to smile about.

Which was why once she ate her surfeit of lobster patties and succumbed to the obligatory hug from the happy couple, she escaped as fast as a thief purloining silver. After all, the sentiment expressed on such a nice day should never be envy or cynicism.

Such had been the case today. She had attended Jack and Olivia's wedding, and they were friends; good friends whose happiness she could hardly resent, their joy hard-won and universally celebrated. Jack had looked handsome and stalwart as he'd said his vows, Olivia lovely and honest-to-God

glowing, as every bride should. Kate had joined wholeheart-
edly in the celebration. And then, at the first opportunity, she
had run.

She refused to think that, in doing so, she'd abandoned
not only her cousin Diccan but her friend Grace. She might
not have forgiven herself if it had only been the Surgeon's
death they'd been dealing with. But then, in a horrific twist
no one could have foreseen, Diccan had lost his father.
Worse, it seemed that Grace had lost her marriage. Kate
would have stayed to help, if she could have done any good.
But the animosity between her and her family would have
only made Diccan's burden worse. As for Grace, Kate kept
thinking that maybe without their friends there to smooth the
way, Grace and Diccan would learn to rely on each other and
rebuild their marriage.

Pulling on her gloves, Kate stepped out of the door of
the Angel Inn and into the gray afternoon. Guildford was
bustling, as always, situated as it was on the main London–
Portsmouth road. Of its two coaching inns, Kate had always
preferred the smaller Angel on High Street with its cozy
half-timbered facade and efficient staff. It never took longer
than twenty minutes to change out the horses and down a
cup of tea.

Today seemed to be different. When she stepped out into
the cobbled yard, her coach was nowhere to be seen. A stage
was being unloaded, with much shouting and banging, and
behind it a curricle waited. Kate tapped her feet, impatient to
be away.

From her left came the sound of a muffled sob. She
smiled. "Bea," she gently chastised her companion, laying a
hand on the older woman's arm. "It is perfectly bourgeois to
continue crying over a two-day-old wedding."

If Kate enjoyed the pomp of weddings, Bea positively

wallowed. She hadn't stopped crying since they'd walked into the tiny Norman church of St. Mary in Bury to find it bursting with friends and late-summer flowers.

"Odysseus and Penelope," her friend inexplicably answered, dabbing determinedly at her eyes with one of the aforementioned flags of surrender, this one edged in the honeybees Bea so loved to embroider on things.

"Yes," Kate answered, giving her a squeeze. "It was particularly satisfying to see Jack and Olivia married, after all the years they'd been apart."

"Devonshire," Bea said, casting soulful eyes down at Kate.

This meaning Kate had to work for. "Devonshire? The duke? Was he invited?"

Bea glared, which on the tall, elegantly silver-haired woman was formidable. "Georgianna."

Kate frowned, wondering what the late Duchess of Devonshire could have to do with the newly minted Earl and Countess of Gracechurch. Georgianna had been married to a cold fish who'd kept his mistress and children in the same house as his legitimate family. All Jack had done was divorce his wife and take five years to rectify the mistake.

"Unfair?" Kate guessed.

Bea beamed.

"To whom?" Kate asked, now cognizant of the looks that passed among the various travelers and ostlers who cluttered up the courtyard. She had to admit, following Bea's unique conversational style could indeed be distracting. "Jack and Olivia? How could it be unfair that they're finally happy?"

This time Bea gave Kate an impatient huff, and there was no mistaking her meaning. Kate, who never got misty-eyed, nearly succumbed.

"Oh, Bea," she said, wishing she were tall enough to give her stately friend a smacking kiss. "How can you think my life is unfair? What more could I want than money, freedom, and my dearest friend to share them with?"

Bea sniffed. "Half loaf."

"Not at all, darling. Or is it you?" She leaned close and whispered. "Do you long for an amour? Mayhap a young *cicisbeo* who would squire you about on his arm? General Willoughby would snap you up in a minute, if you just let him."

Bea's laugh was more a snort, but Kate saw the pain behind the humor. Bea thought no one would want her, no matter her impeccable lineage and bone-deep aristocratic beauty. Not only was Bea into her seventies, but a few years earlier her brain had suffered a terrible injury that left her speech so tortured, many days Kate was the only one who understood her.

But Kate also knew that, like her, Bea couldn't tolerate coddling. So with brisk fingers she pulled out Bea's signature handkerchief and dabbed away the last of the old woman's tears. "Now then, my girl, we need to be going. After all, you're the one who committed us to Lady Riordan's memorial service tomorrow."

Immediately Bea's expression folded into pity. "Poor lambs."

Kate nodded. "At least Riordan has finally accepted the truth and declared her dead. Now maybe the children can move on." She shuddered. "I can think of few things I find less appealing than drowning."

Just then, the coach clattered around the corner, the Murther lozenge shining against the black lacquered panels. The horses were unfamiliar, but they were handsome bays that seemed to be pulling hard at the reins.

"Your Grace," one of the postboys said, bowing low as he opened the door.

Kate smiled and let him hand her into the carriage.

She had just settled and turned to help Bea when suddenly she heard a shout, and the coach lurched. She was thrown back in her seat. The door slammed. The horses whinnied and took off, as if escaping a fire.

Furious, Kate tried to right herself without success. How dare they abuse the horses that way? How dare they leave Bea stranded in the coaching yard, her hand out, her mouth open, still waiting to get into the coach?

The coach turned on two wheels and skidded through the archway. Kate could hear the clatter of the horses' hooves against the cobbles, the scrape of stone against the coach sides. She heard the urgent cries of the coachman and thought, suddenly, that it didn't sound like Bob Coachman.

It took her a few tries before she managed to sit back up. She pounded on the roof to get the coachman's attention. No one responded. The coach didn't slow; in fact, it sped up, the horses clattering up High Street, their tack jangling like Christmas bells. It didn't occur to Kate to be frightened. She was still too angry, too anxious for Bea, who simply could not be left alone in a coaching inn.

"Blast you, stop!" she shouted, pushing at the trap.

It was wedged shut. She pounded again on the roof. The coach sped on, rocking from side to side and throwing her off balance. "I am a duchess!" she yelled, resorting to the title she so loathed in an effort to get his attention. "Do you know what will happen to you if you don't set me down *immediately*?"

In all truth, probably nothing. Her brother Edwin, the current Duke of Livingston, would say she deserved it. Her stepson Oswald, now Duke of Murther, would be delighted by the mistreatment. She had never gotten on well with either. She had to try, though. She had to get back to Bea.

The carriage made another precarious turn and then straightened onto what Kate thought might be a turnpike. She barely caught the strap in time to keep from falling again. She already felt bruised. She couldn't imagine what injuries she would collect before the idiot driving her coach finally brought it to a halt.

That was the thought that finally gave her pause. What idiot? Brought it to a halt where? Why hadn't he paid attention to her? Why hadn't he so much as slowed through a busy town? She could hear shouting outside, and feared for nearby pedestrians. She tried to pull open the window shades, but they wouldn't budge. She heard a crash and more shouting and cringed.

"Are you mad?" she cried, rapping again against the roof. "Stop this thing!"

Could it be a kidnapping? She was certainly wealthy. But who in their right mind would think anyone would pay to get her back?

"Did you hear me before?" she called. "I said I'm a duchess. I'm a *rich* duchess!" It had to be good for something. "Put me down now and I'll double whatever fee you're being paid. Better yet, take me to my brother the duke, and he'll triple it!"

The words were barely out of her mouth before she froze. *Her brother.*

Suddenly her mind shuddered to a halt. Oh, God. Edwin. He'd been threatening for years to put her away for what he considered behavior unbecoming a Hilliard. Had he seen the painting? Was that what this was all about?

Kate refused to panic. She categorically repudiated the idea that her brother had the power to incarcerate her for something she had no part in. And when she saw him, she would tell him so.

On the other hand, it would probably be better all around if she didn't have to face him at all. She needed to get away before he did something irrevocable.

The coach was moving too fast, its balance precarious. She was holding on to the strap, and still being battered around. She would probably kill herself if she leapt. She laughed out loud. There were worse things than a split head, and this little jaunt threatened her with most of them. She would jump and happily take her chances.

She was still too furious to really be properly terrified. Which meant it was time to act. Pulling in a steadying breath, she crossed herself like a papist and reached for the door handle.

It didn't move. She jiggled it. She yanked. She tried the other one. Nothing. Somehow they had secured the doors, preventing her from escaping. Thinking she could at least alert people passing by, she attempted again to pull up the leather shades, only to find them all nailed in place. She was truly imprisoned.

For the first time, she was beginning to realize how desperate her situation was. Damn Edwin to hell.

She needed to get word to Diccan. He would intercede. He could at least threaten Edwin with the kind of public disgrace her brother loathed.

Diccan was thirty miles away burying his father. Too far for a quick rescue. Much too overwhelmed by the sudden death of his father to have any attention left for Kate.

She sighed, hating the shaky sound of it. She hated being out of control. She had long since sworn that she would never be at the mercy of another human being. She would never again know this feeling of helplessness.

She should have known better. She'd never had that kind of luck before. Why should it start now?

"Please," she whispered out loud, knowing it was a prayer that wouldn't be heard.

* * *

Back at the inn, people were just beginning to realize that there was something wrong. The ostlers had certainly seen carriages speed through the archway before. There was an entire generation of young bucks who refused to leave any other way. The bystanders weren't even particularly surprised to see the elderly lady standing flat-footed by the door, her hand still out, her mouth open and emitting garbled noises that made no sense. Obviously the young lady she'd been talking to had departed mid-conversation. Unsettling even for people who weren't dicked in the nob, like the old gal seemed to be.

A few people frowned when the old woman turned back and forth and cried out, "Sabine women," her hand still pointing toward the departed carriage. A few more shook their heads, sorry to see such a pitiful thing right there in public.

But when she started to sing, everybody stopped and stared. It wasn't just that she was singing "Cherry Ripe," which shouldn't have ever been heard on the tongue of such a dignified old lady. It wasn't even that she was singing the wrong words. It was that even with the wrong words in a tune she shouldn't know, it was beautiful.

"Thrasher, come!" she sang, head back, hands out. "Thrasher, come! Lady Kate, follow the way! The carriage has her! Follow the way, Thrasher come!"

And just as if she were making any kind of sense at all, suddenly a motley gaggle of men in crimson-and-gold livery came thundering around the corner from the stables and headed for the old woman.

"That way I say!" the old woman sang, waving toward the street where the carriage had just disappeared. "Four horses brown, a driver strange. Follow the way, Thrasher, go!"

And darned if one of them didn't respond. Without pausing in his tracks, a thin, sharp-featured boy waved at the old girl and took off after that carriage like a hare at the sound of a gun. As for the old lady, she just stood there, tears running down her cheeks as the other men circled her, her own mismatched army. It seemed she was finished singing. The people who had stopped to listen shook their heads and went back to their business.

"Well now," the inn's head groom said, turning back to his stable. "Wasn't that somethin'?"

*   *   *

Kate frantically searched the coach. Not for escape; she knew the coach was too well made to be easily pulled apart. For weapons. It was almost impossible, and she knew she'd be bruised head-to-toe from trying, but even as she was thrown around, she rifled through the cushions and side compartments, ripping and tugging until the inside of the coach looked as if a mad animal had been caught inside.

Not so different, she thought, feeling more frantic as she failed to secure so much as a rusty spring with which to defend herself. She was left with three hat pins and her shoes. On the other hand, she had used hat pins to great effect on more than one occasion.

If only she could rip through enough of the coach to see daylight. The coach was beginning to close in on her, all the sunlight barricaded away, leaving only shadow and speed. Even throwing herself under the wheels seemed to be a better option than simply surrendering herself to the dark.

Bastard, she kept repeating to herself, although of any insult she could rain on her brother's head, that would certainly be the most unlikely. Edwin truly was the one and only Duke of Livingston, holder of all titles and privileges, born to the strawberry leaves, and certainly happy to remind you if you forgot.

He was nothing like their father, who had been a good duke, a responsible man loyal to his people and generous to his community. That duke had truly been mourned when he died. When Edwin went, Kate had the feeling there would be a lot of show and no sincerity.

The problem was, he still had the power. And that meant, since he was head of her family, he was the male legally in charge of her life.

She worked for hours, tearing the coach apart like a starving woman looking for the last bit of cheese. She unearthed two blankets, a writing desk, a tiny bottle of scent she didn't use anymore, three vinaigrettes from Bea's stash, and a stale hunk of bread from behind the cushions.

To that pile she added a handful of coins and a small sewing kit she'd been looking for since the Countess of March's soiree six weeks ago. But no weapons. No escape. No hope. Except she refused to believe that. She would go mad if she considered the places Edwin might want to incarcerate her.

She must have finally fallen asleep, sitting in the well with her head on the ruined seat. All she knew was that when she woke it was deeply dark. It took her a moment to realize that she had been alerted by a change of speed. They were slowing and turning.

Had Edwin had her brought to Moorhaven Castle? Would

he have the effrontery to drag her back home kicking and screaming just as he was burying his uncle in the family vault? For heaven's sake, the Archbishop of Canterbury was supposed to preside. If it was Moorhaven, though, Diccan would be there. It was his father they were burying.

Closing her eyes, as if that could keep the darkness at bay, Kate assessed her options. She loathed the idea of putting her fate in someone else's hands. Especially a man. That had never exactly worked well for her in the past. But she could trust Diccan. No matter the risk to his social standing, he would speak out against Edwin.

The coach ground to a halt. Kate could hear the jangle of harness as the horses settled. She heard men's voices, and the creak of the coach as the driver swung down from his perch. She heard the hollow caw of a raven.

And then, nothing. No movement. No voices. No appearance by someone who would offer explanation. Obviously a move orchestrated to heighten her terror. Considering how dark it was inside the coach, it was working.

Well, she'd be damned if she showed Edwin how frightened she was. Even as her stomach threatened revolt, she straightened her clothing and tidied her hair. Stuffing the horsehair back into the cushions as well as she could, she perched herself in the center of the seat and laid her hands in her lap, a duchess come to call. Except this duchess had a quiver of large, very sharp hat pins tucked in her hand.

She settled herself just in time. The door swung open, and a homely, carrot-topped man in an old fusiliers uniform reached in a hand. "If you'll come out now nice 'n easy, ma'am."

"Not ma'am," she said, assuming her haughtiest posture. "Your Grace. And if you lay a hand on me, I'll hurt you."

He guffawed. Kate stayed put.

"Go on, then, Frank," another man called from beyond Kate's sight. "Haul the old girl out."

Frank sighed and reached in. Kate struck like an adder, sinking the hat pin deep into the meat of his hand.

"Jesus wept!" Frank shrieked, hopping back. "Now, why'd you go and do that?"

Kate didn't bother with a reply. She just glared. "You can tell my brother he can come collect me himself."

He didn't answer. He just tried to sneak in past her reach. She struck again. He howled. His companion laughed.

"It's nothing personal," Kate assured him. "I just believe that a man should do his own dirty work. Now go get him."

Frank shook his head, as if Kate were mad. "He ain't gonna like it." But he shut the door.

Kate turned forward. She didn't want the men to realize how fast her heart was beating, or the fact that it was only through force of will that she still sat there. She wanted to run. She knew, though, that she wouldn't get four steps. So there she sat, a queen on her way to tea in a ravaged coach.

Suddenly the door was yanked open again. It was all Kate could do not to jump. She didn't, though. Proud of her composure, she turned to face her brother, or whatever henchman he'd sent to represent him.

She froze. It wasn't Edwin at all. For a moment, she couldn't say a word. She could only stare, sick with betrayal. *Not him*, she thought. *Not again.*

"Harry," she drawled, hoping he didn't see how lost she suddenly felt. "Imagine seeing you here."

Harry Lidge made it a point to look around the disaster she'd made of the carriage. "What the hell have you been doing?"

Kate didn't bother to look. "Redesigning. You know how easily I bore."

He offered a hand. "Get out."

She didn't move. She hated the fact that his hair gleamed like faint gold in the lamplight, that she could see even in the deep shadows that his eyes were sky blue. He had grown well, filled out into a strong man. A hard man who had survived the wars with fewer scars than most. He was no longer the boy she'd known, though, and it showed in more than the web of creases that fanned out from the corners of his eyes. It showed in the unforgiving rigidity of his posture, the impatient edge to his actions.

But maybe that was just for her.

"I don't think I will," she told him. "Not until you explain yourself. Are you working for Edwin now, Harry? I certainly hope he's paying you as much to kidnap me as my father paid you to desert me."

His expression, if possible, grew colder. "You don't get to ask questions, Your Grace. You get to answer them. Now get down before I drag you out bodily."

"Go to hell, Harry."

Harry didn't answer. Faster than even she could react, he reached in and yanked her out of the carriage. When she shrieked and fought, he tossed her over his shoulder and turned for the building Kate could only see as a deeper shadow in the darkness. She lifted a hand, ready to drive a pin in his back. He swung her around, never letting her down. His expression flat and cold, he wrapped his hand so tightly around hers that it drove the pins into her palm. She instinctively opened her hand, and they fell. She saw Frank scramble for them.

"You bastard," she rasped, her hand bleeding and hurt. "Put me down!"

Harry didn't bother to answer, just swung her back over his shoulder with a grunt as if she weighed fifteen stone, and stalked up the stairs into the building.

Kate was breathless with rage. "Stop this! You're being ridiculous!"

He didn't even slow. "Shut up, Kate."

She tried to answer, but the position cut off her air. She struggled, but it did no good. Harry hauled her into the house, up a dim, grimy set of stairs, and into an even grimier bedroom, where he proceeded to dump her on the bed. She bounded back as if the mattress were on fire and scrambled to her feet.

This wasn't Moorhaven. It wasn't any place she recognized; it was a wreck of a room that looked as if it hadn't been inhabited this century. Suddenly she was truly afraid.

"When did you start doing Edwin's bidding, Harry?" she demanded, straightening her clothing with her uninjured hand. "Are you under the hatches, or do you need another promotion?"

"I don't work for Edwin," he said, his voice dripping ice. "I work for the government. And I have the dubious pleasure of keeping you here until you give us some answers. Where is it, Kate?"

Her hands stilled. She found herself blinking like a child. "The government? *Our* government?" She laughed, angry that she sounded shrill. "Pull the other one, Harry."

He took a threatening step closer, his rugged features as hard as granite, the forest green of his Rifles uniform offputting. "Oh, I think you know perfectly well what I'm talking about. Just before he died, the Surgeon told us. You're mixed up with the Lions. Do you have it, Kate? Do you have the verse with you? Because if you do, we'll find it."

"The verse?" she echoed, stumbling back from him, only

to have her knees fold and land her back on the bed. "You mean that poem we've been searching all over creation for like a lost Easter egg? *That* verse?"

He merely tilted his head.

"I don't have your bloody verse," she snapped, still feeling pathetically overwhelmed. And then the second betrayal sank in. "You believed the *Surgeon*? A man whose favorite pastime was carving poetry into people's foreheads? Are you mad?"

"Not as mad as you if you think I'll fall for your stories again."

He stepped back toward the door, and it was all Kate could do to keep from reaching out to beg him not to lock her in. She could barely breathe in this room. It was infested with shadows and dark corners, just a candle away from darkness.

"Don't," was all she could say.

Harry stopped, his eyebrow quirked with disdain, but she couldn't get another word out.

"What?" he asked. "No clever quotes? No Latin or Greek or German, Kate? What happened? No more ignorant farm boys to impress?"

She found herself blinking again. He couldn't believe that of her. Hadn't he loved that game as much as she? They'd once spent hours teasing each other with arcane quotes and elaborate curses in as many languages as they could learn.

She shook her head. "I certainly see no one here I want to impress."

She didn't recognize Harry anymore. She'd known him once, an open, easygoing son of the earth with a brain too big for farming. She had loved him once, with the passion reserved for a first love. She'd seen him as the hero who would save her from her father's plans.

But he hadn't saved her. He had betrayed her. And over the last ten years, grown into this implacable, humorless, spiteful man.

"Now then, Your Grace," he said as if to prove it, his voice a razor. "You can make this easy or you can make it hard. Your luggage is being searched. If we don't find the verse there, you'll be searched. You can cooperate or not." He shrugged. "Until then, you can consider yourself my prisoner."

"I told you," she repeated, rising to her feet like a doomed Mary Queen of Scots. "I wouldn't recognize the thing if it came up and asked me to dance. Now stop being such an ass and let me go. I need to get back to Bea."

She was furious to hear a note of pleading creep into her voice. At least it stiffened her spine, so she could brace her feet on the floor and confront the enraged stranger she'd once known so well. Or thought she had.

He shrugged and turned for the door. "No."

"You don't understand," she said, stepping closer to him. "Bea can't simply be abandoned. She isn't strong. She'll fret herself to flinders worrying about me."

"Don't be melodramatic, Kate. She was with your staff. Nothing's going to happen to her."

"All violence isn't physical, Major."

"You don't leave till I get what I want. Your hand is bleeding, Duchess. You might want to see to it." He smiled. "And consider the consequences of your own violence."

Kate clenched both of her hands. "Diccan will kill you for this."

He stopped, his stare implacable. "Diccan told me to take you."

Kate wondered whether shock really had a sound. She

thought she heard a whirlwind; she thought she heard the echo of a cold void. "Don't be absurd."

Diccan would never do this. He would never threaten her with imprisonment. He knew...no, she realized, he didn't. Only Bea knew. But Bea wasn't here.

She snapped out of her reverie just in time to see Harry step through the door. She grabbed him by the sleeve. "Damn you, at least get a message to Bea."

"I told you," he said, his voice cold as silence. "Give me the verse and we'll see."

She bit back a sob of frustration. "You'd torture an old woman just to get back at me?"

It was as if she'd snapped some restraint in him. Suddenly Harry spun around and advanced on her, forcing her across the room until her back was pressed against the peeling, dingy wall. He kept crowding her with his body, battering at her with the fury in his eyes.

"*I'm* not the one doing anything," he snapped. "I'm certainly not betraying my country."

"And you immediately assume I am."

She was trembling, the cold wall damp against her back. Her first instinct was to cower, to throw her arm up to protect herself. She knew too well, though, that cowering only made it worse. She held perfectly still.

"Yes," he all but snarled, too close. Too angry. "I do."

She had nowhere to go. Harry loomed over her, heating the air between them. She wanted to spit at him, to laugh and walk away. But inexplicably, caught like cornered prey, her body suddenly remembered. It wouldn't move; wouldn't fight. It began to soften, to open, to *want*, and she hadn't wanted in so long she'd forgotten the feel of it.

Even if she didn't want Harry, her body did. It remembered how she'd hungered for the scent he always carried, horses and leather and strong soap. It remembered how he'd touched her with the raw wonder of an explorer. It remembered how it felt to trust those guileless blue eyes enough to offer him her virginity.

It only lasted a moment, that sense of elation, before she remembered exactly what it was she had once wanted. Before she found herself fighting the urge to curl into herself and hide. And that made her angrier than ever.

Somehow she must have betrayed her momentary weakness, because suddenly he was smiling like a wolf. "On the other hand," he murmured, leaning even closer, too close, only small inches away, "maybe you want me to find it myself. Shall I look for it? Should I strip you until I can see every inch of the skin you bared for that painting? Should I search you, slipping my hands under your breasts to make sure you haven't tucked it inside, where it would be warm and damp?"

She couldn't think. She couldn't tell if it was fury, fear, or arousal, even though her nipples tightened with his words and a light flared in her belly. She couldn't breathe because he was taking the last of her air.

"I could do it," he whispered, his mouth next to her ear. "All I'd have to do is kiss you, right here behind your ear. You'd let me do anything, then. Wouldn't you, Kate?"

Reaching out, he pulled a pin from her hair, loosing a thick curl. Kate shivered, frozen with memory. Suddenly she was fifteen again, balanced on the edge of womanhood. Trembling with possibility, with wonder, with hunger. For the first time in a decade, she remembered what it had felt like to anticipate, and it shredded her control.

"Or would you like to offer a bit of incentive *not* to look?" he murmured into her ear. "I'm sure it wouldn't be difficult. From what I hear, it's your favorite thing to do."

And then, Harry made his mistake. He took that last step as if he had the right, as if she would never think to defend herself.

He wrapped one hand around her throat. Not squeezing, just controlling. It was too much. She felt the familiar wings of terror beating against her ribs. She had nowhere to run.

She did the only thing she could. She rammed her knee straight up into his bollocks.

Chapter 2

Harry made it down three flights of stairs before finally giving in to the agony in his body. Taking a moment to make sure he was alone, he leaned back against the wall and bent over, eyes closed, hands on knees, and let out a long, low groan.

He shouldn't have let his anger get the better of him. He'd had no business picking Kate up. If he'd been more rested, he wouldn't have made that mistake. He would have let Frank deal with her and kept his distance, which had been his intention all along. It would have saved him from not just the fresh pains in his chest, but the hot ache in his balls.

He should never have agreed to this. He should have kept to his original plan and gone home after the wedding. He'd promised himself, lying on that shattered Belgian field among the screaming horses and groaning men, that he was finished with world events. No more Rifles or army or extra little missions he'd found himself taking on during the last ten years. The future would hold nothing for him but the clean, strong lines of construction, the peaceful dust of history, the immutable laws of mathematics.

And yet here he was again. And it was all Kate's fault.

Even so, he owed her an apology for what had just happened. He had never treated a woman so badly. He'd meant to crowd her a bit, push her into an indiscretion. Instead, the minute he'd stepped close, all of his hard-won discipline had disintegrated. Just the scent of her had damn near destroyed him.

It was her perfume, an oddly discordant scent of jasmine and vanilla, and the clean, fresh-air scent of her hair. His body remembered as if he'd held her last only a week ago, as if the betrayals and lies, the years of separation, had never happened. His body didn't give a damn about betrayal. It wanted her just as badly as it always had. It wanted her flat on her back, legs spread, eyes soft with desire, just for him. A duke's daughter offering herself to plain Mr. Harry Lidge.

He wasn't plain Harry Lidge anymore. He was Major Sir Henry Lidge, knighted for conspicuous bravery, friend of Wellington and Rothschild and Nash. The squire's son who had dared to fall in love with a duke's daughter had come far in the world. But she was still a duke's daughter. And he'd lost his taste for dukes' daughters ten years ago.

Except that it seemed he hadn't. Even throbbing like hell, his balls clenched with the thought of having her in his arms again. Even disillusioned and furious with her, he couldn't get the memory of her out of his mind: the old echoes of her surprised sighs when he'd touched her; the velvet-soft span of her skin as they'd nestled close, hip-to-hip, belly-to-belly; her plump, luscious breasts flattened against his chest.

And her eyes. Grass green, with little flecks of yellow that lit like chandeliers when she was excited, that softened to velvet when she comforted or kissed. Those eyes had once been the most beautiful thing about her, as changeable and vibrant as a moor beneath passing clouds. He had fed on those eyes, deliberately inciting mischief and outrage and glee just to see the emotions flare. He had seen the sun in those eyes.

Now, though, her eyes were sharp as shattered glass; brittle, knowing, sly. A much better reflection of the soul within. His memories had been a lie.

Could he truly mourn what he'd thought he'd seen in her eyes? He could. He did. Because that summer they'd shared, he'd thought her eyes reflected everything that was good and bright and possible in the world. That summer he'd still believed in all those things. He'd believed in her.

He'd been such an innocent.

Well, Kate had taken care of that. Kate and the battlefields of Europe. The only thing Harry believed in now was the beauty of a well-laid foundation. The sweep of a simple staircase, the comfort of a well-placed window and a sturdy roof. The elegant geometry of architecture.

He gave a sour smile. Well. He obviously believed in lust. Hadn't he just had an unmistakable example of it? And he hadn't been the only one. He would swear Kate had been just as aroused as he. He'd felt it; her body bowing toward his, metal to irresistible magnet. No matter what had happened before, what would happen next, in that moment she had wanted him just as much as he wanted her. That, at least, hadn't changed.

Fat lot of good it did him.

Sighing, he straightened. He needed to be more careful than ever now. More disciplined. He didn't want to be the one to let the Lions slip through his fingers.

He was just so tired. And Kate was still Kate. It was going to be a long few days.

"Wouldn't you like a bit of a lie-down, Major?" he heard nearby.

He looked up in surprise to find his batman standing not four feet away in the doorway to the library, a lit candle in his hand. "Thank you, no, Mudge. I'm afraid there isn't the time right now."

"I'll watch down here for you, sir," the boy insisted.

Once, on the Continent, Harry had seen a painting of angels by Botticelli. If he didn't know better, he'd swear that one now stood before him: young, lithe, beautiful, with curly brown hair and big, liquid brown eyes that looked as innocent as a child's. Definitely too beautiful to have been thrown into a troop of riflemen without protection.

Straightening as best he could, Harry walked into the room his staff had dubbed HQ. "We have a lot to do, Mudge. Let's get on with it."

"Please, sir," Mudge said, following. "Tell me we're not supposed to stay here."

Mudge had obviously already been in the room. The shutters were thrown open to allow weak moonlight to wash through. Sadly, it did nothing to dispel the squalor.

"Sorry, Mudge," Harry told the inexplicably named angel as he unbuckled the saddlebags that sat on the misused oak desk. "This is our bivouac for a bit. Mr. Hilliard assured me that it's been out of use so long, no one would think to look for us here."

Mudge cast his huge eyes around the room as if he were a Christian martyr assessing the Colosseum. "I'm sure that's all well and good, sir…"

Harry really couldn't blame the boy. The library was just as grim as the rest of the house. What had once been an oak-paneled room, embellished with coffered ceilings and ogived windows, had been reduced to a bookless, water-stained wreck, paint-peeling, musty, and dark. Harry still couldn't believe that Diccan's uncle had lived here until four years ago. It must have taken decades to reduce this place to such sorry shape.

He'd only glimpsed the outside briefly, and it had been no more promising: a collection of mismatched wings badly grafted onto a medieval abbey. Honey-colored Cotswold stone clashed with red brick and, inexplicably, gray flint, all cobbled together like a beggar's coat. Even so, it had good bones. Harry hated that it had been left to rot.

Perhaps if he had some spare time in the morning, he'd take his sketchbook and do a tour of the place, just for himself. It might never be beautiful, but with a little help, Harry thought it could at least be reclaimed. It certainly wouldn't hurt to have something other than his prisoner to focus on.

He thought of the termagant up in that bedroom and sighed. He had a feeling he was going to be spending all his time trying to outwit one small duchess.

"Sir?"

Harry started back to attention, Mudge's worried countenance beginning to annoy him. "How many of the bedrooms are dry?" he asked. Relieving Mudge of his candle, he made his way to the fireplace.

Mudge sighed. "One."

Which had been given to Kate. "Well then, pull some bedrolls into any dry room on the ground floor. Any luck with stores or staff?"

"No, sir." Mudge's voice was mournful. "Nothin' in the pantry but mice and dust. Phillips is out trying to make a dent in the stables."

Harry knelt and pushed his candle into the black maw that yawned beneath the grimy marble mantel. "We've bedded down in worse places." Although even in those, the fireplaces had drawn. As opposed to this one. The candle flickered and died.

"There was a war on," the boy retorted. "Sir."

He couldn't suppress a wry grin. "I don't suppose you know any chimney sweeps."

With a long-suffering sigh, Mudge trudged for the door, ostensibly on the way to look.

Setting his candle down on the desk, Harry took out his handkerchief and wiped off his hands before claiming one of the few undamaged chairs. "Schroeder has money," he reminded the boy. "See where the town is and re-victual. If asked, you can tell them we're thinking of buying the place for a hunting lodge. "

Mudge was already out of sight. "Yes, sir," floated from the darkness.

"Schroeder is here," a woman's voice answered in the clipped consonants of Germany.

Harry looked up to see a buxom blonde stride into his new office.

Hands clasped at her waist in imitation of the best chatelaine, the drably attired beauty smiled. "I have to admit I liked my last position better."

Harry looked up from relighting his candle. "You'll be abigail for a duchess."

"Considering who the duchess is, I think I'd rather be scrubbing pots in Chelsea."

"You've finished going through her baggage?"

Taking out her own handkerchief to wipe off the rickety chair that sat across from Harry's desk, she settled onto it as if she were in a salon. "Nothing...well, unless you count a store of scandalous attire, enough feathers to stuff a mattress, and several very technical treatises on the propagation of tulip bulbs...I don't suppose the evil plot she's involved in is to take over the tulip market. If that were so, then we'd have our man...woman. Duchess."

"Tulips?" Harry asked, as if it would help bring sense to the subject.

Barbara just shrugged. "There was also this," she said, tossing a pristine white handkerchief onto the desk. "You'll notice it is embroidered with Napoleon's symbol."

For a moment, his heart raced. Then he picked up the handkerchief and saw Barbara's mistake. "Golden bees," he said and pointed. "These are black and yellow."

Schroeder shrugged. "So the duchess said. Evidently her companion is fond of embroidering the insect on every piece of lingerie and linen in their store. The companion's name is Lady Bea Seaton, the duchess's sister-by-marriage, if you can believe it."

"We need to search her person," Harry said, momentarily distracted by the soft slide of lawn through his fingers.

Schroeder quirked an eyebrow. "Is this a privilege you reserve for the senior officer?"

He dropped the handkerchief. "Didn't Diccan tell me you were well mannered and obedient?"

She laughed, a pleasant, throaty sound. "He must have been thinking of his horse…No, come to think of it. Gadzooks is the worst-tempered horse in Britain." When he didn't answer, she sighed. "Are you sure you want to invade a duchess's privacy?"

"We don't have a choice. You're the one who works for Diccan. Do you think he would have accused his cousin of treason if he hadn't been sure?"

"What I heard was that it was the Surgeon who made the accusation, and that Diccan was afraid *for* her. Not of her. Sounds a bit less…damning to me."

Harry looked over at the open window. "Trust me, she's capable of anything."

"I take it you know each other."

"We did."

"Not a pleasant experience?"

He sighed. "It was until I discovered that she was amoral, selfish, and manipulative. You'll save a lot of time and energy if you begin there. Now, please. Get her to change and watch her while she does."

"Would you like me to also question her? Sometimes it comes easier from another woman."

"I would like you to find that verse. Nothing else."

With a long-suffering sigh that sounded a bit like Mudge's, she pushed herself to her feet. "I don't feel good about this."

Harry flashed her a tired smile. "If this were going to be easy, I wouldn't have asked for you."

* * *

For the first time in her life, Kate wished for complete darkness. Maybe without sight she could have avoided the truth. But she had the candle. She had enough light to discern every shape and shadow in the room. She held on to enough sanity to recognize them all.

The house was called Warren Hall. A decaying monstrosity that blighted the countryside near Marlborough, it had been the home of one Philbert Ambrosius Hilliard Warren until his too-timely death four years ago. Kate sat in a straight-backed chair in the middle of the master bedroom, a grim, echoing chamber presided over by an even grimmer painting of Philbert himself, a skeletal old man in a badly fitting bagwig. She knew this because after the old man's death, she had taken a tour of the place with the person Philbert had willed it to. Her cousin Diccan.

Harry hadn't lied. Diccan knew where she was. He really had put her in Harry's hands.

No one was coming to save her from the dark. No one was coming to save her from Harry. She had nothing to protect her but an uncertain candle. So she pulled the battered old table up to her and reseated the candle in its dingy chipped plate. And then she watched as the flame slowly failed.

In the corner of her brain that still worked, Kate realized that no more than two hours passed before she heard the key in the door. In the rest of it, though, it seemed to be forever, counted in the flickers of the disappearing candle.

When new light spilled into the room, she came perilously close to sobbing out loud.

"Your Grace." A woman stood in the doorway. "I have come to help you change."

Kate took a slow breath before turning to greet her visitor. It wouldn't do to seem desperate. She recognized the newcomer, a tall, shapely woman with blue eyes and pale blond hair that glowed oddly in the light that silhouetted her. She had impressive posture and hands she kept clasped at her waist, like the perfect servant.

"Schroeder, isn't it?" Kate asked, smiling. Beside her, her candle shuddered with the advent of fresh air. She afforded it a quick glance to make sure it stayed healthy before briefly turning back to her visitor. "You work for my cousin Diccan. As a spy."

Kate heard the rustle of material as Schroeder curtsied. "I aid him in his investigations," the woman allowed. "I am also an excellent abigail. Sir Harry asked me to do for you while you are his guest."

Turning back to her candle, Kate actually laughed. "Please, Schroeder. If you wish to remain on congenial terms, try not to resort to such absurd euphemisms. I am no guest, and we both know it."

"Yes, ma'am."

"If you are here, then I suppose it's true. Diccan is involved in this travesty."

"He offered the house."

Kate nodded, as if she understood.

Schroeder hesitated. "Are you all right, Your Grace? You seem a bit..."

"Tetchy? Think nothing of it. Kidnappings seem to make me fractious."

"This has happened before?"

"No, but once my brother Edwin hears how successful Diccan has been, I'm sure he'll waste no time taking up the idea. Edwin was never much of a leader. He is, however, an excellent follower."

Schroeder took an experimental step closer. Kate didn't move. "May I help you change now? The men will be bringing your baggage up for you."

Kate kept her voice admirably pleasant. "It is nothing personal, Schroeder. But touch me, and you'll limp for a month. What you *can* do is to provide more candles. This one is failing. Or get Harry to open the window."

"I'm afraid—"

"Try not to be afraid. It's such an exhausting emotion."

Schroeder spent another ten minutes trying to get Kate to see the error of her ways. Kate spent the time watching the candle eat away at itself. She could hear her luggage being dragged up the stairs. Once it reached the top, though, silence fell.

Schroeder stood before the door like a warrior. "I'm sorry," she said, sounding truly regretful. "I can do no more without your cooperation."

Kate should have known Harry would come up with an

effective torture. She itched. Her hair felt like a rat's nest, and she wanted to scrub her teeth. But she wasn't about to strip for anyone, especially if Harry was the one asking.

Turning back to the candle, Kate nodded. "I understand. I hold you completely faultless in all of this. You tell Harry that if he wants to see me naked, he can make it worth my while, like everybody else."

Sighing, Schroeder turned to go.

"Schroeder," Kate asked suddenly. "Do you have a first name?"

Schroeder paused. "Barbara, Your Grace."

Kate nodded. "Would you mind if I used it? I despise unnecessary formality."

Schroeder didn't answer right away. "It would be an honor, Your Grace."

"Kate," Kate said, briefly deserting her candle to meet the abigail's uncertain gaze. "Or Lady Kate. *Never* Your Grace."

Still looking confused, the woman dropped a quick curtsy and opened the door.

"I would truly appreciate some candles, please, Barbara," was all Kate said. It annoyed her that her voice had begun to thin out again, and that her hands were trembling in her lap. "What time is it?"

Schroeder turned. "A bit after midnight."

Kate almost groaned out loud. At least five hours to go.

"Thank you." What else could she say? Barbara could do nothing about the dark.

*   *   *

"Something is not right," Schroeder said without preamble when she ran Harry down in the kitchen where he was brewing tea.

"Plenty is not right," Harry said, not looking up. "Did you search her?"

"She didn't move, not once. She could barely look away from the candle long enough to face me, as if that candle were the only thing she could see. Does she have problems being shut in, or being in the dark?"

Pot in one hand, his tin mug in the other, Harry looked up. "How would I know?"

"You said you knew her."

Harry tilted his head. "I never remember her holding still."

Schroeder pulled out a cup for herself and wiped it out with her skirt. "I'm telling you. Something is wrong. Cannot we at least open the window?"

"And have her escape?"

"It's three stories up, Major. She isn't a bird."

He poured Schroeder's portion before his own. "She's a witch. We'd wake up and she'd have vanished with all her luggage and our horses. No."

"Then get her some candles."

"She can have candles. She can have chandeliers. Once she strips."

"You mean once I search her clothing."

His head snapped around. "When we find the verse."

"What if we don't?"

He turned back to his tea. "Then she ate it and we'll have to find a way to make her tell us."

"You're so sure?"

"You don't know her."

"You don't seem to, either. Not if you don't know why she stares at candles as if they are the window out of a prison."

Harry slammed the pot down, sloshing water across the

grimy table. "Schroeder, don't get poetic on me. She's a duchess, not a fairy princess. Now please. Search her."

*   *   *

Kate wasn't sure how much longer it was, except that the candle had worn away to a puddle, and she was seriously thinking of ripping at the shutters with her fingernails. She needed to have more light. The walls were closing in, the darkness thickening, and she refused to face what it hid. More, she knew, since she'd spent that time caring for wounded in Brussels. Another layer of nightmares now lay in wait.

She was so focused on the little flame that she didn't even hear the lock turn. She just suddenly knew that there was new light in the room.

"I'm not a monster," Harry said from the doorway.

She wasn't sure what he wanted her to say. She wasn't sure she could say anything. Sweat had collected under her armpits and between her breasts, making her itch even more.

He walked in, his boots thudding on the floor. "What game are you playing, Kate?"

"You're the one playing the game, Harry. Why don't you tell me?"

She knew better than to goad him, yet she couldn't seem to help it. Once upon a time, they had fought like duelists, trading verbal blows as they'd argued about everything from astrology to architecture, their laughter as sharp as their wit. For a long time now, though, the barbs they'd traded had carried nothing but venom.

"Please, Kate," he said, and he almost sounded sincere. "I don't have a choice."

He stepped close enough that she could smell fresh air and leather. She almost closed her eyes with the sheer pleasure of it, a scent of freedom and summer and hope. Deserting her candle, she considered the harsh angles of his face.

For the first time, she realized that he looked like hell: strained and tired and lined, as if something literally weighed him down.

"Everyone has a choice, Harry," she reminded him. "You *could* believe me instead of a notorious assassin."

"And you could help us find out why he would have made the accusation."

"I would be happy to, if that was what you really wanted. But what you really want is to see me humiliated, and I am not in the mood for it."

"The Surgeon admitted it right before he died," Harry accused. "He said that you had the verse. That you were tied up in this. Diccan told me himself."

She shrugged and returned to her candle. "The Surgeon lied."

Harry didn't move. He didn't speak. Even so, Kate swore she could hear his skepticism.

Fine. Let him believe what he wanted. He always had.

"You like this room so much," he said, "you'll just stay here until you cooperate."

She hoped he didn't see the shudder that went through her. "The longer you hold me, the greater your chances that I'm going to spread this tale all over London."

"You'd become a scandal."

She laughed, relieved that it sounded sharp and dry. "Where have you been, Harry? I *am* a scandal. I'm the woman mothers point to when they want to show their chicks how not to behave."

"Don't make it sound as if you're put upon. You chose the way you live."

"Indeed I did. Which no longer has anything to do with you."

It was his turn to laugh. "Don't I wish that were true. I'm supposed to be selling out right now and going home. I've waited ten years to do it. Ten *years* with no goal in mind but to survive long enough to get out, grab only what I can fit in a rucksack, and wander the world. *Alone.* Without commanders or enemies or lying, manipulative women to stop me from doing what *I* want for a change. You're making me wait, Kate. That's not a smart thing."

Again, as if he couldn't help it, he approached, stepping so close she could feel the heat pulse off him; she could almost taste his breath against her skin. He stood there for the longest time, not quite touching her, not speaking, not moving. Crowding her, though, with sensations, with memories, with the forlorn hope of youth.

For once, she didn't mind. He was distracting her, setting up an almost harmonic resonance in her that seemed to light her body from within. Her skin hummed, her blood slowed and thickened, until it seemed to pool in her belly, until it tautened her nipples and filled her breasts.

For a moment, a long, blissful moment, she forgot about the candle and the dark and the long hours till morning. She forgot Harry's animosity and the impossible task he'd set her. For just that moment, she relived the exquisite pleasure a body could enjoy. A pleasure that lived in the memory of one long ago summer when she hadn't known any better.

Then Harry stepped back and the link snapped. Kate almost shuddered with the loss. Suddenly the dank old room was colder and emptier even than it had been before. All the rest of her life came rushing back to her, and she remembered who she was. What she was. And what she wasn't.

"Your candle's about to go out," Harry mused. "Would you like another?"

She was so proud of herself. Not by the flicker of an eyelid did she betray her distress. "You mean if I help you, you'll help me?"

She swore she could hear his teeth grind.

"I'll give you until noon," he said, and she heard the confusion in his voice. "If you haven't cooperated, then I'm afraid the gloves come off."

As if in punctuation, the candle flame, pulled by Harry's movement, leapt up once and then died.

Don't leave me in the dark, Kate almost begged. But she didn't. She did not beg anymore. Ever. She would survive the dark, just like always.

When the candle flickered out, Harry paused only a moment before stomping over to the door and yanking it open.

"Mudge!" he yelled as if he were in an army camp. "Candles!"

His voice shook, and Kate knew he'd been as affected as she.

It wasn't much. But it was something.

*   *   *

"What do you mean, she got away?" the quiet voice demanded.

The man standing before the desk raked his hands through a perfectly coiffed Brutus haircut. "Someone stole her."

His companion was not amused. "Stole her. Like a pocket watch?"

He sank into an upright chair, his focus on the ornate Turkish carpet beneath his feet. "We waited at the Angel, as agreed. We meant to intercept her coach as it crossed the downs. But—" He shrugged and raised drawn gray eyes. "Someone was ahead of us."

"And you didn't follow?"

"My men are still looking. I felt obliged to come notify you."

"And I thank you. It was wise to come during the funeral. You should not be remarked on." A dry smile crossed the knife-sharp features. "I imagine you're getting your share of commiseration over your own wife's death."

The young man flinched. "My children..."

"Will understand, I promise. You have only done what you need to, after all. We couldn't move without you." A finger tapped against the leather desk blotter. "I'm afraid that this setback will delay everything, though."

The man stood and pulled at his jacket. "We'll find her."

He had barely walked from the room when a hidden door swung open alongside the bookshelves. An exquisite auburn-haired beauty with large blue eyes and a voluptuous figure stepped into the room.

"It is too bad you must rely on such as he," she said, her accent decidedly French. "I could have taken good care of your duchess, me."

"You will undoubtedly get your chance, Mimi."

Mimi poured two glasses of brandy and took the recently occupied chair. "You promised," she said, handing a glass over. "I get to finish it. I have not had any fun, me, since the Surgeon is killed."

Her compatriot took up the brandy and tasted it. It would not do to reveal to the redheaded doxy just how repugnant she was. Ah well, needs must.

"I'm afraid we won't be able to wait for you to dispatch the duchess. However, once it is done, I don't see why you can't enjoy yourself a bit. Would you like to follow in the Surgeon's footsteps and do a bit of carving?"

The redhead actually shivered with delight. "Oh, yes. Mimi, she will like that."

As if she couldn't wait to share the news, she reached beneath her skirt and pulled out a lethal-looking scimitar-shaped butcher knife, lifting it so that the light slithered down the blade. "Her knives are lonely."

"Good. I have the perfect message to leave on the Duchess of Murther."

Oh, yes, a very good one. Suddenly Mimi wasn't the only one shivering with delight.

Chapter 3

"Oh, Mudge," Kate mourned, laying her hand on the boy's arm. "You're wasted on the army. You should come work for me."

The wide-eyed boy blinked as if he'd seen a vision. Kate wasn't surprised. She hadn't recovered her trunks, and she hadn't changed her dress, but she had candles. She felt reckless with relief, and Mudge was a beautiful boy. Which meant that she was enjoying a bit of flirtation with the breakfast Mudge had just brought. After all, Mudge was the one who had saved her.

Oh, all right, Harry had ordered the candles, but Mudge had brought at least a dozen. Kate's first instinct had been to set them on every surface in the room and light each one so she could banish the last of the shadows. She knew better, though. Harry could just as easily order them away. So she lit two and pocketed the rest until she could hide them where Harry wouldn't find them.

It helped that dawn had come and gone. Not that she could precisely see it. But she'd felt it in her marrow, like an atavistic clock, stirring her senses awake, pushing the monsters back into their corners. The light effervesced in her blood, brewing giddiness. Freedom, even the illusion of it, coursed through her like a drug.

"Mudge is immune to you, Kate," Harry said from the doorway.

She made it a point not to acknowledge him. Her attention was on his improbably beautiful batman, who stood staring at her as if she were an exotic species of animal he'd never seen before. "How old are you, Mudge?"

The boy shrugged, his Rifleman green uniform pulling oddly across his shoulders. "Not sure, ma'am. Twenty?"

She nodded, flashing him a blatantly insincere smile. "A good age. The age of wonder. The decade of discovery. You'd love to be in my employ, Mudge. You'd meet such interesting people. See such interesting places. *Do* such interesting things."

She knew she shouldn't torment the boy this way. He wasn't up to her weight. Harry, on the other hand, was, and he was obviously irritated with her. The tighter his brow grew, the more reckless she felt.

"For instance," she said, leaning close to Mudge, "do you know what I've recently acquired from Josephine Bonaparte herself? Well, not from her hand, poor dear. She died before I had the pleasure of meeting her, which I consider a tragedy." She sighed, knowing exactly what it did to her bodice. "Just think of the secrets we could have shared, her the mistress of the most rapacious ruler of our age, and me…"

Chuckling, she quirked her eyebrows. Mudge smiled. She didn't need an interpreter to see that the smile was impersonal. Mudge really was immune. She was glad, actually. She liked the boy.

"Don't," Harry warned her.

She turned her smile on him. "You don't want to know, Harry? After all the effort you've gone to over the years to cement my reputation, at least in your own mind? Of course you do."

She didn't move, didn't turn away from the man who had defined her adulthood. "I got it from her estate," she continued brightly. "Josephine's. Her things were up for auction, and I snagged a real prize. A psyche mirror." Turning back to Mudge, she leaned in close, as if imparting secrets. "Do you know what that is, Mudge?"

Mudge shook his head, looking exactly like a man enjoying a confidence. "Imagine you're about to tell me, ma'am."

She smiled and put every suggestive thought into it. "A psyche mirror," she said, her voice pitched lower, her hands sweeping through the air in punctuation, "is an oval mirror on a stand. A *tall*...oval mirror. The innovation is that in it I can see a reflection of my entire—" She swept her hands down, mimicking her own contours, still smiling. "Self. All at once. Scandalous, don't you think? I keep it in my boudoir."

"Mudge," Harry interrupted.

The boy started and turned, as if he'd completely forgotten that Harry was there.

"Did you get supplies?" Harry asked.

Mudge blinked. "Yessir."

Harry nodded. "How about some food, then? The men will be hungry."

Mudge bobbed his head and turned to give Kate an abrupt, rather clumsy bow that endeared him to her all the more. "Y'r Grace."

She held out her hand as if he were a viscount on a morning visit. "It has been a pleasure. Don't let Harry intimidate you, my dear. He's all uniform and no sword."

Touching her fingers, the boy flashed her a bright grin. Then he fled.

Harry waited until Mudge was well out of sight before stepping into the room. "I'm afraid your efforts were wasted on him," he said, leaning against the doorjamb in a pose of insouciance. "He's not your type."

"Not my type?" Kate retorted with a quirked eyebrow. "You truly think there is a man alive who's not my type? I must be losing my touch."

"He's a soldier in the king's army, and would not be well served by any of the men hearing him called 'dear.'"

Kate strolled over to the boarded-up window, as if she could see out of it. "How on earth did Mudge find himself in the army?"

"It was that or Botany Bay. He was caught stealing bread."

Kate wished she could say she was surprised. "Why, Harry," she said, turning back on him, her own eyes wide. "You've taken him under your wing, haven't you? Altruism? I'm not sure it fits you."

"I reserve it for people who deserve it. Mudge has no idea how to lie."

"And I'm so very good at it, you see no reason to protect me."

"I never said you were lacking in intellect, Kate." Straightening, he offered her a chilly smile. "It's almost noon. Are you going to cooperate, or will this get difficult?"

"Oh..." Kate gave the appearance of considering his question. "Difficult, I think."

He stared at her, obviously fighting for control. She held her breath, not sure what she wanted him to do. She wanted to fight him; to tear strips off his skin for the insults he'd delivered, the assumptions he made. She wanted to get past him and escape.

He shook his head. "Don't push me, Kate. I'm not in a good mood."

She smiled. "Good heavens. If kidnapping your favorite nemesis doesn't put you in a good mood, Harry, I fear you've lost the knack for happiness. Probably a good thing that those two engagements of yours didn't work out, then, don't you think? Think of what their lives would have been like. Especially...Lady Poppy, wasn't it?"

The minute she said it she regretted it. She saw his mouth go white and braced herself.

"You just won't stop, will you?" he snarled.

A shiver of fear chased down her spine; a shudder of anticipation as he stepped right up to her.

"Is that what you want?" he demanded. "For me to lose my control?"

Was it? His eyes, those soft sky-blue eyes, were the color of hot flame. He seemed to fill the room. She stood her ground. Joan of Arc. Boudicca. Except she didn't think those valiant women had been holding out against the confusion of desire.

He stood so close, she could feel the wash of his breath against her cheek. "You want me to take it from you?" he asked. "Is that the taste you've acquired over the years? Would you like me to control you? Maybe tie you up, or get out my riding crop? I know that some women like the sting of it across their sweet little asses. How about you, Kate? Is that what you're waiting for?"

Suddenly the room went cold and Kate couldn't breathe. Her skin crawled; the blood drained from her face, leaving her unpardonably dizzy and clammy. "Thank you, Harry," she managed to say, holding perfectly still. "You've finally made me glad I didn't run off with you."

Harry reared back, as if she'd slapped him. "Just now?" he demanded. "Hell, Kate, I was glad the day I left."

Stalking out, he slammed the door behind him. Kate dropped into her chair, her knees giving out. The only thing that made her feel better was the knowledge that his hand had been shaking as he reached for the door on his way out.

For a long moment, she just sat there, her stomach somersaulting and her head swimming. He was right. She'd gone too far, and she'd been paid back for it. She lifted her hands to see that she was shaking, too, but she really wasn't sure what from. Anger? Fear? Desire? How was she supposed to separate them?

She had to get away. This insane contest between Harry and her would only escalate, which would solve nothing. She had no answers for him, nor did he, it seemed, for her. He certainly couldn't tell her why anyone would think she belonged to the bloody Lions. He would just keep sparking her temper and rousing her body until something very bad happened. And Kate had had quite enough of very bad in her life.

Taking an unsteady breath, she leaned her elbows on the table and dropped her head in her hands. She'd been allowing Harry to take the lead up till now. She had to change that. She needed to get out, and she was the only one who could do it.

First she took the time to hide her candles and flint. Like a starving child with her first meal, she couldn't assume more was coming. Pulling up a floorboard near the grayish rug, she slipped her stash beneath and moved the table over it. Then she scoured the room for tools, for weapons, for weaknesses.

Harry had prepared well. The bed was suspended on ropes, and the chest of drawers emptied of everything but dust. And although a hit over the head with a wooden drawer might surprise or even cut, it would not stop. There weren't any sheets on the bed, nothing but a tattered pea-green brocade that would probably rip from no more than a look. There wasn't even a mirror to smash.

She went over the room inch by inch. She didn't expect success; Harry had been too thorough. So she was even more surprised when only half an hour later, she found her answer.

The shutters. They had been nailed closed, but the hinges were within a good yank of pulling from the wall. All she had to do was pry them loose and she could sneak out that way. She just had to hope that Harry hadn't already cut away the ivy that had once climbed up the old stone walls.

Now for a plan. She needed to wait until deep night, when her guards were at their most lax. What Harry didn't know was that her own country home, Eastcourt Hall, was no more than ten miles away. If she could get as far as Marlborough, she could catch the Bath coach and be there in no time. If worse came to worst, she would just walk.

But until then, what?

Brushing down her gown, she settled into her rickety little chair and thought, absently picking the soft wax from the battered old table. She would have to let herself be searched. She'd known it all along. But at first she'd been too panicked to think clearly, and then too furious. She'd even entertained the idea of making Harry do it.

Why not? she thought, savoring the sharp taste of righteous indignation. Why not hold out so long that she would force him to strip her? Why not stand before him, dignified and silent, as the shame grew on him? Let him be the villain. Let him have to face other people's condemnation for what he did. The minute they caught sight of his cockstand, they'd know just how altruistic his actions were.

She wasted far too much time on the idea. But she just couldn't seem to turn away from the fantasy of Major Sir

Harry Lidge, the hero of the Peninsula, the saint of Salamanca, finally brought down a peg or two.

Climbing to her feet, she began to pace. No, she couldn't do it. Not because she didn't want to hurt Harry. She did, especially after his behavior since they'd been here. But after all she'd been through, she refused to put herself in the position of being a victim ever again, even for the satisfaction of seeing Harry's downfall. She simply couldn't allow him to hurt her.

She would allow Barbara to do the job. For some reason, Kate trusted the woman's knowing smile and quiet strength. Besides, if Kate understood correctly, with the search came access to her trunks. There was extra traveling money tucked beneath a false bottom that would ease her way.

And so it was that when the bar across the door slid back and the door opened, Kate was patiently waiting in her chair as if expecting visitors in her salon.

Barbara smiled as she stepped in, her expression apologetic. "I am sorry to bother you, your... Lady Kate," she said, her accent stronger than before.

"Barbara, there you are," Kate said, climbing to her feet. "If you'll bring in my luggage and close the door, we can get on with this."

She had obviously surprised the woman, because for a moment Barbara couldn't seem to do more than stare, her hands clasped together at her waist.

"And find me a screen, please."

Schroeder frowned. "But, Lady Kate..."

Kate elevated an eyebrow. "Those are my terms, Barbara. Would you really prefer to wrestle a duchess to the ground just to see her titties?"

Schroeder had the grace to look uncomfortable. "I was instructed to... completely disrobe you, Your... Lady Kate. Just in case you were hiding something beneath."

Kate looked down at her dress. "Where? What do you think I did, tattoo the verse across my stomach?"

Still Schroeder didn't move. Standing before Kate, she seemed implacable. But since she was also the head of the group of servants Diccan had collected to gather information, Kate hoped the woman was professional enough to see the benefits of compromise.

"Please, Barbara," Kate nudged. "I would rather have this done before Harry comes storming back in here."

Evidently Barbara agreed with Kate, because after another small hesitation, she bobbed a curtsy, smiled, and turned for the door.

In only minutes, Kate was changed and her travel clothing carried away to be picked through. "Does this satisfy you?" she asked as she rebraided her hair.

"I wasn't the..." Barbara stopped short and shook her head, as if losing an argument with herself. "Yes, Lady Kate," she said instead with a brisk bob. "Thank you. Would you like a bit of tea?"

"Ah." Kate nodded. "With cooperation comes reward? Yes, come to think of it, I would love tea. I believe I am half starved."

Again Barbara betrayed a flicker of surprise. Probably because she expected Kate to continue waging her war. After all, according to Harry, if nothing was found, Kate wasn't going home. What neither Harry nor Barbara knew was that Kate was, indeed, going home. She might as well sustain herself for the trip.

"Yes, my lady." With a final curtsy, she walked out.

Left behind, Kate wasted no time opening her trunk and pulling out the contents. Her money was beneath the false bottom. It wouldn't do for anyone to know. Or to know that in five minutes it would be hidden under the loose floorboard alongside her candles. For the first time since tumbling into her coach, Kate felt a sliver of hope.

*   *   *

Nothing. Not so much as a scrap of lint. Harry went through Kate's clothing as thoroughly and meticulously as if it had been a battle plan. He ran his fingers over every inch of material, from the bright yellow twill of her carriage gown to the silk of her stockings to the lawn of her chemise. Mudge offered to help, but Harry growled at him and the boy retreated. If there was evidence here of a crime, he wanted to be the one to find it. He wanted to be the one to wave it in Kate's face so that this time she couldn't deny it. It had nothing to do with the fact that the cloth was still warm from her body, or that her elusive scent still wafted from the fabric like incense. He was only doing his job.

Even so, he couldn't help noticing how fine the material was, how sensuous. He could see his fingers through her chemise, which fit the Kate he knew now. He couldn't forget, though, how indifferent Kate had once seemed to fine clothes. In fact, she'd always made a point of showing up in her sisters' old hand-me-downs, which had never fit, even before she ruined them going over fences and sitting in the dirt to fish. When he'd asked her why she'd not had a better wardrobe, she'd challenged him with that sharp, bright smile of hers and said, "Why, this is what I wear," as if it would explain all.

Harry had always believed that she'd done it just to be contrary. He'd obviously been right. There were certainly no hand-me-downs in the duchess's luggage.

He wondered if it had been the duke who had taught her to skirt the edge of propriety. She was never vulgar, exactly.

But each time Harry saw her in public, her attire was just shy of being too bright, too bold, too revealing. Her carriage dress was a prime example, cut to hug her figure, when most dresses were as shapeless as gunnysacks, the soft wool a bright lemon yellow. Her evening dresses were far worse.

Funny, though. He would have expected her undergarments to be even more decadent. Just like everyone else, he'd heard about Kate's legion of lovers. Surely a woman intent on attracting a man to her bed would indulge in silk and satin, elaborately embroidered and made to slip off in a hurry. His mistresses certainly had.

The only embroidery on Kate's chemise was a pair of honeybees just beneath each strap. And the chemise wasn't silk. What was it, lawn? The same stuff they made handkerchiefs from. As soft as a whisper, true, and sheer enough to give a damn good idea what was beneath. But...plain. Practical. Not what he would have expected the most notorious duchess in the realm to wear.

How many men had run their hands over this chemise? he wondered. How many had slipped it off and tossed it to the floor in their hurry to get to her body?

Cursing, he dropped the garments as if they'd caught fire. He needed to stop this. He needed distance, time, perspective. Instead he had an aching cock, itchy eyes, and a growing conviction that he was about to walk off a shaky pier in heavy boots.

No matter what had passed between them, the last thing he needed was to join the procession into her bedroom. And yet here he was, fondling her garments as if she were in them, and he was sweating like a fat man in a steam bath.

"Unless you want to cut her open like a cadaver," came Schroeder's voice from the doorway, "I can guarantee there is nothing hiding anywhere on Lady Kate's body."

Harry was sitting at the freshly dusted library desk, Kate's dress spilling over the side like a waterfall of sunlight. He couldn't seem to look away from it, mesmerized by the conundrums it posed.

"Major?" Schroeder said with a cough. "What next?"

Harry yanked himself to attention. "We wait to hear from Diccan."

"You'll be sending a messenger off right away?"

He saw the direction Schroeder's gaze had taken, and realized he was once again running the cloud of lawn through his fingers. Quickly he bunched it up and tossed it onto the desk, where Schroeder recovered it.

"See if Frank is finished in the stables."

"What about the duchess?"

Harry leaned his chair back on two legs. "What *about* her?"

Schroeder tilted her head, her arms overflowing with Kate's garments. "We didn't find anything. Why don't you let her out?"

"Because I don't trust her."

"She doesn't have the verse."

He wasn't about to tell Schroeder that the verse had little to do with it.

"It is obvious you don't get along with her," Schroeder said suddenly. "Is there something we need to know?"

"No."

"Nothing that could impact how you discharge your duties in this situation."

"No."

She stood there, passive, damning in her silence. "Major," she finally said. "If you have credible information that the duchess is part of a plot against the throne of England, then you have my full and unquestioning support. But if this is something personal between the two of you, then I must...wonder."

"We were...close once," he snapped, then shrugged. "We are not now."

Schroeder nodded. "And this happened recently?"

Harry got to his feet. "Ten years ago."

She stared at him. "You can't mean to say that all this noise is over something that happened when you were, what? Twenty?"

"Of course not." He turned away from her and walked over toward the window. "I've run afoul of the duchess enough times to know what to expect from her. Suffice it to say that my experiences with her impressed on me the fact that she is not to be trusted. She is a facile liar, manipulating all those around her for her own pleasure. I wouldn't put it past her to be involved in this plot just for the fun of it."

"Has she committed any crimes?"

He sighed, wishing like hell that Schroeder were a Rifleman who took orders without question. "I was engaged twice," he finally admitted, looking out the window as if he could see past the grime. "She managed to end both."

"The duchess?" Schroeder asked, her disbelief evident. "Ruined your engagements."

He could still see the fury in Lady Poppy Posts's great blue eyes as she threw his ring at him. He'd never even had a chance to defend himself. "Yes," he said baldly.

"Why?"

Why the hell was he having to dredge up the past? Schroeder didn't need to know his personal history to follow orders. "Don't you have work to do?"

"Yes. Helping you figure out why the Surgeon mentioned Lady Kate in relation to the verse. I just thought it might be good to know whether we've locked her up because she is a danger to the Crown, or because you feel the need to exact some sort of revenge."

For a minute, Harry couldn't manage an answer. He did get to his feet. "We've locked up Lady Kate to keep everybody safe until we find out what the hell's going on. That's all you need to know, and more than I usually tell a servant."

She was nodding. "Ah, but you see, I'm not a servant. Mr. Hilliard should have told you that."

"Then what are you?"

She smiled, and Harry was struck suddenly by the quiet confidence he should have seen before. "Somebody who is very good at what she does. Now. I would ask you again. Since we're just waiting around, why don't I see if I can get any answers from her."

Harry kept staring at her. "What does Drake think of you?"

"The earl?" she asked, then shrugged. "I have no idea. We've never met. I work solely with Mr. Hilliard."

Finally, he nodded. "Diccan says you have excellent instincts. Use them on Kate."

And without another word, she walked out, leaving Harry with the uncomfortable feeling that she had been right. He was looking for revenge. He was looking to cut Kate Hilliard down to size. Back to the Kate he'd known before she had added *duchess* to her name and become impossible. Before she'd betrayed him so thoroughly.

Well, he thought, looking around the dim room. He had nothing to do right now but wait for Schroeder's report. He could either wait here, up on his bed, or outside walking the estate.

No question. Right now he needed to be busy.

"Mudge!" he yelled, knowing the batman wasn't far away. "I'll be outside."

And grabbing his sketchbook and charcoal, he left the room.

                         *   *   *

"You truly don't know what the Surgeon meant when he said you were involved?" Barbara asked.

Her calm a hard-wrought facade, Kate sat on her rickety little chair running one of Bea's handkerchiefs through her fingers. Barbara had returned a few minutes ago for a bit of gentle interrogation over tea. "I truly don't."

At least it was keeping Kate occupied. The hours till dark and escape would be long enough.

Barbara, for her part, had the courage to sit on the bed, as if she hadn't noticed the puff of dust that lifted when she sat, or the spiders that danced away over her head. "But Major Lidge said that you were at the wedding last week when the Surgeon was killed," she said.

"Indeed I was. Most entertaining house party I've attended in ages. One should always count an assassin among one's acquaintances, Barbara, if only for the notoriety. But if he told anyone that I was involved, he seems sadly delusional."

"He said you have the verse."

"And we proved I don't."

"You know many people, Lady Kate. Could you know someone in the Lions?"

"I know *everyone*, Barbara, which means that chances are very great that I do. But so far none has suggested I help him drive a knife into Prinny's back."

Kate paused for a bit, her eyes on the shuddering flame as she tried to gather her scattered wits enough to see if she might have ever heard something suspicious. It didn't take long to shake her head. "No. From what I know about the Lions, they sound to be archconservatives; Liverpool's kind of people, who seek order above all else. As you can imagine, that kind of person doesn't frequent my At Homes. I draw those who delight in being scandalous, of course, but only because they befriend artists and literati and such. And people like Byron are much more interested in Greek independence than British insurrection." She smiled. "I believe it is because the costumes are so much more romantic."

Barbara nodded. "Yes. That is what my operatives have surmised."

Kate couldn't help but grin. "Do you really run an army of domestics who spy for the Crown?"

"Indeed I do." Barbara smiled genuinely for the first time. "It was an ingenious idea of Dic...Mr. Hilliard's. After all, the staff know what happens in a house before anyone else. We've been able to gather quite a bit of proof and give the government the names they seek."

"But *you* aren't a domestic."

Barbara's smile became mysterious. "Of course I am. I am an excellent abigail."

Which meant Kate would learn no more. "Tell me what *you* know, then. Maybe new information will spark my memory."

But Barbara shook her head. "I know very little more than you, my lady. Some of the people who have been named, of course. Some who aren't named yet, but as you say, none who would frequent your affairs. I know, of course, that these are in the main aristocrats who think that the country needs a return to the government of the last century, and that placing Princess Charlotte on the throne will accomplish this. There are only about three or four people at the core of the Lions who know all. The rest, I understand, are broken up into smaller...squads, I suppose, who don't know one another except by an identifying sign—"

"Like the verse. Yes. I gathered that."

She was awarded another nod. "There have been no arrests as of yet, although the Earl and Countess of Thornton are reported to have escaped to the Continent along with Mr. Geoffrey Smythe, who worked with them. I know that Mr. Hilliard has spent an inordinate amount of time trying to insert himself into the Lions, although we don't know whether he has been successful yet. And I know that his father the bishop was killed after admitting to his own complicity. From what I gather, his task was to bring the House of Lords into line when the time came."

Kate nodded thoughtfully. "If anybody believed he was more worthy of ruling a country than the king and Parliament, it was certainly my uncle Evelyn. I'm just relieved he didn't survive long enough to be drawn and quartered."

"I don't think anyone will be, if you want the truth," Barbara said. "The culprits are too high-placed. Can you imagine what would happen if they had to try a dozen aristocrats for treason?"

Kate looked up, her stomach taking an unexpected dive. "What do you mean? You think that they'll just...disappear?"

Schroeder didn't even blink.

Well, that certainly gave Kate something to take her mind off her escape. "Do you think it was the Lions who shot my uncle, or the government?"

"I think we'll probably never know."

Kate took in a slow breath. "I imagine I should thank Harry for merely kidnapping me. I have no doubt that he would have much rather shot me and been done with it."

*   *   *

Barbara stayed another hour, but neither woman learned anything new. At least it kept Kate busy. She had been right about those hours she had to wait. They stretched out like a desert road, wearing on her patience and testing her composure. As the house settled around her and all the voices stilled, she changed into the sturdiest dress she had, a dark blue kerseymere gown. Sadly, she hadn't thought to bring hiking shoes to a wedding, so she settled for the strongest slippers she had. Then she waited until she could hear no more voices or movement outside her door. There were rustlings in the walls and weird creaks in the corners, but Kate knew that to be the betrayals of old age and disuse. She would wait another thirty minutes or so, and then she would test the shutters.

She had just gotten to her feet when she heard the most curious sound. It sounded exactly as if someone was tapping on the shutters. Three stories above the ground.

She froze, her heart in her throat. It came again. She jumped to her feet. "Who is it?" she whispered.

The answer came in a dearly familiar Cockney accent, "'Oo d'ya think, Y'r Graciousness?"

"Thrasher!"

Without another thought, she wrapped her hands around the shutter and pulled. The agonized screech of hinges should have woken the dead. She stopped, eyes closed, and tested the silence. When she heard no new movement, she finished the job.

It only took two more good tugs to pull the hinge away from the wall. Swinging the whole apparatus to the side, she unlocked the window and shoved it up a few inches.

And there was that tousled blond head hovering just

above the sash. "It *is* you," she whispered, grinning as she reached out a hand. "What are you doing here?"

Shoving aside the help, Thrasher rolled over the window sash like a tumbler, landing on the floor with barely a sound. "Whattya think?" he asked, giving her a big cheeky grin up from the floor. "Savin' you."

She didn't care how uncomfortable it made him. She dragged the skinny young reprobate to his feet and gave him a crushing hug. "You devil. How dare you risk your life on that wall?"

"Risk?" he retorted, pulling away before she could kiss him. "Wit' all that ivy? Cor, it were like hikin' up a easy hill, which is good, 'cause we gotta go down the same way." With that, he unwound a rope from around his waist and began tying it to the big four-poster.

Kate grinned, flushed with triumph. "Actually, you caught me just getting ready to go out." Gathering her things, she pulled on her cloak and gloves. "How did you find me?"

"Don't be daft," he chastised without looking up. "Never lost ya. That cove what run off wiff ya 'as 'air as red as a Runner's vest."

"Aitches, Thrasher."

He looked up with a cheeky grin. "*Has. Hair*," he corrected himself, giving the rope a test tug. "Orangest hair I ever seen. Was dead easy ta follow. I jus' jumped up on me perch and 'ung on."

"You didn't come here alone, did you?" she objected.

His laugh was breathy. "Nah. Stopped by y'r 'ouse and got t' others."

"Others?" she asked, casting an anxious look out the window.

He waved off in the direction of the dark woods. "Mr.

Finney," he said. "Coupla stable hands 'n that cook o' yers. Wouldn't be left be'ind. Says 'e can be right nasty wit' a cleaver."

Kate almost laughed out loud. Her butler, her grooms, and her chef, all armed and waiting to help rescue her. She thought she might weep.

"What about Lady Bea?" she asked, helping Thrasher tie the rope to the bed leg.

"Bob Coachman took 'er back to Lunnun to wait."

For the first time since being tossed into the coach, Kate breathed a sigh of relief. "Thank heavens. She really is all right?"

The boy grinned, all teeth and big brown eyes. "Mad as a wet 'en. Ready to grab a fryin' pan 'erself. Mr. Finney's the one as eased 'er. Said as 'ow she'd need to be in Lunnon to give out you was sick in bed so's nobody'd know you was nabbed."

Kate nodded, glad. It was the only argument she could think of that would keep Bea from running headlong into danger for her. Finney was about to get a big raise.

Thrasher tiptoed to the window and threw the rest of the rope over the sill. "'Oo was it took ya, Y'r 'Onorableness?"

"That's a long story, Thrasher. We'll talk about it when we get home."

He gave the rope an experimental tug. The heavy old bed didn't budge. "Vines is good climbin' vines. 'Ang on to the rope jus' in case."

She nodded. "You first."

His sharp-featured face folded into a fierce frown. "Don't be daft."

"I won't go down unless you're already on the ground, Thrasher. And if I'm caught, I want you to run, do you hear me? You have to get back to the rest of the staff."

He took a quick assessing look out the window. "Only 'cause then we can come get ya again."

And without further ado, he swung himself over the sill and disappeared. Left behind in the room, Kate took a moment to steady her heart. She wasn't afraid of the climb. She had climbed down many a vine in her day. She was afraid for her friends. If Harry caught them, God knew what he might do.

She took her own look outside to see Thrasher already halfway down the house. At least the windows were dark. Evidently the house slept on. Taking a deep breath, she threw her leg over the ledge.

The descent seemed longer than three stories. By the time she reached the ground, her knees were trembling and her fingers aching. She took no time to recover, though. The minute her feet touched the soft flower bed, she ran after Thrasher.

She made it no more than fifteen feet before she heard the footsteps behind her. She ran faster. She could see Thrasher disappear into the trees. She pulled up her skirts to lengthen her stride. Something slammed into her and shoved her straight to the ground. She knew who it was even before he spoke.

"I probably should have told you," Harry murmured in her ear. "I don't sleep."

Chapter 4

Harry felt as if he'd fallen on knives instead of Kate's soft body, his ribs setting up a grating screech. He wasn't about to let her know, though. She would take advantage, sure as check.

"Sadly predictable," he said, trying his best to sound as if he could breathe past the stabbing pain in his chest. "I expected better from you."

Stretched out along her back, he grabbed her splayed hands and held on, fully expecting a fight. When she didn't immediately move, he took a second in the whispering darkness to assess the situation. Kate had climbed down the east wall and headed for the woods at the far end of the lawn. He could only be thankful he'd heard her, since he'd had to run all the way across the front of the abbey and turn the corner to even see her.

A movement at the tree line caught his eye. Her young accomplice, no doubt. The little blighter had a fast pair of feet. It didn't matter. Harry knew who he was. He'd seen the little urchin riding the back of Kate's carriages.

"So," he said jovially to his captive, "resorting to children for rescue now, are you, Kate? What's the matter? No *cicisbeos* in the neighborhood?"

He was trying his damndest to ignore the sweet pressure of her derriere against his groin, the feminine swoop and swell of her too-lush form beneath him. She'd almost gotten away, and he blamed himself for not anticipating it.

"What?" he asked. "No excuse? No plea for clemency or offer to negotiate?"

That was when he realized that something was wrong. She was too still. He thought she'd shuddered once, but after that she went quiet, emitting no more than a funny, rasping little wheeze he almost couldn't hear over the shush of the breeze.

She couldn't be having trouble breathing. He didn't have all his weight on her. But by now she should have been bucking and kicking, at least cursing him back to the ninth generation. Instead, she was eerily still, her forehead on the ground, her hands limp.

He couldn't have knocked her out, could he? "Kate?"

Nothing. He lifted back enough to give her a bit of room and flipped her over on her back. Not unconscious. Her eyes were open.

"You really have to stop this, Kate," he told her, holding her hands, just in case.

She didn't answer. She didn't look at him. It was as if she weren't there at all. She just...lay there, staring sightlessly past him. An odd chill snaked down Harry's back. Capturing both of her hands in one of his, he tapped at her cheek.

"Kate."

She was beginning to frighten him. Kate was never this quiet. This still. "Kate, answer me or I'll do something drastic."

He knew he wasn't using all of his faculties. He'd actually been half asleep in the library when the sound of scraping against the outside wall had pulled him awake. He still felt groggy. But that didn't excuse his next decision, except that he was beginning to feel desperate, and he could think of only one way to guarantee an immediate reaction from her. He kissed her.

At first, he merely touched her lips, nudging them with his own. Brushing back and forth. She didn't even resist. She was scaring the hell out of him.

He pushed farther, deepening the kiss, stroking her throat with his hand. He nibbled at her bottom lip; he ran his tongue across the seam of her lips. He pressed against her closed teeth.

He wished he could have said he remained unaffected. He wished like hell the taste of Kate didn't suddenly call up too many memories to contain. Good memories, sweet memories, the kind that a man should store up as ballast against all the evil and violence he would face in the world.

It had been his last moment of innocence, that summer, when he'd still believed that the world was his for the taking, when he believed Katie loved him. When he still held out the hope that she really would cast her lot with him.

Too quickly to think, he found himself spinning back there, and it cost him his control. Before he knew it, he was urging her to open for him; he was stroking and soothing and doing his best to incite a firestorm. And she was responding. Her lips began to soften, her body move, tentatively at first, as if she'd forgotten the sensuous duels they had once fought.

Relief swept through him, gratitude. She was all right. He let go of her hands and cupped her face, his body molding itself against hers. He felt her heart against his, and it was thrumming like a hummingbird's. He was in danger of being lost, and he knew it.

And then she bit him.

He reared back in outrage. "Ow! What the hell was that for?"

He reached up to touch his lower lip and came away with blood.

Well, at least he'd accomplished one thing. She was definitely alert. Her eyes were cold as death, the icy green almost vanished around huge pupils. "You have to ask?"

"You enjoyed it as much as I did! You can't tell me you didn't."

"I'm not telling you anything except get off me."

He couldn't; not yet. He couldn't pull himself away from the heat of her body; he couldn't just shut away those memories as if they had never existed. They existed; they'd just been lies.

He wanted to look back on those summer days as the last days of innocence. But there had been nothing innocent about Kate. Nothing pure or true. And he'd paid the price for believing there had been.

She squirmed, trying to push him away. "Get. Off."

"Why?" he asked, suddenly angry. "You've fucked every other man in Europe. Why not me?"

He heard the words come out of his mouth and knew they were ugly, violent things. He saw their impact on her already ashen features, and it shamed him. He was doing it again, hurting her. He kept hurting her, and that was so unlike him. He had never once given in to anger; not in all the long years of soldiering, when the bloodlust of battle too often spilled over onto perpetrators and innocents alike. He had seen the cruelties men inflicted on men, on women and children, and he had held himself sequestered behind a strong wall of discipline. But suddenly the anger rose from deep within him, and he couldn't seem to rein it in.

"You owe it to me," he grated, retaking her hands.

She managed a breathy laugh. "The only thing I owe you is a hat pin in the eye."

He couldn't seem to catch his breath. He was still hard, still consumed by the soft feel of her beneath him. He could feel how taut her nipples were. He could hear the quick rasp of her breathing. And he knew how hard her heart was beating. She was as aroused as he. She *had* responded. And she was belittling him for *his* reaction.

Suddenly he resented the hell out of her. Because of her, he'd spent a decade wading through one battlefield after another. He had faced atrocities no mortal man should ever suffer, been wounded to the point of death, and still carried the cost of that last battle in his chest. And her? She sat atop the dung heap of society, a rich trollop with a title to protect her. He shook with the urge to hurt her. To make her regret every promise she'd ever made to him and broken. Every hurt *she'd* inflicted.

"I hope you don't mean to tell me you're indifferent to me," he accused, so close he could see her pupils dilate even more. "I know you too well. Why not make your incarceration more pleasant? I could certainly find better things to do with our nights."

If anything, her skin grew paler. "I hope you don't think you're offering me a compliment."

"I'm offering you a deal. Don't you think I have as much right as anybody else to finally get what I was promised?"

"Oh, I see," she said, looking away. "This is about your rights."

"Why not?"

She blinked. "Men do have their rights, don't they? Their rights to their house, their horse, their land, their women, their children. Their right to own, to control, to punish." Like a lightning strike, her gaze met his, and he could taste her disdain. "Well, Harry, a woman has only one right, and that is the right to occasionally say no. No, Harry."

And with that, she turned her head away and lay silent as a stone.

As if she'd taken away a light, Harry suddenly felt the darkness again, the chill of the night breeze. He heard a dog barking far off and the slam of a door somewhere in the house. He smelled the grass they'd crushed when they'd fallen. Beneath him, Kate was rigid and still, her gaze once again fixed on nothing.

He flushed with guilt. He'd heard the faint tremor in her voice, and knew that it didn't matter what she had done to him, what he thought she'd stolen. She didn't deserve that kind of disdain. No woman did.

Briefly closing his eyes, he lifted himself away from her. She lay splayed on the grass, her skirts twisted around her legs, her cloak lying half over her dress. Taking a moment, he covered her legs and untangled her cloak. He was just about to push himself to his feet when her cloak shifted, revealing a tear in her dress that exposed part of her breast. Harry saw it and stopped cold. It wasn't the breast that shocked him. It was what he saw on it, round as a coin, almost an inch across, just above the nipple.

"Is that a *tattoo*?" he demanded, not sure whether he was more surprised or outraged that she'd disfigured her beautiful breasts. Perfect, full, firm, milky white. Irrevocably marred.

But he only had a moment to react, because his words incited the oddest reaction of the night. Suddenly Kate rolled over and pulled herself into a ball, yanking her cloak over her. "Yes," she said in a curiously flat voice, her head tucked like a hedgehog's. "It's a tattoo."

Harry was confused. He would expect her to react with defiance or insouciance. She sounded shamed. She looked as if she were trying to disappear.

"What is it a tattoo of?" he demanded, suddenly unsettled.

Kate lurched to her feet and turned away to retie her cloak. Her head was down, her long neck curiously vulnerable looking, as if she were bowed under a weight of some kind. "That," she said, stalking past him, "is information you have no right to."

"Kate," Harry protested, hand out.

But she evaded him, heading back toward the front of the house. He hurried after her, intent on catching her. He had to find out what that tattoo meant.

He reached her just as they broached the flower beds near the south corner. Grabbing her hard by the arm, he spun her around. Kate ducked, arm up over her face, as if warding off a blow.

Harry froze, suddenly even more off balance. He knew that reaction. He'd seen it a thousand times in places of violence, a distinctive cringe into defensive posture. Instinctively he let go of her arm. Still half turned away, Kate cast him a quick, oddly defiant look. Then she turned and ran for the woods.

"Kate, stop!"

It only took six steps to catch her. Again he grabbed for her arm. He caught cloth instead, and it tore. Kate shrieked, batting his hands away. He pulled back, but it was already too late. His hand had brushed against that dark red design on her breast. It was no tattoo he'd touched.

"Let me see," he commanded.

She tried to run again, but he grabbed her around the waist and held on. She fought like a wildcat, kicking, biting, scratching. He knew he was shaming her even more, but he couldn't let her go until he knew for certain what it was he'd felt.

He saw. He let her go.

"That isn't a tattoo," he all but accused, hands clenched, chest suddenly on fire.

She stood before him, trembling and white, her hair falling out of its braid, her hand covering the expanse of breast exposed by her torn dress. Even in the dim light from the stars he could see a sheen of tears he knew she would never let fall.

"No, Harry, it is not a tattoo. Are you finished now?"

He took an instinctive step closer. She retreated. "Kate, that—" He waved an ineffectual hand at the monstrous thing. Raised, red, shiny, the perfect round image of a coat of arms. "It's a brand!"

She tilted her head, and he saw how brittle her defiance was. It shook him. "Yes, Harry," she said. "It is."

"How?"

"Don't you recognize it?" She pulled the material away so he could get a better look. He didn't need to. He could still feel the imprint of it across the tips of his fingers. "It's the crest for the House of Murther."

He blinked. He shuddered, the breath leaving him. "Murther? Your husband?"

"Yes, Harry. My husband. He wanted to make sure I knew who I belonged to."

"But *why*?"

For a moment, she just looked at him. Then, grimly, she smiled. "Because it was his right."

*　　*　　*

Harry wasn't sure how long he stood there, his hands clenched before him like a fighter, his chest on fire. He thought he'd been inured to evil. He thought he'd seen it all. But as he stood there, it occurred to him that the curious honey bee Lady Bea had embroidered on Kate's chemise would have been perfectly placed to cover that brand. But there had been two bees, one on each breast.

Christ. He wanted to vomit.

"Major?" came Mudge's voice from the front of the house. "You need to get back here now!"

Harry closed his eyes. *No more. Please, no more.*

He couldn't ignore Mudge, though. Favoring his ribs, he set off for the front of the house. He didn't see Kate. Had she made for the woods? Could he blame her if she had? He was beginning to wonder if Schroeder hadn't been right after all. It wasn't logical, but the courage Kate had just shown shook his belief in her culpability. She might be outrageous. He was no longer so sure she was venal.

He trotted around the corner to the front of the house to see Kate ahead of him, making for the door. He wasn't sure if he was relieved or not. He didn't know how to face her again.

"C'mon!" a shrill, young voice cried, and Harry looked up to see that a group of men crowded the front door. He couldn't believe it. Kate's tiger was back, bouncing up and down on his toes on the portico, and surrounded by three armed compatriots.

"We don't have time ta waste!" The boy was punching a finger at Mudge's chest. "Let us in!"

Kate had already seen them and was running for the front door. "Thrasher! I told you to run!"

"You stay right there!" Harry yelled at the boy and picked up his own pace.

Kate's tiger caught sight of his mistress and gave a frantic wave. "Get inside!" he yelled, evidently to Kate. "You're in trouble! There's a bad man arter ya!"

"I am not bad," Harry protested instinctively as he closed in on Kate, both of them still at least thirty feet from the door.

"Not you!" Thrasher yelled. "Axman Billy! 'E's right on our 'eels!"

At the name, Kate stumbled to a halt, her head swiveling toward the dark woods. "Axman Billy? *Again?*"

"'E wants ta kill you, Y'r Graciousness! And when he's done that, he's going back t' kill Lady Bea!"

Harry almost ran into Kate. "You know somebody named Axman Billy?"

"He once set fire to my house in Brussels." She started running again. "We have to get back to London."

Splinting his ribs with his arm, Harry followed at a lope. "You are acquainted with the most interesting people."

She had just turned to answer when there was a pinging against the wall by her head, and rock chips went flying. The unmistakable report of a rifle echoed from the woods. Harry took a flying leap and brought Kate to the ground for a second time.

He really wasn't going to survive this. His chest felt as if it were caving in. "You certainly seem to have a way of...annoying people, Katie," he grunted. "What did you ever do to Axman Billy?"

"I'm afraid...," she gasped, squirming beneath him. "I have never been introduced to the gentleman."

Harry heard the thunder of running feet, and suddenly one of Kate's friends was yanking him up. Before Harry could so much as protest, a behemoth appeared and collected Kate like an oversize parcel before running for the portico.

Another gunshot echoed through the valley. Harry instinctively ducked, but the marksman wasn't aiming for him. Thrasher hadn't lied. Another bullet buried itself into the stone near Kate's bobbing head. Mudge, his head swiveling in an attempt to scan the grounds, was ushering Kate and her menagerie in through the studded oak front door. Harry followed, another bullet just missing his beleaguered chest, to find that extra lanterns had already been lit and his personal weapons laid out on the marble hall table. He fully expected Mudge to shut the big door behind them. Instead, his batman turned back out to the night.

"Get in here, you dolt!" Harry snapped. "They have guns."

Mudge nodded, still scanning the darkness. "Yessir." Then in a lightning-fast move the boy pulled a knife from his sleeve by the blade and sent it whizzing straight into the darkness. Harry heard a strangled cry from the overgrown hedges lining the front drive. Mudge nodded with satisfaction and slammed the door shut.

Alongside Harry, Kate stared at Mudge, slack-jawed. "Why, Mudge," she said with a tight smile. "You have unexpected talents."

Mudge gave her a brief bow. "I don't hold with guns, ma'am."

Kate grinned. "You really have to show me how to do that."

"You do," Harry warned, "and you'll be back on the line." It was time, he decided, to reassert control. "Where is everyone?"

"Checking doors and windows," Mudge said, lighting another lantern. "Gathering weapons and supplies."

"Good." Not good enough, of course. This place was a death trap, dozens of rooms, acres of window. "Keep an eye out for surprises, Mudge. We'll need to prepare for trouble."

Mudge picked up a gun and turned for the great hall. "On my way, Major."

"We need to get back to Bea," Kate said, busy patting the arms of the motley group that circled her.

"It'll be easier to just kill Axman Billy here," Harry said. "I assume he is connected to the Lions, somehow? Or do you have other enemies I should know about?"

"We ran afoul of Axman when we were hiding Jack Gracechurch in Brussels," she said, her hand on the arm of the big man who'd carried her. "I've just always assumed he was working for the Lions."

Harry rubbed at the ache in his chest. "Well, Kate, it seems he's followed you to the country. May I assume that these…gentlemen belong to you?"

She flashed a blinding smile at the men who ringed her. "They do. You know Thrasher, and this is my butler, Finney—" A thick-necked man who had the look of an ex-prizefighter and now balanced a Manton shotgun on his shoulder. "My chef, Maurice." A thin little man with pop eyes, a pencil mustache, and a pair of cavalry pistols tucked in his belt. "And my groom George." The behemoth who had carried Kate inside: tall, round, placid, with a moon face, blank smile, and nothing more. All of them positioned to protect their duchess.

"Loyalty is commendable in a staff," Harry said.

"Glad you feel that way," Finney the butler growled, glowering at the tear in Kate's dress. "'Cause, we find any-body hurtin' our lady, we'd take care o' him certain. Not a one of us is afraid o' the nubbin' cheat."

Harry's first instinct was to protest. But the butler wasn't that far wrong.

"We can discuss that later, you and I," he said. "But right now we have Axman Billy to deal with. I don't suppose you know how he found us."

It was Finney who answered. "We're that sorry, Your Grace. We think Billy 'n his crew followed us."

"How many?" Harry asked.

"Eight." Finney shrugged. "Ten. All armed."

Harry nodded. "From those shots, at least one of them is a Rifleman."

"Too bad I didn't tag that one," Mudge muttered from the other room. "Give the Ninety-fifth a bad name."

Harry faced Kate's staff. "You said they wanted to kill Lady Kate. Not take her?"

Thrasher shook his head. "Nup. 'Eard it clear as day. 'Whatever you do'"—he mimicked the rougher accents— "'make sure she's dead. Take care o' the rest later.'"

The Lions had killed their own before, Harry knew. They had at least eight well-armed men out in the darkness who wanted Kate. It was up to Harry to prevent that. He needed to come up with a plan.

Defensive positions. Field of fire. Advantage. Come on, man, think.

He spent a moment calling up the building he'd spent the day walking about. Originally a Cistercian abbey, the main part of the house was built in a square around a central courtyard, with kitchens and storerooms up the west wing, the ruins of the old church along the north, living quarters along the east, and the great hall, which had once been the refectory, taking up much of the south.

The hall opened off the entryway, where they now stood, an echoing, shadowy stone-walled space hung in old tapestries and lined on opposite sides with two stories of ogived windows. Not too big to defend, although there were a lot of windows. Stone walls were good, and the doors were thick wood. They'd take a lot of battering. Even better, the room had a screened, window-lined balcony on the second floor. Better line of fire against invaders.

God knew he needed all the advantage he could get. He might have greater numbers, but four of them were nothing but house staff.

The sound of feet clattering down the main staircase brought him back to attention. Schroeder rounded the corner into the entryway followed by the four men, their arms full of guns.

"They're in the bushes out there, Major," Frank said, his orange hair strangely bright in the gloom. "Saw 'em from the windows. They'll be circlin' the house soon."

Guns were passed out, and Harry shoved one in his belt.

"Are these the only weapons?"

"There's a kitchen full of knives," Mudge said with a lazy smile.

"Get them."

Stepping to the door into the great hall, Harry assessed the position. The room rose three stories, with a vaulted gothic ceiling and ranks of arched windows. The view out to the drive was clear enough that Harry could see deeper shadows moving among the foliage.

"Get all the supplies in here," he said. "Then split up, half up on the balcony. We need a defensive position if they break in."

"Oh, they'll break in," Thrasher said, hopping from one foot to the other. "Nasty lot. Scourge o' the Dials, they are."

Harry saw Schroeder attempting to hand a rifle to Kate and intercepted her. "No," he said, handing the weapon back.

"The whole point is for you to be safe," he told Kate. "Frank, secure Her Grace someplace safe. The wine cellars." He pointed to the west door. "Just under there."

"Why me?" the big redhead protested, stepping back. "She stuck pins in me."

Kate bucked in Harry's grip. "Don't you dare!"

"Don't argue," Harry grated. "Move."

"No!" she cried, her voice oddly thin as she struggled. "I can help!"

Harry shoved her at Frank, who instinctively held on. "We don't have time for this, Kate. It's you they want."

Why the hell did he feel so guilty? He had to do this. She was going to be inconvenienced, but she'd be alive, damn it.

She turned to her staff, obviously expecting help.

"Go on with the man, Lady Kate," Finney said, looking more tormented than Kate. "We'll come f'r you once this business is over so we can go get Lady Bea."

The rest of her staff stood where they were.

A curious sob escaped her. "You're fired, Finney."

He didn't move. "Yes, ma'am."

Her staff's betrayal seemed to snap her resistance. When Frank led her away, she looked lost, a child who'd been deserted. God, Harry thought. He couldn't wait to get free of all this.

"Take a lantern, Frank!" he yelled.

Trying hard to ignore the halting shuffle of Kate's retreating footsteps, Harry grabbed a gun. "To me!" he yelled to his men.

They had no sooner collected around him than a window shattered. Everybody whipped around to see a lantern splinter across the stone floor of the great hall, spilling oil and fire.

"We probably should have told you," Finney said, running with everyone into the hall. "Billy's particular fond of fire."

They'd just managed to stomp out the flames when another window crashed with the same results. The shudder of red and orange washed the high walls and lit the night. With a whoosh, the tapestry to the left of the great fireplace caught.

"Get it down and shove it in the fireplace," Harry snapped. "This is a stone room. The fire won't hurt us. Those guns outside will. Find a window. I'm going up to the balcony. Half of you with me."

Harry had just turned for the staircase when he noticed Finney on his knees before Thrasher, his hands on the boy's arms.

"Come on, now, lad. 'Er Grace needs y'r help."

Eyes wide and glassy, Thrasher couldn't seem to take his eyes off the flames that licked up the wall fifteen feet away. He was shaking his head, and his mouth was silently working.

Harry had seen the reaction before. "Thrasher!" he barked. "Can you load guns?"

The boy started, his attention finally caught. His features were haggard, but he managed a tremulous smile. "Does y'r granny fart?"

Harry grinned. "Get the powder and shot from Schroeder. We need to move."

Still the boy stood frozen, the flames reflected in his staring eyes.

"Now!" Harry yelled in his best parade-field voice.

It worked. The boy still shook, but he let Finney push him up the steps. Closer by, another window exploded with a burst of flame. Smoke curled up toward the high roof, but the worst the fire could do was make them visible to the marksmen outside.

"All right, then," Harry yelled. "Everybody pick a spot. I don't want anybody walking away outside."

He followed his own instructions, taking the stairs two at a time. When he reached the gallery, he saw the moon-faced George punch through one of the windows with his fist. The chef Maurice patted the big man on the back and handed him a fowling piece.

"You sure that's wise?" Harry asked.

Maurice grinned, revealing a gold tooth. "'E knows 'ow to shoot, George."

Harry nodded. "Shoot down on them as they approach the building."

Evidently George needed no encouragement. Even before Harry finished speaking, the big man fired. Harry heard a muffled oath and the crash of bushes. Backing out to hand Thrasher his gun, George flashed Harry a beaming smile.

Choosing his own window, Harry broke it out with the butt of his gun. At least the adrenaline had finally kicked in. His brain cleared, and time slowed. Battleground reflexes kicked in. He knelt and aimed, but he was aware of everything that was happening. Below, his men called back and forth. The snap and pop of rifle fire peppered the night, and behind him Thrasher kept on a constant move refilling weapons. Sighting a moving shadow on the lawn, Harry fired and passed back his rifle.

Harry had just accepted another from Thrasher when Frank thundered up the stairs. "Sir," he called, dropping down next to Harry. "The boy." He was whispering.

Harry looked to where Thrasher was shoving a ramrod down a rifle with shaking hands. Frank seemed to relax a bit. "Her Grace was worried. Said Thrasher freezes in fires. Lost his whole family to one."

Harry handed him a gun and resumed his position. "You sure the duchess is safe?"

Frank accepted the gun and checked it. "As houses, sir. Nobody'll find her."

A shadow moved out on the lawn, and a bullet ricocheted off the stone by Harry's head. "They might overrun the place before this is through," he warned Frank.

"They won't overrun the wine cellar. And I have the keys."

Harry stopped breathing. All around him the night was alive with the hiss and pop of the encroaching fire, the crack and whine of gunshots. But suddenly all Harry could think of was Kate locked in a wine cellar, alone. In the darkest, dampest place in the house.

"You left her the lantern."

"I did."

It was all he could do for now. He had bigger fish to fry. "Take a position downstairs so you can get to her easily."

The fire downstairs cast a very convenient light on the lawn outside. Fire glinted off upraised weapons, and Harry aimed for one. He was just about to fire when he saw someone lighting another torch.

Harry leveled his pistol on the form and pulled the trigger. The attacker collapsed, the fire he'd just lit splattering over his clothing. Harry ignored his screams and tossed the spent pistol to Thrasher, who was crouched on the landing, his supplies splayed out on the wood floor.

Around him Harry could hear the flat crack and tinkle of broken glass. There was the report of a Brown Bess musket and the crack of a window just to his right. He saw a man sprint across the lawn. Shots were fired, but the attacker came on, launching himself through the window. Another followed close on his heels.

To Harry's right there was a grunt and a resounding, "Oh, bugger!"

Harry turned to see Finney fall back against the screen, hand up to his neck. Smoke curled through the screen, and Harry wondered how long this wooden floor would hold. It was now or never.

"All right, then," he said getting to his feet. "I've had enough. Let's let the bastards know who they're dealing with."

And with his motley crew giving a ragged cheer behind him, he ran straight down into the fight.

Chapter 5

Well, Harry thought as he looked around at the carnage in the great hall. One thing was for certain. Diccan had been right. Someone was after Kate, and they didn't care in the least who got in their way. Smoke rose in lazy spirals from the charred debris that littered the hall. Ancient leaded windows lay shattered on the floor, and old Holland covers lay over the bodies of the dead.

Frank had been killed. Finney was wounded, a pad pressed to his neck as he sat against the wall while Kate's chef, Maurice, prepared a bandage. Thrasher was bouncing around helping Mudge collect spent weapons and supplies, but Harry could see that he was camouflaging his own injury, a burn suffered on his arm when he'd tried to help Frank pull the burning tapestries down in an effort to spare the roof.

Harry had to give the little imp credit. He'd faced his fear better than half the men Harry had led. He'd make a hell of a soldier someday.

"Six killed," Schroeder said, pinning up her straggling hair as she approached. She was soot-streaked and weary looking, her dress torn at the shoulder and Frank's blood spattered across her skirt. She pointed to the Holland covers that masked several untidy lumps. "Two inside, the rest out."

Harry rubbed at his neck. His chest hurt again. His eyes were burning, and his legs felt as if he were trying to walk through mortar. And Frank was dead. Frank, who had been such a good man that Harry had trusted Kate with him twice. If Harry hadn't already made up his mind to quit this insanity, that would have done it. He had buried enough good men for a lifetime.

"Major?"

Harry nodded, as if he'd been paying attention. "Six enemy dead, you said." The morning sun was just up, its light pouring in past the shattered glass to chase colors across the littered floor. "You sure there were at least eight, Thrasher?" he called.

The boy looked up from where he was stacking the rifles against the wall. "I counted ten. And Axman in't 'ere." The boy shook his sooty head. "And 'e's not a cove what quits easy, guv."

Harry sighed. "No. I don't imagine he is. We need to get out of here."

"We need to get Lady Bea," Finney insisted.

One of Harry's men looked up. "Frank was in charge of transportation."

And Frank lay under a Holland cover.

"Cor luv ya," Thrasher protested. "George 'n me'll do f'r the carriage. Our job, innit?"

"If we still have horses. Parker," he said, pointing to one of his men. "Go with them. Mudge, gather what we need. We have to go before our friend regroups."

"What about 'Er Grace?" Finney asked.

Harry's stomach dropped. *Oh, hell. Kate.*

"I'll get her," Schroeder offered.

He shouldn't have felt so relieved. It was his job to see to Kate. But she had become one responsibility too many.

"She's waiting in the wine cellar," he said, walking over to where Frank lay.

Keeping his gaze well away from Frank's shattered face, he threw back the Holland cover and rifled through his pockets until he found the keys.

"Meet us out back," he told Schroeder, tossing them to her.

He turned to the rest of his men. "Right," he said, assessing them. "Get everything ready to go. I don't think our attackers will return in broad daylight, but keep a sharp eye."

He planned to already be seated on Beau and waiting alongside the packed carriage by the time Schroeder retrieved Kate. He didn't even make it out of the great hall before he heard her voice echoing up from the stairs.

"...not that I don't appreciate the company, of course. But next time, they can haunt their own nightmares."

Mid-sentence, Kate shot into the hall like one of Whinyate's rockets, her trajectory just as unpredictable, her fuse well lit. Harry swore he could see sparks flying from her skin. On the other hand, the lantern she carried was out.

"Do you know how cold it is down there?" she demanded, as if chastising a tardy lover. "I could have died of ague before you lot remembered me. Tell Frank for me that he'll never be invited to Eastcourt for Christmas. In fact, none of you will."

Harry was going to smile until he realized that she was walking right past him without once acknowledging him. She just kept pacing and rubbing her hand against her skirt, as if wiping something away that stank.

"You can stop now," he suggested. She didn't seem to hear.

Schroeder entered the room behind Kate and walked straight for Harry. "I'm not sure you should put her into a carriage quite yet," she said quietly.

"Why?" He gave in and looked at Kate, who hadn't slowed at all.

Schroeder shook her head. "Somehow the lantern went out. By the time I opened the door, she was talking to people."

"Who?"

She frowned. "I think...dead soldiers."

Harry's stomach dropped. "Stay with her."

"I tried. She's having none of me."

So he wasn't going to be able to ignore Kate after all. Bloody *hell*.

"Let's see what we can do." Handing the rifles he'd collected off to Schroeder, he went after Kate. "Are you all right?" he asked, pacing her.

She never turned around. "I've decided to remodel my house in town," she said, her voice tumbling around the cavernous space like a bright waterfall as she walked along the windows, taking a quick peek out of each. "I had enough time just now to plan the decor. Egyptian, don't you think? I believe the craze for alligator legs died out far too soon. After all, furniture should do something besides just sit there. Let it scare cats and small children. They deserve it. Come to think of it, I can never get my family to visit. Perhaps if I got a sarcophagus or two, the infantry would badger their parents to visit their aunt Kate so they could play hide-and-seek with a mummy." Without slowing, she shook her head. "No, that's probably not going to work. I think my youngest niece is coming out next year. I must tell you, I find it excessively annoying to have siblings old enough to have children my age. Do you know how uncomfortable introductions are? 'Hello, this is my nephew Percy, who held me at my christening.' Positively archaic."

He caught up with her just before she tripped over Frank. "Kate, stop!" he insisted, taking her arm. "You have to stop."

She didn't even look at him. "No, I don't think so. I think I need to go home. I need to check on Bea. I need to shop for drapes. Gold. Maybe purple. With stripes."

She kept trying to pull away. Grabbing the lantern from her and setting it on the floor, Harry pulled off his hacking jacket and helped her into it. She looked down and shook her head. "No, no, not brown. It makes me look sallow. Corbeau, maybe. Or bottle green. I look positively sybaritic in bottle green."

"If you don't stop," he said, his voice sharp, "I'm going to kiss you. If that doesn't work, I'll slap you."

She kept pulling. He could hear that funny, wheezing rasp in her breathing again.

"Kate. I'm sorry. I had to keep you safe. I didn't mean for you to be kept in the dark."

He felt the shudder go through her. Finally, she stopped and focused on him, although he certainly wished he could have missed it. Her eyes were bleak as death. "Really? Where did you think he'd put me? The conservatory?"

"I didn't have a choice. If Axman Billy does work for the Lions, his attack makes it more obvious than ever that you know something."

She actually reared back to box his ears, but he caught her wrist at the last minute. "Bad manners, old girl."

And that got the biggest reaction of all. Full-throated laughter. "Bad *manners*? Good Christ, Harry, try for some originality. I've told you I'm not a traitor every way except singing it accompanied by harp. I'm finished now. I'm not talking to you. I'm not helping you find your bloody verse.

I don't care if Prinny has to live in a monastery in Crete to keep him from being assassinated. I don't care if Parliament tumbles or the Crown Jewels are replaced with paste. I'm finished."

"So you'd sacrifice Lady Bea because you feel insulted?" he asked, goading her farther. "You do remember she was threatened, too?"

It was a low blow; he knew it. He didn't care. He didn't have time to bargain with her. Even so, it didn't make him feel any more heroic to see her face go stark white. He hated the hitch in her breath that sounded too much like a sob.

"Bastard."

He shrugged. "If I have to be. But if this attack does anything, it should convince you that we're not playing games. Real traitors will go to any lengths to stop you, and right now I'm the only one preventing it."

Her head bowed. He knew she was trembling. He wanted to hold her, just like any wounded animal, to pet her until she calmed and promise her everything would be all right. If he tried, she would eviscerate him.

"I assume everyone's all right?" she asked, her voice small.

That was the moment Harry admitted to himself that he really had been a bastard. Not for urging her on. For punishing her for something she hadn't done. Harry had seen a lot of people dissemble in the last ten years, traitors and cowards and criminals of all stripes. He prided himself on being able to smell out a liar. But he couldn't pretend anymore that he'd been fair. He'd let old anger interfere with his judgment.

Kate might have betrayed him ten years ago. But she wasn't lying now. Her reactions were too raw to mistake. She truly didn't know why the traitors were after her. She wasn't consorting with the Lions. She was just trying to get home to her friend.

He'd been wrong. And he'd made her pay for it.

When he didn't answer her right away, she looked up, and Harry felt even worse. Dread darkened her eyes, loss, grief, the last ghosts of terror.

"Finney was winged," he said, clenching his hands to keep from reaching out to her. "Your chef bandaged him right after dispatching the culprit with a butcher knife. Thrasher now holds him in awe. Said it was nice to know the man wasn't 'nuthin' but cheese and bad temper.' But I would advise you to be careful. Thrasher is now completely enamored of all things sharp."

Her eyes glistened with tears she never let fall as she turned to search for her staff. Even before she saw Finney, she was walking that way. "And Axman Billy?"

Harry had hoped they would already be on the road before she thought to ask that. "He left six of his men behind."

She stopped hard, her head up. "You mean he got away?"

Harry sighed. "Thrasher did not recognize him among the dead."

If possible, she went even paler. "My God. Bea. We have to go."

"First I get you someplace safe. Then I'll get Bea."

She turned on him, a lioness again. "You didn't listen to me. We go to Bea."

"You don't have a choice. I'm not letting him get you."

Her eyes grew hard in a way Harry barely recognized. "Trust me when I tell you, Harry. Very little has the power to frighten me anymore. Unless you put me back in that hole, you won't stop me."

Harry shook his head, but he was secretly impressed. "Lord, I can't wait to hand you off to Drake."

It was as if he'd pulled some string. Suddenly seductress Kate was back, her eyes sultry and lazy and insolent. "So do I," she said. "He's far more...*amenable*."

Harry was suddenly furious. "Stop it."

She flinched as if he'd struck her. "Stop what?"

And then he saw it in her eyes, a flicker, no more than a flash of a pain so hard and helpless that it shook him to his core. He wished he'd never seen it, another chink in Kate's bold facade. He didn't want to become more entangled in Kate's problems. He wanted to hand her off and finally be done with her. Be done with everything.

"There's no one here to seduce," he said.

Predictably, Kate answered with a too-bright smile and a sashay over to where her staff had gathered. "And now, Finney, you and I need to discuss who is in charge."

And what Harry was left with, oddly, was a dawning respect for Kate's strength.

Thank heavens, he thought, watching her stalk off, that she was probably innocent. If she threw her lot in with the Lions, Prinny would be chanting matins in Greek by Christmas.

*   *   *

On her way over to Finney, Kate stayed as close to the windows as she could. The sun was up; she needed to feel it on her face. She needed to sate herself on it, especially after that last inexplicable exchange with Harry. He saw too much; he got too close. And then in a heartbeat, he left. She didn't need to survive that all over again.

She needed to stop thinking about Harry and pay attention. She needed to get control of herself. If she didn't, Harry would, and she couldn't tolerate that.

It was so hard, though. No thought would adhere to another. No heartbeat separated itself enough from the one before to ease the rushing panic in her chest. All she could focus on was the idea that if she stopped for a second, Bea would be lost.

Her footsteps echoed away into the gloom as she strode over to where Finney sat, shamefaced and bleeding on the floor. And there were Thrasher, Maurice, and George—singed, a bit bloody, but whole. She let go her first sigh of relief.

"By the looks of you all," she greeted them, shrinking at the shrill tone of her voice, "I had a better time in the cellars. None of you deserves to ride in my coach looking like this."

Looking up from where he was gathering up a pile of equipment, Thrasher flashed her a brash grin. "Cor, Y'r Graciousness. You should see t' other blokes. Proper put 'em to bed wit' a shovel, we did."

"And you, George?" she asked, smiling up at him as she took his hand.

George's smile was incandescent. "Got mine, Katie. Got mine good."

She nodded briskly. "Excellent. I am positively blue-deviled that I had no chance to wield a gun."

"You shoot?" Schroeder asked next to her, looking a bit taken aback.

She flashed a bright smile. "I was taught by a general's daughter. And now, Mudge is going to add dinner cutlery to my arsenal. I am in alt."

Her heart skidded when she saw the state of Thrasher's sleeve. "Thrasher," she snapped, pointing to the singed velvet of his cherished crimson-and-gold uniform. "I forbid anyone to be in my service who refuses to care for himself. Maurice, see to him."

Thrasher went beet red. "Yes, Y'r Worship."

She nodded briskly. "I would like to thank each of you for coming to my aid. You have my undying gratitude...well, except for Frank. He must pay a penalty for thinking I considered an empty wine cellar appropriate accommodations for a duchess."

As she spoke, she looked around. "And where is Frank? I have decided to forgive him. After all, Harry was the one who gave the order. I'll punish him instead."

She noticed that everybody was looking over at Harry, as if expecting him to speak. Then they made the mistake of looking over to where three bundles lay on the floor. Kate looked, too. She stopped, her heart skidding in her chest. The drape had slipped a bit from one of the bundles. A shock of bright orange hair peeked out.

Oh...

For the longest time, she could manage no more than a stricken silence. Another specter to pace the night with her. "You'll furnish me with the direction of Frank's family," she told Harry without looking away from that untidy bundle, so easily overlooked amid the jumble of debris.

"That's not your—"

She leveled an unrelenting glare on him. "It is my life he saved."

"Maybe when we find a safer burrow," Harry suggested. "Right now, the carriage is ready. We need to leave while we can."

"We have your trunk packed, Lady Kate," Barbara offered.

Kate stalked right past her. "Bother my trunk. Just promise to get us to Bea."

Harry tried to stop her. "I told you, Kate..."

"Thrasher," she said, not looking at Harry. "Did Axman Billy threaten Bea?"

Thrasher's nod was emphatic. "'Eard the blighter m'self."

"I heard it, too," Finney admitted. "Said after they killed you, she were next."

Only then did Kate face her nemesis. "That means the discussion is closed." And turning in a whirl of azure kerseymere, she led the way out.

101 28A   0622X70115 09:23AM

Thanks for shopping at
barnes & noble

MEMBER SAVINGS $0.30

CASH CHANGE   0.23
CASH   8.00
TOTAL   7.77
Sales Tax II (8.000%)   0.xx
Subtotal   7.19

(1 @ 7.19)   7.19
(1 @ 7.99) Member card 10%(0.80)
9780446542050   II
Always a fempiress (Book - B. Booker Series
ORDER NUMBER 2274 12510
CUSTOMER ORDER PICKUP

BARNES & NOBLE MEMBER   EXP 06/30/2013

STR:2274 REG:002 TRN:1541 CSHR:Phillip K

Barnes & Noble Booksellers #2274
313 Corte Madera Town Center
Corte Madera, CA 94925
415 924 9016

books made within 14 days of purchase from a Barnes & Noble Booksellers store or Barnes & Noble.com with the below exceptions:

A store credit for the purchase price will be issued (i) for purchases made by check less than 7 days prior to the date of return, (ii) when a gift receipt is presented within 60 days of purchase, (iii) for textbooks, or (iv) for products purchased at Barnes & Noble College bookstores that are listed for sale in the Barnes & Noble Booksellers inventory management system.

Opened music CDs/DVDs/audio books may not be returned, and can be exchanged only for the same title and only if defective. NOOKs purchased from other retailers or sellers are returnable only to the retailer or seller from which they are purchased, pursuant to such retailer's or seller's return policy. Magazines, newspapers, eBooks, digital downloads, and used books are not returnable or exchangeable. Defective NOOKs may be exchanged at the store in accordance with the applicable warranty.

Returns or exchanges will not be permitted (i) after 14 days or without receipt or (ii) for product not carried by Barnes & Noble or Barnes & Noble.com.

Policy on receipt may appear in two sections.

Return Policy

<u>With a sales receipt or Barnes & Noble.com packing slip</u>, a full refund in the original form of payment will be issued from any Barnes & Noble Booksellers store for returns of undamaged NOOKs, new and unread books, and unopened and undamaged music CDs, DVDs, and audio books made within 14 days of purchase from a Barnes & Noble Booksellers store or Barnes & Noble.com with the below exceptions:

A store credit for the purchase price will be issued (i) for purchases made by check less than 7 days prior to the date of return, (ii) when a gift receipt is presented within 60 days of purchase, (iii) for textbooks, or (iv) for products purchased at Barnes & Noble College bookstores that are listed for sale in the Barnes & Noble Booksellers

Chapter 6

It took fourteen hours to reach Mayfair. It might have been easier if they had used the inns Kate frequented on her way to and from nearby Eastcourt, but she had to agree with Harry that it would have made her far too vulnerable. The horses were of lesser quality and the changes less efficient, but the trip passed quietly and without event.

By the time they turned the corner onto Curzon Street, Kate felt as if she would splinter from the effort to hold herself still. She hadn't slept, because she couldn't bear to close her eyes. Darkness sent her head spinning, especially in the carriage's small space. She didn't eat, because she couldn't still herself long enough. She didn't even have her anger to keep her company. Only guilt over Frank, who had tried so hard to be kind, and a grinding worry for Bea, which did nothing but make the miles stretch longer. She was plagued by a growing sense that without knowing it, she had put her dear Bea in very real danger.

From the moment Harry had told her why he'd taken her, Kate had been relying on the assumption that he was wrong. She'd been so sure that the Surgeon, knowing his life was forfeit, had taunted them with lies to distract them from the real prey. But Axman Billy had come after her. If Harry hadn't moved so quickly, she would have been dead. Which meant... which meant she *must* know something. She just didn't know what.

She hadn't lied to Barbara. She did know everyone in the ton, both those she wished to and those she didn't. But certainly no one had whispered secrets in her ear... well, not *those* kinds of secrets. True, her uncle Evelyn had admitted to being a Lion, but she couldn't remember when last she'd spent time with him. Like the rest of her family, Uncle Evelyn had never approved of her.

She obviously didn't have the mysterious verse on her. Could it be in her Curzon Street house? Could someone who attended her At Homes have tucked it away somewhere, thinking it would be safe in a home devoid of political interests?

Harry would expect her to find out. She didn't even know where to start. And in the meantime, she was beset by the image of Bea sitting unaware in the small morning parlor where she so loved embroidering bumblebees onto pillowcases as assassins closed in.

When they finally passed the plain red-brick facade of her house to find it quiet, Kate almost slumped in her seat. She realized she'd almost expected it to be smoking and shattered, much as they'd left Diccan's old abbey.

In the deepening twilight, all seemed peaceful. Light spilled from the fanlight over the door and out the front windows. A few hackneys clattered by, and the occasional pedestrian passed. But the majority of denizens were tucked inside their own homes.

Turning onto Clarges, the carriage swung into the mews that ran along the back of the house and stopped. Thrasher ran to hold the horses as Harry swung stiffly from the job horse he'd acquired two posting houses ago, a rawboned gray that reached around to try to nip him. Harry batted its nose and leaned into the carriage window. "Wait here."

And without another word, he was sprinting up the walk and through the gate into Kate's tidy little garden. She lost sight of him then, but could imagine his course. The library opened off the garden to the right, but steps led down to the kitchen. She'd give him five minutes and then, permission or not, she was going in.

Finally, Mudge opened the carriage door and let down the steps. "He waved us in."

Taking Mudge's hand, Kate lifted her skirt and climbed down into the cobbles. Then she was running, following Harry's path. She opened the kitchen door to find her two kitchen maids chopping vegetables.

"Lady Bea," she demanded.

One of the young maids had the presence of mind to point to the green baize door. "Her parlor, Lady Kate. Lady Kate, y'r brother—"

Her brother could wait. Lifting her skirts, she ran up the servants' staircase to the first floor and down the hall to the yellow morning room. And there sat Bea, tidy in gray merino wool and blond lace, a pair of little round glasses perched on the edge of her nose, a needle and yellow thread in hand.

Harry stood alongside Bea, but Kate had no time for him. She could only see her dear Bea, smiling as if Kate had returned from a sea voyage. Bea looked so placid that anyone could think her unaffected. But Kate saw the results of her friend's embroidery. The bumblebee Bea could normally sew in her sleep looked more like a black-and-yellow cyclone, and her dear friend's hands shook.

Kate dropped to her knees and stilled those hands in hers. "Well, my dear. As you see, I refused to stay away from you. What do you say to a bit of an adventure?"

Tears welled in Bea's eyes, and she pulled a hand free to stroke Kate's mangled hair. "*Mysteries of Udolpho*?"

Kate chuckled. "Sadly, no. Nothing so romantic as ghosts or mysterious monks. In fact, nothing more exotic than Lions. But they do seem to be on our heels, and they seem to think I have that bedamned verse everyone is looking for."

Bea tilted her head, looking like an elegant sparrow. "Legerdemain?"

"I swear, my love. I am hiding nothing. But you need to help me figure this out. I admit I am all at sea. We cannot do it here, however."

Bea nodded, patted Kate on the cheek, and gathered up her sewing. "Foxhunt."

"Indeed," Kate agreed, climbing to her feet. "We'll go to ground. I have no wish to be caught in the open when the next attack happens. I'd rather not have to deal with guns. Although I am to learn the most clever things with knives."

Only the next attack didn't come by gun or knife. It happened by writ, and the writ was brought by her brother.

Kate had run upstairs to collect a few things for Bea and herself, with Harry hot on her heels. Kate's abigail gathered Bea's things while Barbara stayed with Bea. George and Thrasher were poling up a new team of horses while Maurice raided the kitchen for food to sustain them on their flight, and Parker and Mudge watched for invaders.

"We already have your luggage on the coach," Harry protested, stationing himself by the door of her boudoir.

"Nothing practical," she said, throwing a pair of half-jean boots into a carpetbag. "Difficult to run for one's life in *peau de soie* and lace."

As quickly as she could, she gathered sturdy dresses, sturdier half-boots, unmentionables, and cloaks. Focused on speed, she didn't notice Harry's attention wander.

"So this is it," he mused.

She didn't bother to look up from folding clothes. "What?"

"The psyche mirror."

She looked up to see him reflected, boots to hair, in her notorious mirror. He was watching her in the reflection. She grinned, knowing he expected it. "Tickles the imagination, doesn't it?"

He turned his focus on his own reflection. "I'm not sure."

When Kate closed up the carpetbag five minutes later, he was still standing there, looking in the mirror. She couldn't imagine what he found so interesting. "Ready?"

He seemed to startle to attention. "Yes."

Taking the bag from her, he opened the door. Kate had just followed him into the hall when she heard a commotion downstairs. Harry stopped, his arm across her chest.

"Her Grace is not at home," Kate heard Finney say in his most dignified tones.

"Don't be impertinent," came the answer. "Of course she is. I've had someone watching the house. Now let me through. I am her brother, the duke."

Kate gaped down the stairwell. Edwin? Here? Any other time she would have laughed at how Edwin felt compelled to remind people he was the duke, as if he recognized his own inadequacies. But tonight, the sound of his voice set off something ominous in her. Too much had happened in the last few days; she didn't think she could tolerate another surprise.

"Would you like us to escort him out?" Harry asked with a tight grin.

"And be hanged for touching a lord of the realm? He'd do it, too. Edwin is nothing if not jealous of his dignities."

Suddenly Finney's face appeared around the corner of the stairs. "What do I do? He has two constables with him."

Kate froze. Constables? That couldn't be right. She must still be muzzy from being locked in that cellar. "He'll terrify Bea," she said, lurching toward the stairs. "I have to get to her."

Harry grabbed her by the arm. "Wait. You can't just go charging down there. We don't know why he's here. He could be—"

Kate actually did smile this time. "A Lion? Come, Harry. You know Edwin. He hasn't the imagination for conspiracy."

Smiling for Harry, she followed Finney down the stairs and into the salon where Edwin loomed over Bea, looking as uncomfortable as a Methodist meeting a Hottentot. Kate usually delighted in watching an exchange between them, as Bea took great pleasure in confusing the duke. Tonight, though, Bea bore the look of a cornered rabbit, her gaze focused on the two lumbering behemoths who bracketed the salon door.

Kate spared them no more than a glance. "Edwin, what a surprise. You caught Bea and me just on the point of going out."

Edwin spun around as if Kate had ambushed him. He hadn't even removed his hat. For such a bombastic man, Edwin should have been larger, heartier. He looked more like a mole with a receding hairline. Tonight his color was high. He looked...exhilarated.

It was then he seemed to realize that Kate wasn't alone. In fact, that she had a few behemoths of her own. Mudge and Parker took up positions alongside Edwin's men, and Finney stood in the doorway. Beyond him lurked Schroeder and Thrasher.

"Who the devil are you?" he demanded, stepping back. He sounded rather like a cat who'd caught his tail under a rocker.

"Ah," Harry said quietly, in a tone of unmistakable command. "You don't remember me." Then he was bowing. "Harry Lidge."

Edwin lifted his eyeglass. "Lidge? Good heavens. You're not getting involved in this again, are you?"

"Involved in what?" Harry asked placidly, leaning against the Adam mantel.

Edwin wasn't about to be questioned. "Step aside. I am here to see my sister."

"And these gentleman?" Harry persisted, pointing to the two by the door.

"None of your business."

The salon became crowded after that, what with Edwin's oversize companions ranging against Kate's. Kate was having trouble breathing, as if the visitors were stealing her air. If it hadn't been for Bea, she would have been tempted to run.

"Isn't this rather excessive, Edwin?" Kate said, beset by a growing sense of peril. "Even for you. Did I inadvertently walk off with the family rubies last time I was over?"

"This is a personal matter, Kate. I insist these people leave."

She crossed her arms, refusing to sit, which kept everyone else on their feet as well. "And I insist they stay. Say your piece, Edwin. I am late for an engagement."

Edwin assessed the hostility in the room and retreated a half step toward his companions. "You've left me no choice," he insisted in his nasal whine. "Did you think I wouldn't find out?"

She sighed. "I might better be able to answer that, if I only knew what it is you're talking about."

Edwin blinked as if she'd just shone a bright light in his

eyes. She knew better than to confuse him. She couldn't seem to help it.

"The painting," he finally said. "I warned you."

She lifted an eyebrow. "What painting?"

"We need to get goin'," one of Edwin's companions whispered with a nervous glance around the crowd. "You wanna show 'er?"

Edwin flashed him a black scowl. Even so, he reached into his coat and withdrew an official-looking paper. "I don't know what else to do anymore, Kate," he said. "I've tried everything to quell your wildness. But my father was right. You have the devil in you. I should have locked you up as he did before you went too far."

Kate froze. Edwin was going to use that blasted painting as an excuse to take control of her. "What has gone too far, Edwin? I haven't even been in town."

He continued as if she hadn't spoken. "All I had to do was bring a judge to see your latest travesty. One look at that offense to everything decent, and he agreed that as head of the family I had a duty to keep you restrained to stop your madness."

"Restrained?" She couldn't breathe. She couldn't think. She had a terrible suspicion that she was melting and freezing at once. "You have no right."

"I have every right. I am head of the family. I'm responsible for your safety. More, I have a responsibility to my children, to the honor of the Hilliards, which you have endangered. So I had to take it upon myself to rectify that and see you stopped."

"What have I told you, Bea?" Kate asked, struggling to sound nonchalant. "*Vasa vana plurimum sonant.*"

It definitely wouldn't have helped to share the translation: Empty pots make the most noise.

Bea's smile was impish. Kate heard Harry choke back a

laugh. As for Edwin, his reaction was all too predictable. "What? What did you say? I thought Murther cured you of that Latin nonsense."

With an effort, she kept a serene smile on her face. "I seem to have relapsed."

"Well, don't worry," Edwin said. "You're finished with it now. You think you're so smart. Did you really think you could get away with being painted *naked*?"

"But I didn't have myself painted naked, Edwin. Even if I did, though, it is not, to my knowledge, illegal."

"It is, however, sufficient proof that you aren't competent to handle your affairs."

And suddenly, in a devastating instant, it all made sense. "You don't care about your children's morals, you hypocrite," she charged. "This is about Eastcourt."

Edwin flushed an ugly color. "Nonsense."

"Don't lie, Edwin. You have no facility for it. You never forgave our mother for making sure I inherited Eastcourt. You never forgave Father for making sure I got it back when my husband died. You want it for yourself."

"I do not! But anyone can see you don't know what you're doing with it. Who in God's name turns prime pastureland into a *flower farm*?"

"You obviously haven't seen our books."

"A flower farm?" Harry asked behind her. "So that's what the tulip pamphlets were about."

"It's insane!" Edwin shrilled. "And now it's stopped. Here. I have the papers."

She stared at the writ as if it were a snake. He wasn't just destroying her. He was destroying Eastcourt. Bea took hold of her hand, but she could barely feel it. By the door, Thrasher and George made a move to defend her, but Harry held them back.

"You can't commit her," Harry told Edwin. "Not even you."

Edwin turned a glare on him. "I can do anything. And I will, to save my family."

Kate thought she might choke. "I don't think your reputation will survive committing a duchess to Bedlam."

"Don't be absurd," Edwin snapped. "I would never allow you to be so treated. There are excellent private facilities. You can come along, or these men will take you."

"Get out of here," Harry suddenly growled, stepping between her and Edwin.

"How dare you interfere in a private matter, Lidge?" Edwin demanded.

"I dare because this is a grave miscarriage of justice."

Edwin snorted. "She's not being arrested. But for her own sake, she must be...protected from herself. After all, that painting might only be her first real outrage."

"Bollocks," Harry snapped. "You know damn well that painting isn't of your sister. Somebody paid a second-rate artist to put her face on someone else's body."

"You've seen the painting?" Edwin demanded, poking Harry in the chest with the folded writ. "If you've seen it, you can't tell me it isn't her."

"Of course I can. And I can prove it."

Kate's ears were buzzing. She was holding on to somebody; she wasn't sure who. But she heard Bea give a little moan next to her. *No, Harry, no. Even for this.*

"How?" Edwin countered, his eyes narrowed. "How can you prove it?"

Kate closed her eyes again. She couldn't look. She couldn't listen to Harry blurt out the truth. She wanted to curl up and hide. She wanted to run. She wanted, oddly, to weep. She hadn't wept since her sixteenth birthday.

"I assume you mean to tell me that you've seen my sister unclothed," Edwin spat, his voice sounding more triumphant than angry. "Which means that she has not even confined her revels to men of class. She is now disporting with common soldiers. All you have done is cement the judge's verdict of insanity."

"Disport?" Harry countered, leaning over Edwin like a hawk. "I disported with no one. I *married* her."

Chapter 7

Harry heard the words coming out of his mouth and couldn't believe his own ears. What the hell was he doing? Any other time he could have come up with a better defense. But he was exhausted, he was distracted, and the only idea that ran through his head was that the authority of a husband superseded a brother's, even if that brother was the Duke of Livingston.

"Don't be absurd, Lidge," the duke sneered. "Even Kate wouldn't lower herself to marry the second son of a squire."

"The son of a squire who is now a baronet," Harry corrected, his eyes steely. "Knighted for conspicuous gallantry on the field of battle. It is said I took out thirty men and recovered an eagle. I don't remember. I was too...distracted at the time."

He had the satisfaction of seeing Edwin swallow and the two constables exchange nervous looks.

"It's a lie," Edwin squeaked.

"That I'm a baronet? Well, you might ask the Prince of Wales, since he was the one who conferred the honor. That Kate married me? Why not ask her?"

Please, Kate, he thought, *don't contradict me*. He shot her a warning look, but she wasn't attending. Her eyes had gone glassy and flat.

The duke bristled. "I won't allow it."

"You have no say in the matter." Reaching out, Harry took Kate's hand, only to find it limp and clammy. "She is of age and independent. She doesn't need your consent."

"Where is her ring?"

"At the jeweler's being sized. I brought it back from Spain."

"And the marriage lines?"

Harry tried to look bored. "Contrary to Minerva Press novels, Your Grace, I don't carry my marriage lines in my pocket on the off chance I might need them."

Edwin snorted. "You are no more married to her than I am, Lidge. *You* have no say in the matter." Turning, he glared at Kate. "Like it or not, you're coming with us."

Still Kate didn't react. Harry looked over and felt his heart stumble. She was just too still. She looked like she had when he'd taken her to the ground, hollow and lifeless. It made him furious for her. It scared the hell out of him.

"Kate." He took hold of her other hand.

By the door Finney and Mudge were looking back and forth, waiting for a cue from Harry. Thrasher was reaching over to pick up the bust of Athena from the bookcase by the door. The constables had their focus on the duke.

"Your Grace, take her to Livingston House," Harry suggested. "I'll meet you there with the marriage lines."

Edwin's smile was thick with disdain. "Don't try my patience. You're the last person who'd marry her. Now out of the way before you suffer the consequences."

The duke grabbed Kate's arm; then everything happened at once. Bea jumped up to intervene. The duke got tangled in her feet and pushed her down. Kate's staff charged in, yelling, which signaled a free-for-all. All the men were scuffling in an attempt to protect Kate or save Bea. Kate shoved her brother aside in an attempt to get to Bea. Her brother, red-faced, swung at her so hard he knocked her back against the fireplace.

Harry's vision went red, and there was a roaring in his ears he hadn't heard since Waterloo. The next thing he knew, his hands were around the duke's throat and he couldn't stop squeezing.

"No!" he heard Kate yell. "Harry, stop!"

The duke's face had gone purple; his eyes were beginning to bulge. Harry couldn't let go of that scrawny, bobbing neck, even when the duke began to gurgle. It was only when he felt a small pair of hands pull at his wrists that he realized what he was doing.

"Harry, no," Kate said, her voice unbearably gentle.

Something about her voice cut through the miasma of rage. Shuddering, he opened his fingers. The duke, sputtering and wheezing, fell back on the carpet.

"I'll see you hanged for this!" Livingston squeaked, hands to swollen throat.

Kate kept her hold on Harry for just a moment longer. He shook his head and gave her a dry smile.

When Kate saw it, she let go and dropped down to where Lady Bea lay curled at her feet. "Dearest, valiant Bea," she murmured, pulling the old woman into her arms. "Are you hurt?"

Harry helped Kate lift Lady Bea to the couch. The old woman tried to smile, but even Harry could see the bruise rising beneath her eye. "Slippery," she said in a quivery voice.

"Get her out of here!" Livingston told the constables, who were righting furniture.

"Your sister has friends," Harry said, standing by her. "We won't let you take her."

One of the constables stepped forward. "I'm that sorry," he said, looking it. "But we've no choice. We gotta take 'er. It's the law."

Clumsy with discomfort, they moved to either side of Kate. "And take Lidge in," Livingston insisted. "For attacking a peer."

It was odd; in that instant Kate turned to Harry, and he swore she was the girl he'd once loved, eyes bright with emotion, heart open. But then, in a blink, she was shaking her head and smiling, and the smile was as old as artifice.

"Let it be, Harry," she said, standing. "*Vir prudens non contra ventum mingit.*"

"What?" Edwin demanded, pushing forward. "What did you say? Damn it…!"

"I said I'm going with you," she told her brother. Harry couldn't believe it, but she was straightening her rumpled dress and tucking up her hair, as if preparing to go on morning calls. "But only if you drop the nonsensical charge against Harry."

"I will not!"

She faced off with him, a queen before a lumpkin. "You will if you don't want all of London talking about how you attacked an old woman just so you could lock up your sister." She didn't wait for his blustering, but turned back to Harry. "Please, Harry. Care for Bea. She can't be alone. See to my staff."

"We see to ourselves," Finney announced, sounding suspiciously teary.

Lady Bea reached for Kate's hand. "Conciergerie," she sobbed.

Dropping back to the couch, Kate took her tearful friend

into her arms. "Ah, Bea," she whispered, her voice thready. "I'm hardly Marie Antoinette. Don't cry. Everything will be all right. Harry will see to it. Won't you, Harry?"

"I'll come get you myself."

Kate nodded without looking at him. "Of course."

With one last kiss to her friend's bruised cheek, she rose. "Keep Bea safe, Harry."

He nodded, suddenly angry and uncertain. "I promise."

Her expression never changed as she turned back to her brother. Harry saw something bleak and empty, though, and suddenly he couldn't bear it. He did the only thing he could think of. He enfolded her in his arms and kissed her. And for a moment, oddly, everything else went away; Kate's brother and Kate's dilemma and the Lions and revenge. There was only Kate; supple, soft, sensuous Kate, in his arms again, her head tilted back, her lips pliant beneath his, her hands resting against his chest.

Past and present collided, met, melded, and Harry was back in their private glen, where the trees whispered secrets and the river rushed by. She was his girl, and he was her hero, so much taller than she, so much stronger, so certain he would save her.

Too soon, though, someone coughed and broke the spell.

Pulling back, he looked down into her troubled eyes. "I promise," he repeated, and dropped a final kiss on her forehead.

Without another word, she accepted her pelisse from Finney's massive hands and followed her brother out the door. Left behind, Harry battled a terrible sense of déjà vu. He'd parted from her once before with a lingering kiss. He'd promised her, just like now, that he would rescue her. And he hadn't.

What would have happened if he had? Would she have

escaped those scars on her breasts? Would she have made him happy, no matter the lies she'd told? Or would their lives have been an even worse disaster?

No. He'd known then, and he knew now. He couldn't possibly have done what she asked. He could this time, though. He would. If not for her, then for the safety of the nation, which might just rely on her.

Beside him, Lady Bea suddenly began to sob. "Oh, my girl, my girl. Persephone."

Harry felt bloody miserable, but he put his arms around the old woman. She laid her head on his shoulder and wept.

"We'll get her back," he promised rashly, patting her on the back.

"Was that Latin Lady Kate spoke?" Mudge asked. "What did she say? Why did she leave?"

"She told me it wasn't prudent to piss into the wind." Harry battled the unfamiliar sting of emotion. "Guess we'll just have to plan our attack from a different direction."

He looked around the tumbled room. He needed help, and he needed it right away. "Mudge? You're in charge of securing this house. Finney? I need somebody to bring Lady Kate's friend Grace Hilliard here to be with Lady Bea. The last I saw of her, she was at Oak Grove in Sussex. Schroeder? See to Lady Bea until she comes."

"What about me?" Thrasher asked.

"You're coming with me," Harry said, already walking from the room.

*   *   *

"What do you mean there's nothing you can do?" Harry demanded an hour later as he faced Marcus Drake in the library of Drake's Charles Street town house.

Harry knew he should have been more circumspect in approaching Drake. But Harry didn't have time to be clever. Either Drake came to him, or he went to Drake. So while his staff was securing Kate's home, he crept into Drake's house like a sneak thief.

"I mean there's nothing the government can do." Pouring two drams of whisky, Drake handed Harry one before settling into a brown leather armchair. "This is a private family matter, Harry," he said, resting the glass on his crossed leg. "It has nothing to do with us."

Harry measured the dark Indian carpet in impatient steps. It was as if he could hear the tick of every second since Kate had walked out her front door. "Of course it has to do with us," he retorted. "Do you really think it a coincidence that her brother had her committed the same day assassins tried to murder her?"

"It actually might be. Livingston has been threatening it for a while, you know. And what good would it do the Lions to have her protected in an asylum?"

"Who says she's going to be protected?" he snapped, stopping to glare at Drake. "Can you think of an easier place to quietly do away with someone? Hell, man. Who says they have to kill her? They can simply wait till she goes mad. That'll take care of it."

"A little melodramatic, don't you think?" Drake asked. "Do you really think the Duke of Livingston is a Lion?"

Harry started pacing again. "I think anybody could put a suggestion in his ear of how to control his sister, and he'd do it. But she won't be able to tolerate it, Marcus. You didn't see her after she was locked up in that cellar."

God, Kate would use one of Mudge's knives on Harry if she knew what he was revealing to Drake. He didn't care. Drake had to be made to realize the urgency of the situation.

"There are some very enlightened asylums being built," Drake reminded him.

Harry laughed. "And you consider the Duke of Livingston as the charitable and forward-thinking type."

"Not really, no. But I'm afraid the government is in no position to interfere in a private matter. First of all, it would tip the Rakes' hand. If we come charging in wielding the power of the government, we can hardly remain anonymous. Second, the duke, like him or not, is a very powerful man."

Harry stopped by a mounted globe. "Then what can we do?"

His gaze never leaving Harry, Marcus took a sip of his whisky. "Considering how you've always spoken of her, you do seem unnaturally concerned."

"She left me in charge of Lady Bea Seaton. Do you want to care for her?"

"Gads, no. Can't understand a word the woman says."

"She's even harder to understand when she's sobbing."

Drake contemplated his drink. "Kate really didn't sit for the painting?"

"No. I can prove it, but I won't unless things get desperate."

"Do you think the Lions were the ones who had it painted?"

Harry gave the globe a shove and sent it spinning. "Who knows? I can certainly see somebody in her family having done it to force the issue. Especially if, as she says, the duke has always coveted her country estate. But it would be just as effective for the Lions, if they wanted to get her out of the way without showing their hand." He watched the countries pass in a blur as the globe whirred on. "I don't think it's a matter of her having something they want anymore, Marcus. I think it's a matter of her knowing something they just don't want her sharing."

Marcus looked up. "What?"

Harry shook his head. "I don't know, and neither does she. I do know that if we don't get her back soon, it won't matter."

"Kate's a pretty tough girl."

Harry watched the globe spin. "I'm not so sure."

He had begun to suspect the truth when he'd seen that brand. The suspicion had solidified into terrible certainty when he'd stood in front of that psyche mirror in her boudoir. It had been just as she'd boasted, long and wide enough to catch her complete reflection as she passed. The perfect opportunity to savor her own beauty, to show it off for all around her. Except that for all the time she'd spent in that room, she had never once looked into it. In fact, she'd seemed to purposely avoid it. She might have bought the mirror to outrage, but she couldn't bear to look at herself in it.

Harry had realized, standing there as Kate rocketed around the room, that the mirror was an illusion. In fact, her whole life was. He'd seen how she'd reacted when he caught sight of that brand on her breast. She had been ashamed, humiliated. Smaller, somehow. If she hadn't wanted Harry to see, if she hadn't even wanted to accidentally catch sight of her scars herself, how on earth would she have blithely bared them to every second man in Britain?

And if she actually had done that, how could it not be the greatest *on dit* of the decade? There wasn't a man alive who wouldn't dine for months off that little tidbit. *"Disgusting, don't you know. Right there atop those glorious teats, where you can't miss them. Barbaric things. Turned m' stomach."*

No man had seen them. No one had touched her. Kate had perpetrated a myth that she was the most promiscuous woman in London. In fact, Harry suspected she might be the most chaste.

Once, in the middle of the battle of Salamanca, Harry's horse had been shot out from under him, sending him arse over teakettle, the horse rolling right over him, hooves, head, and saddle. He'd been left on his back among the bodies staring at the sky and trying to remember how to breathe. He felt that way now. Tumbled and battered and upended, trying to remember how to think. If he had been so wrong about Kate's hedonism, believing in it so surely, what else about her had he mistaken?

"You were right, you know," Drake said in that annoyingly languid tone of his. "Marriage is the only answer. Are you prepared to sacrifice your future to secure her release?"

No. He had quite another future in mind, one in which a pampered duchess didn't belong. In fact, in which no one belonged but him.

Harry emptied his drink in a swallow. Before him the globe whirred merrily along, continents and oceans blurring past. "Surely there's another way."

There wasn't. He'd known that since the minute he'd opened his mouth back in the duke's salon. Reaching over, he grabbed Drake's glass and emptied that, too.

Drake didn't seem to notice. "A marriage *would* be to your advantage." Leaning back, he crossed his legs. "Kate has quite a tidy fortune of her own, you know. Surely enough to enable you to comfortably leave the army. I know you've wanted to."

"I don't need her money. Between my time in India and the acquaintance you secured for me with the Rothschilds, I don't need anybody's money." Harry looked down at the smiling man. "Would *you* marry her?"

Drake chuckled. "Gods, no. But then, I won't marry

anyone. Besides, I'm not the one who publicly claimed her, am I?"

No, Harry thought. *He* was. And now it looked as if he would have to carry through with it. He crossed to the drinks table by the window and refilled the glasses. He was gracious enough to give Drake one.

"First things first," Drake said, getting up with glass in hand, and walking over to sit at his desk. "We need a special license postdated at least a week." Pulling out pen and paper, he set to scratching out a note.

Harry rubbed at the tension between his eyes. "So you've decided to help after all."

Drake looked up with an enigmatic smile. "Well, I was hoping you'd offer so I didn't have to insist. We really do need to find out what she knows, and that's not going to happen if her brother has his way."

"I'm so glad I could help."

"Better you than Axman Billy." Shaking his head with a grin, he went back to his note. "She does live the most colorful life."

Harry slumped into a chair. God. He really was getting married. He suddenly felt as if he couldn't breathe. "I understand you know the Axman as well."

"He went after Gracechurch when he was in Brussels. Slippery devil. We haven't been able to nab him since."

Harry hoped like hell he'd done the right thing setting Thrasher down in the Dials to catch the bastard's scent. "And the license? I assume you know someone in Canterbury's office willing to perjure his soul."

Drake looked over at him. "Happens I do. One of Canterbury's secretaries. He...helps us on occasion."

That got Harry's attention. "Good God. One of Drake's Rakes is a vicar?"

Drake's smile was gentle. "He'd prefer to think of himself as auxiliary." Folding the note, he sanded and sealed it, then pulled over another sheet of paper. "Now then, after the license, you need a couple of stalwart friends to support you when you go see her brother and get her out of wherever she is. Sadly, I am previously engaged."

"Friends?"

Drake's smile grew. "Chuffy, I think. No one ever thinks to question Chuffy's word. And for a bit of intimidation, Ferguson."

Harry gaped. "Ferguson? Good God, Marcus, I don't need anybody swinging claymores in a duke's sitting room."

"I'll tell him to keep quiet. He's there for size and height."

"And the suggestion that any minute he could go on a rampage."

"Exactly."

Actually, it was probably the perfect plan. Chuffy Wilde was as guileless and friendly as a spaniel pup, pudgy, smiling, and ever in search of his glasses. Ian Ferguson was his antithesis. A great large ox of a Scot, Ian had survived a brutal childhood to unexpectedly find himself the heir apparent to an English earldom. It hadn't eased his brogue, his disdain for "Sassenach fops," or his massive appetite for life. Thankfully, one of the few people he respected was Wellington.

While Drake finished his note, Harry returned to his place by the globe to find it finally slowing on the African continent. There at the top Harry could see the cities of Cairo and Alexandria, Jerusalem and Constantinople. Cities he had planned to explore once Napoleon was beaten and the roads opened. He had survived the nightmares of the last ten years by walking those hot, white streets in his mind, measuring and studying and absorbing the echoes of ancient places. He was going to wade through the bazaars and sit cross-legged in the coffee shops arguing history with old men. He would return to India to seek out the lost cities, trace temple carvings with his fingers, and climb the high mountains to savor the holy silences in flag-adorned temples. And then he would bring all of that experience home to England and draw his own buildings, so that one day someone else might find permanency and grace in them.

Had he forfeited his opportunity with that one impetuous gesture? Did he know how to redraw his life? Did he have a choice?

Behind him the door opened, and a footman came in to collect the notes Drake had written. "This might take a little time," Drake said as the door closed again.

Harry refused to look up from the globe. "I don't think we have time."

"You truly think Kate will suffer where she is. Why are you so certain?"

Harry thought of those obscene scars on her perfect breasts, of the brittle shell she'd constructed to protect her soft center. He thought of women he'd known like her and what those women had been through. There was no question in his mind. If Murther had been enough of a monster to brand his own wife, the abuse hadn't stopped there.

But it wasn't Harry's place to tell Drake the secrets she'd worked so hard to protect. "Suffice it to say that yes, I do think she's suffering, in ways we can't even imagine. And no matter what she's done to me or anybody else, she doesn't deserve that."

"But what *has* she done? You've never said." Standing, Drake returned to his drink and his armchair. "Beyond what I've heard about her interfering in your engagements, of course. But I can't believe you really regret losing either of those ninnyhammers."

Harry's instinctive reaction was to deny that anything more had happened. He had never shared the truth with anyone but Kate's father. It felt odd to think that of all the people he might spill his budget to, it could be Marcus Drake. Drake had certainly never been one of Harry's intimates. Drake had gone to Eton. Harry had been grudgingly accepted to Rugby. Drake sat in the House of Lords. Harry marched with the 95th.

But it had been Drake who had changed Harry's life, giving him his first chance to rise above his role as soldier. Ian Ferguson, then a captain in the Black Watch, had introduced Harry to Drake. But Drake had been the one to accept Harry into the Rakes. He had offered Harry opportunities to broaden his horizons, trusting him with information, with gold, and with lives.

Throughout the years Harry had known him, Drake had never deceived him or lied to him. More than once Drake had even protected him when Harry's word was questioned. Harry didn't take that kind of loyalty lightly.

Besides, Harry realized, he needed an objective ear. For the first time in nearly a decade, he was having doubts about what had actually happened.

He walked over to stand in front of the window. "Did you know Kate's father?"

"The old duke? I did. Great friend of the pater's. I liked him very much."

Harry nodded. "I worshiped him. Him and the duchess both. My family lived near Moorhaven. My father was squire. Not much land, but doing all right. He played chess with the duke every Friday. The duchess was the kind of woman who invited all the neighborhood kids to birthday parties, no matter their rank."

It wasn't hard to pull up sun-soaked memories of laughter

and mayhem and a petite beauty who'd stood at the center of it all like a calm sun watching orbiting planets. He only just remembered the duke smiling at her as if he only survived in her light.

The duke. Yes. Get on with it, Harry. "There was a canal scheme the duke invested in. He convinced my father to join him. When it went bust, the duke lost quite a bit of money. My father lost almost everything." His laughing, rough-housing, red-faced father. "The stress killed him. My brother took over, but it was years before we recovered. During that time, the duke helped support us. He said that since he'd talked my father into the venture, it was the least he could do. He made sure we boys were schooled and the girls had dowries. And every Friday, he invited me up to the castle to play chess." He smiled. "I learned most of my most important life lessons over chess."

"I didn't know."

"He never once made us feel inferior, and he never lied to us. Not even to protect his own reputation. And he loved his family so much." He took a sip of his whisky and considered the next part of his story. "Did you ever know Kate when she was a girl?"

"Not really until after she was widowed."

He nodded, his attention still out onto Piccadilly, where the traffic was thick with drays and hackneys and sleek racing curricles. What he saw in his mind were the verdant glens of Moorhaven. "I knew her brother and sisters, of course. But she was such a late child, and the duchess dying and all." He shrugged. "I knew about her, of course. But she was never brought down when I was there, so I didn't meet her until she was fifteen. I was twenty. I imagine it was inevitable, although I knew better."

He rubbed at his eyes, suddenly feeling so old as he

looked back on that summer when everything had still been possible. When he'd meant to explore the world and hand it to that bright-eyed, sharp-minded girl. When he thought he'd found his soul mate in the daughter of a duke.

"Were you lovers?" Drake asked.

"No. I was the only one who…" He stopped, suddenly uncomfortable. She'd wanted to. She'd wept when he had refrained, mere seconds from taking her. He'd insisted he respected her too much. He'd been so close…

"No. Anyway, one day she came to me, frantic. Begged me to run off with her. She said she needed saving from her father. From what he planned to do to her."

"Her *father*?"

He nodded. "He always seemed a bit distant from her, but the duchess had died in childbed with her. The duke never really recovered from it. But I knew he would never deliberately hurt Kate. She insisted that he would, though. That he was about to marry her off to a dangerous man, and I was the only one who could save her."

"And did you?"

Harry thought a moment on those last days, and he wondered. "No. I didn't. I went to her father. I knew she must have misunderstood his intentions."

"What did he do?"

Harry's shook his head. "He thanked me for coming to him. Told me he should have intervened before I fell victim to his daughter. He seemed…heartbroken." Harry could still see the older man, posture perfect, with his leonine head of hair that had turned white overnight when his wife had died; those sad, sad eyes and sadder smile. "He told me that Kate was not what I thought. That she didn't deserve a good man like me. When I protested, he said…" Harry took a breath, wanting to get over this part quickly. "He said that he couldn't tell me everything. He'd made a solemn promise. But that she'd asked me to run off with her to avoid the consequences of her behavior. He said she was increasing, probably by one of the grooms, somebody named George she'd been sneaking out to see. Her fiancé had been furious when he found out."

"That was Murther? But he married her anyway."

Harry shrugged. "The duke said that Murther loved her. That since he already had heirs, it didn't matter so much. He thought marriage to him could...help her."

Harry thought of that brand and felt sick chills chase his spine.

"And you?" Drake asked.

Harry's laugh was sore. "The duke said he was sorry for me; that I was innocent in all this. He bought me a commission in the Fifty-second and kitted me out."

"The baby?"

"Miscarried."

"And you didn't ask Kate if it was true?"

Harry turned to face Drake and asked the real question. "Why would I? If her father was telling the truth, she just would have lied. And I had to believe her father was telling the truth, or else everything else I'd been taught would have been worthless. Don't you see? I'd only known her two months. I'd known him my whole life."

It was Drake's turn to stand up. Walking over to the drinks table, he poured another whisky. "Yes," he said, and came over to refill Harry's. "I do see. Why have you changed your mind?"

Harry accepted the pour and took a long draught. "I don't know that I have. I still can't imagine her father saying those things if they weren't true. He certainly didn't have to make up lies to get me out of the county. You know perfectly well he would have been well within his rights to have me horse-whipped and handed to a press gang for so much as looking at his daughter, no matter how many times he played chess with me."

"Can you trust Kate now?"

He looked down on the street and realized it had started to rain. "I don't know that, either."

"You still love her."

He smiled, as if his entire body hadn't just tightened. "I'd be an idiot to love her."

For a long moment, except for the distant clatter of traffic, there was no sound but the tick of the mahogany bracket clock on the mantel. The windows groaned a bit with a freshening wind, and somewhere in the building a door slammed. But in this room, inevitability had been reached.

"I don't know if you're a saint or a fool, Harry," Drake said, tossing back the rest of his drink. "But I'll help you get married."

Harry downed his own drink. "It seems the time has come to piss into the wind."

*   *   *

Darkness had weight. It had substance. Kate's nanny had told her that darkness was no more than the absence of light, but Kate knew better. It was a living thing that pulsed, that breathed, that spoke. That slowly, inexorably, engulfed, bearing you down with every memory and fear that gave it life. Darkness had form and mass, as thick as tar, as fluid as oil, as deep as death. It had its own temperature, a cold so deep it burned the bones.

And finally, it had voice. *Helpless*, it whispered over and over again. *Helpless, worthless, helpless*, its voice rising like a child's. Panic sent it soaring, shrill and frantic until, finally, spent and miserable, it disintegrated into a whimpering plea that never changed and was never answered. *Papa.*

Kate knew all this. She had challenged it before, eyes open, and she had succumbed, curled up in an empty corner. She might have survived it better this time if she hadn't just been locked in a cellar the day before. She might have held the panic off longer if she could hear anything beyond her prison or been able to outpace the nightmares. But when she had protested the staff's handling of her, they had put her in a room with thick walls and stout doors and no light. She was completely alone in an unlit box that seemed to shrink by the minute.

She tried to outpace the darkness, but she knew better. She tried to ignore the old memories and newer fears. But it took light to do that, movement, challenge. Spring spent dancing in Mayfair, summer walking the Eastcourt fields, Christmas tucked into her pew at quaint old All Saints listening to Bea spin gold from old carols. Sunlight bolstered her spirits, and music made her believe. And cloaked in the untidy babble of voices, she could imagine that she had won. That she had escaped and triumphed.

But in the dark, the truth was clear. No matter how hard she tried, how much she believed, nothing really changed. So she walked until she couldn't anymore. Until she could no longer silence the keening in her head, a sound of madness, of grief, her hands clenched to her mouth to stem the tide of despair that threatened to pour out.

She shouldn't have bothered. There were no others to hear her. None but the silence and the darkness, and they knew what lived in her head. So she paced. She would pace until the weight of the darkness bore her down and she succumbed.

*   *   *

It took all night to organize Kate's rescue. By the time Harry finally approached her brother, he was hungry, tired, and holding on to his temper by a thread.

Livingston House was on Grosvenor Square, an elegant white four-bay row house with ornate wrought iron at the balconies and windows. When Harry was shown inside, though, all semblance of elegance disappeared. Harry found himself gaping, and wondered if Kate had seen her brother's house. Because if there was ever an Egyptian decor that could frighten children, this would be it.

It wasn't simply the fact that the furniture was adorned with alligator feet, snake heads, and strange, elongated dogs. It was that the duchess had evidently collected every Egyptian couch, chair, and table in Mayfair and crammed them in with a forest of palm trees, like a Cairo ghetto. Harry even suspected that that might be a mummy case standing in the corner.

When he finally picked his way through to the morning room to find the duke and duchess eating breakfast, he almost cost his mission by laughing in the woman's face. He disliked the Duchess of Livingston on sight, a thin, icy blonde with the kind of nose that always seemed pointed upward and eyes the blue of a Russian lake. Braced up by Chuffy Wilde, Ian Ferguson, and the Reverend Lord Joshua Wilton, Harry made his bows to both her and the duke, who still looked like a dyspeptic rabbit.

"What do you mean by this, Lidge?" Livingston demanded, jumping to his feet, a knife and muffin still in his hands. "I said we were not at home."

"I told you I'd come," Harry said.

Beside him, Chuffy stepped to the front. "Knew you

wouldn't be able to forgive yourself if you kept your sister's lawful husband away from her," he said with a wide smile, as if he couldn't imagine the duke not being thrilled to see them.

Rising from her place like Medea on a tear, the duchess assessed Chuffy as if he had just dripped mud on her carpets. "And what matter is it to you, sir?"

"Thought you might need a peachful witness," he said.

"Unimpeachable," Harry instinctively corrected.

Chuffy positively beamed. "Spot on."

Suddenly the duke took a step back. If the sudden pallor on his skin was any indication, he'd just caught sight of Ferguson. "Who the hell are *you*?" he squeaked.

Not an unreasonable reaction, considering the fact that Ian topped Harry by half a dozen inches and was kitted out in full Black Watch regalia with red jacket, black-and-blue tartan kilt, and black bearskin tucked under his arm. With his wild, too-long auburn hair, he was a sight to put fear in the hearts of much braver men. Especially when he smiled, as he was doing now.

Well, at least they'd talked him out of the claymore.

"Ah, don't fesh y'rself about me, laddie," Ferguson drawled. "I'm just here to make sure we come away with the wee duchess." When he saw the blond ice queen blanch, he let go a great laugh. "T' other wee duchess, don't ya ken. The grand one who invited me to her weddin'."

"You will address me as Your Grace," Livingston demanded.

Ian was already shaking his head. "Only man alive I'll give that honor is Old Nosey himself. And that's because he's a braw man in a fight. Are you?"

Patting Ian's arm as if he were a schoolboy, Chuffy intervened before blood was shed. "Ian Ferguson, Viscount

Brent," he introduced him. "Other unimpeachable witness, don't ya know. Thought you'd need more than one, so you could be sure Lidge here wasn't lying." Chuffy blinked. "Although I've never seen him do it before…"

"Chuffy," Harry muttered.

Chuffy beamed and shoved his round glasses up his nose. "Right. Ian, like to present you to Edwin and Glynis Livingston, Duke and Duchess of Livingston. Lady Kate's brother." Not giving Ferguson the chance to loose another insult, he kept speaking. "Now, Your Graces. Lidge here married Lady Kate right after Gracechurch remarried his missus. Friends all there anyway, don't ya know." Reaching into the pocket of his puce-and-gold waistcoat, he drew out an official-looking paper as if it were a magic trick. "Here you go. Knew you'd want proof. Seems important to you."

Harry almost laughed at the outrage on the haughty faces. Chuffy didn't let them get started, though. "Even brought along our friend Joshua, who said the words. Lord Joshua Wilton." He motioned to the third member of their party. "Duke of Greason's son. But you know that, don't you?"

"The *Reverend* Lord Joshua Wilton," the tall cleric gently corrected as he gave a perfect bow. "Your Graces. A pleasure to see you, as always."

Both the duke and duchess flushed an unpretty red. The was no question of Wilton's profession or veracity. Not simply because of the clerical collar, or the cross on his chest. Tall and rangy, Wilton had the ascetic features of a monk. If Harry hadn't heard him belly-laugh at the idea of putting one over on the loathsome Duke and Duchess of Livingston, he would have thought Wilton had never cracked a smile in his life.

The duchess sniffed at the sight of the document. "How do we know this is—?"

Wilton bristled. Chuffy guffawed. "Zounds, ma'am, even the queen herself don't have the nerve to call Wilton a liar. And she'll say it about her own sons. Here." He handed over the paper. "See for yourself. There's my name, along with Kate's friend Lady Bea. Sweet old thing, ain't she? Pats a person on the head like a hound bitch."

In fact, Lady Bea had first refused the pen when asked to sign. It had taken the combined efforts of Harry, Grace Hilliard, and Finney the butler to change her mind.

"Where is Lady Kate?" Harry asked, twitching with impatience.

Livingston looked up. "I think I should have my man of business verify this."

Wilton drew himself up to his not-inconsiderable height and frowned. "I sincerely hope, Your Grace, that you don't find it necessary to question my word."

Livingston's face grew even darker. His wife went rigid. Harry had the oddest feeling that she was far more livid than her husband.

"Our sister was in need of help, Reverend," the duchess said, hands tightly clasped atop drab rose skirts. "Surely you understand our...concern when the man asking for her release is the same...*person* who attacked the duke as he did his duty."

"But that person is her husband," Wilton evenly reminded her. "You must see that you interfered with his rights."

Rights, Harry thought dourly, uncomfortably aware of what Kate would say about that. "Now," he said, holding on to his patience with both hands. "Where is she?"

Chapter 8

It didn't seem like a bad place. An ivy-covered limestone Palladian mansion with three even rows of windows and sloping lawns, the Richmond Hills Asylum looked to have once been a private estate. The public rooms were clean and smelled of strong disinfectant and floor wax. Flowers graced the tables, lace curtains hung in the windows, and the staff wore clean white aprons. Even the administrator, a Dr. Whaley, spoke with an educated accent and wore a signet with a Tudor rose on it that matched the one painted on the sign outside, which made Harry think old family.

He was perusing the paper Harry had handed him. "I don't think..."

"Don't think," Harry suggested. "Just take us to her. As you can see by this license, she is now Lady Catherine Lidge. Which makes me—" He took a step closer, with a grim smile that forced Whaley back a pace. "—most unhappy."

He felt a cautioning hand on his arm and looked up to see Ian Ferguson smiling at the doctor. "Oh, he'll let us in," the great Scot promised in his deadliest voice.

Wilton and Chuffy were waiting out in the carriage. Harry thought that between the 95th and the Black Watch, full-dress uniforms would better convince the doctor of their purpose.

With a nervous look from Harry to Ian, Whaley spun around, his keys jangling like Harry's nerves. Waving off assistance from the attendants, Whaley strode over to a locked door and, after a moment of fumbling, unlocked it. Harry braced himself, not at all sure what he'd see.

More flowers. More lace curtains and a clean, tidy hallway with Persian rugs over the hardwood floors. Comfortable chairs and whisper-footed servants. The place looked like a bloody hotel for diplomats.

The only thing that betrayed its true intent was the fact that women in plain blue gowns wandered aimlessly along the hall, not even looking up when they heard the door open. They didn't seem to notice as the three men walked by, and Harry couldn't imagine anyone ignoring Ian.

"Always thought I'd like my women to be more quiet," the great Highlander muttered, shaking his shaggy head. "I think I'll be changin' my mind."

Harry couldn't agree more. The unnatural silence grated on his already stretched nerves. Even so, in one way he felt much relieved. How awful could it be here for Kate? The only thing he could think she might object to was the color of the carpets. It wasn't as if they'd shoved her in a wine cellar.

"I know I don't have to ask if you're taking good care of her," he told the doctor.

"Oh, excellent care, Sir...uh, Henry. She's so much better today."

Harry pulled the little man to a stop in the middle of the hall. "Better?"

Whaley nodded, both hands wrapped around the keys. "Oh, yes. She was...distressed about being here last night. It often happens." Nodding toward the rest of the hall, he smiled. "But as you can see, our ladies are all very happy here. Once we convinced Lady Kate that cooperation would make her stay much more comfortable, she settled right down."

Harry stared at the women who failed to notice him, pale wraiths in blue, and fought a sudden chill. Surely not.

He turned at the sound of the keys. Whaley had stopped about halfway down the hall and was unlocking a door. "The lock is merely standard procedure for the first two days. After that, unless she causes a problem, she's quite free to mingle."

"Not anymore," Harry said. "She's going home."

Harry's first sight of the room was of gray afternoon light seeping in through another lace-curtained window. His stomach unclenched by inches. There was another thick rug on the floor and nice, if plain furniture, with a bright yellow quilt on the bed. Kate was awake, seated in an armchair in front of the window, groomed and neat as a pin in that ubiquitous blue dress.

"Well, here you are," he said, giving her a smile.

She didn't so much as blink. Harry felt the first cold tendrils of dread wrap around him. Striding across the floor, he went down on his knees next her. "Kate?"

He kept forgetting how tiny she was, not even an inch over five feet. Seated in picture-perfect position, her back not touching the chair, her hands in her lap, her toes barely touching the floor, she was gazing fixedly at her lap. It was the most uncomfortable position Harry could imagine. And yet she didn't budge, like a child who had been admonished to sit straight until her parent returned.

What frightened Harry was that he didn't think he had ever seen her so still. She didn't even acknowledge his presence. It was as if someone had stolen her away and left a wax effigy in her place. He took her hands in his and found them limp and chilly.

"What did you do to her?" he demanded, looking up at Whaley.

Whaley looked affronted. "Why, nothing. We had to isolate her, of course. She tried to bite an attendant when they had to bathe her. But we assured her that she would be let out when she acted in a civilized fashion. Ladies are such social creatures, you see. They can't bear to miss out on the gossip. Eventually, they come to understand."

He was smiling. The bastard was smiling.

Harry squeezed his eyes shut. "Isolation. Were there windows in this isolation?"

"And take the chance of having a patient cut herself? Of course not. There is nothing in the room that could be a danger."

She had to have been in the asylum at least twelve hours. How long had she been in the dark? Harry didn't bother beating the doctor to within an inch of his worthless life. He just scooped Kate up in his arms, his only thought that she felt cold and small. Too small.

She didn't react. Her pupils didn't even constrict. She simply lay in Harry's arms, never blinking or speaking.

"Poor wee thing," Ian whispered, grabbing the quilt and wrapping it around her.

"Come along, little one," Harry crooned, turning for the door. "Time to go."

Wasting no time, he carried her from the building and settled with her next to Chuffy in the carriage. He needed her safe. He needed to get her away from not just this place but these witnesses. The Kate he knew seemed to relish in-spiring outrage. Pity, though, would be an entirely different matter.

"Where to?" Ian asked, leaning in the door.

"Her house. She needs to see Bea."

Across from him, Chuffy nodded. "Nothing like your own bed to comfort you."

"Not her bed," Harry disagreed, the silent weight of her in his arms unnerving. Right now he'd give anything to have her rail at him. "That's not what she needs."

*   *   *

Kate wasn't sure when she began to return. At first, she was confused. Time seemed to have melted, and she was fifteen again. She was down in the glen with Harry, sating herself on sunlight and the beauty in her beau's smile. It was her fa-vorite thing, lying in his arms down by the stream where she could see the tight green leaf-buds begin to unfurl on oak trees and feel the soothing rhythm of Harry's heart against her cheek. Where she could inhale the bluebells' spicy scent and know the fragrance would always bring her back here.

Harry would call her hopelessly romantic. He would tell her that she was only risking freckles lying in the grass with-out a bonnet, and then happily explain how sunlight turned into spots. She didn't care. The air was open, the sunlight free, and she planned to gorge on it like a glutton at a Christ-mas feast.

Besides, Harry was murmuring against her ear. She couldn't quite hear what he said, but she knew he was telling her he loved her. In a moment, after she savored the comfort of his arms just a bit more, she would reach out and trace the hard angles of his square, strong face, and she would whis-

per to him, *Sic itur ad astra*. Such is the path to the stars.
And she would believe it.

"Harry," she murmured, snuggling closer to his chest.
"Kiss me."

She couldn't understand why Harry needed to be encouraged. Yet he'd gone still, as if he wasn't sure what to do.

"Harry, please."

Bending over her, his big, rough hand cupping her face,
Harry put his lips to hers. His lips were so soft, his breath as
quick as the breeze. He nibbled at her lower lip as if it were
a sweet, sucked on it, just enough to taste. His fingers rasped
against her skin, spilling chills before them. Her body, oddly
cold and still, began to thaw, warm, glow. It seemed an oddly
unfamiliar feeling, as if lost for a long time.

She wanted more. She wanted to lift her hand to him,
but it seemed so heavy. *She* seemed heavy; tight, as if she'd
fallen from a horse or tried to run too far. Yet she refused to
investigate. If she did, she might have to leave this perfect
moment.

It was inevitable, though. She had to see him. But even
as she opened her eyes, she knew it was a mistake. The trees
were in the wrong place, and where was the oak? There
were only brick walls and the flash of sunlight on a window.
And there were no bluebells; no wildflowers at all. Spring
was long gone. The roses were blown and the leaves on the
plane trees yellow and drifting through a muddy city sky.
She blinked, prepared to hide, except that she had to see
Harry.

But he was wrong, too. The face that bent over hers belonged to an older man, harder, leaner, with creases at his
temples and eyes that gleamed like ice in the sunlight.

Kate's heart began to gallop; panic seemed to block off
her breath. No, she decided, this was surely not Harry. It was

just another illusion. Another wish withered to grief. She would go back into herself where all was safe and quiet. She closed her eyes.

"Oh, no you don't," she heard the older Harry say, and he shook her. He shook her hard. "Come back here, Katie my cat. Talk to me."

She knew then that it really was Harry. No one else had ever called her that and gotten away with it.

"Open your eyes, Kate. You're safe. You're home."

She couldn't answer him. She didn't have the courage. What if it was a lie? What if she looked up and saw nothing but hard, white walls? She didn't want him to try to bring her back from the safety of her own silence. She simply couldn't risk it anymore.

"Kate," Harry said, his voice brisk. "You're frightening Lady Bea."

The name was like a vinaigrette beneath her nose. She couldn't frighten Bea. "Where is she?"

Was that her voice? It sounded so rusty and tentative.

"Sitting inside the library waiting for you. But I wanted you to feel the sunlight first. Now open your eyes. We're running out of time, and there's business to attend to."

"You're real?" she asked, the truth still barricaded beyond closed eyelids.

"Very real. Are you feeling better?"

Kate almost laughed. She could still hear plaintive, lost murmurs in her head. And something else, another voice. She listened, but it was gone now, left in the corners of a madhouse. For some reason, though, the whisper of that voice nagged at her, as if she needed to remember it.

No. She didn't need to remember anything of that place. She needed to shut it away, just like always. "I'm fine," she said as if she meant it. "Fine."

"Where did you go just now?"

"Where I was safe." She whispered it, afraid again.

"I thought you'd try to stay awake and alert," Harry said, and sounded oddly hurt. "So you'd be ready to get out."

She opened her eyes. "Why?"

He was frowning. "I told you I'd come."

"You've told me that before."

She had meant no malice with her words. They were the simple truth. But they seemed to freeze Harry solid. For the longest time he didn't move, his expression stony.

"You didn't expect to get out of there," he said baldly.

Again, she told him the truth. "No. Why should I? Bea would fight for me, and my staff, I suppose. But who would listen to a confused old woman and a motley crew of servants, most of whom were hired from prison?"

"Is there no one else you can rely on?"

She laughed, as if she found him amusing. "Heavens, no. I gave that up long ago."

"I see."

His voice was tight and dry, and Kate imagined she could hear the relief there. God knew he wouldn't want her to rely on him. No one would.

And then before he could say more, she swung her feet down and lurched upright. She was seated on the wrought-iron bench in her garden, still clad in the asylum's drab blue uniform. She could smell the place on her, not bluebells or fresh air. Madness and fury and despair. Whispering again, just at the edge of her memory. *You have to listen…*

"I need to change," she said, tugging at her bodice with shaking fingers.

She itched again. Her hair felt as if it had been dipped in tallow, and she felt as if she might shake apart. She stared at her trembling hands as if she didn't recognize them.

"You will," Harry promised, helping her sit. "After we have a little talk."

She tugged at the bright yellow quilt someone had wrapped around her. She needed to cover up. "Talk. No, I don't need to talk; I need to bathe."

She needed to collect her composure and button it around her like a woolen pelisse. She needed to remember that voice.

No, she didn't.

Was this what Jack Gracechurch had felt like, she wondered, his memory ragged and incomplete? No, she decided. Jack *couldn't* remember. She didn't want to.

"You must attend, Kate," Harry said, standing. "We've come up with a plan."

She laughed. "That's what I love about the Rakes. Give them an hour and a box of cigars, they'll come out of the den ready for Waterloo. What did you plan?"

"How to keep you safe from your brother."

Kate felt something tilt inside her, as if lead had been poured into an unstable cup. Even knowing how mad it sounded, she chuckled. "My brother. You. The Lions. I declare, Harry, I never knew a girl could have so many people intent on pursuing her. It might be time for me to retire to the country and knit mufflers for the poor. Maybe that would placate everyone and secure my place in heaven."

"I doubt it. You need to be protected, Kate, and this time you need help."

She nodded. "Actually, I was thinking about that. About why I've been targeted." She focused on her blanket, smoothing it over her lap as if it would bring her order. As if her motions could restitch the unraveling threads of her life. "I've really thought hard about it, Harry. But I have no idea what it is the Lions want."

"I know."

Her head snapped up and she stared at him. "You do?"

He looked as bemused as she felt. "Schroeder believes you. And I've found her to have unerring instincts."

She wanted to laugh. How absurd, really. Why should she feel so relieved that he finally believed her? But she did, and it confused her, which made her babble. "Fine. But I can help find out. I have a large circle of acquaintances. I can go over each of them with you to see if anyone seems...oh, I don't know. Suspicious. And Uncle Hilliard. We already know he's a Lion. Why can't I help you search his homes? He never liked me, but the servants were far less discerning. I know they'd let us in."

"Diccan is already searching."

She nodded almost frantically. "Oh. All right. That's fine. What about Uncle's offices in Slough? It's much nearer London, where he must have had most of his contacts, don't you think? Bea and I have actually been there—" Suddenly it was as if a candle flared. She grabbed Harry's arm. "My God. Bea. She's safe? Nobody's hurt her?"

She was already on her feet, and turning for the house when Harry caught her hand. "Kate. She's inside. She's fine. See?"

And there Bea was, standing at the library window, her pale face crumpled with distress, one of her handkerchiefs clutched in her fist. Kate's heart clenched. "I must go to her."

Harry refused to let go. "You must settle this first. Trust me. I have the house guarded, and a keen eye out for Axman Billy. No one will get past us. But you're not safe yet from your brother."

She shuddered. Harry was right. Edwin would not sit still for her being taken out of his control. Maybe if she and Bea got away. The Continent, maybe the West Indies. She could deed Eastcourt to the village, just to keep it out of Edwin's hands, and then she and Bea could disappear...

"Kate," Harry said, turning her to face him. "You need a husband."

She reared back, feeling as if she'd been struck. "A what? No. Oh, no, thank you. I had one. We did not get on."

"You don't need to get on with this one. You only need to take his name so your brother loses his right to commit you."

Kate laughed, panic squeezing her chest. "Whose name? Yours?"

He wasn't smiling. "It's what I told your brother."

She tried to pull away. "Don't be absurd. No one will fault you for making such a wild claim. I'm certainly not going to demand you make such a sacrifice."

"*I* will," he retorted, looking furious. "It's a matter of honor."

She glared, panic gestating into terror. "Oh, bollocks. You don't want to be tied to me for life. You told me yourself. You're going off alone. This would ruin it."

She looked up just in time to see his eyes go hollow, but only for a second. "Not really. You live your life, I'll live mine."

She was already shaking her head. "I would still be your property. No, thank you, Harry. I'm perfectly happy being in charge of my own affairs." She sucked in a breath, as if it could stabilize her racing heart. "No, we'll find some other way. Prinny owes me a favor."

"He owes your brother several thousand pounds."

"The Archbishop of Canterbury is a cousin. He can intercede."

"In baptisms and communion. Not in the courts of Chancery, where your brother will seek your estate."

She lurched into motion, almost going right over on her

nose from shaky knees. Harry reached to help, but she batted him away, catching herself on the back of the bench. She grabbed the blanket just before it sagged to the ground.

"I'll sue Edwin," she said, taking a few tottering steps along the walk. She hated it that her hands shook so much, that she walked like an octogenarian. If she were going to stay out of any kind of prison, she had to be strong.

"You don't have time," Harry said, sounding regretful. "Don't you think it's a bit suspicious that your brother came after you so soon after the attempt on your life?"

Kate stopped, the path crunching beneath her toes. "You think he's a Lion because he tried to commit me?" She laughed. "Oh, Harry. He's wanted to commit me since I set his hunting pack loose when I was six. This is nothing new."

"The painting is. Someone painted it and made sure your brother saw it. I think someone knew all too well he would think this the perfect excuse to put you away where no one would ever hear from you again. The only thing keeping your brother from putting you right back in Richmond Hills is the fact that he thinks you're already married."

Kate opened her mouth, but she just ended up closing it again, uncertain suddenly of what would come out. Harry was right. She could well have permanently disappeared into that tarted-up madhouse, a victim of Edwin's jealousy and greed.

For a moment she was back in the darkness again, hearing that whisper, the thin edge of fear in the dark. *They'll never let us out.* They wouldn't have, either.

Still, she shook her head. "I told you before," she said, her voice unpardonably shrill. "Thank you, but no. I won't marry you."

"But you *have* married me," he said, standing before her. "At least that's what it says on the special license Josh

Wilton and Chuffy Wilde have dated the same day as the Gracechurch wedding. They're in the front salon with Ian Ferguson."

Her heart stumbled, and she battled a fresh wave of dread. "They've seen me?"

"They helped me get you out."

She wrapped her arms around herself, rocking back and forth, the shame washing through her like acid. It was too much. She couldn't face him. Couldn't face any of them. After this she wasn't sure she could set foot from her parlor ever again.

"Please," she said, shaking her head. "I can't talk about any of this until I am...together."

Recognizable again, at least to herself.

"Grace is seeing to your bath," Harry said. "She came to be with Bea. But don't worry about anybody else. They understand."

"No!" She felt so humiliated, and hated Harry for it. "They don't understand. I don't *want* them to understand."

"They've been very good to you."

"I don't care." She was trembling now. "They can't force me to marry."

His answer was quiet, implacable. "Then you'll go back to the asylum."

Helpless.

Tears, now ignominious and painful as they crowded the back of her throat. She pressed the heels of her hands to her eyes, forcing them back. "You're a bastard, you know that?"

His voice, when it came, was quiet. "I'm not any happier about this than you."

She had no more strength. She sat back down on the bench. "You really have a license."

"Signed and witnessed." He flashed a fleeting grin. "By

the way, did you know that Finney does a very credible copy of your signature?"

"Of course I do. I'm the one who taught him." She looked up, hating the need to beg. "We have a license. Surely it's enough. Why make this travesty worse?"

Harry shook his head. "Joshua Wilton is an honorable man. He wouldn't pre-date the license unless we made the marriage real. Do you know the risks he took?"

She sighed. "I do. And damn your eyes, even I couldn't serve him such a turn."

She assessed herself, thinking she should be reacting more. Violent shakes, nausea, rage. Those would all come, she knew. For now, though, the tears had faded and she seemed to have slipped into the numb limbo of shock. Everything around her seemed to have gone gray.

"You wouldn't just get me, you know," he urged gently. "You'd get all of my family. You know you'd love that. You were always perched in the kitchen talking to Mam or running about playing with the little ones."

He paused, as if giving Kate time to be seduced by the idyllic picture. She had haunted Harry's home at The Grange; his had been a real family, squabbling, laughing, hugging, often at the same time. She'd felt like a beggar being given a glimpse of a feast, but she hadn't been able to stay away. Those memories were often enough to get her through her own day.

"You really wouldn't turn down a chance to let Mam spoil you, would you?" Harry asked. "You know she'd be over the moon."

For a moment Kate shut her eyes, besotted by the idea. But she knew Harry couldn't really want that. She knew she was right when she looked up to see the conflicting emotions skim across his eyes like clouds before a noonday sun: anxiety, regret, hesitation, resentment, and finally resignation. And she couldn't blame him in the least. He'd risked more than anyone. He was giving up everything. Harry, who was passionate in his loyalty, his excitement, his anger. Who radiated sensuality and power and command.

Who deserved better, no matter what he'd done to her.

"No," she said, wrapping the quilt tighter. "I won't do it."

He stiffened, as if she'd insulted him. "We've just been through this, Kate."

She couldn't face him. She turned away, only to see Bea's anxious face again. Ah, Bea. The last thing Kate wanted to do was betray Bea. If she didn't marry Harry, she would be leaving Bea alone and vulnerable to an unforgiving world. How could she put her dear friend in such a position? But how could she be party to this fraud?

"I won't..." *Look at the sky. It's endless, open, blameless.* "I won't lie with you, Harry." Her hands began to sweat just with the thought. "I won't lie with any man."

"I don't blame you," he finally said, his voice so quiet and calm. "I promise I won't expect anything of you until you're ready."

She looked up at him, stricken by the understanding in his eyes. More shame. More guilt. "But that's just it," she retorted and turned to see his jaw working. "I won't ever be ready."

Still his voice stayed quiet. "I think you're wrong."

"You don't know..."

"Oh, I think I do." Sitting next to her, he cupped her face in his hands. He didn't even seem to notice her instinctive retreat from the touch of his fingers. "I'm not an innocent, Kate. I think I know just what happened to you. I think that monster hurt you, and kept hurting you. But I think..." He began to stroke his thumb along her cheek, and just as always, her body woke. "*This* hasn't changed. No matter how we've felt about each other, we've always had this spark." His smile was wry. "Bloody inconvenient most of the time. But maybe...maybe if we remember how nice it can be, it could be a start."

She was trembling with the new warmth that swept through her. Her womb, that dry, wasted space she had long since given up hope for, seemed to soften. If she'd been another person she might have imagined it was ten years ago. That with a wish she could reclaim the wonder and hope that trailed from Harry's fingers.

But she wasn't that girl anymore. Revulsion surged, nausea, dread. She pushed him away so hard she almost knocked him over.

"No." She hated it that she couldn't catch her breath. "Never."

He raised an eyebrow. "Why not?"

Harry's eyes were still dilated. Kate could see the bulge in his breeches. It sent raw fear coursing through her veins, propelling her to her feet, hand out.

She refused to weep. "Because when you make me feel like this, what I remember is that after bringing me to the point of giving you everything—" She clenched her fists so tightly she thought she'd drawn blood. "You left it for Murther to finish."

Harry looked as if he'd been struck by lightning.

Kate couldn't bear to face him. Gathering up her blanket up, she walked away. "I won't, Harry. I won't."

She was already to the door before he answered. "Then you won't," he said, his voice clipped. "But you will say your vows."

*   *   *

By the time Kate and Harry stood before Joshua Wilton in her front salon, Kate knew she was on her last reserves. She had been bathed and powdered, curled and corseted, and now stood up in a deceptively simple azure *peau de soie* dress with silver acorns embellishing the hem and sleeves. She held a quickly gathered bouquet of blue asters and white carnations, which amused her, since in the language of flowers they meant innocence and daintiness. The sun glinted yellow off the mirrors and warmed the pale green silk wall coverings. Grace Hilliard sat quietly by the window, her plain face composed, and Kate's staff shifted uneasily in hastily assembled chairs.

Bea took up her place behind Kate in gray moire, a pretty lace cap atop her head and fingerless gloves covering her restless hands. Harry stood at parade attention, the very picture of a British officer of the 95th Rifles, his shako beneath his arm, his boots shining like black water. Kate thought he looked more handsome than she had ever seen him; she was not about to tell him, though. There was only so much she would sacrifice for this wedding.

As witness for the groom, Chuffy Wilde presented himself in tobacco brown and fawn, his waistcoat an amazing canvas of parrots and palm trees. As ever, Chuffy was smiling, his glasses halfway down his nose.

As if he weren't quite sure Chuffy was up to the job, Ian Ferguson stood just behind him, his kilt gently swaying around his knees, the bearskin beneath his arm. Even Mudge had dredged up his Rifles uniform, although on him it looked odd, like a young god trying on human form for the day. None of the maids seemed to mind.

The only person conspicuously absent from the hastily gathered group was Barbara, who had stayed only until Kate's own abigail had arrived. Kate wished there were some way she could have kept Barbara around. She thought she'd miss her.

Clad in a hastily recovered chasuble and holding the Book of Common Prayer in his elegant hands, Joshua Wilton looked a bit strained as he took up his place in front of the Adam fireplace. In a Minerva Press novel, the wedding would have been accompanied by either birdsong and rainbows or ferocious thunderstorms to portend danger. No portents accompanied these vows, just the sounds of neighbors wending their way home for tea and a sniffle or two from Kate's chef, Maurice.

One day, she thought as she listened to Joshua recite the time-worn lyrics to a song she'd sworn never to sing again, she would compare this wedding with the last one and laugh.

"Repeat after me," Joshua said to Harry, which snapped Kate back to attention. "I, Henry Phillip Bryce, take you, Catherine Anne—"

"Dolores."

Joshua blinked. "Pardon?"

Harry turned surprised eyes on Kate. "What?"

She gave a false smile. "I thought you knew. My name is *Dolores* Catherine Anne. Did you sign it that way on the license?"

Everybody looked around. "No."

Kate wasn't sure if she was excited or disappointed. "Does that mean we can void the whole thing?"

Joshua smiled. "Sorry. We got most of it right. It will stand."

"Your first name is Dolores?" Harry asked Kate, not looking nearly as amused as Joshua. "Your father named you 'sorrow'?"

"Yes, well, he was distraught. After all, I'd just killed his wife."

"Not!" Bea cried.

Kate smiled for her friend. "Of course I did. I didn't intend to, of course. But it seems that even then I insisted on having my way. I wanted to be born, whether she was up to it or not."

"Probably a discussion for another time," Grace said from where she sat.

Kate smiled gratefully at her friend. "Yes, indeed," she said, casting a quick look at Harry. "'If 'twere done, then 'twere well it be done quickly.'"

Harry only stood straighter. Everybody else turned back to the reverend.

"Repeat after me, then," he said. "I, Henry Phillip Bryce, take you, Dolores Catherine Anne..."

She made it all the way through the service, even holding still as Harry slipped a beautiful gold filigree ring on her finger. *Fine*, she kept thinking. *We're finished. I can escape now.*

Of course it couldn't be that easy. Joshua had barely finished the service with the quite depressing admonition that whatsoever God united could never be separated when Kate heard Bea stir behind her.

No. Oh, no, Bea, she thought, turning on her friend. *Not now.*

But Bea's eyes were closed. And before Kate could protest, Bea began to sing.

The room fell into stunned silence. Joshua sucked in a gasp at the ethereal sound of Bea's voice, filling the room. Ian's jaw dropped. Maurice sobbed. The minute Kate recognized Bea's choice, she closed her own eyes. Oh, God. It only wanted this. Of all the songs she could have chosen, it had to be Thomas Moore's "From This Hour the Pledge Is Given." The next time she saw the ubiquitous Moore, she would box his ears. Especially for the last bit.

> *When the proud and great stood by thee,*
> *None dared thy rights to spurn;*
> *And if now they're false and fly thee,*
> *Shall I, too, falsely turn?*
> *No;—whate'er the fire that try thee,*
> *In the same this heart shall burn.*

The last note drifted off and silence returned, profound, almost stricken. By the front window, Mudge had tears streaming down his face. Kate could hear Maurice blow his nose. And poor Bea, hearing it, opened her eyes and looked around, anxious. What could Kate do? Emotion clogging her throat, she pulled her friend into her arms.

"What would I ever do without you?" she whispered, holding her tight. "I should have had you sing at my first wedding."

Bea let loose a watery laugh. "'Down Among the Dead Men,'" she said.

Kate gave her another squeeze and laughed back. "Much more appropriate."

She was trembly and nauseous, she was so exhausted. Frozen with shock; liquid with relief. She had not another gram of strength.

"Well then," she said with a bright smile. "Thank you all for your help. I know you'll agree with me when I say thank God it's all over. Now, I believe I'm for a nap."

Unfortunately, no one moved.

"You haven't told her?" she heard from behind her.

She turned to see that Drake had stepped into the room.

"Told her *what*?" she asked sharply.

The scowl on Harry's face sent Kate's stomach dropping. "I haven't had a chance to get her alone," he said.

Kate felt the ground slipping away beneath her. Good Christ, what more could possibly go wrong? "Thank you, everyone, for coming to my wedding," she said, her eyes on Harry. "Now, if you'd give Harry and me a few moments together."

Her staff well knew that tone of voice and fled as if the ceiling were about to collapse. Harry's friends, correctly interpreting the migration, followed. Only Bea and Grace had the courage to stay. And Drake, who approached carrying a brace of official-looking documents in his hand.

"Congratulations, Kate," he greeted her with a kiss to the cheek. "I'm sorry I missed the ceremony."

Kate backed away, her attention on the papers. "You seem to have been busy."

"A friend alerted me to some covert activity down at the Chancery Court." He lifted the papers. "Your brother has been busy. And your stepson."

She blinked, certain she was in the midst of a nightmare. "My stepson? *Oswald?*"

"Drake sent a message just before the ceremony," Harry said, taking Kate's hand.

If she'd had more sense, she would have shaken him off. "What do you have to tell me, Harry?"

He gave an uncomfortable cough. "It's not."

"What?"

"Finished."

He actually looked to Grace, as if she would help him. Grace crossed her arms and kept her silence. Finally setting down his shako, he took up Kate's other hand, as if it would help her understand.

"The license isn't enough," he said, sounding as if he were announcing a death. "Nor the ceremony."

It took her three tries to get the words out. "What are you saying, Harry?"

It was Drake who answered. "Your brother and stepson have both filed to have you named incompetent to administer your estate," he said holding up one of the writs.

Kate shook her head. "Didn't we just put an end to that problem?"

Drake held up the other writ. "Your brother has charged you and Harry both with fraud. He claims the marriage is nothing more than Harry's attempt to get your money."

"He certainly didn't waste time." Shaking her head, she sighed. "What do we do?"

Drake shrugged. "You convince the world that you and Harry are completely besotted with each other."

Chapter 9

All Kate could think was that there should have been thunderstorms after all. Maybe if she'd had a portent, she could have anticipated the disaster.

"I sincerely hope, Marcus," she said, her voice trembling unpardonably, "that this is a result of your reading too many gothic novels. If so, I have to tell you that I expected better from you." She turned to her suspiciously silent husband. "You knew about this?"

"Not all of it. I've been more focused on the direct threats to you."

She stared at him. "There are more of those, too?"

"No. Just Axman Billy. Nothing you need worry about."

Kate fought a sudden rage. "Worry? Of course I'm not worried. Grace, can you think of a reason I should worry?"

Grace, who had been poisoned while all the men around them had told her she needn't worry, was wise enough to stay silent.

It was enough that Harry flushed. "I'm handling it, Kate. You need to focus on this threat from your family."

"But you're leaving," Kate protested. "You've waited ten years to go."

"The world will still be there in a month."

"Harry and I have taken measures to protect your wealth," Drake assured her.

Another jolt. Her wealth. Not her wealth anymore. Harry hadn't given her time to consider that, and here she stood irrevocably married. "And quite a nice estate it is," she said, unable to keep a bitter note from her voice. "You forgot to ask, Harry, but you've done very well for yourself today."

Harry waved off her claim. "I don't want your money. But your family is another matter."

"They've resubmitted to Chancery to have you declared incompetent on the basis of your marriage to Harry," Drake said.

Kate felt herself blanch. "Then why in blazes did we waste our time on this farce?"

Harry glared. "Because it isn't a farce. All we have to do is prove that this marriage is real to stop them in their tracks. If we can do that, the petitions are moot."

"The only way to prove that is to invite the Almack's patronesses into our bedroom, Harry." She glared right back, feeling panicked and cornered. "And even I am not willing to go that far."

"You need not be that...thorough," Drake said with the suspicion of a smile. "Merely look charmingly in love in public and speak as if this were a long-term thing."

As if it were as simple as that. Kate fought to mount some kind of argument, but she felt as if she were barely treading water, her brain sluggish and thick. "Are you sure? I mean, even for the pleasure of ruining me, I can't see Oswald and Edwin working together."

"Eastcourt," Bea blurted out, wringing her hands.

That one word took the strength from Kate's knees, leaving her sitting on a side chair. "Eastcourt. Of course." Swamped by dread, she rubbed at her temple. "Edwin will do anything to get it back. Even deal with Oswald." She laughed, the sound bleak. "He must have had a seizure when he realized that it's now in your hands instead."

Her beloved Eastcourt. All her hard work and commitment and...yes, dash it, love. For naught. How absurdly funny that the one compensation she'd received for six years of hell should now be the noose that could well choke her.

"I told you," Harry snapped. "I want nothing from you."

Why, thank you, she thought, standing. A woman couldn't hope for a better testimonial on her wedding day. "It doesn't matter," she retorted. "You have it. With all the benefits and problems. Enjoy it, Harry."

She saw his face and braced for a punch. He didn't move, though. "Do you really think I want to take control of you?" he demanded. "Are you mad? I should be in bloody *Paris* right now, sketching the Tuileries and drinking champagne! Not being nanny to a spoiled child who is more afraid of what's going to be taken from her than what danger her friends and her nation are in!"

She would not cry. She would *not*. He would never understand, no matter how hard she tried to explain. He would never have something taken away simply because he was a man. "Well," she quietly said. "Thank you for the clarification. It saves me time fretting over how you see this marriage." Brushing down her skirts, she assumed a position of dignity. "On the off chance it will make a difference, you and I will become more devoted than Abelard and Heloise. At least until I buy your ticket for the Dover-to-Calais packet. Now then, I hate to act the spoiled child, but I have need of a lie-down."

At least he looked chagrined. "Good," he said with a stiff nod. "Drake and I will take care of things down here."

She stopped dead and sighed. "Take care of *what* things?"

"Security. We're replacing your staff with ours so that we have reliable protection for the short time we're here, and then we're trying to figure out where we're going to put you to keep you safe once we've established our undying love."

For a long moment, she just stood there. Then, looking from Harry to a suspiciously quiet Drake where he still stood in the doorway, she shook her head. "No," she said, breathless with this latest betrayal. "You're not."

Now Harry looked bemused. "Not what?"

"Not any of it, certainly not replace my staff with strangers."

He tried to smile. "Do you still consider Mudge a stranger?"

She pulled herself up to full duchess height. Her head had begun to hurt; a small knife had begun to dig into her right temple. "This is my house, Harry. You aren't allowed to just come in and take over. You certainly aren't going to lock me up again without my permission."

"But it's not," he retorted. "Your house. It's mine now. Not only that, it's my job to keep you safe, and I'll do whatever I must to do that."

She felt as if he'd struck her. No, she would have preferred it if he had. Of course. How could she have forgotten so soon? He was making a mockery of the control she'd fought so hard for. And now he was sweeping her last vestige of self-reliance out like unwanted trash.

"I may have signed away all my rights," she warned, her voice growing ragged, "but if you act without my knowledge and consent, I will make you pay for it. And you know I can, Harry." She was trembling, seething. "You know I can."

"He only wants to keep you safe," Drake said.

"Shut up, Marcus," they both said at once, never looking away from each other.

"Whatever you think of me," she told Harry, "you will not insult my staff who fought alongside you by shoving them aside. And you *damn* well won't insult me by doing the same."

Harry shot Drake a quick look, but Drake just smiled. Shoving his hand through his hair, Harry shook his head. "Don't you understand yet? There are people who want to lock you up, and people who want to kill you. And they're not even the same people. You can't know who to trust!"

She laughed, feeling more frightened by the minute. "You truly think I can't trust Finney or Maurice or George? Don't be an ass, Harry."

"Fine," he snapped. "Stay. Share every opinion you have. But after that, leave me to do the job I was asked to do."

*   *   *

From that moment Harry did exactly what Kate most feared. He took charge. It wasn't an overt thing. He didn't thump his fist or swing a riding crop as Murther had, but as he gathered her staff and his in the main salon to instruct them on the new security measures, there could be no question that Harry had led men into battle. He was quick, he was organized, and he was, in his quiet way, ruthless.

After making it a point to participate in the meeting, Kate sat by his side and tried to convince herself that she was maintaining her authority. Increasingly, though, she was beset by a sense of loss. Nothing physical had changed. The walls of her salon were still hung in light green silk; the furniture was still Chinese Chippendale, with its gold cushions and the wood carved into delicate tracery; her walls hung in the Constables and Canalettos she so loved. Her staff kept an eye on her, as if reassuring themselves, and Thrasher sat cross-legged by her feet, just in case she needed him.

She wondered, though, how soon Harry would begin to change it all. First a chair removed because it cluttered up the room, the paintings changed for his own, or the morning room taken for an office. The tulips on the estate forsaken for rye, familiar faces replaced for strange, until finally she didn't fit into her own life again, nothing familiar left to her but frustration and fear.

Her bankers would no longer meet with her. Her estate manager would bring his problems to Harry. Her staff would turn to him for instruction and ask his preference. And Harry, naturally, would assume responsibility. He would take care of her. He would take care of everything, not even realizing that he was robbing her of the only thing she'd ever wanted. Control over her own life.

And once he'd done that, he would leave for his life around the world. And return without notice, only to start the cycle over again. She couldn't bear living like that.

As if she heard everything in Kate's head, Bea reached over and held her hand. Kate gave the gnarled fingers a gentle squeeze and smiled for her friend. Her head was beginning to feel as if it would split in two. The world around her had taken on a watery tone, as if she were listening to what went on from the bottom of a lake. She needed to be alone. She needed to walk through her house, to mark out her haven as if she could protect it, a cat marking a fence to warn the rest away.

Only the cat she wanted to warn away was now her husband.

"Is that acceptable to you, Kate?"

She looked up, blinking. "Pardon?"

Her entire staff was watching her. Harry, his lecture evidently ended, stood four-square before the fireplace, hands behind his back, head forward just a bit, as if it would help him ram his way through opposition. It exhausted Kate just to look at him.

"My arrangements," he said, looking strained. "Are they acceptable?"

She gave a careful nod. "Yes, thank you." At least he'd kept her staff in place. "I'm certain we will be revisiting them when necessary, of course. *Malum est concilium quad matori no potest.*" It is a bad plan that cannot be changed.

He sighed. "Kate..."

It seemed to take every ounce of her strength, but she rose to her feet. "Thank you for including me in your planning session. Now that we're finished, I believe it is finally time for me to see my bed."

Everyone stood as Grace and Bea followed to their feet. Thrasher jumped up as if he'd been spring-loaded, his elbow out for her hand like a swell. It was all Kate could do to maintain her poise. She was so very tired, and her hands were shaking again. With a final nod to the assembled staff, she set her hand on Thrasher's arm and followed Bea and Grace from the room.

She knew Harry was following her, probably just to make sure she was all right. It didn't make her feel any better. Even so, when she reached the staircase, she stopped. Whether she wanted to or not, there was one more thing she had to do.

"Harry?"

He strode up and bent over her. "Yes?"

It took every ounce of remaining poise, but she looked up to see the concern writ large on his face. And she smiled. "You truly did save me. Thank you."

He looked surprised, but he smiled. "It was my pleasure."

It wasn't the fact that Harry raised her hand to kiss it that almost broke Kate's composure. It was that briefly he looked as sad and lost as she felt. And there was absolutely nothing she could do about it.

*   *   *

Grace Hilliard owed her life to Lady Kate Seaton. At least, that was the way she thought of it. After the battle of Waterloo, Kate had taken her in, helped bury her father, treat the wounded, and prepare for her new life. Kate had never pressed or smothered or insisted on Grace's gratitude. She had even stood by Grace during the short, turbulent weeks of Grace's marriage.

Grace wanted so much for Kate, and she thought Harry Lidge could well be the man to offer it. Grace had known Harry most of her life. He was brave and loyal and funny and kindhearted to little girls. But he had never gotten along with Kate, and Kate had ever been vocal in her disdain of him.

Grace wished with all her heart that her two dearest friends could have liked each other. But she, more than most, knew that wishes like that were pointless. You could only deal with reality. And the reality was that two people who detested each other had just married. And the only support Grace could give was to help Kate make her way up to bed.

"I am only allowing you lot to make me look vaporish because it will increase Harry's guilt," Kate said in a small voice, her eyes closed as they mounted the stairs.

"Excellent thinking," Grace said, seeing that Harry hadn't moved. "He looks stricken."

Kate gave an infinitesimal nod. "Then I am content."

What Kate looked, Grace thought, was pulled to the point

of snapping. It seemed to Grace an upending of the natural order that Kate should need help. She was a force of nature, not a self-indulgent society queen.

When they reached Kate's suite, Thrasher took up a position outside, as if expecting Axman Billy to follow them up the stairs. Grace followed Bea and Kate inside, all the way into Kate's bedroom, where they helped her disrobe. Bea was an able conspirator in getting Kate to bed, communicating with expressions rather than words. Bivens, Kate's abigail, took one look at her white-faced mistress and took off for the kitchen to brew one of Bea's tisanes, leaving Grace behind. Grace was surprised. It had always been one of Kate's little idiosyncrasies that Bivens was the only person allowed to breach the bedroom door.

It was when Grace was helping undress Kate that she understood why. They were slipping off Kate's petticoats when Bea shot Grace a warning look. Grace quirked an eyebrow in question. Then she turned back to Kate and saw what Bea had meant.

Grace had seen enough violence in the years she had followed the drum with her father, much of it against women. But when she helped slip off Kate's chemise, she exposed scars so obscene she almost cried out in rage. How could anyone treat Kate so?

Of course she said nothing. She helped Kate into a lemon-yellow night rail and waited for Bea to brush out Kate's thick mahogany hair before slipping her friend between the cool sheets on her tidy four-poster. Bivens forced the tisane down Kate's throat and laid a cloth soaked in lavender over her forehead.

For any other woman, Grace would have closed the curtains to attract shadows. But it was an edict in Kate's house that the curtains never closed and candles never went unlit.

Kate always claimed that light was more healing for her than all the laudanum in the city. For the first time Grace wondered if that were the only reason.

"Finally," Kate said in an unnervingly frail voice from beneath her scented cloth, "I am truly acting the part of a lady. Shall I regale you with my complaints and call the Regent's doctor to physic me?"

Tidying up the room, Grace smiled. "That's better," she said briskly. "For a moment I was worried about you. Will you sleep?"

"Since the sun is up," Kate answered. "Otherwise I would have you sit by my bed reading improving religious tracts to me."

Bea snorted. "Heretic."

"Indeed not," Kate murmured. "I am a married woman again and must remember my place."

"You are married to Harry," Grace said. "Your place is where you make it."

Kate lifted a corner of the cloth. "A passionate defense."

Grace blushed. "I've known Harry since I was ten. I think of him as a brother."

Down went the cloth. "I've known him for just about as long, and I think nothing of the kind."

"Then it's a good thing you're the one marrying him and not me."

Kate offered a small smile. "I don't believe I implied I thought of him that way, either."

"He's a good man," Grace protested, unable to mistake her own defensiveness.

"And so he must be," Kate answered, "to have earned your loyalty."

Grace was sorely tempted to ask how Harry had forfeited Kate's loyalty, since she knew exactly how strong that force was. After spending time with Kate, she also knew that Kate had been motivated by more than petty malice to have interfered with both of Harry's engagements. There must have been a terrible falling-out between them.

It was as if Kate heard her. "The complaint between us is old," she said. "Surely a childish thing. I *was* only fifteen." She smiled then, a pale ghost of the notorious Kate Seaton grin. "I did pay him back, though. It was some of my best work."

Grace looked to Bea, who shrugged. "Exactly what kind of work?"

Kate shrugged. "A well-considered word put in the correct ear that caused his two fiancées to reconsider their choice in husbands. Easily done."

Grace shook her head. "Then too easily done, if that's all it took."

"And so I always thought. I don't believe, however, Harry saw it that way." She shrugged. "Ah, well. We have our entire lives to quibble over it."

Grace heard the resignation in her friend's voice and ached for her, for them both. If only Kate and Harry could find a way through the resentments they both hoarded. They were married; nothing would change that. But they could build a real marriage. Grace would have given every shilling she had, every acre of land to have that chance.

She'd had so little time to protect her own marriage. She'd worked so hard, even knowing that a man nicknamed The Perfection would never have chosen a great gawk of a girl like herself. And she thought he really had come to hold her in some esteem.

It hadn't been enough to bridge the distance, though. When Diccan had had the chance to get out of the marriage, he'd taken it. And Grace had been left with bittersweet memories and an empty house she'd once thought to make her home. She didn't want Kate and Harry to suffer the same fate.

Grace was startled to feel Bea lay a hand on her arm. She looked up to find Kate curled on her side like a child, already asleep. She had the most absurd impulse to drop a kiss on Kate's forehead, which made her smile. Kate would box her ears if she tried. So she followed Bea's lead and turned to leave.

As she moved, Grace made the mistake of looking out Kate's window. She stopped on the spot, her heart suddenly thundering. There, back by the mews, she saw a man. A man she knew. He had spent days watching her house, just like this.

He was dressed differently. When he'd loitered outside her house, he'd been dressed as an aristocrat on the prowl, Stultz jackets and gleaming top hat. Today he was in a workman's homespun with a slouch hat. It didn't matter. She would recognize his jaunty posture and lanky frame anywhere. The last time he had stood outside a house she was in, she'd been poisoned.

She was just about to turn away when he straightened. Bowed with a flourish that made her think he'd seen her, too. Heart pounding, she ran for Harry.

Fortunately, Harry was waiting for them at the bottom of the stairs. "What's wrong?" he demanded, straightening to attention.

She grabbed his arm. "Harry, there's a man behind the mews watching the house. I recognized him. I don't think he works for you."

Harry didn't hesitate. "Mudge!" he yelled, running toward the back of the house.

Mudge appeared out of nowhere, tossed Harry a pistol, and followed him out.

By the time Harry returned, Grace had settled a worried

Bea into the Yellow Salon and was pouring tea. Harry came straight to them.

"Nothing," he said. "You're certain you recognized him."

"And he, me," Grace assured him. Setting down the Sèvres teapot, she looked up at him. "Kate really is in danger, isn't she?"

Harry walked over to the drinks table to pour himself a whisky. "She really is. Which is why I need you to help us keep her inside this house where we can protect her. She can't just go swanning around as if nothing's wrong. She won't listen to me, though."

Grace couldn't help a smile. "Your talents don't really lie in diplomacy, Harry."

He tossed off his drink and set it down. "Which is why you get to do it. I have places I must be."

Out of the corner of her eye, Grace caught him wincing. An old hand at soldiers' stoicism, she took a closer look and was chagrined that she'd missed how pale he was. "The only place you should be is bed, Harry. You look terrible. Which wound is it?"

He shot her a half grin. "Waterloo. I caught some shrapnel from a canister, and it tends to catch me unawares."

She'd seen Harry like this before, and it worried her. "You're not sleeping."

He shook his head. "Don't fret. I'll be fine. As soon as this assignment is over, I'm going home to have my mother fatten me up."

"Will she be happy about Kate?"

That brought Harry to a standstill. He looked out the window, as if seeing his family on the street. "I don't know. She blames Kate for my army career."

"Will she blame Kate when you head off again on your travels? You haven't changed your mind, I assume."

It had been a dream of Harry's as long as she'd known him. She caught a quick flash of guilt in his eyes, a new uncertainty. Still, he shook his head. "No. I haven't."

As if in response, Bea suddenly stood. "Parlay," she said.

Harry stared at Bea. "She wants to talk to you," Grace said. "Might as well sit."

He flashed Grace an impatient look, but he did just that, helping Bea back down onto the settee. It still took Bea a moment to form her ideas.

"China," she finally said, her face screwed up with effort. "Bone...fine...china."

Grace felt her heart melt. She could see the confusion on Harry's face. "I think," she said, "that what Lady Bea is trying to tell you is that Kate is more fragile than most people realize. She's asking that you care gently for her."

Harry looked insulted. "Well, of course I will."

Bea just cocked her head, pursing her mouth in disbelief. And Harry, whom Grace had seen stand off a cavalry charge and infiltrate twenty miles behind enemy lines to rescue a fallen comrade, quailed before the gentle woman's quiet skepticism.

Leaning forward, he put his hand over Bea's. "No woman has ever suffered by my hand," he assured the old woman. "Lady Kate is now my wife. I can assure you we'll argue. But I will always protect her, and see to her best interests."

Lady Bea nodded anxiously. "Queen Bess," she said. "*Needs*...realm."

It was Grace's turn to frown. She had become quite proficient at interpreting Lady Bea. This one, though, was beyond her. Poor Harry was looking positively befuddled.

Lady Bea huffed, waving her hand to take in the room. "Domain."

For some reason, that did the trick. Grace had a flash of

the scars she had seen on Kate's skin, of the broad swath she cut through a jaded society, the quiet hand she'd always had with a staff most society women would have shunned.

"I think Bea is asking you to give Kate a bit of room," Grace said, her attention on the anxious old woman. "Kate's marriage was...unfortunate."

"From what I've seen," Harry snapped, "I'd say it was an unmitigated nightmare."

Then he *had* seen what Grace had on Kate's skin.

"The public sees one face of Kate," Grace told Harry thoughtfully. "You don't see the private Kate. You don't see what she's built all on her own. The Duke of Murther drained every cent from Eastcourt. Kate has turned it back into a showplace. She has a multitude of schemes to help her people to become self-sustaining. As for her staff, you've seen them. Who else would hire them? But they would die for her."

"All right," Harry conceded. "She has my respect."

"But you have complete control of her now, don't you see? After what her life has been like, it will seem unbearable."

He looked back and forth between Grace and Bea. "But there isn't anything I can do. It's the law."

Bea huffed. "The devil quotes the Bible to his own purpose."

Harry blinked in surprise. Grace smiled. No need to interpret that.

"I can't in good conscience delegate matters of security," Harry said. "As for my marriage, I can only promise my best."

Again Bea searched his face. She must have found what she wanted, because finally she smiled.

Harry seemed to sigh. "I know this has been difficult for

you, Lady Bea," he said. "Which is why your singing meant so much to me. I'll never forget such a gift." Lifting her hand, he kissed it.

Bea flushed furiously. "Pandora's box."

Harry frowned over at Grace. "The container for all the world's evils?"

Bea looked at Grace. Grace smiled. "It also held its hope, Harry."

Harry looked almost as uncomfortable as Bea. "You will stay with us, won't you?" he asked the old woman. "I can't imagine how Kate could get on without you."

Great tears welled in Bea's eyes. "Gooseberry."

Harry scowled. "You are not a gooseberry. You're family."

It took a minute, but finally she patted Harry's hand. "Family."

Giving Bea's hand one last squeeze, he got to his feet. "And you, Grace? Could you stay for a bit to help keep Kate from chafing at her restrictions?"

Grace thought of the work she'd begun at her home in Longbridge, of the people she'd left in such a hurry. But then she thought of how silent that house was after the sun went down. How empty. And what Kate had done for her. "I'd be happy to."

He nodded. "Thank you both. I imagine you'd like a bit of a rest yourselves. Just do me a favor. Promise none of you will leave this house until I get back. Tell Mudge if you spot your friend again. And no one but Finney answers the door."

"Of course." Grace helped Bea up. "What about you, Harry? What's on your agenda?"

"Me?" His smile this time was dark. "I believe it is time to see a man about removing an offensive painting of my wife from his club."

*   *   *

It didn't take Mudge long to help Harry effect his change from army officer to man about town, trading the green uniform for blue jacket and pearl-gray trousers, with a silver waistcoat and single fob. After the special work he'd done for Wellington and Scovell on the Continent, Harry knew how important the correct disguise was.

He stepped out of his door fifteen minutes later, intent on leaving. Instead, somehow, his feet took him to the end of the hall and Kate's double doors. She'd had such a bad few days. He just wanted to make sure she was all right.

The master suite stretched across the back of the house, two adjoining bedroom suites connected by a center sitting room. The good *and* bad news was that the sitting room and each bedroom had a door opening out onto the hallway. The first thing Harry did was to check to make sure the bedrooms, at least, were locked. Then he slipped into the sitting room to find Kate's abigail sitting by the window working on some sewing.

"Can I help you, sir?" she asked, getting to her feet.

Harry motioned to the closed door into Kate's bedroom. "How is she?"

Bivens, oddly enough, looked out the window. "Oh, asleep."

Harry nodded. He still walked over to the adjoining door and turned the knob.

The door was locked.

"What's this?" he demanded.

Bivens, a blowsy bit of blond tart Harry bet hadn't started life as a servant, placed herself between him and the door. "Her Grace don't like to be disturbed," she said.

"You can't lock her in," he protested.

"I don't. She locks me out."

He looked around, as if answers lurked in the corners. "But that's absurd. What if something happens to her? Surely there's a way in."

Bivens's eyes strayed toward a small secretary in the corner.

"You have a key," he said and held out his hand. "Hand it over. I need to make sure your mistress is all right."

Bivens puffed her chest out like a broody hen. "Nothin' happens to my lady what I don't know about it."

Harry didn't even bother to answer her. He just kept his hand out until, with a huff of outrage, Bivens retrieved the key and handed it over. "She doesn't know I have it," she said. "I go in through the boudoir." Pronounced *boo-DWIRE*.

So did Harry, passing right by the infamous mirror to get to the bedroom door.

It was the first time he'd been let into the holy of holies. He had to admit he was surprised. Every other room in Kate's house was decorated in tasteful pastels. Even the boudoir had been done in pale blue and silver. But within the private sanctuary of Kate's bedroom, a rose garden ran riot. The blush of sunset warmed chintz curtains and covers and chaise longue. The walls and rugs ran to soft, comfortable shades of leaf green and rose pink, red and white, with real roses overflowing a low bowl, scenting the air with their faint attar. A whimsical bower. More a young girl's room than a siren's.

The only odd note was her four-poster bed. Not positioned in the center, as expected, but shoved against the far wall. He didn't understand why until he finally caught sight of Kate, lying on her side, her back against the wall.

Harry didn't realize he'd moved until he found himself at the edge of the bed. God, he thought, his chest hurting with the sight of her, how could she look so small? So young? Her hair had been braided, strands already straggling over her flushed cheek. Her eyelashes were long and sooty, her mouth lush. She could have been fifteen again if her forehead hadn't been pursed and her hands tucked close. She placed herself in a defensive position and slept as if bracing for attack; it woke a new ache in Harry's chest.

He'd never imagined he'd feel the need to protect Kate. He'd never pictured her being soft and vulnerable enough to need him. Kate was all sharp angles and brittle surfaces, with no cushion to comfort a man. And yet suddenly he was beset by the feeling that a dangerously soft heart lurked just beneath her unyielding surface.

He felt an overwhelming urge to wake her. To demand answers for all the incomprehensible questions that circled around his brain like leaves in an eddy. He kept hearing her voice, thick with condemnation. *You left it for Murther to finish.* She couldn't have meant that she'd gone to Murther still a virgin. It was cruel enough to know the life she must have faced. But if she meant...

No. He'd had the word of her father, and the only man he trusted more on earth was his own.

In the end, it didn't matter. What mattered was the promise he had just made, to honor her; to protect her. To cleave himself only unto her.

Oh, God. What had he done? It was only now that the full impact of this day hit home. He had married a woman he didn't trust. A woman who had betrayed him more than once. And she'd just told him that she would never allow him into her bed.

And yet, for the first time in his life, as he looked on her sleeping alone in this vast bed, he knew she was going to need him. Not just his strong arm, but his patience, his support, his common sense. And how could he provide that half a world away?

But how could he stay? He would never have the big, noisy brood he'd always half imagined. His house would be silent, populated only by ticking clocks and the whisper of servants' feet. His holidays would be sterile and his nights cold.

His parents had shared everything: laughter, anger, grief, attraction. No one could have spent more than five minutes in the rambling, cluttered Lidge household without knowing that Big Jim and Nancy Lidge couldn't keep their hands off each other. Harry had always expected to find a marriage like that. If he couldn't soften Kate's defenses, though, his chance was lost before he started.

First, though, he had to decide if it was worth it to try.

Outside, a church bell tolled the hour. Birds chattered on their way to sleep, and a last flower girl touted her violets in a singsong voice. The light was fading fast, and Harry had places to be. But for a long moment, he stood looking down on the woman he'd once loved and wondered what would become of them both.

Chapter 10

Kate swore it was the voice that woke her. *They'll never let us out...*

She looked around, almost expecting to see the woman it belonged to, even though she'd only ever heard her in the asylum. But there was no one in the room. It was pitch dark outside. Kate's unerring internal clock told her it was about three AM, long past the witching hour. Bivens must have snuck in, because all the candelabras were lit, the flames casting wavering banners across the walls like sunlight through young trees. At least that was how Kate chose to see it.

Outside the streets were quiet, and a stiff little breeze lifted the curtains. Normal. All normal. But her heart was racing and she tasted the metallic tang of fear on the back of her tongue. She hated this sudden, stark waking when nothing was certain. When nightmares still had form, and the morning seemed so far away. She wanted so badly to close her eyes and rest. But it was too dark to manage it. Besides, she was remembering the dream that had woken her. She had recognized the voice that had been plaguing her. She knew who it belonged to. It was just a matter of believing it.

And then a matter of proving it. If she spoke, it might just be her ticket back to that white, silent room.

I know this sounds ridiculous, but do you remember Lady Riordan? The sweet young viscountess who drowned out on the Solent last year? You know her. They just had the memorial for her at St. George's. Weeping children, loads of black crepe? Oddest thing. Two days ago she was sitting in the room next to mine at the Richmond Hills Asylum.

Even more awful, Kate thought, Lady Riordan had claimed to be the wife of a Lion who had put her away to keep her from betraying his activities.

Lady Riordan. God, if that were true, then her own husband had locked her up and told everyone she was dead, even her two children. Kate had met Lord Riordan. He'd seemed nice. Not very exciting, but stalwart. Could he really have been so despicable?

She could be wrong. God knew her mind had been taxed. She was cold just thinking about it. But if she was going to bring an accusation this absurd to Harry, she had to support it. She *had* to try to remember everything she could.

She tried, she really did, deliberately walking back into the shadows of that grotesquely charming madhouse. But no matter what she did, her memory skipped about like rain on a roof, unable to settle. She could capture images, lightning flashes of distress: the bruising grip of the constables as they'd forced her up the steps into that innocuous gray country house. The discordant symphony of shuffling feet, jangling keys, and whispers, always whispers. The sharp sting of lye soap, impatient hands, and hard voices, as they scrubbed her down like an urchin from the stews. The satisfaction of sinking her teeth into that fleshy hand.

She managed a smile at that last, but she was shaking and nauseous, sweat pooling beneath her breasts just at the memory of that stark white room. The echoing thud of that closing door. She simply couldn't go past, even for answers.

She had to wake Harry. She had to tell him her tale and risk seeing that careful, placating light dawn in his eyes as he realized just how mad she sounded. She rubbed her eyes, as if that would ease the panic. Damn it. Why did it have to be Harry?

She had no choice. Sitting up, she climbed out of bed and donned a robe. Her body ached in the oddest places, as if someone had thrown her down the steps. She still felt thick and stupid with exhaustion, but she knew that she would never be able to sleep now that she was up.

Tying her belt, she unlocked her door and left the suite. She was already in the hallway when it occurred to her to wonder where Harry had bedded down. She needed to ask one of the men patrolling the house. She'd just turned for the main staircase when she stopped, caught by a shadow curled against the wall.

She squinted. "Mudge?"

The boy's head turned. He was sitting on the floor across from the other master suite door, arms atop his knees. "My lady," he greeted her, struggling to his feet.

"Sit," she ordered, approaching. "Did we not allot you a room?"

He continued up, until he towered over her. His smile was breathtaking. "'Course you did, ma'am. I'm...watching."

She heard a groan. Faint, chilling. Then a man's voice, talking quickly, urgently. Coming from the direction of the bedroom that adjoined her own in the master suite.

"What's going on?" she demanded, turning for the door. She'd just about reached the doorknob when Mudge caught her hand. "Please, ma'am. Don't. He just got to sleep."

She stared at Mudge as if he were mad, her heart stumbling over itself. "Who? Harry? Is that Harry in the master suite?"

She tried to shake Mudge off. "I don't want him sleeping next *door*."

Harry was still talking, clipped, urgent, as if giving commands.

Mudge refused to let go. "If you wake him, we'll never get him back to sleep."

She stopped pulling. "He's asleep?"

"First time in at least a week, I'm thinkin'."

"But who's he talking to?"

"His men. I think he's goin' back up the redoubt at Ciudad Rodrigo."

She felt the words sink into her chest like tendrils of ice. Nightmares. Harry had nightmares. He'd brought his own ghosts to her house. Kate couldn't stop the shiver that snaked through her.

"Shouldn't you wake him?" she asked.

"Only makes it worse."

"Then what are you doing here?"

He ducked his head, hands behind his back. "Just makin' sure he's ... safe."

Kate had a feeling he'd guarded Harry before. She wondered if Harry knew.

"I appreciate that, Mudge," she said, patting his arm. "But I have to talk to him. I have information he needs."

Or evidence that her mind was truly pulling loose.

Mudge took his own look at the door, through which they could now hear Harry yelling at someone to keep moving, keep moving, damn it. He sounded so desperate, so tired, as if in his dream he already knew that he was exhorting dead men.

"I'll tell you what," she said, shoving her hands into her pockets. "Can we get word to Lord Drake? He can handle this just as easily."

Mudge actually looked relieved. "I can go."

Kate knew she should wait till morning, when reality took solid form. But she was plagued by the feeling that she couldn't waste time. So she returned to her sitting room and the marquetry writing desk by the window, where she jotted a note to Drake.

"Thank you, Mudge," she said, sweeping back out to hand the slip of paper to him.

He was still watching the door. "I don't like to leave him alone."

Kate waved him off. "I'll stay."

Mudge frowned. "I can get somebody up here."

"Somebody who's sat with him through nightmares?"

Mudge's expression gave him away.

"Since I'm probably responsible for at least a few of those nightmares," Kate said, hand on his arm, "I'll stay. Now get along before he wakes up and finds me here."

Reluctantly, he pocketed the note and left. Kate settled herself on one of the hall chairs. She wished she hadn't volunteered quite so quickly. It was dark in this hallway. Even with all the wall sconces lit, the shadows seemed to writhe and leap in tune with the rise and fall of Harry's voice. She didn't want to hear him. She didn't want to think that he could be carrying the kind of pain that could only work itself out in the dark. It was so much easier to hate him when he was strong and sure.

Another moan rose, eerie in the flickering light, a sound of such despair that Kate found herself up and walking to the door. She stood there, hand hovering an inch above the door-knob for what seemed forever, fighting the impulse to enter. She knew better than to breach Harry's room. Hadn't Mudge just told her?

The compulsion was too strong. She had to measure Harry's nightmares against her own. She needed, perversely, to see if Harry had really earned his. She opened the door and walked through.

The minute she stepped into the bedroom she knew she'd made a mistake. Dear God, she thought, her feet rooted on the ground. He was naked, splayed out across the mattress as if he'd run far and just fallen for rest, an ivory statue in repose.

She couldn't breathe. She couldn't move. The boy she had loved had been lean, like a whippet. This was a man's body, a man who had worked hard. His shoulders were broad and taut, his chest hard. He had a horseman's thighs and the lean hips of an athlete. And bisecting his chest, that tantalizing line of hair she had once run her fingers through, pulling her eye inexorably downward. Right down to that devilish nest of hair at the juncture of his legs.

Once she saw his cock lying across his thigh, she couldn't seem to look away. Even dormant it made her shiver. Once she would have reached out to touch it, to tease it into reacting, just to see if she could. She would have anticipated what it would feel like inside her. In fact, she had, all those years ago. She'd thought it could bring her great pleasure, transcendent joy. Now it only seemed a serpent that struck without warning. How could she have known then that something that small could cause such pain?

Well, she thought, inevitably comparing Harry with her husband. Not *so* small. Still, she thought, capable of bringing woe and pain to any woman who was foolish enough to get too close. Especially, she thought with another shiver as she considered the strength inherent in that body, a man with such power.

She should go. She should leave Harry to his dreams. She should cover him up. It was cold in this room, and she could see a sheen of sweat across his chest. But the blankets were bunched beneath his hips, and she wasn't about to disturb him.

She managed to turn away. But as she did, she caught sight of something else, and it stopped her again. And this time there was no question about her reaction. She was appalled. Sickened. Oddly, frightened.

Scars. Not one, but a dozen, scattered across Harry's body like a road map of his career. A long, puckered slash along his right shoulder, a constellation of raw dimples and mounds from what Kate suspected was shrapnel in his chest. A gunshot to the thigh and a burn to his forearm. Sweet Christ, she thought, shivering in the sudden chill of night. How had he survived? She'd helped tend the injured of Waterloo, and she knew what these wounds had cost him.

How odd, she thought, stricken by the sight of those marks. She'd never really thought of what Harry's life had been the last ten years. She knew he'd escaped Moorhaven; it had been enough. Whatever his life was, it had to be better than hers. Suddenly, sharing the darkness with him, she wasn't so sure, and it left her shaken.

As if to remind her that all scars weren't physical, he began to move again, his hands opening and closing, his legs moving. "Come along, Forlorn Hope. Up with you!"

Forlorn Hope? He couldn't mean he'd led a Forlorn Hope. Just the thought stopped the breath in her chest. How could he have so despaired as to volunteer for sure death, leading the first group of men over the walls in a siege? How had he survived?

A moan, mouth open, face taut, hand out. She couldn't stop herself. She hurried up and took his hand. "No, Harry, it's all right. You made it. The Forlorn Hope is up."

God, what was she doing? She had no business here, not in Harry's bedroom, and certainly not in his nightmares.

"No...no, they're down. They're down!"

"Keep moving," she urged, as she'd heard him do. "Keep moving; you'll get over."

She could feel him relive the assault in muscle twitches and gasping breaths.

"It's done," she murmured, reaching out to brush her fingers across his forehead. "See, Harry? The army's following over. It's time to rest now."

He still held her hand in a grip that threatened to break her fingers, but the rest of him paused, relaxed. Kate breathed a sigh of relief. Maybe now he would sleep.

Oh, Harry, she thought, the unfamiliar sting of emotion crowding her throat as she looked down on those once beloved features. *I have enough nightmares of my own. I don't want yours as well.*

And yet fate had played the great game and done just that. No matter how they chose to proceed, she was tied to this man for the rest of her life. This man who had so betrayed her that she still couldn't look at him without wanting to hurt him. This man who kept risking his life to save hers, even though he couldn't seem to abide her, either.

Her marriage forced her to be reliant on a man who had already said he couldn't wait to leave. Damn him. Damn them all for doing this to them both. She had been so happy...well, content. Yes. Content. Just her and Bea and the people of Eastcourt Hall, where she was actually making a difference. She had been free for the first time in her life. She'd been living life the way *she* wanted, without male interference or domination or disdain. And now, in a matter of days, of hours, it was gone.

She tried to gently pull her hand from Harry's, but he didn't seem to want to let go. She looked around, searching for a bit of help. All she saw was Harry's trunk tucked at the end of the bed and his brushes on the dresser. No help at all. Simply evidence that Harry had felt comfortable taking the master's place, pushing her a bit farther out of her own life.

She couldn't do anything about that right now. Not if she was going to let him sleep. Pushing her straggling hair from her forehead with her free hand, she pulled over a chair and sat down. Maybe if she sat a few minutes, he would let her go.

Unfortunately, once she sat, she didn't know what to do. It was, she realized, the first time she'd had a chance to be still for more than a few moments in a safe place since being locked into a runaway carriage—how many days ago? She sighed, rubbing at her scratchy eyes. It all seemed so unreal, a melodrama made for footlights and costumes.

Unfortunately, it was all too real. And only beginning.

She was going to need a chance to calmly, rationally decide what she needed to do next. But she would need to get away from Harry to do it. *Calm* and *rational* weren't in their shared lexicon. She looked down at the filigree ring on her finger, almost expecting it to glow. Now that she was quiet, she could feel it again, that strange current of electricity that leapt between them, that so easily flared into flame. The same humming heat that had once seduced her; that now unnerved her.

She was surprised, really, that it had lasted through the years. That it still seemed as sharp and vital as when they'd been young. And yet it did. Sitting here touching only Harry's hand, she felt a surge of power spiral through her, a sweet, hot light that spread across her skin and warmed her belly. She couldn't believe that her body remembered. That it yearned, even for Harry. *Especially* for Harry.

It wasn't that he wasn't still attractive. He was a striking man; not handsome, so much. Handsome had long since been chiseled away into starkness, jaw and cheek and forehead: weathered now, creased from squinting into the sun. His sandy hair was a little shaggy; his ears stood out a bit. But his throat was a work of art, etched in moonlight, arms crafted for protection and care. He'd been drawn in sleek lines of sinew and bone, with the faint gleam of sweat on chest and belly, and she could smell crisp linen and fresh air on him, the faint hint of horses and a tang of tobacco. A man's smell. Harry's smell.

At least she was safe from his eyes. She had so loved those eyes. Once upon a time she'd seen the sky reflected there, impossible, endless eternities. She'd lived to see his eyes go languid with hunger, brighten with impish humor as they'd fenced with arcane quotes from dead authors. She had loved the bright, trenchant intelligence that lit them as he'd expounded on weight and load and line.

Was Harry right? Was there a way to cobble a life together? Even after what he'd done? What *she'd* done? Could she possibly have that much courage? Already her heart was stumbling, but was it with fear or anticipation? Harry said he could help her get past what had happened. He could give her back the matchless, breathless freedom of pleasure, separate it from the pain. He'd said that. He'd also once said he would save her.

She closed her eyes, and the world shrank to Harry. To that odd, restless lightning in their hands. She tasted it, champagne on the tongue; heard it, the quickening stutter of her heart. She didn't fan the feeling; that would have been foolish. But she warmed her fingers in it, tempting herself. Daring herself.

Harry was asleep; he need never know. The heat was just too tempting; she'd been cold for so long. If she could maybe just stay here for a while, quietly, and drink in a bit of life. If she could remember what it had been like. That shivery, anxious feeling of wanting, of expectation, of fear. That breathless catch of wonder, when fingers touched, when a hand, callused and broad, slowly swept down her skin, shoulder to belly to thigh, setting everything in its path alight like a mad brushfire. The sharp wonder when eyes met, hot, dark, heavy with hunger. The wild, soaring exhilaration of possibility that only complete trust inspired.

Had it really felt like that? Had she been so sure it would simply go on? She couldn't quite remember now. She only remembered the jagged flashes of lightning that stunned her body to life. The way her nipples had tightened and her blood slowed to a deep throb that echoed in her ears. She remembered that Harry had looked on her as if she were his personal treasure, seduced her without a word. Without a promise.

Most of all she remembered the feeling of soaring exhilaration, knowing that Harry would always be there to catch her if she fell. That he would hold her dreams for her, her secrets, her discoveries, as if he were a schoolchild's grubby tin box full of buttons and feathers and sparkly rocks collected from a beach.

With him to shield her, she had begun to believe that she might be more than the unfortunate child who had killed the most beloved woman in the county. She had begun to believe

that her father was wrong; that she deserved more than isolation and silence.

Inevitably, though, that final memory slipped through to
mock her. Her last day with Harry in the glen; frantic, fumbling, begging him to believe her. To save her. So sure that it
would be all right, because Harry promised. Even if he hadn't
made her his, he would claim her. He would fight for her.

Instead, when she'd slipped out into the whispering,
moonlit garden later that night, it had been her father waiting
for her. "I think I knew that one day you'd come to this,"
he'd said, his sad eyes so much sadder."But did you have to
include an honorable boy?"

Impatiently she shook herself to attention. It would not
do. Remembering would solve nothing. It only left her trembling and cold. She needed to get out of here.

She pulled at her hand. This time, it popped free. Jumping
up, she ran for the door.

She was too late. She was struggling with the knob when
she heard his voice, muddled and sleepy. "Kate?"

"Go back to sleep, Harry," she said without turning,
"Everything's fine."

"What the hell are you doing in here?"

"Leaving."

"Kate," he said, fumbling with the sheets. "Wait."

She didn't.

*   *   *

Harry was confused. His chest was on fire, and his head hurt.
He swore he could still hear cannon fire, and he had the oddest memory of Kate urging him up the Forlorn Hope. The
cannon fire was easy to explain. He'd heard it every night
since Waterloo. Kate was more problematic.

"Stop!" he yelled and rolled out of bed.

He didn't even think to pull the sheet around him. He had the oddest feeling he couldn't let Kate go just yet. Just as she was opening the door, he slammed it closed.

"Kate," he said, grabbing hold of her arm.

He saw her instinctively duck, her free hand up, and stopped dead in his tracks.

"Kate." He made sure she didn't hear the anger in his voice. He didn't want her to think it was directed at her. "I'm sorry. I didn't mean to startle you. I just wanted to know what you were doing here."

She wouldn't look at him. "You had a dream. Believe me. I won't make this mistake again."

He couldn't help smiling. Only Kate would sound surly about being kind. "I appreciate the concern. The dreams are nothing new, though. They don't hurt me."

She looked over her shoulder, and Harry was struck by how large her eyes were, how very young she looked with her braid coming loose over her shoulder.

"How can you not mind?" she asked.

He shrugged. "Comes with the job. You have nightmares, too."

It wasn't a question. He refused to insult her with pretense.

She looked away again. "Doesn't everyone?"

"Not like yours, I think." Taking a second, he assessed the night. He could hear early birds, which meant it was after four. He'd only had about five hours' sleep, which left him muzzy, and Kate's exotic scent was doing damage to his self-control, which was going to be painfully obvious in a minute. He needed to recover his banyan.

"Let me go, Harry," she said, pulling against his arm.

Should he? She was a bit softer now, tentative. Was this

his chance to begin chipping away at her formidable defenses? Did he *want* to? Did he really want to risk falling prey to her again?

He didn't know. But he had the most irrational feeling that if he passed up this chance to soften her barriers, he'd never get another.

"Come back and lie down," he urged. "It's chilly out here."

"No!" She gestured toward his rapidly chilling body. "And not like that."

He looked down with a grin at his nakedness. "It does put me at a disadvantage, doesn't it?" Letting go just long enough to grab his robe, he shrugged into it. "Just lie down where it's warm. That's all. On my honor as a gentleman."

Her laugh was sharp. Harry bristled, the laugh setting up old hackles. How dare she? Didn't she realize how bloody honorable he'd been to her?

One look down at the round shadow on the swell of her breast deflated that balloon. They had both served time in hell. He just wished he better understood why. He wished, not for the first time, that the Duke of Livingston had been a man who lied.

Reaching around, he opened the door a crack. "You're free to go at any time," he said. "But we need to talk together before we face the rest of the world."

She stared at him, as if she'd never heard the word *talk* before. "Why?"

He shrugged. "To find out if we can ever again deal well with each other."

"I thought I wasn't going to have to deal with my husband. Aren't the Tuileries waiting?"

He came so close to just saying yes and letting her go. Because if he didn't, if he forced her to stay, he might be taking an irrevocable step toward something he didn't want.

Hadn't he done enough already? Wasn't he entitled to his own life, now?

"Possibly. But possibly we'll learn to like each other and come to another solution. Whatever happens, we need to learn to trust each other, or marriage is going to be hell."

She laughed even more loudly this time. "I'm not long on trust, Harry."

Harry bristled at the sound, because he heard his name implied in the accusation. Still, it wouldn't help to snipe. "But I think you're beginning to trust me."

She stiffened like an outraged virgin. "*Vestigia nulla retrorsum.*"

He chuckled. "Case in point. You may think that there's no going back, but if I'm correct, you haven't been making use of your rather unorthodox education in the last ten years. Yet suddenly you're quoting Homer again."

Harry regretted his flippancy when her face lost its color and she swayed. He tried to pull her closer, but she shoved at him as if he'd hit her. .

"What did he do, Kate?" Harry asked. "Just how did your husband convince you to give up Latin?"

She managed to yank her arm out of his grip, but she didn't leave. "That's not anybody's business but mine."

"I disagree. If we are to have any chance, it has to be my business, too."

Her head shot up, and she impaled him with a look of derision. "Your *right*?"

He was swamped again with the feeling that he needed to hold her. "No. You've taught me that lesson well. But how can I know how to live with you if I don't know what's off limits?"

She seemed struck. "Live with me? You think you want to live with me?"

Harry didn't feel complimented by the acid in her voice. "What did you think? That I'd take all your money and run?"

She quirked a cold eyebrow. "You really plan to settle on an estate in Gloucestershire and grow flowers."

He knew his hesitation was damning. Of course that wasn't what he planned. But they were still a long way from that discussion. "We need to start somewhere."

She gave him an assessing look that took in his entire un-clothed body. "Why don't we start with you going back to bed? We can do the rest in the morning."

"No. Right now. By morning you'll have your armor back on." With a brief grin, he reached over and flicked at her braid. "You should wear your hair like this more often. It makes you look like that girl I knew at the castle."

She stiffened, her nostrils flaring. "Don't ever make the mistake of thinking I am," she said, her voice cold. "I haven't been that girl for a very long time. She was unfor-givably naive."

Harry almost laughed out loud. If there was one word he would be hard-pressed to use about Kate, it was *naive*. He needed to get her where he could talk to her, though. Quickly grabbing her hands, he pulled her back toward his bed.

Her eyes got even wider. "You are *not*…"

"Kate, my feet are freezing. Please. I promise on my mother's plum duff that I won't touch you. I just don't want to come down with the ague on my wedding night."

"There'll be no wedding night," she retorted.

"Not a wedding night any red-blooded male would recog-nize, certainly." Gently, inexorably, he drew her away from the door. "Come."

With a quick look out the window to make sure that only his own men patrolled the area behind the mews, he nudged her on. He wasn't quite sure how he did it, but he managed to get Kate into bed alongside him, the covers tucked up to their chins, like twins in a trundle.

"See? Isn't this nice?" He was getting hard just from the shared heat.

She lay frozen, her hands at her sides. "I hope you don't mean for me to fall asleep. I don't fall asleep in the dark."

"That's fair." He shrugged, carefully keeping his space. "I don't fall asleep at all."

She huffed. "So I found out. Tell Mudge he doesn't have to sit outside your door. He isn't getting any sleep, either."

"I have. It doesn't do any good."

They'd been lying side by side for a while when suddenly Kate sighed. "I loved your mother's plum duff."

Harry hoped she didn't see his relief. "It won another ribbon at the county fair."

Another silence, this one shorter. "She's all right? I don't get back there anymore."

"She's blooming. I think she gained at least two stone since last I saw her. She has all those grandchildren to cook for now."

He felt Kate's head turn. "Grandchildren...oh, my. Of course everyone is grown."

"All but Carrie. She's holding out for something better than Perseus Cleaver."

Kate chortled. "The miller's son? Tell her if she needs a champion, I would be happy to help. Percy outweighed your mother by the time he was ten."

"Tell her yourself when you see her. You don't think I can get married without showing you off."

He felt her stiffen and reached over to take her hand. "I won't deny my mother the satisfaction of seeing me married, Kate."

She didn't answer. Harry thought of the times she had

shown up at his kitchen door, as if unable to stay away from his mother's massive hugs. He'd often wondered what a duke's daughter could prefer in that haphazard house by the millpond. Then he'd wondered how she could have so blithely thrown it away for a quick tumble with a groom.

"Why didn't you tell me, Kate?" he asked before he could change his mind.

She looked over. "Tell you what?"

He took a breath. He couldn't believe he was forcing this. But he'd wanted to know for years. He needed to understand before he could take another step toward committing to a marriage of any kind.

"The baby, Kate. Why didn't you tell me about the baby?"

He couldn't help himself. He looked into her eyes and expected to see hesitation; guilt; anger. Maybe resentment at being forced to face her misdeed.

She only looked bewildered. "What baby?"

He wanted to shake her. "Please, Kate. It's time we told each other the truth. You wanted me to marry you that summer so George's baby wouldn't be a bastard."

He spoke for effect. Again, she surprised him. She didn't slap him or stalk off or weep, as if tears now would wash away his anger over old sins. She just blinked at him, as if he were making no sense at all.

"George who?"

Chapter 11

Harry quelled a sudden rage. Sitting up, he turned on her. "I'm too tired to be playing this game, Kate. If you don't want to talk about it now, just tell me."

She kept staring at him as if he were speaking Hindi. "I'm happy to talk about it, Harry. I just have no idea what you're talking *about*."

That brought him right out of bed. Circling to Kate's side, he held out a hand to her. "Come on."

She flinched. "Come on what?"

"I can't fight you lying down."

She pulled away. "Fight? I don't want to fight."

"Discuss, then. Clear the air." Losing patience, he picked her up, covers and all, and settled her on one of the armchairs.

"Move and I'll come after you," he warned. Then to give him a chance to get his temper under control, he crouched to prod the fire into life.

She took the opportunity to jump up and try to stalk off.

Harry caught her before she escaped and pushed her back into the chair. "I told you to sit," he snapped, leaning over her. "I understand, Kate. I really do. You were desperate. I was handy. I don't blame you anymore. I just want to understand."

"Understand *what*?"

Kate was confusing him. He understood denial. He understood out-and-out fabrication. But something about the oddly frustrated expression in Kate's eyes made him question his assumptions.

"Why did you really beg me to marry you, Kate?" he asked, sitting across from her.

"You know perfectly well. I loved you. And my father was going to marry me to Murther."

"What about George?"

"George? Which George?"

He struggled to keep his patience. "You had a groom named George."

"Well, yes, of cour..." Shock dawned in her eyes; confusion, anger. "Oh, my God," she breathed. "You said *George's* baby?"

She looked suddenly fragile as isinglass, hurt in ways Harry couldn't even understand, and it unnerved him.

"I'm afraid you need to explain this to me, Harry," she said, her voice perilously thin. "In simple terms. Why do *you* think I asked you to marry me?"

Harry sighed. "There's no reason to dissemble, Kate. Your father told me."

"Told you... *what*?"

Harry stood and wandered over to the fireplace. He hated to speak so baldly. "He admitted that you were promiscuous. That you'd been indiscriminate."

"Promiscuous." She laughed, a bleak sound. "Of course you believed him. After all, *you'd* certainly been under my skirts."

"Don't be crude."

She actually gasped. "Crude? You just called me a slut."

"Your *father* called you..." He faltered to a halt when he saw the anguish bloom in her eyes.

"What else did he say?" she asked, her voice hollow.

Harry turned away, unable to face her with her father's words. "He said there was something...wrong with you. That you were unmanageable. Were you?" He looked over his shoulder to see her staring into the fire. "Unmanageable? Please. I have to understand. I only knew you that one summer."

She laughed again, the sound grating like ground glass. "Oh, Harry. *Now* you want to understand. You couldn't have thought to simply ask back then." She began picking at the fringe at the end of the blanket, her focus on her fingers. "Unmanageable." She sighed. "How can I know? I don't think so, but then, I wouldn't be a judge, would I? I know I was forever trying to sneak away to see my father. Every time it happened my nannies and governess would get called onto the carpet, so I imagine they protested. But father left punishment to them. Nanny Dodd liked the library. She made me stand with books on my head. It was my governess Miss Frazier who thought of the priest hole."

Harry looked up. "Priest hole?"

She glanced at him sharply, as if surprised by her own words. "Yes. In the library."

He sat down in the chair next to hers. "You were locked in a priest hole?"

Kate shrugged, pulling the blanket higher. "Once Frazier realized that my stints in the library were only helping me learn Latin, she decided the priest hole was a much better idea. Not so many books."

Harry saw her shudder and felt sick. "I thought it was your husband..."

She looked up. "Who inspired my odd relationship with the dark? Oh, no. Although he was happy to take advantage of it."

"But your father..."

She looked down again. "I'm sure he never knew."

The last word Harry would have ever used about Kate Hilliard was *vulnerable*. And yet he found himself aching for that lonely, frightened little girl. He remembered the first time he'd seen her lurking about the back of the Grange, as hesitant and anxious as a fawn. He'd thought she was one of the orphans from over at the workhouse.

She went on, as if Harry weren't even in the room. "I finally realized that my father simply didn't want me around. I asked why, once." She kept pulling at the fringe with quick, jerky movements. "It was the only time my father hit me."

Harry had an image of the sprite he'd met that summer, all flowing hair and dusty skirts, eyes brimming with wicked intelligence and devilish humor. She'd had such a bright, impish smile. "You seemed so happy," he said. "So...fearless."

Briefly she looked at him, then back at the flames. "I was."

Harry got to his feet and stood there a moment, struggling with the direction of this conversation. Afraid, suddenly, to see it to the end.

"What made you think I was having George's baby?" she asked, never looking up.

Harry walked to the window and looked out into the empty darkness. "Your father told me. He said you'd been sneaking off all summer with George, and the inevitable happened. That he was just the...latest."

She let out an abrupt laugh, a high, eerie sound. "And my father swore to this."

"Of course. Why else do you think I agreed with him?"

He turned to see her shake her head. "Indeed," she said, her voice too quiet, her focus on nothing. "Why else?"

He stood there for a long few minutes, but she didn't say any more. "Kate?"

She didn't answer, didn't so much as acknowledge him. She kept shaking her head, her eyes too bright and glassy, her face stretched into an odd rictus, as if she'd been stripped of everything but skin and bones. But when he reached for her, she pulled away, tightly clasping her hands in her lap. She looked, Harry thought, oddly like an abandoned child.

Stalking back over, he crouched by her chair. "Kate."

Suddenly she was lurching to her feet. "Get your pants on, Harry."

He stood as well, now completely confused. "My pants?"

"I need to show you something."

"Kate, it's four in the morning."

"Then we're just in time."

And without another word, she spun around and headed for her room. Left behind, Harry couldn't think of anything to do but dress.

He met Kate outside his door five minutes later. "Now what?"

She didn't answer. Clad in a dun brown round gown and cloak, her braid pinned up out of the way, she led the way down the hall and through the dim house, not stopping until they walked outside to the mews, where Harry saw lights and heard one of the grooms whistling. Kate threw open the door to the stables and walked right in.

Giving her bobbing staff a distracted smile, she made her way to the back, where Harry heard someone crooning to one of the horses. As they got closer, Harry recognized the big, vacant fellow who'd helped them rout the Lions back at Diccan's. He topped Harry by a good four inches and positively dwarfed Kate.

"'Lo, Katie," he said with a wide grin, doffing his cap.

She took the big man's hand, and he smiled as if she'd brought the sun. He had his cap in his other hand, held over his heart. Harry remembered that his movements were halting and abrupt, his manner child-like.

"Harry," Kate said. "I'd like you to meet George." She flashed a smile up at her companion. "George is my cousin."

Harry felt as if he'd been kicked by a mule. Good God. *This* was George? "Impossible," he protested. "You'd *never...*"

"No," Kate said, her voice derisive. "I would never. George, you know my friend Harry."

George nodded enthusiastically. "Helped him save you, din't I?"

She flashed her cousin another of the sweetest smiles Harry had ever seen. "Indeed you did. I don't know what I'd do without you, George."

George blushed. "Couldn't do without *you*, Katie."

"We'll leave you to your work, now, all right?" she said, patting his hand.

George bent for Kate's kiss on his cheek and watched as she strode out of the barn. Harry followed, more by rote than anything.

"George's mother was one of the dairy maids at the castle," Kate was briskly saying. "My father's brother Will had a notoriously wandering eye." She briefly looked back over her shoulder. "George has always been happiest with his horses."

Harry was numb. He felt as if in these last few minutes, Kate had swept his feet out from under him. Her father had lied. Not just lied, made up the most damning accusations about his daughter out of whole cloth.

But *why*? If it had been Diccan's father, the duke's brother, Harry could have understood. The bishop had been a petty, controlling, unhappy, condescending bastard. The Duke of Livingston had not. He had been the definition of noble, generous and caring for his family and fields and every last person on his lands. He'd stood up in Lords and sat on the privy council, and he had done it all with a kind of unconscious humility that had marked him a great man.

Then how in God's name could he have maligned Kate unless she really had deserved it?

Harry came to a dead stop. "He couldn't have lied," he insisted. "He *never* lied."

Because if he had, then Kate *hadn't* lied. Murther had been the one to take her virginity. And Harry had condemned her to it.

"My God, Kate, I'd revered your father my whole life!"

Kate stopped just shy of the kitchen door. "And you'd only known me a matter of weeks."

He searched her face for the truth and saw it. All of his beliefs, the cornerstone that had anchored his anger all these years, was crumbling. "It all happened so fast. I was so overwhelmed by you. I thought you must have blinded me."

She stood silently for a moment, the predawn breeze fingering the curls around her face, the uncertain light making her look young and vulnerable. Harry couldn't take his eyes from her. He wondered if he'd ever really seen her before.

"Well," she said, turning away. "At least you got a commission out of it."

He reached over and caught her by the shoulder. "You

think that I *wanted* that commission? Do you? Did I ever once express a desire to go for a soldier?"

Now it was Kate's turn to look uncertain. "My sister Frances said you were delighted. Swanning your uniform around the neighborhood and boasting of your luck."

"How else could I convince my mother that I wasn't being sent into exile as punishment for casting my eyes too high? I couldn't have stayed there. You know that. Your father just made it possible for me to make my way somewhere else."

"But you've never left the army," she protested.

"I'm good at it," he snapped, knowing how disgusted he sounded. "While your father was alive I owed it to him. He could so easily have ruined my entire family for my having the temerity to court you."

"And since?"

It was his turn to shrug. "I couldn't leave the job half finished."

For the longest time, she stood perfectly silent. Then, shoulders slumping, she shook her head. "*Difficile est saturnam non scribere.*"

It is difficult not to write satire.

She couldn't have been more right. Ten years. Ten *years*, destroyed by a single moment, by a man Harry had always believed would never injure another living soul. Harry simply couldn't comprehend the scope of it. He was shaking with shock. And he hadn't been the one trapped into a nightmare of a marriage, caged and beaten and thrown in the darkness.

Oh, God. How could anyone repay Katie for what she'd lost?

"Why?" he demanded, shock still freezing him. "Why in God's name would your father do such a thing to you?"

Kate didn't move. "If you find out," she said, "would you please let me know?"

She sounded so lost; so suddenly, completely alone. Harry couldn't tolerate it. He couldn't bear to think of what these last minutes must be doing to her. The father she'd adored had accused her of sins that would have shamed her. And the boy she'd loved had believed him.

Even as he watched, Harry could see her drawing herself up, her posture growing rigid as a wall. There were no tears, no wailing or cursing, when any other human would have disintegrated at tonight's revelations. Not Kate. Right before Harry's eyes, she was disappearing back into that hard, impervious facade she'd built to protect herself.

He couldn't let her do it. She would only grow more brittle, more outrageous. She would encapsulate all that betrayal and grief and anger within the outrageous persona she'd created, and it would eat away at her until it destroyed her. He would never forgive himself if he allowed it to happen. There had to be a way to exorcise her grief.

He knew she would fight him. He'd be lucky if she didn't eviscerate him. But it was a penance he was willing to pay. Before she could escape, he pulled her into his arms. And before she could express the outrage that sparked in her eyes, he kissed her.

Chapter 12

For Harry the reaction was instantaneous. Not just the usual spark that flared between them; something sweeter, softer. Something that bound them. She fit so perfectly beneath his heart, her body so soft and pliant, her hair like silk. Her scent had changed. She had once smelled of summer flowers and sunshine. Now she was exotic flowers, a scent that made a man's mouth water. Her mouth, that wide, laughing, sharp, sensual mouth, caught his like a pillow, and he sank into it without a sound.

Here in the deep night where the darkness had begun to pale on the eastern horizon, he swore he could hear the old stream tumbling by in their little glen. He could almost feel the sunlight on his shoulders, when it was too early for dawn. Bowing, his body molded itself to Kate's, as if he were melting into her arms.

It all happened to him in a second. In two, she was fighting. Even though he'd expected it, he was still surprised at her ferocity. She used knees and elbows and fingernails. She bucked and kicked; she growled, deep in her throat like a feral cat. Not in fear, not in panic; Harry knew well the sound and feel of those. In anger. In despair. In pain at what had been done to her, at what she'd been left with.

And all the time, Harry held on. Not with force; Kate would never suffer a bruise at his hands. He simply withstood her fury, hoping that when she wore down she would realize that his arms were a bulwark against fear and pain, not a prison to create them.

He didn't know how long she fought. He knew he was going to show bruises in the morning, but he held on, gently, firmly, caressing her mouth from corner to crest, kiss after kiss, claiming every small inch, soothing as he would a wound, massaging with lips and tongue. Softening, seducing, waiting, one arm around her waist, the other cupped at the back of her head so she had to stay.

He knew it was a risk; she might end up hating him. She might never let him close again. But he couldn't let her escape back into her hard, desolate shell. He had to make her know that she wasn't alone anymore.

He felt her surrender in minute steps, her force waning, her protests dying. He felt her lips soften, finally open, just a bit, just enough to offer welcome. He felt a tremor build in her, muscle by muscle, bone by bone, as her fearsome control began to disintegrate. And finally, finally he tasted the salt of tears on his tongue, and she began to sob.

It was only then that he released her mouth. Gently, deliberately, he pulled her face against his chest and held her tightly to him. He said not a word; words would have been intrusive. He held her as her whole body shook beneath the force of her sobs. He held her as ten years of pain and loathing and fear bubbled up and spilled free. He held her as she mourned for what had never been, what had been suffered and forfeited. He had failed her before. He wouldn't this time.

As if she had fallen all the way to the bottom of a long

hill and was preparing to rise again, Kate began finally to regain her poise. Harry could feel it as if she was rebuilding, a block at a time, straightening, reclaiming her strength and posture and dignity. He knew that he only had moments more to comfort her before it became too uncomfortable, and he savored every small moment. The curl of her hair against his cheek, the tears that still dampened his neck, the fierce pride that shored her up when everything else had been lost. He realized he was humming, like a mother did to a hurt babe, deep in his throat. He was stroking the silken tangles of her hair. He was inhaling her exotic bouquet and hoping she accepted his warmth.

Even if he hadn't known her, he would have held her. He had certainly held grieving women before. But to hold his Kate this way again, after all they had shared and lost, was both honor and burden. It was a privilege he knew only a very few had been accorded. If she never let him this close again, he would have to be satisfied.

Before he was ready to let her go, Kate pulled out of his arms and turned to the side. "I must ask you to excuse me," she said, much on her dignity as she surreptitiously scrubbed at her face with trembling hands. "I am not usually one for waterworks."

Harry couldn't help smiling down at her puffy, tear-stained face. "*Est quaedam flere voluptas.*"

Her laugh was abrupt. "Ovid now? Well, he's wrong. There is no pleasure in weeping. Only a thick head, puffy eyes, and a quite disgusting need for a handkerchief. I vow, I'll be laid low with cucumber slices over my eyes for a week."

"You can't be," he said, tucking a damp curl of hair behind her ear. "You're obliged to present yourself to the public in order to convince them we're inseparable."

Before this, Harry would have resented the moue she

made. "Not today, I think," she said, straightening her skirts with still-trembling hands. "I believe after everything that has happened, I am entitled to a day of the vapors."

Harry was smiling again, relieved to hear the sharp edge of her tongue. "I heartily agree. Shall I buy you some gothic romances to peruse?"

She shuddered. "Vile things. All ghosts and monks and fainting women. I should write my own. The heroine would never wait for the hero to rescue her. Heroes are so unreliable." She stopped, shut her eyes. "Sorry, Harry. Hard habit to break."

He took her hand and kissed it. "But they are unreliable, Kate. At least they have been, during which time you have more than magnificently cared for yourself and Bea."

She shook her head. "You wouldn't say that if you'd seen me five years ago."

"You survived," he insisted. "You had the last laugh."

Her head came up, her surprised smile a bit smug. "I suppose I did. Murther is dead, and I am still a duchess and the daughter of a duke, which is more than enough. After all, it gives me precedence over my sister-in-law Glynis, which makes her livid. Every time I walk into dinner before her, I can almost hear vessels burst in her head."

She sounded better, but she was still thrumming like a tuning fork; Harry could feel it, not even touching her. He simply couldn't leave her like that. Reaching down, he cupped her face in his hands. She instinctively stiffened, tried to pull away.

"Sssssh," he whispered. "I'm just going to kiss you. I promise from now on I'll always try to tell you what I'm going to do before I do it."

Her eyes looked huge. "What if I don't *want* you to do it?"

Her pupils had grown. Her breath had shortened. Harry smiled. "Then you will tell me and we'll discuss it. I will never force you to do anything you don't like or that frightens you, Kate. But if we're going to make a show of how great this marriage is, we have to at least look comfortable together. The more I can touch you, the better we'll pull it off. If you let me simply kiss you now and then, you'll become more used to it."

She made a little huffing noise. "I'm not as convinced of success as you are."

He smiled, using his thumbs to wipe away her tears. "You don't need to be. You just need to close your eyes."

The trembling increased; for a second she betrayed the terror that must still shadow every memory. Then, like the valiant woman she was, she took a deep breath, closed her eyes, and lifted her face to him.

Harry was humbled by that simple show of courage. Two days ago, he wouldn't have believed he would ever see it. Dipping his own head, he brought his mouth down to hers, brushing lightly over her lips, her eyelids, her nose. He wanted so badly to stay, to deepen the kisses into something warmer, more intimate. He wanted to run his tongue along her lips, coaxing them open, coaxing *her* open.

He was the one trembling now. His body wasn't used to restraint. It wanted her with all the swift hunger of a starving man. He knew better, though, so with a final kiss to her forehead, he straightened and dropped his hands. He was selfishly glad when she swayed a bit, as if regretting his loss. And when she opened her eyes, he was relieved to see uncertain wonder hovering there.

"It's still early," he said. "Would you like to return to my room for some rest?"

She was already shaking her head. "Maybe tomorrow or the next day."

He dropped a final kiss on her brow. "Tomorrow."

*   *   *

Kate felt as if she were splintering into a million pieces. Emotions she hadn't allowed in years surged through her, taking her breath, her balance. Grief, anger, shame, and oddly, on hearing that Harry hadn't been quite so thoughtless, relief. Confusion mixed them all into an unpalatable stew. Had Harry actually held her? Had she let him? Had it really felt like coming home after surviving a storm?

She didn't know. She didn't *want* to know. She just wanted to get inside her room, where she could be alone. Where no one could see the toll this night had taken, or suspect the maelstrom it unleashed.

So when Harry opened the kitchen door, she swept past the sleepy tweeny who was just building up the fire and hurried up through the baize doors into the main house. Thankfully, Harry let her go on alone.

As usual, the halls were well lit. It was still early, though, when shadows held sway. They made her run up the stairs a bit faster, her focus more on getting to her room than how she did it. She wanted to get there before anyone intercepted her.

She had just set her foot on the second-to-the-top step when she realized that something was wrong with the stair. Her foot never took hold. Before she could catch her balance, her foot shot straight up and catapulted her backward.

Out of the corner of her eye she saw a shadow shift at the top of the stairs, but she never had the chance to identify it. Shrieking at the top of her lungs, she went over backward and tumbled all the way down the stairs.

Chapter 13

J esus, Kate! *Talk* to me!"

Oh, she was going to regret whatever it was she'd just done to set Murther off. She felt as if she'd fallen down a...oh.

Kate opened her eyes to find herself lying on the marble floor of the entryway. Above her bobbed various heads, and beyond, the entryway ceiling with its cream-colored rotunda and skylight, which was beginning to lighten. Her head was in Harry's lap, and it hurt. "Finney," she said, surprised at how faint she sounded. "Call in the painters. The cornice work has begun to peel."

Reaction hadn't set in yet. Her body was still numb with shock, not yet deciding where to hurt. The terror of those last seconds, the shattering realization of what had happened, still hovered just beyond reach. She was too familiar with the progression to be surprised by it, which helped her sound calm as she braced for the inevitable.

Harry let loose a harsh bark of laughter. "You scared the devil out of me!" he protested. "Can you move?"

She made an attempt and awoke a million nerve endings. "Under protest. Harry, something's wrong with the steps."

"No there isn't," he assured her. "You were in too big of a hurry and missed one."

She shook her head and instantly regretted it. "No. There's something slippery on the second step down. Grease, I think, if the speed of my descent was any indication."

She turned her head gingerly again. "Don't let anyone up those stairs until it's checked."

Finney straightened. "I'll do it meself." Kate had the most distressing suspicion there were tears in his eyes.

"I'm fine, Finney. Although I will be sporting bruises on very delicate places."

Other staff came thundering in as Finney turned to carefully mount the stairs. Kate was mortified. They'd probably all thought that they were seeing their paychecks evaporate, poor things. Harry busied himself feeling Kate's arms and legs for breaks, which she was sure she should resent more, especially when he hit a sore spot. She was oddly comforted by the panic she'd seen on his face, though.

"I really am all right," she assured him, reassured by her own assessment. "I'll bruise, but only in places no one will see. I seem to have the luck of the devil. At least that's what Edwin is forever telling me."

He didn't seem comforted. "How could you do something so silly?"

"I didn't." A memory surfaced, threatening her breath. She instinctively looked up past where Finney was bent over that second stair, but the hallway was predictably empty. "Harry, somebody was up there when I fell. I saw a shadow."

Harry was just about to deny it when Finney turned, his eyes wide. "There's a big pool of grease up here, like somebody spilled a skillet."

Predictably, Maurice was insulted. "No grease leaves the

kitchen of Maurice!" he protested, waving one of his larger knives. "He will not have it!"

But Kate was looking at Harry, who seemed to reach the same conclusion as she. Someone in her house had made sure someone would take a header down the steps. Possibly someone she or Harry trusted.

"Come on," Harry said rather briskly as he gathered her into his arms. "You're for bed and the doctor while we clean that stair off."

"I can walk," she protested, although she found herself wrapping a sore arm around Harry's neck. "I don't want to frighten the staff."

"Too late," she heard and looked over to see Thrasher white-faced.

He could break her heart, that one. "Hold the call for the undertaker, Thrasher. He's not needed." She flashed him a cheeky grin. "Besides, he'd just overcharge us."

She wasn't convinced she had made the boy feel any better. After the life he'd led, she wasn't sure she could. She needed to hide herself away before she scared everyone. The "shock shakes," as she called them, were beginning to set in. Finally giving in to the inevitable, she laid her head on Harry's shoulder. "Watch out for that second step."

*   *   *

"He got in the *house*!" Harry yelled, leaning over Drake's desk. "The house!"

"Are you sure?" Drake asked. "It wasn't just an accident?"

Harry slammed a fist on the desk. "I'm sure. Kate was almost killed, because an assassin got past all your men and strolled into my bloody house! It wouldn't be so bad, but I'd just told you about the man Grace saw."

"You did," Ian Ferguson agreed from where he was sprawled over one of the armchairs. "I heard you myself."

"And me," Chuffy agreed from his place by the window where he'd been counting the passing curricles. "Heard you say you'd take care of it. Didn't. Five."

Drake offered a wry smile. "My men suspect the butler."

Ian guffawed. "Finney? Oh, laddie, I want to be there when you tell him."

"Well, you won't," Drake said agreeably. "You're off to France in the morning."

Ian gave a great gusty sigh. Harry turned on him. "France?"

Ian showed him teeth. "Haven't they decided that there's nothing for it but that I protect the big man himself?"

Chuffy choked. "Bigger than you?"

Ian glared. "Wellington, ya daft bugger."

Harry frowned. "Then who's going to help me protect my Katie?"

"*Your* Katie?" Drake countered drily.

It was Harry's turn to glare. "You're the one who made sure we married. You should be relieved that I'm trying to acclimate to it."

Harry wasn't about to share the new feelings Kate had unleashed in him last night. Her sobs had torn something loose in him, something that had long since scarred over, and he could feel it bleed. It made this newest threat to her unbearable.

"I'm just relieved you haven't killed each other," Drake admitted. "Since you're here bellowing in my ear, can I assume the lady didn't take much injury from her fall?"

Harry shoved a hand through his hair. "How do I know? You can't tell a thing with that woman." Actually, if he'd understood Lady Bea correctly, Kate was used to batterings like the one she'd had that morning, which made him feel even worse. No one needed to know that, though.

"I'll come help," Chuffy offered. "Like Kate. Six...oh, wait. That's a tilbury."

"We all will," Drake said, and pulled out a thick file. "In fact, I already have. I have histories on every one of Kate's employees."

"Bet it's interesting reading," Chuffy said.

Drake scowled. "Like a Fielding novel. The reason we were looking at the butler is because he came to Kate's employ from Newgate. He was hanged for murder."

"Since he's walking around, I assume they did a shoddy job," Ian said.

"Also worked as a fortune-teller, the half man half ape at Tim's Tiny Circus..."

Chuffy laughed. "*That's* where I know him. Quite convincin'."

Drake scowled again. "And boxer. You want to know about her chef?"

Harry grabbed the file. "No. Remember, I fought alongside these men, and they were certainly no worse than the soldiers I've fought alongside for ten years. It's not her staff. Find out who it is. I don't suppose you've had any better luck finding Axman Billy than I have."

Drake shook his head. "Your Thrasher has the best nose in the Dials, and he's come up empty. We'll increase the watch on your house until we get lucky."

For the next fifteen minutes, the four of them tossed around ideas on Kate's security, until Harry felt his fears for her ease a bit.

Drake must have seen his growing impatience, because he finally set down his pen and stood. "I'm sure Harry thanks us for our diligence, gentlemen. But for now I believe he wants to get back to enjoy his wife."

He didn't have to tell Harry twice.

*   *   *

Kate hated lying in bed. She hated being passive. She hated hurting. Mostly, she hated wondering why. Not why she'd been helped down the steps. That was easy and understandable. She was a danger to someone, and they'd tried to stop her.

She hurt a little bit everywhere, and that shivery, nauseous feeling of shock plagued her. But those were old acquaintances. She'd suffered worse from Murther after a bad night at cards. But those injuries had never kept her in bed, no matter the cost. She had always refused to admit that Murther could hurt her so badly.

Today was different. Her injuries weren't bad, as injuries went. Her emotions were much more problematic. Suddenly she was prey to the most unpardonable urge to cry, and over something that had happened all of ten years ago. Surely a killer in the house should trump that.

Evidently, it didn't.

She supposed she should have felt surprised by what Harry had revealed about her father. Shocked. What shocked her was that she really wasn't that surprised at all. She was just crushingly sad. Afraid. Ashamed.

Why had Papa said those things? What had she done that could be so bad, he would accuse her of whoring herself at only fifteen? And with *George*, for God's sake. No matter how hard she tried, she couldn't recall a transgression so great that it would turn her own father against her.

Surely she should have easily remembered such a moment, for it would have changed everything for her. But her life had never changed. From her earliest memories she'd lived the same way. Cook had petted her, and George had hugged her, but mostly it had seemed as if she didn't exist. As if she were being shunned, but never told why.

She had tried so hard to break through that invisible wall, especially with Papa. She'd left painstakingly written letters for him, earnestly drawn pictures. Carefully collected sparrow's nests. Wildflowers tied into limp little clumps, and a lopsided sampler that said HONOR THY FATHER AND MOTHER. He had never even acknowledged getting them.

Aunt Maude had told her that her father couldn't look at her because she bore such a resemblance to her mother, whom she'd killed. But Kate had always known better. After all, how could he know she looked like her mother? He'd never known her mother when she was nine.

Kate had always suspected it was something more. A defect of some kind that was only discernible on closer acquaintance. It was the only reason she could think that a man so beloved by everyone couldn't seem to love her. Was there something in her that repelled good men and turned mean ones into monsters? Was Murther all she deserved after all? She had never had the courage to ask.

No, that was wrong. She had screwed up her courage twice. The first had been when she was being called to account for calling her sister a bird-witted harridan. She'd been standing in front of Papa's big oak desk, hands behind her back like a good girl, her face scrubbed and her hair neatly tied back with a grosgrain ribbon. She hadn't known whether to be thrilled to be with her papa or terrified of his displeasure.

"Dolores Catherine," he'd said, barely looking at her. "Your sisters are grown women with families of their own. They deserve your respect and obedience."

"But Frances says that you hate me," her eleven-year-old self had said and trembled. "She said that everybody hates me."

Ah, there it was, she thought, looking back. That unconscious flinch, the fleeting grimace, as if the emotion provoked was intense, unpleasant. The long, stiff silence.

"Nonsense."

She couldn't remember. Had she quailed, or had she thrown her shoulders back in defiance of the truth? "Why would she say that?" she'd asked.

But he'd told her their interview was over and sent her away still not knowing.

When she'd asked a second time, he'd slapped her.

She knew she was being unpardonably maudlin. Her father was dead these four years. She would find no answers there. But suddenly she felt small and insignificant and alone, and she didn't know what to do about it. *Helpless*, she heard in her head, as if she'd been sitting in the dark. *Worthless.*

Promiscuous. Thank God George would never understand what his beloved uncle had accused him of.

And Harry. Oh, God, what did she do about him? How could she hold on to her resentment when he had never been at fault? How could she blame him? He hadn't stood a chance, not when her own father condemned her.

He had said he loved her once. But he'd only known her for six weeks. What would happen when he was forced to live with her for years? Did she have the courage to wait day after day for him to follow the way of her father? Or should she send him off as soon as she could and spare them both?

Oh, hell. She was crying again. She *hated* crying. It was such a pointless sport, useful only for prodding gentlemen into buying trips to Rundell and Bridge. Only Harry wasn't the kind of gentleman who frequented jewelers. He had given her something different. Not jewelry. Strong arms and silent support. Something she'd finally identified as comfort.

The memory of those moments were what finally propelled her out of bed. When she stood up, her breath hissed out of her throat at the pain. It didn't stop her, though. She had to walk off the memories of the night before.

He had been so kind, so understanding. He'd held her in his arms as if he would be her shelter against a storm. Kate had seen Harry's family hug, of course. They had never been able to pass one another without tapping, patting, holding, kissing—especially when someone was hurt or sad or frightened. She'd watched their generosity like a vagrant looking for warmth.

But she didn't know how to accept it. She didn't know why Harry had done it. She had more trouble accepting that one gift of warmth than the worst beating Murther had ever given her.

Damn. Fresh tears. Striding over to her dressing table, she snatched up a handkerchief and swiped at her eyes. It was time to think of something else. Something she could understand. Something she could affect. After all, Harry would leave and take his hugs with him. She needed to find a way to go on alone. She needed to help bring the Lions to justice so Harry could go. Because if he had to wait, she might learn to rely on him, and as she knew all too well, that simply wouldn't do.

Chapter 14

She was standing at the window assessing every social acquaintance she had for a possible connection to the Lions, when she heard the door to the suite open behind her and Bivens's distinctive footsteps tapping on the hardwood. The abigail didn't even bother to quiet her approach for the assumed invalid. Kate smiled to herself. Bivens was on a mission.

Swinging into the room as if nothing was out of the ordinary, the abigail set out evening attire. "You going to swan around here all week, or can the maids get in and clean?"

Bivens was the only member of the staff who had worked under Murther. So she knew exactly how Kate dealt with injury.

Her gaze out on the rainy gardens, Kate smiled. "Swan, I think."

The abigail huffed. "Don't be daft. Lyin' about looking interestin' never worked for you. You know it makes you tetchy." Bivens had to have seen that Kate had been crying.

"Bivens," Kate admonished, glad her abigail had breached

her fortress. "You know perfectly well that I am never tetchy. It is simply too common."

"Besides, you're scarin' Lady Bea, and Thrasher won't leave the top o' the stairs, in case you slip again."

She turned around. "I thought he was out hunting down Axman."

The only answer was a shrug. "Water's heating for a bath, here are your togs, and you'll eat your dinner, or Miss Grace, Lady Bea, and me'll shove it down you with a spoon the way Miss Grace says they feed those great, awful snakes she saw in India."

"Charming image."

"Your choice. I mixed a good headache powder for you, and there are cool cloths for your eyes," Bivens continued, as if this were a daily routine, as once it had been.

"I'll take a tray up here," Kate said, stretching her stiff limbs.

"You'll eat like a Christian at a table with your friends. Miss Grace needs some kindness after putting up with *your* guests this morning. She also wants to talk to you. Something about the man who poisoned her watching the house."

That got Kate's attention back out into the waning light. "What are you talking about?" She didn't see anyone out there but George, leaning against the mews munching on what looked like an apple.

Bivens shook out Kate's second-best petticoat. "I'm talking about none of us bein' able to go outside for fear of bein' murdered. House is crawlin' with armed ex-soldiers, and some o' the major's friends are tearing up your library."

Kate had the most disturbing image of books thrown in piles on the floor, their pages fluttering in a breeze, and her private correspondence tossed haphazardly around the house like confetti.

"And the major?" she asked, walking toward the hall door.

"Don't know that, do I? He's been in and out all day. He did leave ya something. In your boudoir. Said it's a peace offerin'."

Kate nodded absently. "I'll look for it later."

Bivens laughed. "Won't take much lookin' for. Trust me."

Bivens knew just how to get Kate moving. She could rarely ignore a mystery. Slipping on her wrapper, she took a minute to peek out into the corridor. There was Thrasher tucked up against the far wall, arms crossed, expression fierce. "Do me a favor," she said. "Go down and make sure those men aren't destroying my books."

He jumped to his feet. "But what if..."

"I'll have Bivens help me down the stairs. I promise."

That was all it took. Thrasher tore off down the stairs, and she limped into her boudoir. All was quiet. Gray afternoon light reflected from the psyche mirror, and a fire crackled merrily in the grate. But Kate barely noticed. Bivens had been right. Harry's gift was impossible to miss.

She couldn't help it. She laughed. What else was a girl to do when faced with a life-size portrait of herself smiling back at her without a stitch of clothing? Actually, she thought, tilting her head for a better view, she should be insulted. It was one thing to stick her head onto someone else's body, but really. That woman had breasts like bread loaves, and the hips of a heifer. Kate looked down to reassure herself that her own breasts were far more attractive, firm and pale, with much larger nipples.

The true insult, however, was that whoever had commissioned this nonsense had obviously hired a second-rate painter. How anyone could have thought she would allow a rank amateur to immortalize her was beyond her.

"Should we hang it in the library?" she heard and turned to see Harry leaning against the doorway.

Her breath caught in her chest. Clad in tobacco brown and cream, with glossy riding boots, his wheat-colored hair wind-tousled and a riding crop in his hand, he looked the epitome of a Corinthian. Kate felt absurdly shy, as if he'd seen her naked. How could she bear to talk to him when she would always know that he had seen her at her worst? How could she trust him not to speak of it?

Kate felt the tension ease a bit when she saw the same uncertainty in Harry's eyes. She felt something sweet wrap around her.

"Are you mad?" she retorted brightly, trying to ignore such an alien feeling. She tilted her head toward the painting. "That thing should be burned. I refuse to have anyone think I actually look like that."

"I believe the point was made last night at McMurphy's."

"Did you rescue her, Harry? I'm grateful. I couldn't bear having anyone think me so completely devoid of taste."

Harry's bark of laughter surprised her until she saw the mirth dancing in his eyes. And the direction of his gaze. It was only then she realized that Bivens had handed her the magenta, marabou-lined wrapper. Feathers shuddered from her throat to her toes and along her wrists. It was the robe she always wore when bruised up.

Drawing herself up to her full height, she shot Harry a haughty glare. "I'll have you know that this is in the first stare of fashion," she challenged. "I may be outrageous. But only in the best of taste."

Harry's smile was infectious. "Thank you for clarifying. I agree with you about the painting. Sadly we'll have to wait until your brother is no longer a threat before disposing of it. This is Exhibit A in the case for his collusion."

Kate huffed. "She can wait in the attic with all the other second-rate castoffs."

Before she turned, though, she found herself considering all that naked skin. That naked, unmarked skin, which was the real joke. It was the only improvement on reality. Pointless, of course, but oh, she resented it.

"Did you find out how on earth it ended up at a gaming hell?"

"The painter, according to McMurphy. We've been unable to locate him."

"Undoubtedly hiding from his critics. I'll have Finney get this monstrosity moved. In the meantime, I believe it is time to dress."

He straightened up. "How are you? Bea said you'd been abed all day."

She looked up, afraid Harry would approach. She couldn't have borne pity from him on top of everything else. "Perfectly fine. If I hadn't spent at least a few hours looking sufficiently fragile, Bivens would have felt cheated. She never gets to fuss."

"All right."

He fell silent. Kate felt like fidgeting, which just wouldn't do. She didn't know how to deal with this new Harry. How did she go on when he no longer deserved her disdain? Lord, did that mean she'd have to apologize to him for those engagements?

"Well," she said, feeling absurdly gauche. "I think I'd better be off."

"Not yet," Harry said, pushing away from the door. "You need to know about some decisions that have been made."

Kate couldn't help it. She stiffened. "Yes?"

"We'll stay in town three days. Then we're going to Drake's hunting box, where you can be watched."

She was already shaking her head. "No, *we* aren't. You may go with my blessings, but I have to get back to Eastcourt."

"We can't be assured of your safety there."

"Don't be silly. My people would protect me with their lives."

"One of your people tried to break your neck."

She stiffened. "It wasn't one of my people, and you know it. It's been a very long time since I was fifteen, Harry. I do know what I'm doing."

"If you did, you'd leave this to the experts. Don't argue, Kate. I'm doing what's best for you."

She tilted her head. "Funny. That's what my father said when he handed me to Murther."

Kate saw his jaw working as he fought to control his temper and instinctively braced for impact. "I just want you to be safe," he said, throwing her off balance yet again.

She almost apologized. "As do I, Harry. But I can't simply ignore my duties."

She was just turning around to go when he cleared his throat. "You should also know that I've forbidden locks on your door." Kate spun around, ready to protest, but Harry forestalled her. "Just listen for once, damn it. It isn't practical. If something happens in your room, I can't take the time to break down your door."

She couldn't help casting a look at the door into his dressing room. "I'm still not quite certain how you came to be there."

"I'm your husband. Besides, after the attacks on you, I felt that any other room was too far away."

A perfectly reasonable explanation, yet Kate couldn't help feeling a renewed resentment at how blithely he assumed control of her life. "I see."

She tried to turn away again, but he caught her by the

arm. She instinctively ducked away, hand up in defense. He immediately let go and stepped back.

"*Merde*," she hissed, hot with distress. Turning away, she brushed down her skirts, as if that would calm her suddenly racing heart. "My apologies, Harry. I seem to have fallen back into habits I thought myself rid of years ago."

She felt humiliated and angry and even more resentful. She loathed betraying any weakness, but in the space of a few days she'd fallen back into a defensive posture.

"You can't be surprised that you're a bit jumpy right now," he said, hands in pockets, as if to reassure her that he wouldn't importune her. "Any other woman would be having strong hysterics."

She made it a point to look down her nose. "Don't be silly. Hysterics are messy, self-indulgent, and ultimately pointless."

Predictably, he smiled. "I want you to know," he said, his expression suddenly hesitant. "Unless I suspect you to be in danger, I will never open this door without your permission. You'll be the one to make that decision. Never me."

She felt his words lodge in her chest, making it suddenly difficult to breathe. She blinked, certain she'd heard him wrong. "So if I never open the door it's all right."

His smile was thin. "I'm not sure I'd go so far as to say 'all right.' I'll try to understand, though."

Kate couldn't look away from him, not knowing how to believe him. "Thank you, Harry. This is a first for me."

"I was afraid of that." Dipping his head a bit, he shared a slow, knowing grin. "I should warn you that I do reserve the right to try and change your mind."

She blushed. "Why? You know that I don't..."

Harry took her hand. "You'll never know for sure unless you try."

She felt her stomach clench. "I *will* understand that…" God, she couldn't believe how callow she felt. "That you must inevitably find solace elsewhere."

It took him a second to answer. "We'll see what happens. But I think you should know that I've always thought that one day I'd want children, a marriage like my parents." He shrugged. "I'm not sure I've decided to give the idea up."

She truly didn't know how to answer. His words incited panic, fear, envy, and, amazingly, longing. She wanted those things, too. But it was a dream she'd given up on long ago. She had no idea how to resurrect it. She pulled back her hand, as if it could protect her from wanting, but it just made her feel isolated.

"Well," he said, as if they hadn't just been speaking of plans. "I have an appointment at Horse Guards, then a meeting with some friends. I'll see you tomorrow?"

She smiled. "Since it is my At Home, I don't see how you can avoid it."

He nodded. "Keep Finney within reach." Then, without a word, he kissed her.

She anticipated him this time. When he reached out for her, she let him. When he set his hand beneath her chin to tip up her face, she met his gaze. And when he kissed her, a brief, brushing caress of a kiss, she didn't pull away. She never once betrayed the shivery, anxious feeling he left her with, or the way her heart raced. She certainly didn't admit that she wouldn't have minded another kiss. She wouldn't have minded at all.

"See?" he said. "Not so bad."

She scowled at him. "Survivable."

He smiled. "Well, practice makes perfect. I'd be happy to oblige anytime."

*   *   *

Kate was still feeling upended twenty minutes later. Bivens had just eased a peach-and-green tunic dress over her head when there was a quick tattoo on the suite door. Kate had no trouble identifying that sound, either.

"Come in, Thrasher!" she called, shaking out her skirts as Bivens tied up the tapes.

The door swung open and Thrasher trotted in, looking unusually serious.

"The blokes what tossed y'r library 'r eatin', and a new shift is on. They brought this with 'em." And with a flourish he'd evidently learned from Chuffy, the boy made a leg and handed over a folded note.

Kate accepted it with a smile. "You'll make someone an excellent butler someday, Thrasher."

The boy, already almost as tall as Kate, snorted. "'S if I would. I'm f'r coachin'."

And before she could respond, he was gone again. Kate opened the note to see Drake's signature.

Message received. We're looking into it now. Apprise Lidge, pls.

For a second Kate stared at the words as if they were in code. Message?

Her stomach dropped. Oh, God. In everything that had happened, she'd completely forgotten about the errand she'd sent Mudge on the night before. Poor Lady Riordan.

Apprise Lidge. Oh, no. Now that she thought about it, she was much happier to leave Lady Riordan with Drake. He wouldn't care if Kate turned out to be mad as a mongoose. Kate wasn't sure at all how Harry would react.

She turned for the door and then stopped. She still felt too fragile to face him with this. It was bad enough that she felt desire curling through her like smoke, that her body glowed just being in the same room with him. But she found herself wanting to tuck into his arms again, to let him be her shield against pain. She didn't want to marry him; she didn't want to marry anyone. But she was beginning to grieve his going.

Just what would happen if he found out she really was mad as a mongoose? Surely someone else could tell him. Maybe that way it wouldn't sound so bad.

"You goin' in or not?" Bivens demanded, hands spilling over with diamonds.

Sucking in a deep breath, Kate strode through the boudoir to Harry's room. Giving the door one good knock, she opened into his changing room door. And stopped dead in her tracks. Harry stood before her, and he was half naked.

Chapter 15

She'd seen him naked before, she kept thinking. Of course she had.

But he'd been on his back. He'd been asleep. Now his legs were braced, as if he were standing on the deck of a sailing vessel, and his muscles were alive with movement.

Clad in nothing but uniform trousers, he had one arm over his head, a rag in his hand, scrubbing under his arm. It should have only embarrassed her. After all, she was intruding. But somehow the sight of water sliding down his ribs, of that strong, raised arm, and the naked, hair-dusted expanse of rippling torso, struck her deep in the belly, in the knees, in the blood that rushed to her face and thickened in her veins.

Oh, dear sweet heavens. She couldn't look away. She couldn't breathe. All she could think of was Harry's promise to seduce her into his bed.

"When I extended the invitation," Harry finally said, "I didn't expect you to take me up on it so quickly."

She managed to shake her head. "I...um..."

She did finally see how wicked his smile was as he slowly lowered his arm to his side. She saw that he hadn't dried off the soap or water, which made her want to grab a towel and do it for him. She heard the rasp of his sudden breath. Or was that hers?

Finally, as if moving underwater, Harry picked up a towel and dried himself off. "I'm sorry, Kate. What did you need?"

She managed to clear her throat. She had to clench her hands, though, to keep from reaching out. "I'm sorry. I should have...uh..."

"You did knock."

"Waited."

She swore her skin was buzzing; she could hear her pulse, and her breasts seemed to swell against the slick silk of her robe. She was suddenly sensitive to everything. She had the most inexplicable urge to rub herself against Harry's chest like a cat looking for a good stroking around the ears, and it frightened the stuffing out of her.

"Kate?"

"Hmm?"

"I have to be at Horse Guards sometime this evening. And," he said, grabbing a shirt and throwing it over his head, "I can't do that till I dress. Can this wait?"

The scintillating flush died a terrible death as she thought that maybe, yes, they should postpone it. They shouldn't talk about it at all, so that he never again had reason to look down on her in pity.

She would never forgive herself if she succumbed to cowardice. "No," she said, straightening. "I don't think it can."

It had been so easy to tell Drake her suspicions. Maybe she should send Harry a note. To be read at Horse Guards. Or Naples. Keeping her eyes down, she walked into his bedroom and dropped into one of the cream armchairs by the crackling fire. Looking completely bemused, Harry followed.

She kept her eyes focused on the feathers that wafted along her wrists. "Drake asked me to tell you about the note I asked Mudge to take him last night."

Harry looked back toward the door. "Mudge didn't say anything."

"I think Marcus asked him not to." She drew in a steadying breath. "Something happened in . . . in the asylum. I heard someone. A woman who had a room by me, I think. At least, that's where I remember hearing her."

"Do you know who?"

She managed a thin smile. "Well, that's the issue. You see, I believe I heard Lady Pamela Riordan in the asylum. But Lady Riordan has been dead these six months. Drowned at sea."

For a long moment, Harry didn't move. He seemed to be studying the Stubbs over the mantelpiece. "You're sure."

"No. How could I be? But I know her voice. We were on several committees together, and I swear it was she. She kept saying that she was Lady Riordan and that she'd been locked in that room where no one could find her. She kept saying she didn't mean to find out." Kate swallowed, hating the memory of that sad, small voice.

"Did she say who put her there?"

She looked up now, bracing for a verdict of madness in Harry's eyes. "Her husband. He's a Lion."

"She said that?"

Kate shrugged. "She kept promising Richard—it's her husband's name—that if he'd let her have her children, she wouldn't say a word about the Lions."

Harry was silent for such a long time that Kate came perilously close to losing what certainty she had. She suddenly felt suffocated by dread. Would they search, just as she'd asked, only to find nothing but her own ghosts? Would it be Harry's turn to lock her in a room?

"Do you think she's the only wife who's been put away?" Harry finally asked, startling her.

Kate blinked. She hadn't even considered the idea. "I'm not sure."

"Any other wives die mysterious deaths recently in the ton?"

Well, this was something Kate did know. Bea adored memorial services almost as much as weddings.

"Sally, Baroness Sanbourne. Died of smallpox. Miss Mildred Weaver-Fry. A fall down the stairs." She thought, but could come up with no others. "I'll ask Bea."

Harry was already shaking his head. "Sanbourne? He's assistant to the exchequer. Did you tell Marcus?"

She shrugged. "No. Just about Pamela. It never occurred to me about the others."

Getting to his feet, he grabbed his uniform tunic. "I'd better tell Marcus. Lord, if these women are alive, it could be a treasure trove of information."

Kate's head came up. "You believe me?"

He looked rueful. "I don't know. I do know that it isn't a possibility we can overlook. If it's true..." He shook his head. "It opens incredible possibilities."

"And if it's not?"

He lifted a hand to cup her cheek. "Then it's not."

This time Kate was too preoccupied to anticipate Harry. When he pulled her to her feet, she all but bolted. He never gave her the chance. His mouth was gentle, but the kiss was deep. Kate tasted coffee and peppermint. She smelled fresh linen and leather and man. She fought the whirling giddiness that threatened to engulf her.

Then he lifted his head, and she was caught by the intensity in his eyes. "A nightmare is still only a nightmare."

She felt shaken to her toes. How could he say this so blithely?

"How about sharing a bit of warmth tonight?" he asked. "Maybe the nightmares will ease for us both."

She was suddenly so tempted. There was something so seductive about being held. She might actually get to like it.

Which would only make it worse when it was gone.

In the end, she only had enough courage to say she'd think about it. Harry dropped another kiss on her forehead and ushered her through to her boudoir, leaving her with her awakening, anxious body, a bad painting that reminded her too well of what she'd lost, and an invitation to take a first tentative step forward.

*   *   *

Not far away in a lane off St. Martin's Lane, the door swung open to the Black Cat pub and a man stepped out. He was unremarkable for the pub or the area, deep in the Seven Dials, where commerce was conducted in used clothes and produce, and the poor held on to respectability by a thumb. Of medium height and coloring, the man wore a collection of mismatched clothing he'd taken off his victims: brown hacking jacket, greasy emerald-green waistcoat, six watch fobs, and a brand-new bell-shaped rough beaver hat. He was whistling, as if he hadn't a care in the world, but his eyes never stopped moving along the crowded, dingy street. He had just pulled out a shiny gold pocket watch and clicked it open when a beautiful redhead sauntered up to him.

"*Ah, bonsoir,*" she cooed, smiling. "You are Monsieur Mee-chell, *oui*?"

Mitchell jerked to attention, his eyes growing wide. "Do I know you, ducks?"

With a conspiratorial smile, she took him by the hand and led him away. "I 'ave been told by *les Lions* that you and your friend are to kill the Duchess of Murther. But *you* were the bold one to go in 'er 'ouse and show 'er the way down the steps."

After a quick look around, Mitchell grinned. "Never knew I were there. Billy says as how I should make it look like an accident, and that's just what I did."

Stopping in the side alley, she ran a delicate finger down the front of his bright green vest. "Mmmm, yes. Most daring. 'Ow sad she did not die. *Les Lions* asked that I, Mimi, give a message to Billy about this valiant but sadly failed attempt."

She looked up, the whites of her eyes faintly gleaming. Mitchell was smiling so widely that he forgot to protect himself. By the time he thought to run, his throat was slit from ear to ear and his brand-new hat lay in a puddle of blood. It took Mimi only five more minutes to carve the quote into his forehead.

*   *   *

The next afternoon, Harry was in the library talking to Thrasher when Finney popped his head in the door. "'Scuse me, Major. You wanted to know. We 'ave guests."

Damn. Flipping open his watch, he saw that it was one. He'd meant to talk with Kate alone before the meeting Drake had arranged with all the Rakes at three. It seemed that he was going to be sipping tea with society dames instead. "On my way."

" 'Ey," Thrasher protested, motioning to his crimson-and-gold livery. "You can't desert me now. I got all tarted up to talk to you, din't I? Took a baff and ev'ryfing."

"So you did. But Lady Kate looks much better tarted up. So quick with you. What do you know?"

Thrasher scratched his near-white-blond hair. "Right. Ain't...*haven't* cast me glims on Axman Billy. Unless he's takin' the dirt nap, he's layin' real low."

Harry nodded. It fit with the information Drake had. "My thanks."

He was halfway to his feet when the boy objected. "But that's not all!"

Harry leaned his hip on the desk. "What? Quick with it, now."

"Well, Axman ain't...*hasn't* been heard of, but two o' his bully boys has. Dead, they was, in the Dials, slit from ear to ear."

Harry shrugged. "Not much of a surprise in the Dials."

"Word is that them two was seen 'ereabouts the last coupla days. An' 'ere's the weird part. They had words carved in their skin."

Harry sat up. A shiver of portent snaked down his neck. "Words? What words?"

"Two-finger Martin, 'oo works for Charlie the coster-monger, said it was somefin' like—" Thrasher screwed up his freckled face in concentration. " 'Ambition should be made of some kind of stuff.' "

"Sterner. Ambition should be made of sterner stuff. It's from Shakespeare." But that was impossible. It was the Surgeon's signature to leave a quote carved into his victims. And the Surgeon was dead.

"Martin was sure?"

"Handwritin' was real clear."

Harry rubbed at his forehead. They had a new player, and Harry had no idea who it was. "You think they got in here somehow?"

Thrasher shrugged. "Mitchell the Mouse was the slickest second-story man in Lunnon. Reckon he could sneak in Windsor and make off with the crown, 'e wanted."

Harry nodded. "I need you to take a message to Lord Drake. The back way, now. No one can know."

Thrasher scowled. "Teach y'r granny to suck eggs."

Harry dashed off a note, folded it, and sealed it. "I know I don't have to tell you to be careful. Lady Kate would fair skin me alive if I let anything happen to you."

"Got that right." The boy chortled. "She likes me better 'n you."

After Thrasher bolted, Harry took a moment to double-check his own new livery: mulberry jacket, buff inexpressibles, Coachman knot, and riding boots. After all this time in his Rifles green, he felt uncomfortable in Weston and Hoby. But this was his new uniform, designed to camouflage him among the upper reaches of society.

The outfit highlighted what a fish out of water he was. Oh, he had friends in the ton. Men he'd known through the army or the Rakes. But trusting a man with your life tended to blur class distinctions. He was about to step out of that comfortable pond onto hostile territory, where he would be scorned for marrying so far above him. If he stayed, he would face a lifetime of snubs, a daily battle with small-minded aristocrats who would delight in telling Kate how unfortunate she was in marrying him.

Did he want to do that to himself? To her? Should he leave before she got used to him? Or should he just kidnap her and toss her on the first ship out of England? Would his dream accommodate a wife?

Wife. He shook his head. When had he begun to think of Kate that way? Had it been when she'd wept in his arms? He'd definitely felt protective. He'd found himself wanting to make it up to that girl who had left bouquets for her father on an unwelcoming desk.

But she wasn't that young girl anymore. She was harder,

sharper, as wary as a wild fox, living in expectation of the hounds. Just like him, she bore scars that would never fade. Had she changed too much for them to reclaim their relationship? Had he? Was she enough to make him sacrifice the life he'd been planning for the last ten years?

Why, for God's sake, had her father made such accusations? *Was* there something in her to fear? And why, Harry wondered, hadn't he at least faced Kate with her father's accusation all those years ago? What an arrogant ass he'd been.

Well, he thought, shooting his cuffs. That wasn't a mistake he could undo. All he could do right now was get on in and act the besotted husband.

He heard the female chatter long before he reached the Chinese Drawing Room, where Kate held her At Homes. Standing in the hall, his white-gloved hands looking like wrapped hams, Finney scrunched up his doughy, misshapen features.

"You want I should announce you?"

Harry frowned. "Good God, no. Notice anything unusual today?"

"Quiet as a whorehouse on Sunday."

Harry nodded. "I'm expecting several guests coming in the back. They're for the library. Tell Mudge, and make sure we're free of suspicious lurkers."

Briefly he filled Finney in on what he'd learned and waited for him to lumber off in the direction of the kitchen to apprise the staff. Then, taking a breath, he turned back to the room.

If he stood just shy of the door, he could see the room reflected in the mirror on the front wall. Seated on the red sofa, Kate was handing tea to three women who'd obviously dressed to impress, with plumed, high-crowned bonnets and fussy pastel dresses. He'd been right, he thought. Kate had once again donned her strongest armor. Nodding and chatting as she passed a plate of little cakes, she glowed in one of her signature dresses, this one emerald with a high ruffled neckline and long sleeves to hide her bruises. She'd wound a matching ribbon through her piled-up hair, which succeeded in making her look like a deb fresh on the marriage market.

Harry knew he should get in there, but he couldn't take his eyes from her. Something about her carefree smile caught him square in the chest. He would have bet his commission that no one in society had a clue as to what lay beneath Kate's glib, flamboyant personality. God knew *he* hadn't. For the first time in years, Harry was able to appreciate the skill involved in her performance. He was able to admit that he wasn't only amazed at her, he was proud of her.

Well, she shouldn't have to face this alone. Giving his jacket a final tug, he headed into battle. "My dear, I'm sorry for being late," he said with a smile as he strode into the room. "Marcus Drake challenged Beau and me to a race against his Charger, and we took longer than we'd expected."

Kate actually looked briefly startled at his entrance. Had she not expected him to show up? Not yet bothering to acknowledge the three dames occupying the Chinese Chippendale chairs around the tea table, he bent over her hand with a lingering kiss.

"Why, thank you, Harry," she said, recovering quickly with a droll smile. "It always soothes a woman's *amour propre* to know she's been stood up for a horse."

He met her knowing gaze with a grin. "No, no. I did it for you. You've sacrificed enough for me. I couldn't let anyone think you'd married not only a commoner, but a coward as well. So I beat him to flinders for you."

He surprised her into laughter. "Oh, well done, Harry. You've put me firmly in my place."

"Where are Grace and Lady Bea?"

"Visiting Grace's patients at the Army Hospital. I believe Bea made them handkerchiefs and Grace bought rum."

Harry heard a sniff from one of the ladies and winked at his wife. "Gifts for the body and the soul," he approved. "Now, will you introduce me to your friends?"

"Why I'd be delighted." She smiled. "Harry, have you had the pleasure of meeting Lady Jersey, Lady Sefton, and Mrs. Drummond-Burrell?"

Oh, Lord, he thought, turning to where the three women sat. The all-powerful patronesses of Almack's. The big cats had evidently come to the watering hole to feed.

It was time to pull out his rusty charm. "Of course I know you by sight and reputation," he said, bowing over one hand after another. "I'm afraid I've spent more time in wardrooms than ballrooms, though. I could never have hoped to be introduced."

"Of course not," Mrs. Drummond-Burrell sniffed.

Harry glanced at Kate, afraid she'd be hurt. He was astonished when she let loose with a laugh. "Oh, Clementina, please. He's faced down a full French cavalry attack. He's not going to be afraid of you."

"Speak for yourself," Harry retorted, and won smiles from the other two ladies.

"We were just discussing how romantic your wedding was," Lady Jersey said, her expression avid. "It being so sudden."

Well, it seemed they were going to wade right into it. Good thing Kate knew what to say. "Only ten years in the making," she said. "Harry and I grew up together."

"Childhood sweethearts?" Lady Sefton asked. "I wonder your father allowed it."

Harry ground his teeth. Kate smiled with delight. "Not nearly so romantic. We squabbled like siblings. It was only recently that we began to understand our feelings."

"Well, you've certainly surprised your sister-in-law," Mrs. Drummond-Burrell said, her face wreathed in disapproval.

Kate quirked an eyebrow. "Glynis? What does she have to say to the matter?"

Mrs. Drummond-Burrell wouldn't be gainsaid. "Your brother the duke certainly must have something to say."

Leaning forward, Lady Jersey cut her off. "Glynis says that he's been worried to exhaustion about your behavior, but that marriage to a common soldier was beyond their comprehension." Harry couldn't help but notice her frankly assessing look. "Although how she can call him common is beyond me."

"Poor Glynis," Kate drawled, much to her guests' delight. "She simply doesn't have the constitution for surprises."

"If she doesn't like your behavior, she can stay home," Harry said, and went to pour himself a drink to fortify himself. He knew less lethal snipers. "I find it delightful."

Kate flashed him a look that doubted his word. Harry made it a point to smile and was surprised at the shaft of pleasure he felt when she grinned back.

"Perhaps you should confront her," Lady Jersey suggested, her attempt at subtlety falling miserably short. "In a neutral place. Almack's, for instance."

Kate laughed out loud. "Not worthy of you, Sally. I sincerely doubt Harry is interested in providing your entertainment for the season. He's a bit busy."

It was a testament to Kate's skill that the patroness grinned right back.

The other two women turned to Harry. "Of course. You

now have new estates to see to, don't you?" Lady Sefton softly asked. "Does that mean you'll be selling out?"

Harry tossed back his drink. "Don't know," he said, because he couldn't say, *You three are making me reconsider.* "We haven't discussed it yet."

"We've been a bit...preoccupied," Kate said.

Harry looked over to see her smile growing brittle and hoped she understood his look of support. No one was going to know that they'd snuck in under Kate's guard. He leveled a smile of pure lust on her, as if he was even now enjoying memories he couldn't share in public. He was surprised to see her blush.

He obviously wasn't the only one to notice. "That settles it," Lady Jersey crowed. "Any person who can make the Duchess of Murther blush simply must entertain us on Wednesdays. You'll come with her, of course."

Harry was surprised to see Kate's expression soften and shift, giving her a surprising look of pride. "I'm sorry to correct you, Sally," she said, never looking away from him. "But the Duchess of Murther won't be going anywhere. Lady Lidge will."

It was such a small moment, one easily overlooked. For some reason, though, Harry had the feeling that something fundamental had changed. A commitment had been made. So profound did he feel the shift that he was only half aware he and Kate had scored their first major victory against her brother.

Lady Sefton was chuckling. "Poor Glynis," she said. "Here she's been going around insisting that the marriage is a sham. I'm afraid she will be most displeased."

"Displeased?" Lady Jersey countered with a grating laugh. "She'll fall into strong fits. I say we go there next."

Setting down her teacup, she stood, pecked Kate on the cheek, and led her cohorts to the door.

Left behind, Harry looked over at Kate just as she looked at him. They both burst out laughing.

"Does that mean we won round one?" he asked.

She wiped at streaming eyes. "I'd call it more of a draw." With a wave of her hand, she gingerly got to her feet. "I release you from further duty for today, Major."

He immediately frowned. "How are your injuries?"

She smiled. "Progressing from red and purple to green and yellow. I am a veritable artist's palette. And yours?"

He shrugged. "Fine."

"Which means they hurt all the time, so why comment on it?"

He liked to see that impish sparkle in her eyes. "Precisely. Now you know exactly how to deal with an old soldier's war wounds. Ignore them."

They had just turned toward the door when Finney appeared, looking a bit flustered. "Visitors with boxes, Your Grace."

He'd barely stepped aside when a veritable procession of Rakes marched in with Drake at their lead, each one carrying a large, covered box.

"Were we expecting you?" Kate asked, eyebrow quirked.

"Not bearing gifts," Drake assured her, dropping his before one of the front windows.

"Kate," Harry said, watching the rest of them follow suit. "You know Chuffy and Drake. I assume you also know Kit Braxton, Alex Knight, and Beau Drummond. I have no idea what treats they've brought with them. I assume they do realize that they missed the Almack's patronesses by mere minutes."

Kate looked a bit bemused. "Moving the club headquarters, gentlemen? You could have at least let me know. I would have re-covered the chairs."

Chuffy grinned like a child. "Sorry to barge in," he panted, wiping his hands on a handkerchief. "Drake's idea. Said you'd want to help."

"Tell me what you need help with," Harry said, showing Kate to the sofa. "And we'll let you know."

"Don't be daft, Harry," she said, settling her skirts. "I'm dying to help. Finney!" she called, although the doorway was empty. "The good whisky!"

There was no answer, but by the time the men were settled in their seats Finney was passing around filled glasses, the last going to Kate.

"It's Diccan," Drake said, leaning forward. "He's caught down in the country."

"He's not moving in here," Harry protested. "We already have his wife."

Kate swatted his leg. "Hush, Harry."

Drake indicated the boxes cluttering up the room. "These are his father's things from Slough. Since Diccan can't get here yet to search them, we were hoping you might, Kate. We've made one pass at them, but we found nothing remarkable." He shrugged. "But we don't know what the ordinary was for Lord Evelyn."

Harry almost groaned. "Why didn't you just take these to your hunting box for when we arrived?"

He'd never get Kate to a safe location now.

Drake was already shaking his head. "Diccan is already in the hinterlands. We need you to stay until you've gone through these. We'll bring extra help."

Kate immediately forgot her whisky and was on her feet. "Oh, excellent. This will be easy. Especially since I have nothing else to do."

"Not even go home to Eastcourt in two days?" Harry asked.

"Not fair," she protested, her eyes on all those boxes, her heart obviously yearning for home. "I'll be finished by then. My uncle was a most methodical man. This will be fun!"

She was wrong, of course. It was a nightmare.

Chapter 16

Most of what Kate learned didn't surprise her in the least. Uncle Hilliard was methodical, pedantic, and a crashing bore. Even his sermons; especially his sermons, which he had cataloged by reading, holiday, and specific moral lapse. Her favorite was The Wages of Christmas Lust.

Harry was a great help, along with Grace and Bea, who unpacked boxes and organized the material into piles according to type: sermons, bills, correspondence liturgical, and correspondence laic. And most of it was as boring as his sermons. But then, as she was running her finger down a list of office supplies Uncle Hilliard had ordered, she heard Grace gasp.

"You've found the verse?" Kate asked hopefully, her already abused body even stiffer from leaning over the dining room table, where they'd spread everything out.

Grace's head shot up. "Uh. No. It's...uh, some personal correspondence."

At the look of distress in Grace's soft gray eyes, Kate's heart began to stutter.

"Why don't you let me take that?" Harry asked, moving to intercept.

Kate never acknowledged him. She just held out her hand to have Grace reluctantly set a bound packet of letters in it.

One was already open. It was from Uncle Hilliard to Kate's father. Just the sight of the salutation squeezed her chest with longing.

"...it is the only way to control an abomination like her. Give her into the hands of a righteous man who will recognize her for what she is."

Her uncle Hilliard had been the one to find Murther. To recommend him to her father and so consign her fate.

"Spiteful old hypocrite," Kate heard and looked sharply up, for the scornful words had come from her placid Grace, who was looking more fierce than Kate had ever seen. But then, Kate knew what that spiteful old miser had tried to do to Diccan, what he had done to destroy the marriage between Diccan and Grace.

Kate got up to hug Grace, but Grace was ahead of her, bending down to wrap her arms around Kate. No more than days ago, Kate would have bolted like a feral cat. But then, she realized, holding her friend, Harry had held her and she hadn't died. In fact, she'd liked it so much that she wished she could find a way to do it again.

"Good thing he's dead," Harry said behind her. "Or I'd spit him like a pig."

Kate smiled for him, and for Bea, who was twisting one of her handkerchiefs with distress. "He is no matter to me. How can I take the feelings of one sour old man to heart? Everyone else loves me." She flashed a hard-won grin. "I know, because I asked."

She firmly believed that until she found her father's answering letter, agreeing with his brother.

*   *   *

She refused to let the letters between her father and his brother bother her during the day. Between social obligations and the search of the bishop's things, she didn't have the time. But every word her uncle put to paper resonated in her, a coating of cold snow over the fragile state of her heart. The rest of her father's letters, polite inquiries and updates on family matters, left her feeling more isolated from them than ever. He never wrote her name. Not once. And he'd only mentioned her in that flurry of letters that arranged her engagement. Even then he'd only called her by pronoun. *She. Her.* As if she weren't quite real enough to him to warrant a name.

Maybe, she thought that evening as she lay in bed, she hadn't been. Maybe the staff had been more honest than she'd thought when they'd called her the castle ghost.

With that sharp reminder of what she could expect from any man, she decided to keep her distance from Harry. Just sitting next to him roused confusing emotions she didn't think she was ready to face. The memory of his kisses interrupted the most banal thoughts, and when she was quiet she wondered at the alien sense of safety she'd felt in his arms. She'd never experienced anything like it in her life, like a haven from the storm, only the storm had been in her. She'd always had to keep herself so tightly restrained, until she could have almost believed that she no longer felt strong emotions.

Obviously she did, and it should have terrified her. But Harry had been there to protect her from them. But could he protect her from his own defection? She was too afraid to find out. She was angry and sad and upended, and she didn't know how to unravel it all without admitting that Harry had a place in her life. Because if she admitted that, she had to begin wondering when he would go.

That evening they attended a ball, and Harry held her hand. She wasn't sure she carried off her side of the bargain, though. She knew she looked stretched and tense. She fared no better in sleep, waking a dozen times with her heart pounding and the sound of Murther's rage echoing in her head. Worse, she woke to the same aches, which provoked more memories and stole her sleep.

She thought of Harry's offer to have her sleep with him. Just sleep, with his arms around her to protect her against phantom fists. As much as she wanted to, she didn't know how to trust him. So, dry-eyed and wary, she lay with her back to the wall, her gaze on the connecting door, half expecting Harry to storm in and demand his rights. She knew better, but the shadows ruled. And somewhere at the back of her cowardly heart, she almost wished he would. It would relieve her of the decision, and put him in her bed where he might hold her against the night.

He was a gentleman, though. He didn't come.

He didn't come the second night, either. Nor did she sleep. She tried. She closed her eyes only to have them open again and again throughout the night, as she ricocheted from the asylum to the duke's bedroom to one very bad nightmare, where she was crouched beneath her father's desk as he told his brother what an abomination she was.

She made no noise; she'd long since taught herself silence at a high cost. But she found herself wishing Harry would hear the screams in her head and come calm her. She wished, perversely, that he would do something to provoke her. But Harry kept his word, even though she once again heard the heartrending moans coming from his room.

By the third night, she couldn't stop wondering whether it would be easier for both of them to join forces, just at night. Just so Harry would be able to get some sleep. He'd rested when she'd been with him. Maybe she could help him again.

When she woke panicked and breathless the third time, she decided that it was time for her to help Harry. Her heart galloping in her chest and the shadows reaching out to grab at her legs, she opened the door into the connecting rooms and walked through. When she opened the door to the dressing room, she almost fainted in shock. Harry had dragged a chair into the little room and was sitting there in slacks and shirt, his hair disheveled and whiskers roughening his jaw, a flickering candle at his elbow.

He was looking down at his lap, where a sketch pad lay open. For a second Kate wondered what he'd drawn. Then she saw the look in his eyes. Naked longing. Anguish. And she knew that he was looking down at a sketch of the future he'd planned for himself as far back as childhood. The future she might have already destroyed.

She was about to retreat when he lifted his head, and she felt worse. For only an instant, a flash, his eyes held such grief that she felt it, sharp as a razor, scoring her heart.

"I'm sorry," she said, trying to turn.

Jumping up, he let the book fall to the floor. "No. Don't go."

Warmth swept up from his hand; their curious spark still leapt from finger and palm. But she had seen too much. Harry Lidge would never be happy growing flowers in Gloucestershire. His heart would always wander those foreign lands.

"Are you all right, Kate?" he asked.

She almost shook her head. "Surprised," she admitted. Taking a deep breath, she turned back to see the grief safely tucked away. "What are you doing here?"

His smile was thin. "Trying to work up the courage to knock on your door."

She went still. "Why?"

He waved a hand in the direction of her room. "I've been in here listening to you having nightmares, and I can't tolerate it."

For a long moment, she couldn't manage an answer past the odd knot in her throat. He truly looked concerned.

"I've been listening to you, too," she said, mortified that her voice shook. Ashamed that she wasn't going to leave him in peace, even after what she'd seen in his eyes. "It seems silly to suffer alone."

When he looked up, she saw that the ghosts that occupied his sleep were at least as frightening as hers. "How about I get some more lights?"

They settled in side by side, like before, not touching. Evidently it wasn't enough for Harry, because after only a few minutes he reached over, pulled her against his chest, and wrapped his arms around her. Her first instinct was to fight. He was smothering her. Surely she couldn't breathe being held so closely.

"Sssssh," he crooned in her ear as he gently stroked her arm. "It's your turn to be taken care of."

She tried to push against him, certain she hated this. "Oh, no you don't. I don't like you."

"Of course you do. But even if you didn't, it wouldn't matter. I'd be here."

She knew she was probably hurting his feelings, but she couldn't relax. She wouldn't. She couldn't get used to this kind of thing. Not even if it was warm, and cozy and comforting to have her cheek tucked up against his chest so she could hear the steady murmur of his heart throughout the night. Surely she would hate it.

It wasn't a panacea. She had at least two nightmares. But instead of waking in panic to darkness and cold, she was soothed by a gentle hand and a gentler voice. "Ssssssh," she heard just above her, "you're safe now. Sleep."

And, amazingly, she did. She even fell back asleep after Harry had a nightmare of his own and almost knocked her out of bed trying to get to his men.

"You got them," she crooned, stroking his chest with the flat of her hand. "They're safe. You got them."

Neither mentioned those incidents when they woke the next morning and separated to their own rooms to change. But Kate knew that by unspoken agreement, she would return that night.

*   *   *

She did return, still feeling stupid and childish for needing a strong arm, only to find Harry's bed empty. She wasn't sure what to do. It seemed pointless to be here without him. But even after only one night, she didn't want to face her nightmares alone. Not that she needed Harry's help. She just found it easier to have somebody else there.

She was standing undecided in the doorway when she saw the sketchbook lying on the nightstand. She had no right. Even when they were young, Harry had protected his privacy like a jealous duenna. But it was becoming vital to see what her competition was. With one last furtive look to the hall door, she sat on the bed and opened the pad.

She smiled. Here was the Harry she remembered. Rude churches and cathedrals, fortified castles and a blasted farmhouse with the thatch roof caving in. A street in Brussels with its odd stepped roofs, all meticulously recorded with notes about style and function and tradition. Château Hougoumont, still intact before the battle, a jumble of red brick and roof tile surrounded by high white walls.

And then, more exotic locales. Ornate temples and austere homes tucked like bouquets amid a riot of foliage. Mud huts and rough-cut canoes. Dusty streets teeming with dark-skinned men in white arguing with their hands, and the elegant decay of a Venice canal, each conveyed with precision and power, the simple lines enough to convey permanence, magnificence, wonder.

She turned one page too many. Instead of the pristine lines of a church, the sketch was hurried, harsh, visceral. Kate had seen a battlefield, but only after the killing had been done. Harry had recorded the battle in progress: horses rearing, smoke blinding, men twisting, mouths agape in agony, eyes wide, caught at the moment of death. Just from these quick sketches she could hear the chaos; the deafening thunder of cannon, the shouts, cries, screams. The clanging dissonance of metal striking metal. She could smell the smoke, the crushed grass, the peculiar musk of a destroyed body.

She turned the next page, and the next and next, and the scenes continued. Carnage, pain, devastation, one after the other, as if Harry had been purging his memory of the horrors he'd witnessed as quickly as he could.

With the blinding force of lightning, Kate saw again the streets of Brussels in those days after Waterloo: thousands of injured and dead littering the squares, medical tents where sawed-off limbs were tossed like so much firewood onto macabre piles. She shuddered with the memory of it, with the ghosts of those boys who had pleaded for help, for succor, for relief she couldn't give.

As if it would shield her from the sight, she squeezed her eyes shut. Harry had been through ten years of this. How could he have survived?

She knew, of course. His secret lay in those other sketches, the ones of order and beauty and silence. The dreams she threatened to take away.

"'God fashioned hell for the inquisitive,'" she heard and snapped her head up.

Harry was standing in the doorway, clad in trousers and shirt, no more. He looked like a lost angel with his tousled hair and sky-blue eyes.

She shook her head. "St. Augustine was right. I'm sorry." Still, she couldn't seem to close that record of war. "I had no right."

He crossed his arms. "You never used to apologize for sneaking peeks at my sketchbooks."

"You never drew anything like this before." She looked down on an image of men firing from atop a burning building, men she knew would never make it off that roof alive. "Can I assume your nightmares look something like this?"

"Very much like."

She flipped pages until she found order again. "And this is what your dreams are."

She wished it were possible, but there was no mistaking his reaction. The loss in those eyes scored her heart.

"Harry…" But she didn't know what to say, how to face this new desertion. Even though it wasn't really a desertion. She was an interference.

"Let's not think too far in the future," he said, before she could apologize, or, worse, cry. "Let's just enjoy the fact that we get along better than we could have hoped." He brushed her hair back from her face. "After all, anyone else would run shrieking in fright at the noises you and I make at night."

Lifting her face, he dropped a quick kiss on her lips. Kate felt an unexpected *frisson* of awareness sneak down her back. How odd. In that moment, she felt closer to Harry than any other person in her life. He was right. They shared a connection, not just the pain and nightmares, but the fact that both of them had survived. She couldn't believe it, but for the first time in ten years, she felt a true affinity for Harry Lidge, and it had been born in battle. His public, hers private.

"Well, I suppose," she said. "Seeing that you don't snore. I had to make Bivens move from my dressing room. Woman sounds like a hibernating bear."

Comfortable together for the moment, she and Harry slipped into bed and slept.

Chapter 17

The next afternoon, Harry and Kate took a break from the tedium of her uncle's life to wade through the tedium of marital settlements. When the lawyers finally took their leave, scratching their heads over their contrary clients, Harry poured two glasses of Madeira and settled next to his wife on the library sofa. She looked melancholy, he thought, a bit displaced. Not surprising, really. The lawyers had spent a long time cataloging what she didn't have anymore.

Harry had never really thought of it before, but Kate was correct. Men had the right to everything, no matter what was best. And there wasn't a thing Kate could do about it but mourn its loss. Harry had set some remedies in place, but for now all he could do was try to lighten the mood.

"You have a knack for surprises, madame," he said, raising his glass in a toast to the extensive enterprises she'd nurtured, both for her estate and its people. Flowers were evidently more lucrative than he'd thought. She sold tulips as far away as Ireland.

"Me?" she countered, clinking glasses. "I don't believe I'm the one with shares in everything from diamond mines to steam engines." Cocking her head, she took a sip. "I don't suppose you get samples from time to time."

He lazily slipped his arm around her shoulder. "Of course I do. Although what you'd want with a steam engine..."

She playfully smacked him on the chest. "A steam engine would scarce go with my new gold tissue ball gown. Which, by the way, I will wear tomorrow night at the Hampton ball."

Harry grimaced. "I suppose you expect me to go."

"We would be expected to dance."

"I can dance," he protested. "Wellington insisted. I just thought that once I sold out I wouldn't be called on to galli-vant around a ballroom anymore."

She turned to him, her expression thoughtful. "Is it so dis-tasteful to you?"

Harry thought of all of his plans, the carefully considered ones and the ones he'd sworn to amid the madness of com-bat. Kate might have seen the pictures the night before, but not the context. Every one of his dreams had sent him off alone, somewhere he could savor the silence, where no one relied on him, where no one else could be lost to him. Where the lingering violence of battle would have the chance to fade peacefully into extinction as he wandered through the undemanding halls of empty buildings. The dancing he'd planned to do looked nothing like the waltz.

"I imagine I'll grow used to it with a pretty woman in my arms," he hedged. When he looked down at her, he knew he wasn't fooling her in the least.

"One of these days," she said as if she'd heard every thought in his head, "we're going to actually have to discuss our future."

"I expect we will." *But not yet*, he wanted to say. *For now, let me enjoy this nascent peace that has surprised me in this unorthodox place. Let me have a bit more time to draw my wife out from the shadows, like coaxing a deer from the woods.*

"When you imagined traveling," she said, sipping at her wine. "Did you see yourself taking your wife along?"

"Actually." He fortified himself with a sip of his own. She deserved nothing less than the truth. "No."

For a moment she was quiet. "Your engagements are beginning to make more sense. I'm even more glad I interfered. Those were two girls who would have pined."

Harry didn't know how he'd gotten into this conversation. "As opposed to you?"

"Pining," she said with an imperiously arched brow, "is beneath me."

He grinned. "I am well aware of that, Kate."

She sat for the longest time, just sipping, her focus on the dingy gray day outside the window. Harry knew he should interrupt, should steer the conversation away from dangerous shoals. He couldn't seem to open his mouth.

"Then that is what you must do," she said suddenly, still gazing at the window.

He went very still. "What is it I must do?"

"Get as far from the nightmares as you can. Walk distant roads and study the great cities and timeless buildings. Give yourself a second chance to live your dream."

The breath seized in his chest. He actually felt dizzy. She was offering him everything he'd ever wanted. He should kiss her, jump up and get the hell out. Instead, he found himself forcing a smile. "Can we find the traitors first? I'd feel quite deficient as a hero if I left you to be slaughtered just because I want to sketch a bazaar. I might even mind it if Wellington were hurt."

She turned on him, her forehead pursed with intent. "But don't you see? There will always be something. The government, or me, or Eastcourt, or . . . oh, I don't know. One day you'll look up and your chance will be lost. I couldn't bear that."

He cocked his head. "Really?"

She huffed, as if she couldn't believe he'd doubt her. "Really."

Again, he had a choice. And he couldn't allow himself to make it. "I'll tell you what. Once we assure your safety, I'll rethink the issue. Especially if you're so eager to kick me out." He rubbed at the tension in his temple. "Not that I blame you. I know damn-all about tulips."

She dipped her head, unrecognizably uncertain. "I'm sure you'd rather not have to put up with me."

Setting down his glass, he turned to her. "Maybe so," he said, setting his fingers under her chin. "But I'd like to be given a chance to find out."

Her eyes seemed huge and glistening. She had the oddest look in her eyes, as if she'd been holding her breath for a long time. He had no idea where the impulse came from that compelled him, whether it was a true expression of affection or just a desperate bid for distraction. He kissed her neck. She jumped.

"Sssssh," he said, holding her still. "I'm practicing."

"You're taking . . . liberties," she protested in a breathy voice, suddenly still.

He didn't blame her. He was suddenly feeling a bit breathless himself. He could smell that exotic flower scent of hers, as if she'd brushed frangipani along her throat. He tasted the faint tang of salt on her skin. He felt the silken sweep of her hair against his cheek. And suddenly, it was as if his body had decided to throw off ten years of restraint.

"Harry . . ."

He nibbled at her shoulder. "Do you want me to stop?"

"Oh . . . that's unfair."

He smiled. His body, completely unconcerned with tact or patience or control, was tightening, thickening. It was fruitless, he knew. But he couldn't help hoping he was making some headway. She arched her neck, just a bit, as if at war with her own body.

"Relax," he instructed.

Setting down his glass, he took hers as well, reaching across her to put it on the table. Instead of sitting back, though, he let his hand drift gently across the lovely swell of her breasts, watching his fingers rise and dip. He could hear the rasp of her breathing; he saw her nipples tighten and press against the muslin of her gown. God, he wanted his mouth on them, his tongue. He wanted to suckle until she shrieked. He settled for just brushing his fingers back and forth, back and forth, so lightly he knew she couldn't complain, so slowly he couldn't frighten her.

"Is this all right?" he asked. "Since we're going to be dancing, I figured we'd be…touching."

"Touching…" Her eyes were drifting closed, her head drooping back against his arm. "Yes. I see."

Her fingers were opening and closing on her lap. Harry hadn't meant to become even this intimate. He wasn't certain how far she would allow him to progress. His heart had begun to thud in his chest, and his groin was a giant ache. He was going to be in for a long cold bath tonight.

Bending over, not even breathing for fear he would startle her, he laid his lips against the swell of her breast. Her reaction was instantaneous. She gasped, twisting and pushing at him. It didn't take Harry a second to understand. But instead of backing off, he held her. He could hear the rasp of her breathing, saw the wild look in her eyes. But he knew that he wasn't frightening her. She was shamed. Humiliated. He had come too close to those terrible scars.

He knew he could do only one thing. Freeing one hand, he pushed her sleeve down. She flinched, not breathing, staring at anything but him, her eyes big as saucers. He looked down on that obscene design burned into her milk-white breast, a snarling wolf, and wanted to kill her husband all over again. It took immense effort, but he didn't curse at the man's perfidy. Instead, he leaned over and laid his lips back down on her, this time atop the brand.

She froze. He moved to the other breast and repeated his action. He felt a sob catch in her chest.

"You have never been more beautiful, Kate," he assured her. "It's a wonder I can keep my hands off you."

She said not a word, but he felt her stiffen. He kissed her again, at the juncture of her throat. She softened a bit. Reaching down, he cupped her hand in his and sheltered it as he tasted her exposed skin. One kiss, then another. A quick brush of the tongue against that soft, satin expanse that left his cock rigid and painful. Her breasts were so firm, so high, her nipple clearly outlined against the delicate material of her dress. He licked across her breast and then, gently, blew until he saw goose bumps. Until he felt her pulse begin to speed and her breath grow shallow, until her eyes slid completely closed and she trusted him enough to rest against his arm.

He was shaking with the effort of control. He was dying with hope. He remembered an erotic little constellation of freckles on her right breast. He wanted to uncover them; he wanted to see if her nipple was still as deeply pink, long enough to flick with his tongue. He wanted to span her waist with his hands and dip his fingers into the wet, tight heat of her. He wanted to taste her and taunt her and stoke the passion he knew flowed beneath the ice of her fear.

He couldn't. Not yet. Not if he wanted her to trust him, because suddenly that was more important than the hot

arousal she was unleashing. It was more important than pleasure or relief or peace. Suddenly he knew that he wasn't
finished with his responsibilities. The responsibility might
well kill him, but sweet Christ it would be worth it if he
could set her free.

Lifting his head, he gazed down on the lush beauty of her
face, now flushed and softened with arousal. He bent close to
her, breathing so that she could feel it on her cheek. Gently,
so gently she might think it her imagination, he met her lips
with his.

"Open for me, Kate," he commanded softly.

Her eyes flew open. Her pupils were huge, almost drowning the spring green of her eyes. He saw a flash of fear; he
saw hunger. He knew she was fighting her terrors and decided to help. Bending back to her, he dropped a kiss along
the very corner of her mouth. She instinctively turned to
him. He deepened the kiss, searching her lips with his own,
pressing, savoring the luxury of her mouth. He pulled her
lower lip between his teeth and sucked at it.

Her heart was thundering now; he wasn't sure whether
in fright or arousal. He prayed for arousal. He decided to
chance it and slid his tongue along her lips, wetting them, savoring their taste, gently, insistently, begging entry. And just
when he thought he would never breathe again, she opened.

His body all but seized in excitement. His own heart was
matching and outdistancing hers. For God's sake, it was just
a kiss. He couldn't remember when last he'd spent so much
time simply exploring a mouth. But this mouth was special.
Breaching these defenses was a triumph.

Slowly, he leaned back, bringing her with him so that she
lay half on top of him. He turned his head to fit her mouth
better, moved his hand so that he could winnow his fingers
through the silk of her hair, cupped her face with his other

hand, and as gently, as carefully as a butterfly collecting nectar, he slipped his tongue inside her mouth and plundered it.

He felt her hands come up as if to push away. He refused to stop, searching out the hot, slick recesses of her mouth. He tasted wine and lemon and something smoky. He inhaled her surprised little gasps. He fought to control himself, in case she truly meant to stop him. But her hands, hovering just a moment between them, settled on his chest as if seeking balance. Her fingers curled into the collar of his coat. Her body began to melt against his, even as he could almost hear her instincts crying caution.

It was one of the most difficult things he'd ever done, but he held his passion in check. Even as his own body screamed for more, as his fingers ached for her breasts, her belly, her sleek, strong legs, as his heart thundered in anticipation of climax, even as he savored the lightning unleashed by the flicker of her tongue against his, he began to gentle his movements. He drew back from her, stroking her cheek with his thumb, stroking her lush hair, dropping kisses along her forehead, her closed eyes, her ear, her throat.

She whimpered in protest when he drew her head down to his shoulder and just held her. He could feel her body tremble with the passion he'd stirred. He wished to God he could coax her into continuing. But it was too soon. She was still too raw, her memory too intrusive. He needed to bring her along slowly until she could trust him more than that jackal of a husband.

"I'm sorry," she whispered, sounding heartbreakingly young.

Harry immediately lifted her face to him. "Unless you've just ruined my riding boots or shot my horse, I never want to hear you say that again. Do you understand?"

Her smile was a bit thin. Harry didn't mind. He couldn't

quite take his eyes away from her deliciously swollen lips. "It has to be so hard for you," she said.

He couldn't help it. He laughed. "You have no idea. But it's more important for you to get used to intimacy again. We have all the time in the world, Kate."

The minute he'd said it, he knew it was wrong. They hadn't come to that decision yet, had they? The closer he got to Kate, though, the hazier those dusty roads he'd planned to trek grew in his mind, and it unnerved him.

Even so, he was delighted by the sly humor in her eyes. "Well, we don't have *all* the time in the world, Harry. Inevitably, one day your power will wane."

He kissed her nose. "All right. We only have sixty years or so."

And then he shifted, which just brought his cock into contact with her stomach. She flinched. Then she looked down.

"Wait," she said, scrambling out of his embrace. "I can take care of it."

"Take care of what … ?"

But her fingers were already on the placket of his pants. Harry almost swallowed his tongue. "What the hell are you doing?"

He was sitting up now. She knelt between his legs, a curious purpose in her eyes. "You're hard as a rock. I'll solve it."

Harry grabbed her hands. "Stop that."

She tried to pull away. "But this is something I *can* do."

Harry's body begged him to say yes. His cock threatened to burst his breeches, and his heart was about to jump out of his chest. And she was looking at him as if he were a rug that needed to be beaten.

"It is something I will not do," he told her, trying to ignore how his hands were shaking. "Not like this."

She looked around. "Then like what? The only women

around here are my staff, and if you try to relieve yourself on one of them, I'll gut you like a carp."

"Kate..."

"You could handle it yourself, but I know that isn't satisfactory."

He couldn't allow her to continue. Jumping up, he pulled her to her feet and held her. "Kate," he said. "Of course I'd like you to...finish this. I'd love it. But not like this. Not unless *you* want to."

She blinked as if he were speaking a foreign language. "It won't take a moment."

He laughed; he actually laughed. "No it won't, because it's not going to happen."

She looked truly confused. "But if you aren't relieved, you could suffer an injury."

"Who told you that?"

"*You* did."

He actually felt himself blushing. "Well, I didn't teach you *that*," he protested, gesturing toward the general vicinity of her former position.

It was her turn to laugh, only Harry heard little humor in it. "Of course not. Murther did that. He preferred it. Actually," she said, shadows darkening her eyes, "so did I. But it would be much easier with you, Harry. After all, you bathe."

Harry saw that memory in her eyes and wanted to hit something. "Why didn't you just bite him?"

She paled and sat down. "Because he would have retaliated."

Harry sat next to her. He couldn't imagine anything more terrible than the desolation in her eyes. She looked so suddenly young, stripped of the brittle shell she donned for the public. Beneath it, she was still so bruised and wary.

"He would have hurt you," Harry said.

She shrugged. "The staff. Bea." She took an unsteady breath. "Poor Bea. She suffered so much for me."

She'd surprised him yet again. "Bea?"

She looked up. "How do you think she was so grievously injured? She tried to stop Murther and he shoved her down the marble staircase." Her smile was grim. "I always considered it poetic justice that he died going down those same stairs."

"Was he pushed?"

"Sadly, no. He was drunk and lost his balance."

Just from the too-brisk tone of her voice, Harry wondered if there was something more to the story. He wondered if Murther had met his fate trying to hurt Kate. But she wouldn't enlighten him. She simply rubbed at her eyes with a hand that shook just a bit. "So then, you refuse to take me up on my offer?"

"Regretfully, yes. Especially if there is no reciprocation." He tilted his head, smiling. "Have you ever had it done to you?"

Now she was staring, as if he'd just slapped her. "Had..." Impossibly, her eyes grew bigger. "Good God. Are you serious?"

He shook his head. "Oh, Kate, the things you have to learn." He couldn't help it. He kissed the tip of her little nose. "I promise that we'll reinvestigate this area of lovemaking if you'd like. But only at a time and place when we can take our time and truly enjoy it. And only when you go first."

She swallowed hard. "Women *like* that?"

"I know you don't believe me, but I guarantee it."

For the longest time she just sat there, her gaze unfocused, as if imagining the act. Finally, she shook her head. "Harry, you're an education."

"I'll certainly try to be," he said, and pulled her back into his arms. "Now let's get back to lesson one. Kiss me, Lady Lidge. I think I need more practice."

* * *

In the end, Kate didn't get much sleep that night, either. Harry refused to accept a good night without a generous amount of kissing that seemed somehow more exciting lying in his arms. She had never known a tongue could be so clever. But Harry seemed to have surprising talents, which incited a lot of giggling and not a little sighing before he finally kissed her eyes closed and told her to go to sleep.

She lay in his arms for the longest time smiling into the flickering candlelight and thinking how amazing it was that she could smile at the thought of relations. Sex. Lovemaking. She'd stayed away from the words all these years, because none of them fit what had gone on in her house. It was much easier to use words that distanced herself from the act. She was beginning to hope that wouldn't be necessary anymore.

She was drifting to sleep when there was a scratch on the door, and Harry stiffened. "What?"

Kate opened her eyes to see Mudge opening the door, still clad in a darned old shirt and pants, hair sticking straight up. Obviously woken as well.

"Sorry, sir. You're needed downstairs. Matter of some urgency."

Harry bolted up so fast Kate wondered if he remembered she was there. He did kiss her on the head as he grabbed for his robe. "Stay here."

She burrowed into the pillows as Mudge closed the door behind them. She listened to the sounds of the house, but heard nothing until the front door closed.

Harry didn't return. When another half hour passed and he was still absent, she climbed out of bed, grabbed her own robe and slippers, and followed downstairs.

He was sitting in the front parlor, where she received guests. Only one candle flickered at his elbow, and it was cold in the room. And dark. Kate shuddered, stepping into the room as if wading through the moors at night. There were too many shadows.

"Harry? What's wrong?"

His head jerked up, and she saw a disturbing glassiness in his eyes. Without hesitating, she walked over to the drinks table and poured him a stiff tot. He didn't even seem to notice her return until she handed him the drink.

"Now," she said, sitting next to him. "What's wrong?"

Again he looked over at her. This time, he shook his head. "It's Ferguson."

"Ian?" She sat abruptly and took his free hand. "What happened?"

"I don't know. The official word cannot be the truth. I won't believe it."

"What truth?"

He blinked. "I've known Ian for years. Fought alongside him. In fact, he saved my groats more than once when I'd given myself up for a goner. I don't know a more honorable man."

Her stomach had begun to crawl with dread. "Harry. What happened to Ian?"

"He's dead."

She grabbed his arm. That wonderful, outrageous Scot. Dead?

"How?"

When Harry looked up, his expression was flat with shock. "He was shot while trying to assassinate the Duke of Wellington."

Chapter 18

Harry said the words, but he didn't believe them. He thought of that mad Scotsman facing off with Kate's brother, kilt swinging, eyes alight with manic energy. He thought of that last bottle they'd shared after Quatre Bras. Ian had drunk every other man under the table and then climbed atop it. Brandishing his battle sword over his great red head like a Scottish berserker, he'd bellowed out a fine rendition of "Scots Wha Hae," and then demanded every man in the room raise a toast to Wellington, "T' only bastard with cods enough to pull us through Waterloo."

"What happened?" Kate asked. "Is the duke alive?"

Harry startled, almost forgetting Kate was there. "He was unharmed. It seems Ian was stopped in time. It's a bit muddled. It happened at night. They were at sea, on the way home for a quick visit. Wellington had come on deck to blow a cloud. Several shots were exchanged. Ian and two of the ship's crew, they think." Harry looked down at the drink in his hand, not exactly sure how it got there. "Ian was shot and went over the side. So far he hasn't been found."

"Then he could be alive."

Harry shook his head. "He was shot through the heart."

Kate squeezed his hand. "Take a drink, Harry."

He did. He was glad she didn't express her sympathies. He couldn't have tolerated that. "I've lost my share of friends. God, Waterloo alone took too many, good men all. But somehow this is worse." He shook his head, the shock spinning around so fast that the facts couldn't gain purchase. "I swear Ian was the best of us."

It just wasn't right. Ian had made it home. He should have been safe. Tipping back the glass, Harry let the whisky sear his insides.

"How can I help?" she asked, her hand still in his.

He shook his head. "You don't know the people involved. I have to convince them that they're wrong. Ian wouldn't have done this. I have to at least send someone to search for his body, and I have to notify his family."

"Where did they search for him?" Kate asked.

"They were about to put into Portsmouth."

"Why don't you go on down and search for yourself? You need to know for sure."

He blinked, feeling stupid and slow. "You know I can't."

She smiled. "I'm better protected than the royal family," she said. "And I have quite enough to do to keep me busy. Heavens, I haven't even made it past Uncle Hilliard's haberdasher bills."

He kissed her hand. "Thank you, Kate, but I can't. I need to be at the Home Office. Ian wasn't the only news. One of the undersecretaries for the Home Office was also found murdered last night and his offices and home ransacked."

He looked up, suddenly, realizing that he hadn't told Kate about the new assassin. He didn't want to. She shouldn't have had to add this fear to her load. But it wasn't safe to keep her ignorant of any new threats.

"Kate, you need to know that his throat was slashed."

Her eyes widened. "Oh…"

"And a quote was carved into his body."

Kate blanched, but didn't quail. "But the Surgeon is dead. I saw him myself."

"He evidently taught someone else his craft. We have to be even more careful, Kate. I want you to stay in."

She was already shaking her head. "For how long? If I cower in the house, people are going to think you've coerced me into this marriage. I need to be seen enjoying myself. And you need to be seen enjoying yourself with me."

Harry wanted to laugh. How could he enjoy himself? He rubbed at his eyes, wishing he could climb back into bed with Kate. It was pure hell lying with her in his arms all night without doing anything, but it certainly took his mind off everything else. And he needed his mind off Ian for a while. He couldn't do anything about him yet. He couldn't even relegate him to that amorphous netherworld of nonexistence where Harry had hidden all of his other comrades who hadn't come home. Not until he knew what really happened.

"Come on, Harry," she said, her voice dry. "You need some sleep."

He was shaking his head, even as she helped him to his feet. "I need to be…"

"You're sure Ian is dead."

He nodded.

"Is an extra hour going to bring him back?"

He didn't know how she did it, but she helped him undress, all the way to his boots, shoving Mudge back to his own bed, and then she coaxed him back into that soft marshmallow of a bed and for an hour, held him. And when he felt her tears sliding down to his neck, she let him hold her as well.

As he lay wrapped in her warmth, Harry felt something

old and tight in him loosen. Something that had protected him from hurt. He didn't want to lose it. He didn't want to feel this shaky and uncertain. He didn't want to feel anything, but it was far too late for that.

"There is one good bit of news I can give you," he said.

She didn't move. "What's that?"

Fingering her hair, he smiled. "You're not crazy."

Her head shot up. "Lady Riordan?"

"Is just where you said she was. One of Diccan's household brigade managed to get a position at the asylum."

"Has she been rescued?"

Harry heard the stain of old fear in her voice, and wished he could reassure her. "I don't know what the government plans to do."

Kate shuddered. "Poor thing."

Harry pulled her into his arms. "If it weren't for you, she wouldn't have a chance."

She laid her head on his chest, as if it were the most natural thing to do, and Harry burrowed his face in her hair.

"One more thing," he said, feeling even worse.

She nodded against his chest. "Wellington was attacked," she said sounding unsurprised. "So you were wrong. The Lions aren't waiting for the verse to move."

"If they've already made an attempt on the duke, then who knows what else they're getting ready to do? We're running out of time."

And we still don't know, he thought, sharing the tense silence with her, *why they want you dead.*

*   *   *

Kate was distracted the entire next day. Harry was still off at Horse Guards, and she was stuck with boxes of minutiae.

Harry needed to get to Portsmouth. He needed to defend his friend's memory, but as long as she was in danger, he was caught here. And the only thing Kate could do to help was rifle through a dead man's life. She had begun to hate the search of Uncle Hilliard's things, because it was beginning to look pointless. There just wasn't anything to him. Besides, it gave her far too much time to think, and what she thought of was Harry. Old Harry. New Harry. The Harry she'd kept in her head, who had abandoned her on a whim to live a better life, and the Harry he'd actually been: dedicated, driven, honorable, and kind. The Harry who was now determined to stand up for his friend.

She wanted to help him. No matter what he'd done to her in the past, he was trying to become a real husband to her now. He was being kind and understanding. The least she could do was to support him back.

But how? She felt so at sea. It had been so long since she'd *wanted* to comfort a man; ever since her father died. And heaven knew she'd never been successful comforting him.

But Harry? She wished she'd had more time to hold him after he'd gotten the news about Ian. She wished he would come back so she could sit with him, just that. Just hold his hand or wrap her arms around him until that stark shock left his eyes. She wanted, unbelievably, for him to hold her back.

Harry was changing her life. Not in obvious ways; in little quiet ones that seemed completely alien to her. Kisses that seemed to go on forever without expectations. Disagreements that didn't involve fists or feet or the cold silence of isolation. Laughter. God, would she ever have expected laughter in a marriage? And the quiet courage of a man who kept his nightmares in a used-up sketch pad, and yet rose every morning to face the world without hesitation.

Compared with him she was a coward. She hadn't accepted her nightmares and moved on. She had let them cripple her. If Harry hadn't forced his way into her life, she would still be locking her doors and trying to fend off the night with her candelabras. She wouldn't have known how to change, how to expect more.

How much did she want, though? she wondered as she pulled out another of her uncle's boxes. Did she want a marriage, even though the thought frightened her to her toes? Did she want Harry to go on his travels, leaving her to the life she had always wanted, or did she want him to forfeit his dreams and share hers? Or did she want to go along with him? Did she even know how to ask?

It wasn't a question that was going to be answered now, however. Now her focus had to be on playing the part of besotted wife well enough that Edwin lost his case. She had to help Harry pull lion's teeth. Only after that happened would she have the chance to decide what to do about her marriage.

And so when she followed Grace and Bea up the steps to the Hampton ballroom that night, she was smiling, her hand on Harry's sleeve. She was surprised at how proud she felt of him in his sleek black evening attire, his wheat-blond hair neatly trimmed, and his neckcloth a perfectly tied Mathematical. Bea had called him Brummel when she'd seen him. Grace had told him that she would always prefer his Rifleman green, but that his formal civilian uniform befitted him well. Kate couldn't agree more. She just wished the shadows were gone from his eyes.

"Why, Kate, marriage must agree with you," Lady Hampton greeted her, hands out. "You're glowing."

Kate chuckled and took the countess's hands. "Don't be silly, Clare. It's the peach. The color always makes me look healthy."

Actually, tonight, it made her feel lovely, which was another revelation. She couldn't remember ever feeling quite like that before, and it unsettled her even more.

The dress shouldn't have made such a difference. Usually new clothes did nothing more for her than provide a bit of provocation. But this new dress made her feel tender, young. A deliciously soft moire silk tunic over an eggshell-white underdress, it was deceptively simple, embellished only with crystals across the low rounded bodice. A pearl and egret-feather aigret in her hair and diamond parure completed her costume.

"And this is your new husband?" Clare asked.

Kate turned to Harry. "Clare, may I introduce Major Sir Harry Lidge? Harry, this is a friend from the Military Widows project, Lady Clare Hampton."

Clare, a blond dumpling of a woman who could take credit for six children and three marriages, tilted her head and smiled. "I hope you can keep up with her, sir."

"I don't think anybody can keep up with her, Lady Hampton," Harry said with an engaging smile as he bent over her plump hand. "I plan to just hang on for the ride."

Only Kate could see the pain that still lurked in Harry's eyes. He had yet to have any success unearthing the truth about Ian.

The music had begun by the time they reached the main ballroom, a vast, echoing space decorated in white and gold that ran across the entire back of the Hamptons' home. Harry made both Grace and Bea promise him dances before settling them into chairs. Kate saw General Willoughby marching up to Bea, side whiskers bristling, and knew her friend would be entertained. Turning back to Harry, she found that a number of her own stalwarts had already lined up beneath the great chandeliers.

"Not tonight, gentlemen," Harry said before she could hand around her dance card. He pulled it from her hand and ripped it cleanly in two. "Tomorrow or the next night, you may return. But for our first ball, I claim a husband's prerogative."

One of Kate's most faithful *cicisbeos*, a painfully young tulip named Tommy, glared at Harry through an ornate quizzing glass that matched the silver embroidery on his blue velvet coat. "Not at all the thing to sit in your wife's pocket, old man."

Harry gave the boy a wolf's smile. "Undoubtedly something better known to those who haven't spent all their time on the field of battle."

Kate almost burst out laughing at the boy's goggle-eyed reaction. "Tommy," she soothed, a hand on his brocaded arm. "Humor him. He'll probably run out of patience in an hour or so and scarper for the card room."

Before Tommy could answer, Harry swung Kate into a waltz. She admitted surprise. Harry really did know how to dance. Even better, she felt as if she could relax in his arms. Any other man would have been fencing with her, trying to either seduce her or see who it was she was being seduced by. Or, like Tommy, participating in the popular pastime of enthusiastically laying his heart at the feet of a notorious woman.

Harry claimed every dance and walked with her in between. It was immediately obvious that her family had already begun their campaign of poison, because more than one back turned as she and Harry passed. A few of the more marginal members of society, who survived by knowing the way the wind blew, defected from her camp to Glynis's, and a few high sticklers reduced their greetings from smiles to chilly nods. Predictably, the Rakes had made a strong presence and acted as if nothing were unusual.

Kate could not have cared less for herself. She was furious for Harry, though, who was worth more than the vast majority of the people in this room put together. Every time a sharp-tongued matron lifted an imperious eyebrow in his direction, she could feel him stiffen, as if instinctively defending himself from blows.

"How efficient, Harry," she said, returning the smile of young Lady Finster. "You are culling out the wheat from the chaff tonight with amazing skill."

"I believe you have that the wrong way around," he said. "I seem to be the chaff."

"Bollocks. If a man who fought at Waterloo cuts you, I will take notice. Otherwise, we're succeeding in rather tidily reorganizing my standard guest list."

In the end, Kate was encouraged by the fact that the friends she would have regretted losing stood by her side. Since the rest hadn't interested her on their best day, it all worked out well. And of course, she had her faithful court. Fortunately, Harry understood their place perfectly well, especially the puppies who circled her like uncertain satellites.

"You are poetry in motion, Your Grace," her faithful Tommy gushed, kneeling at the side of the chair she'd taken alongside Bea. "How could I hear a note of the music when your radiance shone...shined...shoned down on us?"

"Harvest moon," Bea muttered.

Kate laughed. "Darling girl. Not at all. Nature doesn't have the wherewithal to be wearing a fortune in diamonds."

"I will write a poem," young Luddy Clarke said, hand to heart for his goddess. "The legendary beauty rewarded for her faith by the return of her love after ten long years. I will call it, The Return of Odysseus. Cannot you see how your story parallels that of that great hero? Kept away for ten years, while the faithful Penelope weaves?"

Kate caught the wicked glint in Harry's eye and saw the perfect opportunity to distract him from Ian. "Oh, Lord, Luddy, don't compare me to Penelope," she objected. "She was a ninnyhammer. And she waited twenty years, Luddy. Not ten."

Harry chuckled. "Why, Kate. You used to think *The Odyssey* the most romantic book in literature."

"You've read *The Odyssey*?" one of the court asked, looking a bit flummoxed.

"In Greek," Harry said, an amused twinkle in his eye. "She loved to quote it."

Kate scowled. "I was also fifteen. Everything is romantic at fifteen. After further study, however, and—" She cocked a wry eyebrow at Harry. "—*much* experience, I've decided that after what Odysseus did, Penelope should have fed him to her own pigs."

Now they had an audience. But Kate was focused on Harry, the exhilaration of debate rising like champagne bubbles in her blood.

"After what he did?" Harry echoed drily. "What? Win the Trojan War?"

"Don't be silly. I'm talking of course about how *quickly* he dashed home to be with his ailing mother and faithful wife, who, silly nit, kept herself chaste for him while he caroused with every siren and witch in the hemisphere. He didn't deserve her, and so she should have told him."

Harry's eyes were twinkling. "But he was ensorcelled. He couldn't help it that he was Calypso's lover for seven years."

Kate snorted. "How like a man. 'Couldn't help m'self,'" she barked like an old general. "'Bewitched me and all that. You understand, old girl.' Pull the other one, Harry. And then he has the gall to test Penelope's faithfulness. I repeat. Pigs."

Tommy blinked. "I say." Luddy looked vague, as if already translating her diatribe into rhyming verse. Someone clapped.

"Don't encourage her," Harry protested, laughing.

"He doesn't have to encourage me," Kate retorted, giddy with the sly challenge in Harry's eyes. "I've been saving up opinions for ten years."

"God's teeth," he groaned. "And I married you before I knew it."

They were still both sizzling with exhilaration from their challenge when the next waltz struck up. Harry swept her onto the dance floor, and she felt her spirits fly.

The music seemed sweeter suddenly, the room a lovely kaleidoscope of color and fire from within the safe enclosure of Harry's arms. She could get used to this, she thought.

"You underestimate yourself, Harry," she said, her eyes closed with the sweet pleasure of the moment. "You have a real talent. I insist you only waltz with me."

"Is that the only thing you'd like to reserve?" he whispered, bending his head to her ear.

She almost stumbled. "Pardon?"

She opened her eyes to see a dark smile on him. "I've been thinking," he said. "I believe it's time I taught you a new lesson."

She felt a flush surge up her throat. "Lesson."

There could be no mistaking the smoke in his eyes. "It's the only thing that's gotten me through the day. I've been working on a plan to reacquaint you with pleasure. I think lesson one should be the breast. Amazingly sensitive things, breasts."

She swallowed hard. "And here I was just thinking how nice it was to be able to dance without anyone trying to seduce me."

He gave her a soft smile. "I would never try to seduce you. I would expect your full participation."

"Why?" she countered, suddenly feeling cornered. "So I can begin to enjoy it? Then what? You go away, and I'll be stuck here *pining*. I told you, Harry. Pining is beneath me."

"Is it so awful?" he asked, obviously meaning to be charming. He sounded sad.

She couldn't disappoint him. "I suppose it's better than bad poetry. I get a surfeit of that."

He laughed. "Oh, I can do that, too. 'There was a young woman from Kent...'"

She smacked him on the chest. "There will be none of that."

"What about this?" Harry nipped her earlobe.

She almost lost her footing right in the middle of the floor. "Stop that!"

Heads turned. Harry chuckled. "Smile."

She smiled. Oddly, it didn't take much effort. Something effervesced in her chest, something light and giddy, as if the challenge of a moment ago had metamorphosed into light. She thought she remembered it, long ago. She didn't know what to do with it now.

"Don't you remember what it felt like when I drew my tongue over your nipple?" Harry asked, capturing her gaze.

She stumbled over his feet. Her nipples had tightened just with the words.

"When I took your breast in my hand and lifted it to my mouth? Remember how you felt?"

She might have nodded; she wasn't sure.

"You always loved that, Kate." His smile deepened. "At least I think you did. You used to make the most lovely little growling sounds in the back of your throat."

Uncomfortable heat had blossomed in her belly, between

her legs. She didn't like it; she didn't like wanting it. She hated the wasted energy of hope.

"Please," she begged, her smile more a rictus. "Don't taunt me here."

Harry looked taken aback. "Taunt you? God, is that what you think I'm doing?"

"What else?"

He looked so amazed it made her want to cry. "What else?" he echoed. "Simple. I want to finally make love to my Katie."

She was already shaking her head. "I've told you, Harry. I'm not that girl anymore. There isn't any of her left."

He didn't answer right away, just swept her into tightening circles as if no one else shared the dance floor. Finally, when he settled them back into a smooth pattern, he squeezed her hand. "You're too strong to let him take away your passion, Kate."

She jerked her head up, to see a direct challenge in the sky blue of his eyes. Just then the music ended, and they slowed to a halt, face-to-face in the middle of the ballroom, Kate's heart battering at her chest and her knees weak. She was afraid Harry was only trying to distract himself. She was tumbling off a high ledge, with no safe landing.

"Am I a project then, Harry?" she challenged, afraid he would recognize a retreat when he heard one. "Like the Widows' Fund?"

He tilted his head. "If you'd like. Would you like to be my project?"

She straightened. "I am no person's charity."

"Would you prefer to be my obsession?"

The words lodged in her chest. "I think that might become very uncomfortable."

He shrugged. "I'm not sure either of us has a choice."

It might have been a distraction for him, something to keep him from fretting about his friend. But when they returned home and Harry sent Bivens off so he could play abigail, Kate couldn't seem to manage a protest. Was it fear or arousal that had stolen her breath? Did she really trust Harry enough to lay herself open to him again? She looked to the bed with its cheerful chintz and shuddered.

"You're looking at the bed as if it's a pagan altar and you're the daily sacrifice," Harry said with a slight smile. He'd removed his jacket. He was unbuttoning his waistcoat as if he were used to doing it in her presence.

Kate's laugh was sharp. "It's rather how I feel."

Harry stopped, his fingers on his buttons. "Then tell me what you want to do."

She was about to beg him to leave when she looked up to see something stark and needy in those eyes. A longing she understood too well. He needed her to need him. Harry, who had spent years planning to escape, wanted nothing more at that moment than for Kate to come into his arms for comfort, for security, for connection.

She instinctively shied. She had never done well trusting in other people, laying her loneliness in their hands and hoping to see it transformed. The idea of trying again terrified her. After all, she was doing all right as she was. Harry was doing all right. What did they need to rely on each other for? What would it change?

Everything. And that was what frightened her.

She could back away. He was giving her the option. She could make a joke of the whole thing and escape. But she could still see Ian's death weighing on him. She could almost hear the impassioned defense Harry must have made on his friend's behalf, even knowing it to be futile. How terrible to be forced to defend a friendship forged in the heat of battle to men who had never known the sounds of the big guns or the bowel-melting terror of attack. What must it have been like to be the only one to believe in a person, no matter the evidence? What was he left with when no one believed him?

He needed her.

She hoped she had the fortitude for what Harry wanted. She prayed she would survive the inevitable pain.

"My breasts?" she asked, her voice unpardonably small. "Just those?"

She saw a shudder go through him and felt terrible that she was tormenting him this way.

"Just those."

She opened her arms and he stepped into them. "Well," he added, resting his head atop hers. "Your shoulders. And throat... and definitely your ears. I love your ears..."

She actually wanted to smile. "Are you sure you don't want me to—"

"Yes. I'm sure. I won't lie to you, Kate. I have been far from celibate the last ten years. I have given and received a great amount of pleasure."

It was her turn to shiver.

"But I think that means," he continued, lifting her face to him, "that you have ten years to catch up on."

It was too much. Her body felt suddenly insubstantial, a fragile shell of light and sensation, held together only by his arms, by the assurance in his voice. Taking a deep breath for courage, she lifted her head. She didn't say a word. She didn't know how.

Harry's smile absolved her of cowardice. Bending down, he swung her into his arms. Kate held on as he carried her over to the sofa by the fireplace and settled her into his lap. When his arms came around her, she panicked. But he was just reaching around to untie the tapes at the back of her dress and then the corset beneath. By the time he dropped a kiss on her shoulder, she was dizzy.

He leaned down and nibbled at her ear. "It's much more fun if you breathe."

Kate chuckled, a high, thin sound. She needed to close her eyes; she felt as if she were balanced at a great height. But if she closed her eyes, she couldn't brace herself against surprises. Against blows, even though she swore Harry wouldn't hurt her. It seemed protective instincts couldn't be shed like so much clothing.

She watched as Harry slipped her bodice off her shoulders and down her arms. When he followed with her chemise, trapping her against him, she panicked. She didn't like being held down. But then he kissed her, a lingering, delicious kiss that somehow stole her resistance. And when he raised his head again, Kate realized that her dress was down at her waist and her breasts bared to the night air.

She saw the brands, of course. She wanted to turn her head. But again, Harry kissed them. And instead of lingering, he moved on, dropping kiss after kiss up the line of her throat, behind her ear, across her shoulder. His lips unleashed cascades of chills, sparks, sunlight. She could barely stand to hold still, and was finally glad for the arm that held her close.

Oh, she thought, her heart stumbling, *I remember this.* The delicious abrasion of whiskers against her tenderest skin. The erotic chill when air cooled skin laved by a tongue. The almost painful jolt as nipples tightened, as breasts filled, as breath and tongue and lips followed fingers down the slope of a breast, cupped the bottoms, then, finally, slowly, maddeningly began to circle closer and closer to the nipple.

She almost shouted at him. *Please! Now!* But she didn't. She curled her hand into his hair and brought his head closer, his heat, his clever tongue. And then, oh, then, yes, there, his tongue, circling, bathing, flicking her nipple, his mouth, oh God, his mouth. Had it been this sweet before? This unbearably sharp? Had she begged him to take her nipple in his mouth and suckle?

Lightning ripped through her; exquisite explosions. She felt sparks skitter to the tips of her fingers and deep, deep into her belly, sinking between her legs, there where Harry swore she would like to feel his mouth. She couldn't seem to hold her knees together. They seemed to want to open as her body began to bow, to arch into his hands. She heard the oddest whimpering and realized it was her.

Harry left off one breast and then took the other. He stroked and explored with his big, rough hand. He held her close with his free arm and smiled into her eyes, his own so dark with arousal the blue all but disappeared.

"Will you let me show you, Kate?" he asked, laying his hand against her ankle. "I want you to remember how much pleasure you can feel."

All she could think to say was yes. Her body was trembling, her heart galloping, her body alight and wanting. *Wanting*. And he gave it. Slowly, so he didn't frighten her, he slid his hand beneath her skirts: up her leg; her knee, the tender skin of her inner thigh, lingering just long enough to make her want to scream. She could feel herself hot and weeping, dying for his touch. She remembered the frantic need, the breathless pause at the brink of the precipice. She let her legs fall open, and Harry rewarded her. His mouth at her breast, suckling, nipping, licking, he parted the wet, curling hair with his fingers and slipped inside of her, and she thought she'd die. She was panting, scrabbling at him, yanking at his shirt to be able to feel his skin, to run her hands up and down his chest, wrap them around his back and measure his arms. She wanted to comfort herself with his , to delight herself with his beauty. She wanted to share this mad, reeling passion.

She couldn't bear it. Her body was screaming for relief from the pleasure that had become pain, from the sharp edge of uncertainty. He was tormenting her, his fingers circling, diving, sweeping, pinching. He tortured her with the rasp of his tongue.

"Please," she sobbed. "Oh, please."

"Trust me, Kate," Harry murmured. "Give yourself over to me. Trust me."

She wasn't thinking. She was feeling. She was battling for something, desperately seeking the far land she could barely remember, even now with her body threatening to splinter apart. She was bracing herself for the moment Harry moved over her and blocked the light. When all the hurt returned.

"Relax," he said again and again. "Just relax and enjoy it."

She tried. She tried, warming her hands on his belly and reassuring herself with the breadth of his back. Trying to let her defenses go. And finally, just when she'd given up hope, when she almost shoved Harry away and ran to hide alone where she didn't have to face her failure, it happened. The lightning he unleashed with his fingers, his mouth and clever tongue, coiled in her, tightening, building, glowing like the trenchant core of an inferno, taking her breath, her heart, her mind, until all of her seemed to glow, to pulse, to swell, until she cried out, furious with impatience, and Harry laughed.

And suddenly, as if his laugh had been the trigger, her body disintegrated into light, into sound, into color and music. The explosion took her by surprise, shattering through her, to the very tips of her fingers, forcing the air from her lungs, melting her body and re-forming it as something completely different. Something soft and pliant and glowing. Something she had never thought to feel again as long as she lived.

She laughed. She couldn't stop laughing, even as tears rolled down her cheeks and Harry crushed her to him and called her his brave girl and laughed with her, as if they had both just rolled down a steep hill together. She wrapped her arms around him and hung on for dear life, knowing that she had just walked through a door only Harry had known how to open.

Everything changed when she realized just how hard the pressure of his rod was against her. It had to be painful. She couldn't let it end like this. It wasn't fair. Harry had given her a miracle. The least she could do was accommodate him.

Just the thought, though, stole the rest of her breath. The incandescent joy that had swept her body dulled and winked out.

Harry noticed right away. "What's wrong?"

She felt new tears slide down her cheeks. "It was so wonderful. But it's you who should be…comforted. Not me."

Harry held her tighter. "I can think of nothing more comforting than feeling you come apart in my arms. I promise. The rest will follow, Kate. But tonight is too soon. I took you much farther than I had a right to already."

She shook her head. "It's not fair," she insisted.

She wasn't sure if she was reassured or infuriated by the gentle smile on Harry's face. "And will you enjoy it?"

She froze. "Of course," she said, knowing it was the right thing to do.

He laughed. "Oh, Kate. How do you ever win at cards? You would rather have your toenails pulled out."

She couldn't quite face him. "So what? I'm sure all

women feel the same. And yet, from the size of the British population, they obviously get the job done."

Harry hugged her tight and kissed her forehead. "I don't want to sound smug, my dear, but no woman has ever had to 'get the job done' with me. I make sure of it."

She shuddered again, still not certain what from. She did know that her body had begun to feel restless again. "Braggart," she told him.

"I refuse to make love to a woman who isn't enjoying herself."

Kate looked down at the obvious strain against his pants. "I think you might just be too chivalrous for your own good, Harry."

He laughed and set her on her feet. "To bed, young lady. Tomorrow is a busy day."

But Kate couldn't rest. She knew without asking that Harry was still painfully hard, even after they had both climbed into bed and he'd tucked her beneath his shoulder. She was beginning to realize that Harry would wait forever rather than frighten her again. And she couldn't let him. She had to be braver than that.

She looked up to see his eyes closed. But she knew he wasn't sleeping. Not with his heart still thundering away and his chest slick with sweat. He wouldn't sleep until he found relief. Kate was shocked to realize that she wanted to be the one to provide it. As long as they stayed lying just like this.

Before she could talk herself out of it, she reached down and laid her hand against the straining placket of the breeches he insisted on wearing to bed.

Harry jumped a foot. "What the..."

He reached down to pull her away, but she batted his hand away. "Please, Harry. Don't forbid me. I want this."

His hand stilled atop hers. She could feel his member

twitch and swell even more beneath her palm. "Are you sure?"

She began running her hand up and down, measuring the length of him with her fingers. "Oh, yes." She was shaking; she knew he felt it. Her hands were undoubtedly cold. But something about having him in her hand gave her an odd sense of power. She was the one in charge. She could please him or she could hurt him. It was her choice.

She reached the first button of the placket and popped it open. "You wear breeches so you don't frighten me with your...uh..."

"Cockstand." There was an odd humor in his voice.

"Precisely." The second button pulled open, and the third. He groaned, which spurred her on. Even shaking, she got the placket open. And there, fitting right into her hand, was Harry, hot and hard and velvet all at once. Sleek. Alive. Pulsing, the plum-shaped tip already weeping just a drop of fluid. She found herself running her finger over it and sliding down the shaft. She was fascinated by the unfamiliar weight of it, by the life in it. By the sudden, breathtaking need for it.

He wasn't Murther. There was no way she could ever mistake the two.

She felt Harry's breath hitch, his body stiffen; she heard his heart accelerate. "Are you all right?" he asked, and she giggled.

"Are *you*?"

He chuckled back, although his voice sounded as tight as his body. "Oh, yes."

She swept her hand down to cup his sac and felt how tight it was, how firm, as if his life forces were vital and strong. She traced contours from base to tip and found that she sought to hear his breathing catch. It made her feel...in control.

She turned a bit, freeing her other hand, and wrapped it around the shaft, one hand still on his balls, and slowly, deliberately, she began to stroke. Tightening, loosening, tightening, squeezing his sac until she heard him groan. Until her own body began to respond again, mirroring the changes in his. She almost bent her head and licked him with her tongue. Instead, she licked his chest. She ran her tongue around his nipple, delighted to see it pucker. And when he began to stroke her, she stopped.

"No," she said. "It's my turn."

Harry's chuckle was no more surprised than she was. But she was beginning to understand the attraction of performing this act on someone who didn't demand pleasure, but deserved it. She closed her eyes, savoring the sounds of Harry's excitement, the taste of salt on his skin, the scent of man and the musk of arousal. She tightened her fingers and pumped, and pumped and pumped, smiling when Harry's body arced against her hands, as the guttural groans of pleasure mounted in his throat. As his head dropped back and his hand clutched her arm for balance. As his entire shaft began to pulse, and his body rock, and his voice deepen, until in gasping, laughing spasms, he emptied himself against her hand.

When she felt him collapse, she smiled and kissed his chest, feeling a greater sense of accomplishment than she had in years.

"Harry," she said minutes later as she lay with her hand atop his heart, where it could comfort her. "Thank you. I think you changed my life tonight."

Harry rested his head atop hers. "I know you changed mine."

*　　*　　*

By the next afternoon, Kate was heartily weary of her uncle's life. Not only was he delaying her return to Eastcourt, but the search was proving fruitless. Surely no man could be quite this boring, she thought as she set aside another folder worth of admonishing letters, these to tithe-skimping aristocratic patrons. The words *the example of my illustrious ducal family* appeared more regularly than *sincerely yours*.

Harry worked next to her. At the far end of the long table, Grace was reboxing everything they'd gone through and conversing with Bea, who was sitting in the corner sewing bees into the tablecloth. Kate could have thought the scene had rustic charm, if she didn't feel so hemmed in and restless.

The problem was, she wasn't quite sure where she wanted to go if she could get away. Out to the park or up to bed. Her body was still humming, as if someone had electrified her skin, and every time she looked at a boring letter or even more boring sermon, she saw instead Harry's expression at the moment he'd spilled into her hand. Ecstasy, agony. Her own body had recognized the power of his pleasure and sung in response.

It was all so amazing. So breathtakingly new, as if she had just walked off a ship into a world she hadn't believed existed. Was it too much a cliché to say colors were brighter? Sounds sweeter? Every angle on Harry's face more compelling?

Yes, she thought with a private smile. It undoubtedly was. She couldn't help it, though. It was how she felt.

"Amazing," she said, turning over yet another letter to erring clerics. "Uncle Hilliard had the unhappy knack of making even sin sound boring. No wonder Diccan ran."

Harry grinned. "I'm glad you said it. I keep thinking how glad I am I never lived in his house. Our house might not have been grand, but you can't deny, it was lively."

Kate laughed, suddenly wistful. "Chaos. That's what I remember. Unbridled chaos." Most of it involving laughter. "Although I do admit that when I set up my house at Eastcourt, I did model a few things on your mother's design. Especially the kitchen."

She set aside another file. Harry looked over at her. "Tell me about Eastcourt."

Kate paused, her hand on the box. "Oh, I think you'll like it. It's a rambling old place, all warm and yellow, of Cotswold stone, with dormers and a lovely little cottage garden. When I saw it, I felt as if for the first time in my life, I'd come home."

She could remember so clearly that moment she'd first stepped out of the carriage and looked up to see the house, as untidy and cheerful as an ugly granny, and thought, *Finally.* It had been one of the few times she'd allowed herself to cry.

"No wonder you're so fiercely protective."

She graced him with a bright smile. "Edwin has no idea the fight he's let himself in for. Eastcourt is everything to me."

Except the minute she said it, she knew it wasn't true. Not anymore. She wanted Harry to see it; she wanted him to love it as much as she did. She wanted, for the first time, for a man to share her home, and it frightened her.

Not nearly as much as the arrested look on his face, as if he'd just run into a wall. Kate was afraid all of a sudden, and she couldn't say why.

"Tell me about where you plan to go," she said on a wild hunch.

Immediately his head came up and she saw a flash of guilt. She was suddenly afraid he would never see Eastcourt as home.

"I'd start with Europe," he said, returning his attention to his work, as if he couldn't quite face her with the dreams he feared were slipping away. "Lisbon, Oporto, Madrid, Salamanca, I want to wander cities that aren't under siege for a change. Paris, Prague, Rome. There is so much magnificent architecture to study. Centuries of it. And after that, I'd study the great Mohammedan architects, the Hindus, the Far East. There is so much to learn."

Kate felt his words collect in her heart like stones. He sounded like she did when she spoke of Eastcourt. Dreamy, passionate, infatuated. For a long time, she couldn't even look at him. She focused on her box instead and contemplated the idea of wandering the world with him. She wanted to want it as much as he. Anticipating what would be around the next bend, savoring a warm Italian sun, feeding on his passion as he looked upon the Pantheon like a rake would a beautiful woman.

But the idea frightened her. She'd just found her home, just made it completely hers. How could she abandon it? Where would she feel safe? And what about Bea, and Thrasher and Finney?

"And after that?" she asked, trying to sound casual. "Didn't you plan to study?"

File in hand, he stopped, as if struck. "Study. Yes, I imagine I will. John Nash has seen some of my work and has offered a place. He's working on the Regent Street plan."

Kate came far too close to reacting. *Perfect!* she wanted to say. *Stay here and learn. Build your new world from a base at Eastcourt.* It terrified her how much she suddenly wanted it.

"It's funny, though," he said. "It's been so long since I've thought past getting as far from the army and familiar old England as I can, I can hardly imagine it."

Kate saw the naked yearning in his eyes and thought of

those nightmares, and she turned away. She couldn't take that away, could she? Even the profound experience of the night before didn't erase ghosts.

At the bottom of her box lay a small pile of pens, sanding boxes, sealing wax, a letter opener shaped like a bishop's staff. And, Kate saw, gathering them up to catalog, a small jeweler's box. Hmm, she thought. Could Uncle Hilliard have had an inamorata he hadn't wanted Aunt to know about? Secret meetings in the manse, maybe, a tidy little house in Chelsea?

But when she popped open the box, it was to find no more than a bouquet of tie pins. She should have known. Uncle Hilliard would never waste his resources on someone else. Setting the pens aside, Kate lifted each pin. A topaz, an onyx, a ship copying the Livingston crest with a diamond at the prow, and one that was a large intaglio cabochon carnelian that looked like a signet. A copy of the Livingston signet, maybe, for a second son jealous of his brother's rank?

Just to make sure, Kate hopped up and ran to the library, where she kept a magnifying glass.

"Did you find something?" Harry asked when she got back.

"I'm sure I didn't," she assured him, plopping back down in her chair and picked up the pin. "It's just my blasted curiosity, that's..."

The carnelian came into focus. Gooseflesh prickled her arms. A Tudor rose. Where had she just seen a Tudor rose? And there was an inscription surrounding it.

"*Non omnis moriar.*" The gooseflesh spread. She knew those words. Why did she know that quote? Not all of me shall die. But it was wrong. How did she know that?

Harry was peering over her shoulder. "Family crest?"

"No. Our family crest is a sailing ship and *Audere semper*. Be always daring."

She lifted the pin and the glass for him. "But I know this. I've just seen that symbol and I know the saying, but they don't go together. Where have I..."

Harry lifted the glass and bent over the pin. Suddenly the breath hissed out of him.

"Oh, my God!" Kate gasped at the same moment he looked up.

"Richmond Hill Asylum," he said, his voice tight. "The administrator had a Tudor rose on his ring. But the quote is correct, Kate. It's Horace."

She was shaking her head. "No. I mean, yes it is, but it's also from something else. A poem." Her eyes wide and her heart thudding, she grabbed Harry's arm. "Harry. I think we've found the verse."

Chapter 19

They packed to finally leave for Eastcourt. Once Drake stopped by to pick up the pin, Grace announced that it was time for her to head home as well. Kate fought her; she hated the idea of Grace going home to an empty house when she could be surrounded by her friends. But Grace was afraid of running into Diccan before she was ready, and Kate understood that all too well. So at a time when she should be sitting to tea, she and Bea kissed their friend farewell and ushered her into the Murther carriage for her ride home.

Kate was glad she was busy so she didn't have to dwell on it, or on what would happen when she and Bea showed Harry his new home. Would he fall in love with it? Would he hate it and want to leave all the sooner? Would she be able to live there without him?

The only social obligation they had left to fulfill was an invitation by Chuffy for the theater. There was a new actress imaginatively named Mardryn who was to debut in the melodrama *Lover's Vows*. Harry accepted without asking Kate, which frustrated her even though she was ready to see someone else suffer through a melodrama for a change.

They might have refocused the Lion investigation away from her, but the Chancery Court had scheduled a hearing on her case in a month, which effectively stole her peace of mind. She and Harry met with the solicitor, and he met with an investigator in the hope of digging up some dirt on Kate's relatives. The only thing left to do was show up and do her best to keep from spitting at her brother while on hallowed judicial ground.

Claiming to be committed to easing Kate's strain, Harry had spent the night before extending Kate's sensual horizons, which left her more tense than ever. She couldn't lie and say she hated the sensory banquet Harry brought to her bed. He had spent hours waking her body in ways she couldn't have imagined, carefully and generously lavishing attention on her. It had been a wonder to rediscover the delights they had once shared, and she had loved returning the pleasure Harry brought her.

Only one thing prevented her total enjoyment. They still stopped short of his taking her. Not that she was yet sure she wanted him to. Considering how much better endowed he was than Murther, she couldn't imagine how he could manage the thing without tearing her asunder. She couldn't imagine how any man could be gentle or kind or thoughtful in the act, certainly not when it was one of domination and surrender.

The problem was that she simply didn't *know*. And no matter how thoroughly Harry pleased her, igniting sensations she'd never thought to experience in her life, peaks of pleasure that robbed her of breath and thought and sense, when she rested in his arms, she still felt...unfinished. Cheated, somehow. And she didn't know how to ask him for more, especially when every time he so much as balanced himself above her she panicked like the veriest coward and resorted to pleasuring him with her hands.

So she pretended she was content with matters as they were and ignored the fact that they still hadn't spoken of their future in more than general terms, which made everything she did more fraught with peril. Especially succumbing to Harry. He had enough control over her life. How could she let him assume even more? Even now there were things she needed to do, places she needed to go, and her staff refused to let her, at least until the master said so.

The master. How she hated that word, even though it meant nothing more to them than a courtesy. To her, it carried untold negative memories. And then, one of the few friends she had allowed herself was gone, leaving her to steer her own way through the days to come. Which, she hoped, would begin and end with her very public appearance with Harry at the theater.

At least, she thought, as she climbed the grand staircase on Chuffy's arm, it gave her a chance to sound Harry's friends. "Is there any news of Ian Ferguson?" she asked, her voice low enough that only Chuffy could hear.

Chuffy's benign face folded into creases of distress, and he shoved his glasses back up his nose. "Terrible thing. Don't understand it. Grand fellow."

"Could there be any mistake?"

"Hope so. Bad enough for Ferguson's sisters without havin' him called a traitor. Good girls, what I hear. Don't deserve it."

Kate looked over. "Are they in town?"

He shrugged. "Nowhere else to go. Cousin inherits. Don't get along."

She nodded. "I'll try and stop by."

Chuffy's smile was angelic. "You're a right one, Lady K. Trumps. Would go meself, but never been introduced. Not the thing to show up now. But with Harry worrying at Horse

Guards like a terrier, hopefully we can give 'em better news. Have one question, though. About the verse."

Kate looked around to make sure no one was listening, but the crowd was too busy trying to get to their seats in time to comment on the other theatergoers before the curtain went up. "Yes, Chuffy?"

"Drake is sure this is the verse."

"It's *a* verse, certainly. They've already found it and the Tudor rose on incriminating correspondence. The bishop was evidently head of his group."

Frowning, Chuffy nodded. "Why did they think you had it?"

An excellent question. "I don't know. I think it's more that they thought I'd recognize it, which I did. I'm just not sure where from. It's one of the reasons we're going back to Eastcourt. I have my complete library there. The one I have here is only a partial collection."

Chuffy goggled at her. "You have *more* books?"

Chuffy had been on the search team. Kate couldn't help but grin. "Aren't you glad we're not dragging you along to go through that lot?"

The box was comfortable, on the second tier about halfway down the theater. The play wasn't as good as the advanced notice would have it. As usual, the Rakes kept close company. At one time or another they all came through the box to offer respects. Usually it made Kate feel better to know that they were there to back up Harry. Tonight, for some reason, they added to her feeling of being hemmed in, especially since they seemed delighted to provide an audience for her normal court, who insisted on being particularly cloying.

By the third interval, she was battling what she called a patience headache, born of having to exert such control over her tongue in response to well-meaning acquaintances. Especially her puppies. Glad for a bit of fresh air, she took Harry's arm and followed Chuffy and Bea out into the ornate lobby for champagne.

Suddenly, on the other side of Chuffy, Bea made a rude noise. "Ahoy!" she said. "Sail on the starboard bow."

Harry looked around. Kate didn't have to. She sighed. "Well, it was inevitable."

"What was inevitable?" Harry demanded, now staring at Bea, who had gone back to genteel silence.

Kate scanned the audience. "My family."

Chuffy nodded. "'Course. Ducal crest a sailing ship. Well played, Lady B."

Glynis intercepted them like a frigate stalking a ship of the line. "How dare you?"

Kate sighed. "Hello, Glynis. How nice to see you."

Her sister-by-marriage looked as if she were going to burst, her famously porcelain cheeks a hectic pink, her hands clenched at her sides. "You have no business being here, and you know it. How dare you flaunt this...creature in our faces?"

Kate ignored the jab. "I believe you've met my husband, Major Sir Harry Lidge. Harry, may I formally introduce Glynis, Duchess of Livingston. I would claim kinship, but I don't want Glynis to have a seizure in the middle of the theater. Oh, and there you are, Edwin," she said to her brother, who stood just behind his wife. "You must speak up, or no one will see you."

Kate then leaned close to Harry, as if imparting a secret. "You bow over her hand, Harry. But don't lick. It's common."

She saw that Harry was trying not to smile. "My pleasure, Your Grace."

"You really don't care who you destroy, do you?" Glynis said, never taking her eyes off Kate. "I wouldn't be surprised if you didn't pick this time for your outrageous stunt for the sole purpose of ruining Elspeth's engagement."

Kate raised an eyebrow. "Little Elspeth? My, time really has flown. I hope you like her fiancé."

"That can have no interest for you. And what are you doing in those emeralds?"

Kate admitted surprise. True, it was the first time she'd donned the set since the family lawyer had dropped them off, but Kate wasn't sure they should cause resentment. Although, after what she'd learned about her father, she had trouble understanding why he'd left them to her. They had been her mother's parure: bracelets, eardrops, collar necklace, and an emerald-and-pearl tiara tucked into her upswept hair.

"Well," she said, selfishly enjoying the martial light in Glynis's eye. "I don't think rubies would have gone nearly as well with my dress."

If possible, Glynis looked even more outraged. "Those emeralds belong to the duchess and you know it. Edwin, how did she get hold of them?"

Kate waited, just to see what he'd say. "Well, er…"

"No, no," Kate demurred, suddenly delighted. "Let me, Edwin. You see, Glynis, evidently Edwin didn't think to tell you when he sent them over that my father left them to me in his will."

"The *lawyer* sent them over," Edwin snapped. "And it was *Mother*…"

Red-faced, he went dumb. For a minute, Kate couldn't go on. Her mother. So maybe the emeralds weren't such a mystery after all. Her mother had also been the one to make sure Kate got Eastcourt.

"Of course," Kate said, determined she wouldn't succumb to tears before her brother. "See, Glynis? You should feel better. If it had been up to Edwin, I never would have seen them. How inconvenient that Father's lawyer was so thorough. But enough about this silly necklace. Tell me about Elspeth."

Glynis wasn't playing. "You should have been locked away by now. You should be somewhere you can no longer humiliate your family."

Kate was going to say something, but suddenly Harry put a foot in front of her. He didn't make an aggressive move, but Kate felt a shiver go through her at the quiet threat of his voice. "It seems to me that her family is quite capable of humiliating itself. You're lucky my wife is more gracious than you. If it were up to me, I'd expose you."

"Expose us?" Edwin countered. "For what, protecting my family? How dare you?"

"How dare *you*?" Harry retorted. "A man is supposed to protect his sister, not terrorize her. Thank God you'll never be able to get your hands on her again."

Glynis's color neared purple. "You threaten *us*? Who do you think you are?"

Completely smitten by the cold fire in Harry's blue eyes as he stood up for her, Kate grinned. "Why, he's my husband. And I, Glynis, am the daughter of a duke *and* the widow of a duke. Which, if memory serves, is one more duke than you."

She knew she shouldn't have said it. Glynis was sensitive about the fact that her father was only a baronet. Kate came within ames ace of apologizing, especially when Glynis began to sputter, so enraged Kate thought she would resort to physical violence. "Your *father*—!" she snarled.

But before she could finish, Edwin grabbed her by the

arm. "It is beneath you to brangle with her, my dear. Come. We can certainly find more pleasant company."

It was as if Edwin had yanked a cord in Glynis. Suddenly she stopped, straightened, considering Kate as if she were a mouse caught in her cupboard. "Indeed, Livingston. I have far more important issues to occupy me than your sister's cupidity. Her comeuppance is approaching, and I for one relish it."

And without another word, she turned on her heel and stalked off. Kate was still staring after her when from behind her, she heard a low whistle.

"Your brother's wife seems to spend an inordinate amount of time red-faced," Chuffy mused.

"Harpy," Bea snapped.

"They were certainly no match for Harry," Kate agreed, and pulled her husband down for a smacking kiss that made him grin. It was quite enough to break the mood.

Kate would have thought that to be her quota of family for the night, if an hour later she weren't accosted a second time as she and Harry followed the crowd toward the exit. She was turning to Chuffy to thank him for the evening when, from out of nowhere, a flash of white muslin and white-blond hair threw herself into Kate's arms.

"Auntie Kate! Oh, I'm so glad you're here. You heard about Adam, of course. You must meet him. You, too, Lady Bea. Oh, and you must be the major." Her green eyes sparkling mischievously, she smiled up at Harry. "I've heard *tons* about you. Come!"

And before Kate could protest, Kate's niece Elspeth was dragging her, laughing, down the corridor. Looking back to make sure Harry followed, Kate submitted herself to Elspeth's rambling monologue about her engagement, her fiancé, and her wedding plans.

"Mama is having a country weekend for both families to meet, which I admit quite terrifies me." She leaned close and whispered. "Lady Chatham is quite a dragon. Makes my mama seem positively placid by comparison, I swear."

Kate laughed. "Don't let her hear you say that," she warned. "You're skating on thin enough ice consorting with me. If she catches you, we'll both be boiled in oil."

Kate couldn't understand it. Her own father had doted on her siblings, and yet they had turned out to be stiff-rumped and disagreeable, especially toward her. Yet somehow Edwin and Glynis had borne two delightful daughters and a stalwart son, whom she liked immensely. But then, their nanny had been a deceptively placid creature with a head full of mathematics and Greek heroes.

"Now, Kate. Here is Adam. I insist you adore him."

Kate was already smiling when she was introduced to the Honorable Adam Thorne, a gangling, loose-limbed redhead with an open, happy countenance. Smiling down on the tiny Elspeth as if she were made of spun sugar, he bowed.

"Your Grace," he said, taking Kate's hand.

Kate scowled.

Elspeth giggled. "My aunt is remarried, Adam. It is now Lady Lidge." Elspeth leaned close to Kate again. "Well done. My parents almost burst blood vessels when they heard the news. I haven't seen them turn that color since my brother, Michael, was blackmailed by his inamorata."

Kate was back to smiling. "Desist, you scrubby brat. You shouldn't speak that way of your parents. It is not your job to set their backs up. It is mine."

"Well, no one does it better," the girl agreed, all but twirling on her toes. "Come to our weekend, Kate. You could save it from being deadly dull."

Kate glared as if she meant it. "So you would have me

immolate myself on the family altar just to keep you from being bored?"

Elspeth blinked her big green eyes. "Why, yes. Because when I get bored, I become quite susceptible to irresistible impulse."

Kate hadn't realized that Harry had caught up to them until she heard him laugh. "Definitely related to my Kate."

Introductions passed without incident, and Kate found herself becoming envious of the enamored pair. "And listen, you two," she said, holding each by the hand. "If you need a refuge during the madness, you know where I live. I'll never breathe a word to any of the parents."

Elspeth's giggle was like a waterfall. "Can I see the infamous painting?"

"Absolutely not," Kate said, laughing. "It makes me look like a cow. Now, off with you two before your mother catches us plotting against her."

Harry was escorting Kate through the crowds out on the street a few minutes later when he looked down at her. "I'm very glad your mother made sure you got her emeralds," he said, his voice low.

Kate looked up to see a softer smile in his eyes. "What? Why?"

"Your mother was a saint. Kind and generous and happy, with a joy for life that seemed to include everyone. I'll tell you sometime about her summer parties for all the neighboring children. She was a mean cricket player. She laughed constantly, and everyone adored her."

Kate quirked an eyebrow, bemused by the conversation. "I believe you had a tendre for my mother, sir."

"Worshiped her with every bit of my four-year-old heart."

Kate tilted her head, her heart slipping oddly in her chest. "What made you think of her now?"

His smile broadened. "You're very much like her."

"Oh, yes," Kate agreed. "I look just like her."

But he shook his head and smiled. "I'm not talking about your looks."

Kate slowed to a halt right there in the middle of the jostling crowd, Harry's words catching in her chest. Her eyes burned with emotion; her defenses shuddered. He looked so sincere, so proprietary. How could he mean it? She had been terrible to him. She had protected herself by constructing a wall of distance around her and tried so hard to keep him out.

"Harry," she said, coughing to clear the constriction in her throat. "About your engagements..."

Suddenly someone cried out next to Kate and slammed into her. She stumbled back, her arms flailing, as the crowd shifted again. She was terrified she would fall beneath the passing coaches. Before she could, though, Harry was there, and she was in his arms. He stumbled and grunted, and she thought he'd pulled something. Behind him an orange girl tossed a bright orange in the air to a laughing young dandy and skipped off. The rest of the crowd closed in again.

"You all right, Harry?" Kate asked, brushing off her dress.

"Sore ribs," he said brusquely. "Think I pulled them."

Kate looked around for Bea and Chuffy, who had become separated. She couldn't see them anywhere.

"Harry," she said. "You're tall. Can you see Chuffy?"

She had just put her hand on Harry's arm for balance as she went up on her toes when Harry swayed and stumbled again. She glanced up to see an odd look on his face. "Harry?"

He peered down at her. "I think..."

He swayed again. She reached out to grab onto him and

he flinched. She slid her arm under his so she could grasp his waist. Something was wrong. Harry's coat was wet. She pulled her hand away and looked at her white kidskin glove.

"My God, Harry. You're bleeding."

He stared at her glove, which was stained and glistening. "Oh, bugger," he muttered, and that quickly his knees gave out.

Kate didn't scream. Kate abhorred screamers. She yelled. "Chuffy! Drake! Braxton! Bea! Help!"

She didn't know why she called them all, except that they had been orbiting all night. As if choreographed, they all materialized out of the crowd.

"It's Harry!" she yelled, down on her knees, trying to support him. "He's hurt!"

Bea dropped to Harry's other side. "'Is this a dagger which I see before me?'"

"She's right," Harry said, sounding bemused as he sat on the ground. "I believe...I've been stabbed."

"Get me some brandy!" Kate called up to the men. Instinctively she rooted through her cloak pockets with her free hand before remembering that she no longer had her own flask. Drake had made off with it back at Olivia's wedding.

"You're not stripping me in the middle of Katherine Street so you can pour brandy on a stab wound," Harry said, his voice weakening.

Supporting more and more of his weight, Kate fought a flood of panic. "Don't be absurd," she snapped. "The brandy's for me. I get sick at the sight of a man ruining his good clothes by lounging in the dirt. Oh, why did I let Drake make off with my flask? Chuffy! Get the coach!"

"I didn't see who stabbed him," Kit Braxton protested. "I swear. I stayed close to make sure no one tried to hurt Lady Kate."

"Someone was stabbed?" somebody asked.

Kate didn't hear an answer. By now there was shouting and confusion, people running toward and away from a possible attack. The Rakes gathered around Harry and Kate to keep them from being trampled in the excitement. The surreal light from gas lamps cast weird, undulating shadows across faces, and glinted off gems. Chuffy was in the street waving his arms like a bowler, and Bea was tossing bee-embroidered handkerchiefs at Kate like giant snowflakes. Harry was telling everyone that he was all right, truly he was, even as his voice faded along with his color. And Kate, one hand pressing a wad of snow-white handkerchiefs against the slash in the back of Harry's coat, was suddenly, completely distracted. Somebody had just pressed a chased silver flask into her free hand. She couldn't stop staring at it.

"Oh, my God," she breathed. "I was wrong. We really did have the verse all along."

Chapter 20

It's nothing," Harry kept insisting, even as they all but carried him up to his room. Finney met them all at the front door and sent a footman off for a doctor, and Mudge met them in Harry's room, already carrying hot water. Kate began pulling at Harry's neckcloth the minute he reached his room and didn't finish until she had his bloody coat, waistcoat, and shirt in her hands.

"It's a stab wound, old man," Drake informed him, bent over Harry's back. "Deuced close to your lung. Can you breathe?"

"I'm talking, aren't I?"

But he grunted every time he moved. Drake was right. Harry had missed mortality by less than an inch. Maybe not that far, if he kept losing blood. His shirt and jacket were saturated, and the neat slice below his ribs was still freely bleeding. Kate had spent two months caring for the injured after Waterloo. It had never made her feel as sick and giddy as the sight of Harry's bleeding back.

"Lie down, Harry," she said, standing in front of him. "You're swaying so much, you're making me dizzy."

"You're not going to become vaporish on me, are you?" he asked with a wan smile. "Mudge has hurt me worse shaving."

"Right there, Major," Mudge agreed equably as he cleaned off the wound. "Almost took off your nose once, sir, a mornin' you was worse for the night spent at the colonel's card game. Couldn't hold still to save your life."

The boy sounded so calm, one would be forgiven for thinking he was unaffected if one didn't notice his expression. Kate couldn't help seeing the flash of pain and fear in his eyes, as if he were the one injured.

Merde, she thought, wishing she weren't so shaky. This was unacceptable. She did not want to spend her life fearing for Harry's. She didn't like the hard, hollow dread that had exploded in the pit of her stomach when she'd seen him go down, the instinctive need to hold him as tightly as she could, as if she could protect him after the fact. She didn't *like* feeling sick with fear.

"I have ceased to be amused, gentlemen," she announced, pulling off her bloodstained gloves and tossing them in the corner. "We need a different entertainment."

Off came the eardrops and bracelets. Kate barely noticed Bivens collect them from the dresser. She was busy helping Mudge ease Harry down onto his side.

"Harry," she asked, kneeling down so she could hold his hand and meet him eye-to-eye. "Do you think you can refrain from dying long enough for me to change into a dress more suited for surgery?"

He was deathly pale, but he grinned. "I told you, sweetheart. I have no intentions of cutting my stick. And I wish you didn't have to change. I'm quite partial to that gold."

Kate scowled. "The color doesn't go at all well with blood. Now behave yourself. I'll be back."

She had already turned for her room when he stopped her. "Kate?"

She spun back around.

"Did you really say you knew where the verse is?"

"I did."

Suddenly everybody was staring. "Well, where the hell is it?" Drake demanded.

Kate's smile was hard. "You have it." And then she walked out of the door.

                    *   *   *

Harry hated the liquid, insubstantial feel of injury. Not the pain; he was used to that, even though this pain was beginning to set in with a vengeance. It was always the same with piercing injuries. At first, all you felt was that sudden shock, the sensation that your defenses had just been breached. It wasn't until minutes later that the nerves realized what had just happened. And when they did, they set up the burning, howling agony that rode on every breath. Especially with Mudge pressing something that felt like gravel against the wound to stop the bleeding

He hated to be an infant, but he was glad he was already lying down. It would have been positively humiliating to swoon in his wife's arms. And wasn't it just like Kate to drop her bombshell and exit the room like an actress at the end of her scene?

"Kate!" Drake yelled, already stalking after her. "Wait!"

"Touch that doorknob, old man," Harry growled, "and I'll be forced to have Chuffy mill you down."

Looking apologetic, Chuffy nodded. "Have to do it, too. Not the thing. Lady *en dishabille*."

Drake wheeled around on them. "Did you hear her? What did she mean?"

"I'm sure she'll remember until she's had a chance to change."

"Says *we* have it," Chuffy reminded Drake as he walked over to poke the fire into flames. "Don't suppose you remember where we put it."

"Don't be an ass, Chuff." Abruptly Drake sat down. "If I knew where it was, I wouldn't have been waiting around on Lady Catastrophe in there."

"Careful with the monikers," Harry warned, feeling muddled enough that he couldn't seem to focus. The best he could do was lie there watching the door to Kate's room until either she or the doctor arrived.

"Mill you down again," Chuffy warned Drake, who just smiled.

"Didn't anybody else see anything?" Kit Braxton asked. "I swore I kept an eye out, and the crowd looked perfectly normal. No furtive movements, no lurking cutpurses."

"Must have been somebody," Chuffy mused. "Harry's stabbed, after all."

"But who?" Kit demanded, leaning against the fireplace.

"The orange girl," they suddenly heard from the doorway.

Harry saw Kate sweep through the door clad in a surprisingly practical gray dress topped with a big cook's apron that was oddly complemented by the tiara she hadn't taken the time to remove from her lusciously piled hair.

"What orange girl?" Drake demanded, his pacing halted mid-stride.

Kate stopped, hands on hips, head tilted. "I was knocked over. Just as Harry caught me, the orange girl bumped against him. Didn't you see her flipping the orange to the fellow in the crowd?"

Chuffy nodded enthusiastically. "Lovely color." He saw the grins and blushed. "Orange."

Kate nodded, checking Harry's forehead with the back of her hand. "I think she also had a knife."

Harry was distracted by the cool brush of her skin. He didn't think he'd ever felt such a soothing touch. "Why stab Harry?" Chuffy asked.

Harry saw understanding dawn in Kate's eyes and wanted to hold her. She suddenly looked so vulnerable. "I don't think she meant to," he said. "I got in the way."

Kate didn't let her gaze rest on Harry long enough for him to reassure her. Lord, was that guilt blooming in her eyes? "Kate. She missed."

"But it was a knife," Chuffy protested. "Ain't that the Surgeon's habit?"

"It seems there really is another one," Kit mused.

Kate tilted her head. "And it couldn't be a woman?"

They all looked back and forth at one another.

"What color hair?" Drake asked.

"Blond," Chuffy said immediately. "Couldn't see her eyes. She was laughin'. Was thinkin' she'd make a lovely *chère amie*." He quickly ducked his head. "Sorry."

Harry couldn't help it. He laughed, because he couldn't think of anything else to do. "You're absolutely...right, Chuff. She does."

Drake looked sick. "Minette?"

"The woman who shared half the Rakes?" Kate stopped, closing her eyes to concentrate, which just stole Harry's concentration. She looked so like a young girl when she did that. "Yes," she finally said, eyes opening. "It could very well be. She certainly had breasts like pomegranates."

Drake blinked. "What?"

She waved him off. "I need to focus on Harry right now. Mudge," she said. "Get me something to lay under him. He's ruining a perfectly good bed with all that blood. Kit, would you mind telling Finney to get cook started, and to round up some spirits? I have a feeling we'll need them."

"I certainly do," Harry managed. "You're making me...dizzy. Slow down."

She immediately came over and crouched before him again, her expression taut. At least until she saw that Harry was watching her. Then, like a curtain lifting, she gifted him with a dry smile. "If this marriage is to remain felicitous," she said, brushing his hair off his forehead, "you must not think to become more interesting than I."

He quirked an eyebrow. "Knives bore me."

"Only if you're the one on the receiving end. I promise. By the morning, my parlor will be packed with the curious trying to winkle the story out of Bea."

"You'd subject Bea to that nonsense?"

She waved him off. "She loves nothing better than confounding them all. The ones who understand will stay. The others will give up and leave us in peace."

"And you?"

"Will obviously be up here spooning restorative broths into my wounded hero's mouth." She never moved, never took her gaze from Harry's, which made him oddly giddy. "Might as well. We won't be getting to Eastcourt tomorrow."

If possible, Harry felt worse. "Sorry."

She flashed a too-bright grin. "Drake, you have been inordinately patient. Should I tell you about the verse?"

Harry could hear Drake shuffle, as if holding himself back. "If you please."

Still, she didn't look away from Harry, which was doing odd things to his heart. It would have done odd things to his poor, unfulfilled cock if he'd had a bit more blood in him. He'd been so good the last few days: patient, understanding; *generous*, damn it. He had done everything he could to make Kate comfortable with lovemaking before taking it to the next step, all the while denying himself what he wanted with a fierceness that stunned him. He wanted to sheath himself inside her. Open her, literally, to his invasion, to his domination, to his vehemence. He wanted fire and passion and mindless need.

And yet, the minute he'd seen the first flash of terror in her eyes, he'd held back. He kept holding back, until he thought he'd go mad. He wanted her. He wanted all of her. More than the feel of her coming apart in his arms, although that was pure heaven. More than the torture of her fingers running up and down his shaft. She brought him to a climax; it wasn't hard to do these days. But he could do that himself. He couldn't bury himself so deeply in her that he might never find his way back out.

And now, thanks to Minette, he was going to have to wait even longer.

"Harry?"

He startled, realizing that he'd wandered off. The sight of those keen green eyes was enough to tighten his body all over again, even though it would do him no good. Not now. Probably not for days. Damn it.

"Yes, Kate. I want to know what you were going to tell Drake."

She smiled and turned to Drake. "'Is not the fruit sweet, my first love?'" she said.

For a minute, silence reigned in the room. The words were familiar; Harry could hear them. He could almost see them. He also saw the sweet slope of Kate's breast, and thought about putting it in his mouth.

He blinked. Coughed. Not the time for that. He had to pay attention.

"Devil fly away with me," Chuffy suddenly said, jumping up. "Gracechurch's flask! The mistress."

Kate's smile was almost beatific. "Indeed, Chuffy. That line—'Is not the fruit sweet, my first love?'—is what is inscribed across the miniature on Jack's flask. A miniature of the woman who was both Jack Gracechurch and Diccan's mistress. The ubiquitous Minette. Drake helped himself to it back at Gracechurch's."

Giving Harry a quick kiss, Kate stood and walked out of his vision.

"Hey!" he protested, feeling her loss in the deepest recesses.

"Hush," he heard behind him. "I am about to minister. Don't distract me."

And without any more roundaboutation, she evidently took whatever Mudge had been using to apply pressure to his back and pressed with all her might.

"Ow!" Harry howled as she ignited a fresh wave of pain.

"Hush, you baby," she said, her voice preternaturally bright. "Do you want to have all your friends think you a fribble?"

"I don't care what my friends think. That hurts!"

She dropped a kiss on his shoulder and almost distracted him. "Better?"

He huffed. "It's a start."

"But what does it mean?" Drake demanded.

"The verse?" Chuffy asked. "Does it have to mean anything?"

"You're sure there wasn't anything else inscribed on the flask," Drake said.

"Not that I ever saw," Kate assured him. "I recognized it, though."

"What about the bishop's pin, though?" Drake asked. "Was that a mistake?"

She shook her head. "No. No, I think it's part of the same

poem. *God* I wish I could remember where I've seen it. Because both lines are off by just a bit."

"How do you know?"

She shrugged. "Haven't a clue. Maybe if I looked again. Where is the flask?"

"I turned it over to Baron Thirsk," Drake said. "He wanted his lads to look at it."

Harry could hear a carriage clatter up to the house and stop. Obviously the doctor. Harry hated doctors almost as much as he hated injury. More than once he'd only held off amputation by refusing to sleep. Bastards were far too happy to be lopping things off. In fact, last time, it had been Ian Ferguson who'd chased off the surgeons, letting loose a Scottish war cry that had cleared the tent.

Something nudged at Harry's memory about Ian. The flask.

"Damme," he breathed. "Ian."

"What about him?" Drake asked.

"When did you give the baron the flask?"

Drake thought a moment. "I don't know. Last week."

"And the attempt was made on Wellington's life right after that," Kate said, catching on right away.

Harry nodded and regretted it when his back set up a howling. "Exactly."

"You can't think Thirsk has anything to do with it," Drake protested.

"I assume he's some kind of government person?" Kate asked.

"I can't officially admit to that," Drake said.

"I can," Harry said. "The government gets the verse we were told was needed to commence the attack on Wellington, and suddenly the attack has commenced."

This silence wasn't stark; it was sickened.

"No," Drake insisted immediately. "Not possible."

"What do you think, Harry?" Kate asked, leaning over him.

It did seem inconceivable. Thirsk was quiet, efficient, humorless, and thorough. Harry knew that the man was the government liaison to more than one shadow organization. During his time working for Scovill, Harry had reported to Thirsk on more than one occasion and found him cold, collected, analytical, and conservative. But a Lion? Harry just couldn't see it.

"Find out who he gave it to," he suggested.

"Might even ask for it back," Chuffy mused. "See what happens."

The discussion ended there, because Finney opened the door to usher in Bea and a surprisingly young man with big shoulders, bigger hands, and a brisk attitude. Harry only saw his face briefly, as he disappeared around his back.

"Quite an audience you have here, Your Grace."

"Mike!" She greeted him as if they were old friends. "Glad you were available. My husband has gone and gotten himself stuck like a pig on a spit."

"Not another member of your adoring train," Harry protested.

"Good heavens, no," the doctor said with a booming laugh. "I help out with the orphanage."

Harry tried to look behind him. "Orphanage?"

He caught Kate grinning. "Just something to keep Bea and me busy when the tulips are dormant. Dr. Michael O'Roarke, meet Major Sir Harry Lidge."

"Nice to meet you, Major. Guards?"

"Ninety-fifth."

"Ah, a real unit, which is obvious from the road map you carry on your body. I wouldn't be surprised if you didn't come through my tent one time or another. Go hold his hand, Kate. You're making me nervous."

"Just don't lop anything off," Harry warned.

The doctor laughed. Harry tried his best not to flinch, but as gentle as the doctor was, he was brisk. Kate came around and took Harry's hand. He wished she hadn't. Her hand was cold and clammy, which made him feel guilty. She was afraid. His Kate had been afraid far too often for his liking. She kept watching him, as if she were balanced on his pain. So he winked.

"Good news and bad news, Major," the doctor said, straightening. "You missed all the important bits, but there's too much bleeding. I'm going to need to open this a bit wider and cauterize it."

Kate paled. Harry held more tightly on to her hand.

"Do you have to?" she asked, sounding more uncertain than he'd ever heard her.

Harry didn't hear the answer. Considering that Kate paled even more, he didn't have to. He gave her hand another hard squeeze. "Out," he said. "Mudge will help the doctor. You go sit with Bea."

She pulled herself together. "No. I'm not leaving."

"Yes," Harry said, holding more tightly. "You are. I've done this before. You haven't. I'd much rather not have to pick you up off the floor."

Her laugh was dark and brimming with nightmares. "I told you before, Harry. I'm finished with people shoving me about. I'll stay."

"No," Chuffy disagreed, grabbing her hand and pulling. "Man doesn't like his lady love watching him squeal. And Lidge is about to squeal like a farmyard sow."

"A sow?" Harry echoed, scowling. "I couldn't at least be a boar?"

"Not a bore at all, Harry. Quite an interesting fellow."

Harry groaned. Kate tried to pull away from Chuffy. Smiling like a child, Chuffy ushered her and Bea right through the door just before Drake locked it.

"Wish I'd had him at Mount St. Jean," O'Roarke mused. "Just think of the officers I could have evicted. Now, Major. I assume we have brandy? You're going to need it."

Harry closed his eyes and wished he were the kind of fribble who passed out.

*   *   *

Kate hated surrender. The sound of that lock turning almost sent her running for the hall door. But the minute she saw Bea and Bivens hovering in her room, she knew she wouldn't be allowed back in with Harry.

"Spend our time thinking of the verse," Chuffy suggested, pulling off his glasses so he could mop his brow.

Kate felt guilty. "Not one for surgeries, Chuff?"

He vigorously shook his head. "Delicate stomach."

Kate couldn't help it. She kissed his cheek. "Then you're a good friend."

Just then she heard a strangled moan coming from Harry's room. She instinctively lurched in that direction, only to be caught again by Chuffy.

"Seen all those scars?" he asked, pushing up his glasses. "Done this before."

Kate nodded absently. It was quiet again. Had he passed out? Was he...dead?

Suddenly her legs gave out on her and she sat in her slipper chair. What was happening to her? She had seen people in pain before. She had seen people tortured, and she'd seen them lying on the ground, their insides lying on the street next to them. One yelp from Harry and she was weak-kneed and shaky. He wouldn't die on her, would he?

He wouldn't leave.

Of course he would. If Harry wasn't killed playing his shadow games, he would take off and wander the world, just as he'd promised. She might as well prepare herself for it now. She might as well remember what she had worked so hard to learn. The only person she could really rely on was herself. It didn't matter if she loved him with all her heart. It didn't matter if he was the best man in the world. The time would come when he left her to fend for herself. She might as well get used to it now.

Brave words. They didn't stop the shaking or the terrible, searing pain in her chest at the thought of Harry suffering in there without her to hold his hand.

"Catalog," Bea said, sitting on a chair beside her.

Kate blinked up at her. *Not now*, she wanted to say. *Let me alone*. She was still straining to hear any sounds from the next room, still willing Harry to be all right. To be past the pain. She couldn't waste time on anything else.

Bea patted her hand impatiently. "Catalog sonnets."

Catalog sonnets. What the deuce did she mean?

"You mean the verse?" Chuffy asked, still mopping his brow.

Bea nodded, and Kate gasped. "Do *you* recognize the verse?"

The old woman shook her head. Kate looked up, trying to pull the words from her memory. *Is not the fruit sweet, my first love? Not all of me will die.* They were wrong. In the wrong order, missing a word; something.

"'My library was dukedom enough,'" Bea said, looking curiously intent.

"That's from *The Tempest*," Chuffy offered.

"Library," Kate echoed. "Of course. Let's go. Bivens, if anyone asks for me, tell them where we've gone."

"But where have we gone?" Chuffy asked as Kate swung open the door.

"My library," she said. "I have stocked every book I've read in the last five years in there. We'll look there first."

Chuffy sighed. "Fonder of the stables."

Kate gave him a gentle shove out the door. "Precious few books in a stable."

As much as she knew she should get downstairs, Kate couldn't help walking the other way, just to see if she could learn anything. "I won't go in," she promised Bea. "I just want to..."

She heard it before she saw him in the room across the hall. Taking a second to shoo Bea and Chuffy down the stairs, she stepped into the empty bedroom to find Mudge bent over a chamber pot casting up his accounts.

"Is he all right?" she asked.

Mutely he nodded.

"Are you?"

He managed a half grin. "Never get used to it, do I?"

Which was when Kate realized that the reason Mudge had no interest in Kate's flirting was because he truly did love another. For that moment, she hurt worse for Mudge than she hurt for herself.

"Does he know?"

Mudge's eyes grew huge, and he paled. But he shook his head. "He's not like...me. I understand that." Taking a shaky breath, he got to his feet. "Will you send me away?"

"Only if you ask. It's a difficult thing to love someone when you realize he'll never love you the same way. I know."

Wasn't it funny? It took this sad little scene with Mudge for her to realize that she'd never fallen out of love with

Harry after all. All the turmoil she'd felt when she'd held him during his nightmares, when she'd seen the blood soak his shirt, when she'd wished with all her heart that she could be a complete woman, wasn't going to go away. In fact, it would only get worse because no matter what happened, she would have to love him until the day she died.

And the only one who understood was this exquisitely beautiful boy with the sad eyes. "Well, Mudge," she said with a shaky smile. "Shall we muddle on?"

For a second, the pain in the boy's eyes was indescribable. But when he nodded, he smiled, and it was heartfelt. Kate gave him a quick, hard hug. And then she turned away.

"Can I go in?" she asked.

"Wouldn't do no good. Doctor gave him laudanum and brandy."

She smiled. "Then I'll go down and do my part. But I'll be back up, and no one is going to keep me out of that room."

"Yes'm."

What did she do now? she wondered as she walked down the steps. Would it be easier living with Harry or harder? Would his kindnesses feel like blessings or fresh wounds? Did she have the kind of courage Mudge did to live in Harry's shadow without letting him know what he really meant to her? Just how many times could she watch him walk away without being destroyed? Already the old wound was opening, bleeding, the scar she'd thought she had built up over these long years no protection at all. All it had taken was his being injured and she was that fifteen-year-old girl again, hanging her happiness on his well-being. He was hurt and she lost her balance, her purpose, her composure. Would it be long before she found herself just like Mudge, physically sick every time Harry stumbled?

She *hated* this. She had worked so hard to be free of it; to stand apart from the emotions that had held her in such thrall. And yet, within days of being back with Harry, her distance was gone.

She should leave, take Bea and run to Eastcourt, where she could assume control of her life again. She should offer Harry his freedom before he demanded it and see him off on his way to the rest of the world. She should, damn it.

She knew, though, that she wouldn't. So when she walked by Finney, she smiled and told him to call her the minute Harry woke. And then she buried herself in the library, knowing instinctively that the needle she sought was not in this haystack.

*   *   *

Eight miles away, the windows of the Richmond Hill Asylum were dark. The matron of the east wing, knowing her patients' habits, caught a few winks before it was time to rouse her charges. It took a keen eye to spot her transgression, as she slept bolt upright at her desk.

Someone else was familiar with her habits, though, and crept past her on soundless feet. A staff member clad in the gray serge uniform with its plain lace collar, she was an unfamiliar face on the hall. Her pale blond hair shone in the shadow, and her lush figure strained the seams of the borrowed uniform. In her hands she clutched the master keys. She walked on crepe-shod feet, and she knew where she was going. The fourth door down the right side of the hall.

It wasn't until she had noiselessly opened the conveniently soaped door and knelt beside the low bed with its bright yellow quilt that she made any noise. Taking a second to assess the generously curved blond woman who lay beneath the quilt, she nodded. They did look alike. Gently she laid her hand over Lady Riordan's mouth.

"Sssssh," she whispered. "You need to stay quiet. I'm here to help."

The patient jerked awake, eyes huge in the darkened room. "It's all right," the lady in gray said. "My name is Schroeder. I can help you escape."

The woman gave a little gasp. "My husband?" she asked, barely making a sound when Schroeder's hand was removed.

Schroeder gently shook her head. "Lady Kate. She told some people who wish to stop the Lions."

Lady Riordan hesitated. "You're Scottish."

"My brogue gives me away, I see."

Lady Riordan drew back. "I won't betray my husband."

"We won't ask you to. But you know of others?"

She got an anxious nod. "They put Lady Sanbourne in here, too."

"We know. Are you ready to leave?"

The pretty young matron looked anxiously around, as if expecting help to materialize. "But how will you get me out without them seeing?"

"I won't," Schroeder said, getting to her feet. "You'll do it yourself."

"But how?" she asked, climbing out of bed.

Smiling, Schroeder began to unbutton her uniform.

"By walking out the front door."

Chapter 21

The search of Kate's library ended up taking three days. Not only did Kate have a surfeit of books at her disposal, since books had long since been her only comfort, but from the moment Mike O'Roarke met with her to share his conclusions about Harry, she didn't have two hours of uninterrupted time.

"He's a hard man, your husband," Mike said. "Survived a lot."

Kate handed him a glass of Madeira and took up a seat across from him, trying her best to seem calm. She swore she hadn't breathed since she'd been yanked out of Harry's room. "Will he survive this?"

Mike took a contemplative sip. "We're up against two problems. Loss of blood, and fever. He gets past those, he should do fine. We should have already known if he nicked a lung. A kidney might take a bit longer, of course."

Kate understood now why Mudge had needed that chamber pot. "You are a veritable ray of sunshine, Mike."

He shrugged. "You want me to lie?"

"I want you to tell me what to do."

So he did. And for the next three days, Kate did it. When Harry's fever rose, she dosed him with willow bark and lashings of barley water. When that didn't bring the fever down, she bathed him with cool water. When he became delirious and tried to get up to find his men, she and Mudge talked him through it. And when he managed to get past them and fall, reopening his wound, Kate helped Mike sew it back up.

Bea stopped in to beg her to sleep. Drake demanded she look for the poem. Cook pleaded for her to eat the fortifying soups and delicate pastries he sent up to her. And Harry demanded that she leave him alone.

She wished she could. But as odd as it sounded, that wound seemed to tether her to him. She tried to take strolls around the garden and found herself right back upstairs wringing out a rag and wiping the sweat from Harry's body. She urged him to eat and forgot to do it herself. She watched his eyes constantly moving beneath his closed lids as he refought old battles and reclaimed dead comrades, and held his hand as he tossed his way through the night. And when on the third day he woke more clear-eyed, she sparred with him, trying to ignite that devilish spark in his eye, which meant he was stronger.

"What do you mean you've read *Ars Amatoria*?" he demanded, carefully feeding himself some of cook's soup. "Who in the devil allowed you to read Ovid?"

She hooted as she wandered the room straightening up. "Don't be silly, Harry. I think Ovid should be mandatory reading for every girl. Not only does he reveal all a man's secrets of seduction, but he teaches her to enjoy her life. 'Have fun while it's allowed, while your years are in their prime.' Sounds like good advice to me."

Harry scowled, but Kate finally saw humor. "Sounds like trouble to me," he said. "Men have little enough ad-

vantage in this world. We don't need Ovid
playing field."

For a moment Kate almost cursed at him. Little advantage? Was he mad? They had all the advantage. Just in time she saw the teasing light in his eyes. "Poor men," she scoffed. "Nothing to their credit but law and property and strength and arms. Women, on the other hand, have intelligence, wile, and breasts." Grinning, she looked down. "For some reason, breasts carry disproportionate weight in balance."

Harry closed his eyes on a groan. "Not fair," he protested. "Not when I'm debilitated."

Debilitated, she thought, almost snorting out loud. How could a debilitated man look so compelling? Even pale and bristly, he was all hard angles and power, his bare arms rippling with every movement, his belly flat and his taut chest dusted in golden hair. The bandage didn't detract from his power or his scars from his beauty.

It wasn't fair. She was trying so hard to protect herself. And yet her body positively ached for his. Even as she wandered his room as if not even noticing his naked chest, her heart was picking up speed and her eyes kept straying. She wanted to tangle her fingers in his tousled hair, wrap her legs around his, and lay her head against his chest. She wanted...she wanted *more*, and she didn't know how to ask for it. She, the notorious Lady Kate, didn't know how to ask her husband to bed her. Ovid would say to use all of a woman's arts, looks and voice and coy flirting.

"On the other hand," she continued briskly as she straightened Harry's dresser, "Ovid gives over two sections to instruct men and only one for women. Does he seek to keep the advantage, or think we don't need as much instruction?"

Harry chuckled. "I'm sure each of us will have a different opinion on that. What made you think of Ovid anyway? It certainly can't be my recent amatory feats."

"I was searching the library for the poem those verses come from."

"You haven't found anything?"

"Not yet. I have another section left after you finish your meal. Finney and Mudge are pulling all the books for me now. Again. The staff have worked very hard."

"Your library is extensive," he admitted, casting her a sly glance. "For a woman."

She tossed at towel at him. He caught it midair and grunted with pain.

"Don't think I'm going to apologize," she said, even though she knew he could see the worry in her eyes. "You deserved that."

"Were you the one who gave Mudge *Vindication of the Rights of Woman*?"

She grinned. "He's a very bright boy. And it's a very small book."

Harry harrumphed. "Small in size, oversize in ideas."

"You don't like it?"

He tilted his head. "This is a test, isn't it?"

"Yes. I consider Mary Wollstonecraft a genius."

He scowled. "So does my mother. She made all of us read it." A corner of his mouth quirked. "Although she does part ways with Wollstonecraft over the woman's rather colorful life."

"Geniuses are allowed to be different," Kate stated grandly.

"If you say so." He scowled down at his empty bowl. "This mortal is just hoping to attain a regular diet again. I need a nice juicy beefsteak."

Kate came over to retrieve the tray. "Maybe tomorrow."

Before she could leave, Harry grabbed her wrist. "Sleep with me tonight."

Kate froze, her hands full of tray. "I don't know if it's a good idea."

His eyes were so blue, so intense. She could drown in those eyes.

"I miss you," he said softly. "You quiet the nightmares."

If she were intelligent, she would take a figurative step back and refuse. One look at the real need in his eyes undermined her resolve. Worse, it seemed to prompt her to take an unforgivable step forward. "On one condition."

No, don't. It will hurt so much worse when he leaves again.

"Anything."

She looked away, her heart suddenly racing. "When you're...stronger," she said in an unforgivably hesitant voice, "you must stop avoiding your duty and...and *finish*."

Harry went dead quiet. Kate swore he had to hear her heart; it was thundering so loudly in her chest, she thought it would simply tumble out. She wasn't sure she was breathing. She didn't know what she wanted him to say. Now that she'd blurted that out, she wasn't sure anymore what she wanted. She thought of the exquisite joy she felt in Harry's arms; but the fear always lay in wait, lurking just out of sight until he made one wrong move, shattering the joy and freezing her mind.

"Are you certain?" he finally asked, his hand tighter on her wrist.

She couldn't help laughing. "I don't think I'm certain of anything anymore. But I'm going mad with waiting. The specter of it grows impossibly larger, but at the same time the frustration over not...doing it is driving me mad. I want to know if I can manage it, Harry. I *want* what you promised me ten years ago."

She was stunned to see him close his eyes.

"Harry?"

"I'm not sure I can remain in control," he said, eyes opening to reveal a heat that threatened to scorch Kate right there. "I've tried my best to be gentle, to be patient. But..." He shrugged. "I have a feeling that our joining will be cataclysmic."

She shuddered at the impact of those words. "Will you promise not to beat me?"

Harry dropped his hand, looked stunned. "Good God, what do you think I am?"

She wouldn't relent. "On your honor. No riding crops or fists or feet. No..." She swallowed. "Ropes."

Harry's mouth dropped. Then, once again claiming hold of her, he took in a shaky breath. "One day," he said, "I hope I can show you how pleasurable it can be to give up control to your partner. As I've promised before, though, on my honor, not till you're ready. And it will never...*ever*...involve riding crops, fists, feet, or ropes."

A sudden shock of lightning arced between them, just with his words. Kate felt her breasts tighten and her knees weaken. "And you'll show me about...?"

Harry's smile was immediate and delighted. "It would be my great privilege and pleasure to continue showing you just how beautiful and responsive your body is." Lifting her hand, he kissed it, almost bumping his nose on the tray. "Especially," he added, "when stroked by a tongue."

*   *   *

In the end, Harry took his cue from Ovid. After all, the translation of *Ars Amatoria* was "the art of love." Art, indeed.

One phrase kept repeating itself. *There's a thousand ways to do it.* He just had to think of one that wouldn't terrify Kate into flight. Kate feared domination and pain. That just left it for Harry to let Kate be the one to dominate.

"You want me to what?" she asked when the time came.

It had begun innocently enough. She had all but finished scouring the library that day, and come to bed frustrated and anxious. Harry had taken the precaution of taking a leisurely bath, washing away the last traces of injury and illness so that Kate wouldn't hesitate. He didn't worry about performing. Just sitting in the tub planning the night ahead, he'd had an erection that threatened his returning blood supply.

But he wanted it to be as perfect as he was capable for his brave girl. She had been through so much: first her home, and then her husband. And briefly, in between, a callow boy who'd considered himself far more sophisticated than he'd actually been, who might have hurt her worst of all. That boy owed her joy. He owed her pleasure. She needed to know that every man wasn't Murther.

So he welcomed her into bed with open arms, and she snuggled against him. He was already hard enough when her knee slid onto his thigh. Then his cock reared, ready and throbbing. Praying for the control to make the experience beautiful for her, he began to stroke her. Her skin was so soft, her hair as sensuous as silk, even contained in the braid she wore, as if any man would be put off by it. He immediately pulled it loose and winnowed his fingers through the sweet-smelling strands.

"Where do you get your perfume?" he asked. "It smells like tropical islands."

She lifted her head to kiss his throat. "Floris. Do you like it? It's my special soap."

He lifted her hair to his nose and inhaled. "I would recognize you in the dark."

Tropical islands, lush rain forests, exotic Indian havelis intricately painted in hot colors, the floors piled with brilliant silk pillows, the white muslin curtains wafting in an evening breeze. He'd have to take her there someday so she could share it all.

"I like your scent, too," she assured him, fanning her fingers across his chest and sending lightning shooting through him.

He growled into her hair. "I don't wear a scent."

"Oh, yes you do." As if to illustrate, she buried her nose into his neck and inhaled, which did further damage to Harry's control. "Horses and fresh air and...and...*man.*"

He'd found her breast; round, firm, pert, filling his hand and more, all but daring him to take it in his mouth. He couldn't get enough of the weight of it in his hand.

"I'd better not smell like that. I just took an inordinate amount of time in the bath."

He could feel her smile against him. "I know. I think I've been very patient. And you do smell like man. If you didn't, I don't think I would be nearly as anxious."

She was stretching, arching into his hand, the whisper of silk she wore as a night rail slithering up and down her generous curves. It was a delicious feel. The first thing he did was pull it off over her head.

"Oh, good," she whispered with a giggle. "Now you."

"No—" But he never finished. Her delicate fingers were at the drawstrings of his unmentionables, with predictable results. He felt a sheen of sweat cover his chest, the night air an erotic kiss against it.

He lifted her mouth to his. "Open for me, Kate," he whispered, taut as a bowstring. "Welcome me."

She was trembling; her eyes were huge, the pupils as black as night. Harry couldn't look away. He loved those eyes. He loved the whimsy he saw there, the fierce intelligence, the fiercer indomitability, the sly humor. Kate's eyes were a symphony of seduction all unto themselves, cat green with flecks of yellow so that it seemed they glowed otherworldly in the shadows. He couldn't resist them.

Even so, he kissed them closed and then kissed her mouth open, tilting his head so that they fit together as perfectly as their bodies. Sipping, nipping, nibbling her plump lower lip, tracing the sweet sweep of her upper lip, he sank into the comfort of her mouth like a sybarite settling into a harem. She tasted of wine and honey and Kate, and he sated himself on her.

As he kissed, he caressed, memorizing her plump breasts, her long, taut nipples that responded so quickly to his eager fingers. He swept in to her waist and dipped his finger into the sweet little dimple of her navel. He spanned her hips and cupped the lush globes of her bottom, pulling her full against his side. Close, but not connected yet. Not fully flush against the aching prod of his arousal.

She was hot, damp, nubile, more seductive than the cleverest houri, and he wasn't sure how much longer he could hold out. He kept hearing her taunt in his head. *Finish.* Oh, God, did he want to finish. He kept imagining himself sheathed in her, deep and tight and wet, her head thrown back so he could see the moonlight wash down the arch of her throat, so he could take one of those straining breasts in his mouth and suckle so hard she shrieked in pleasure.

He was panting, his body screaming for release. He was desperate to press himself against her, for his cock to acquaint itself with her contours. To torment himself with the rasp of those delicious curls that veiled the ultimate prize. He was shaking as he struggled to remain in control. *Finish.* He couldn't agree more.

"Please," she panted, undulating like a nautch girl against him. "Please…"

He took that as a command and nudged her knees apart, tracing the sleek line of her leg from calf to knee to soft white thigh, all the while knowing that her breaths were becoming as short and ragged as his. He swore he could already feel her juices on his fingers long before he slipped inside of her. Ah, there, hot as fire, slick as sin, already trembling with arousal. And her clitoris, that deliciously responsive bud that felt like hot satin against his fingers. Relentlessly he circled it with the pad of his thumb, his fingers deep inside of her, inciting her to explosion, the sharp scent of her arousal rising like smoke between them. She was gasping and whimpering, her body in constant motion, her hands frantically mapping his body, until she finally laid claim to his cock.

His instinct was to rise, to shove her knees wide and plunge deep, to pull a climax from her, mouth-to-mouth, chest-to-chest, taking her like a marauding berserker until he exploded into her, planting his seed so deep that none other could claim her.

It took every ounce of control he'd ever known, more energy than he thought he yet had, and the will to ignore the shafts of pain that had begun to gather at his back, but he held back, claiming her only with his mouth, plunging his tongue deep, sucking hers into his mouth where he tormented it, stoking her with his fingers, with his body, with words that seemed to pour out of him in between kisses.

"Yes, sweetheart, yes, come on, you're almost there, enjoy it, take it, take it now…" His voice was a counterpart to her growing cries, the contractions that were beginning to sweep through her muscles, the trembling heat of her skin. "Come on."

"Harry, *please*," she begged, all but bowed right out of his arms. "Finish this."

He should have waited. She should feel her own satisfaction first. But maybe if she was this distracted, she wouldn't let the fear find her.

"I can't move," he panted, his own body screaming in protest. "I can't support myself, Kate. I want you to climb on top."

She almost seized to a complete stop. "You want me to *what*?"

He grinned, his hands already on her hips. "It's easy. And, I understand, quite fun."

Before she could think to protest, he easily lifted her, hoping she didn't call out his lie about weakness. "Take me in your hands, Kate," he panted. "Guide me."

If there was one thing he could say about his Kate, she was quick to learn. "Like this?" she asked, wrapping her fingers around him and positioning him at her entrance.

"God yes." He could barely breathe. "Now ride me."

"Wha—?"

Before she could get the words out, he grabbed her hips and pulled her down. He almost came right then. Every muscle in his body seized with the sudden heat of her capturing him. His cock shuddered and filled. He swore he almost passed out from pleasure. And then he looked up to see the astonishment in her eyes.

"Ride," he instructed. "Just like a horse."

She dipped her head, briefly catching his gaze as if she was still too uncertain to share the sensations that were obviously set loose in her body. Harry thought he saw tears glint in her eyes before she dropped her head and let her hair brush against his chest. He wasn't going to be able to take much more.

"Kate," he begged. "Please."

And then he saw it: that smile. Surprised, delighted, bemused, as if she'd never experienced anything like it before. Which, Harry realized, she hadn't. Wonder appeared and grew, like a fire that spread inside her, and suddenly she began to move. Tentatively at first, her hands balanced on his chest. Back and forth, measuring him inside of her, testing the pleasure of friction. Gaining confidence, her movements evening out, until Harry thought he would just die right there of the pleasure. Finally she looked up, met his eyes with a rapturous smile.

"Would you like to taste my breasts?" she asked, her eyes coy and mischievous.

She didn't even wait for his answer, just leaned forward until the long tip of her nipple settled right against Harry's mouth. He wrapped his hands around her shoulders and brought her closer. And as he began to move in rhythm with her, he suckled, deep and long, pleasuring her with his tongue as she pleasured him with her gathering cries and the contractions that were even now beginning to squeeze his cock into oblivion.

"Oh, Harry," she whimpered, pulling her breast free only to replace it with her own mouth, so Harry could taste her excitement, her amazement, her pleasure.

He held out just long enough, just until she threw her head back, the moonlight washing down her neck, and cried out again and again, shuddering around him, flying apart, her eyes wide to the night, her voice astonished and laughing. She had barely begun to relax when Harry followed, his body disintegrating in mindless pleasure, pumping into her, against the very edge of her womb, emptying himself until there was nothing left, nothing. Not energy or frustration or hunger. And for a very long time, he lay there, still inside of her, with Kate resting against his chest and his arms around her so that he could feel her heartbeat ease against his.

"So *that*," she murmured, "is what all the fuss is about."

He wanted to tell her how sorry he was that it had taken so long to get to this point, but he didn't want to spoil this perfect moment of communion. He wanted to tell her that the mature Kate was infinitely more compelling than the fifteen-year-old Kate, vastly more complex and fascinating, so brave that she humbled him. He wanted to tell her that he would stay in England just for her and raise tulips. He didn't know, though, whether he could. He didn't even know whether that was what she wanted. And after what she'd been through, she deserved to have what she wanted. So he held her quietly, tucked next to his heart, her head against his shoulder, and he listened to her breathe.

"Where do we go from here?" she asked, proving herself more courageous than he.

"Where do you want to go?"

She chuckled, and he felt it in his chest. "I want to do that again."

He smiled. His cock was already signaling its enthusiastic agreement. "Would you like to try it in a chair?"

She lifted her head, her eyes wide. "Really?"

He smiled and reached up to brush her hair back. "Aren't you the one who read *Ars Amatoria*? 'There's a thousand ways to do it.'"

Her eyes grew even wider, and once again she was that young girl, poised on the brink of discovery. "Is that what he meant? Good heavens."

Harry couldn't help laughing. "Just wait till I show you some of the books I brought back from India."

They made love three more times that night, once in a chair, once on the rug, and once in the bath. Harry felt triumphant; he felt thankful. Mostly, he felt tender for his wife, who, after suffering the kind of abuse that could have crippled her forever, had finally learned what pleasure there was between a man and a woman. She was coming, he thought, to trust him. It wasn't everything, Harry knew. But it was finally a beginning, and he wanted to spend every minute with her discovering together what could lie ahead.

Just before dawn came, Kate confirmed her growing trust by letting him blow out the candles. As the last darkness of night slipped into the bedroom, Kate, nestled against Harry's chest, whispered, "I love you." Harry, more stunned than he wanted to admit, fell asleep wondering how he should respond.

*   *   *

Kate never slept that night. Not after she gathered up her courage, there in the darkness and spoke. Harry had given her a miracle; she could at least have the courage to give him the truth.

"I love you," she'd whispered.

She pretended that the reason he didn't answer was that he'd fallen asleep before she'd spoken. She knew, though, that it wasn't true. She'd felt the instinctive stiffening of Harry's body at her words. She could only imagine what he was thinking. *Good Lord. Give a girl a good rogering and she thinks you're devoted for life.*

She should have known better. If Harry hadn't loved her enough ten years ago to challenge her father, how could he

suddenly love her more now? He was kind and pa——
more generous than Kate could have imagined. He had freed her from one of her worst prisons, and she would always love him for that. It didn't mean he suddenly wanted to put his slippers by the Eastcourt hearth.

She basked in the sweet afterglow of pleasure that hummed through her body. She cherished the memories Harry had given her to supplant the old; exquisitely tender caresses, luscious kisses, the stunning sense of fullness. Not pain, but possession, passion, wide-eyed wonder. She wanted to sing, to spin around with the sheer joy of freedom. It truly had been lovemaking, even if Harry wasn't *in* love with her.

For now, it was enough. It had to be. After what Harry had given her, the least she could do was give him his freedom. She could step back as he walked those long, silent miles he thought would banish his nightmares. But she would always wish he had chosen her instead.

When Harry slipped out of bed the next morning, Kate savored the beauty of his strong, sleek body. She allowed herself to remember the feel of it in her hands, between her thighs, inside of her. She spent a few moments battling tears, furious with herself that she was suddenly having trouble controlling her emotions. And then, because she didn't know how else to manage, she got up and began her day.

Her first step was to don her brightest day dress, a wonderfully flowy poppy red sarcenet with gold embroidering. Then, after sending Harry off on his mission to return her uncle's boxes, she breakfasted with Bea and returned to the library to check the last of the books for the verse.

It took no more than an hour to admit defeat. "Not here," she said, plumping down on a chair, William Blake's *Songs of Innocence* in her hand. "What next?"

Bea looked up from perusing Shakespeare's sonnets. "Hatchards."

Kate sighed. "I can't believe Hatchards has any book I don't." She nodded to include the room. "These are the poets I read."

"Always?"

"Of..." Kate looked up, startled by a new thought. She looked around, but she was no longer seeing this library. She was thinking back. "These are the poets I collected over the last five years," she mused. "But before that..."

She closed her eyes to better call up her memories. Oddly, that was what did it. The dark. She saw it, suddenly, as clearly as if she'd just set it down, hidden away in a little niche she'd fashioned in the corner of the priest hole, her purloined candle probably still tucked in beside it.

"I know," she said, stunned. She should have known all along. She should have recognized those words. "I know where it is."

Bea didn't seem surprised. "Moorhaven?"

Kate nodded, still back in the dark, tucked over her purloined treasure. She had felt such a rebel, keeping such forbidden fruit in her cell. Could the book still be there? Surely other children had found her niche.

"I used to sneak books into the priest hole," she told Bea. "I found this one way up on the shelves tucked behind...oh, Gassendi's *Life of Epicurus*." She chuckled. "Nobody read Latin history but me, which was why I guess somebody thought it was safe there. It was a book of poetry by one of my ancestors, all bound in very pretty maroon leather with gold embossing. William Marshall Hilliard. There were three copies tucked up where they would be out of sight of women and children."

"Radical?"

"Heavens, no. Lewd. Let me think. " She tilted her head, trying to recall the forbidden text. "It was titled something like *Virtue's Grave*, after a line in a Marvell poem. I think the Marvell line was, 'Seest that unfrequented cave? That den? Love's shrine. Virtue's grave.' Very wicked stuff for a thirteen-year-old girl. Execrable poetry, but very titillating." She grinned. "My ancestor's. Not Marvell's. His was marvelous *and* titillating."

"Meaning?"

"Now?" Kate shook her head. "I don't know." For a moment, she sat still, memories crowding her, the attar of fear and loss, daring and secret triumph. That book had helped liberate her. It had been her testament to survival, her proof that no matter what was done to her, she could still win. "I can't think the book exists anywhere else, except in a Hilliard domain. Uncle Hilliard must have found it. As obscure as it is, it's probably the perfect code template."

"Arcane," Bea said.

"Exactly. Who else is going to recognize it but another Hilliard so bored she's read every book in the library? And there simply weren't that many Hilliards who fit the description."

"Town crier?"

"Well, we'll need to share the news, certainly. We need Diccan to look for a copy down at his estate. I might as well go tell him. Harry won't miss me."

Kate must have given something away. Bea quirked an eyebrow. "Falling-out?"

Kate blinked. "With whom? Harry? Heavens no. Blissfully contented."

Bea snorted like a horse. Kate got to her feet and replaced *Songs of Innocence*. Didn't it just figure? She wouldn't get back to Eastcourt anytime soon, but she would probably end up back at Moorhaven, the last place on earth she wanted to be.

That was when it struck her. If she was right, if this was, indeed, the answer to their puzzle, then the investigation was over. The verse they'd been looking for was found, which mean that the Lions would have no more reason to kill her. She would be safe. And Harry would be free to go.

She couldn't move. She squeezed her eyes shut, a hand up to her chest, as if she could ease the anguish that sheared through her. He *couldn't* go. Not yet. She'd just found him. She loved him. She needed him.

It changed nothing. He needed to go, and she had no right to stop him. It would be unfair, and she simply couldn't do that to him. But oh, suddenly she wasn't so sure she would survive this.

"Kate?" Bea's voice sounded small and anxious.

Kate shook her head and opened her eyes. Bea needed a smile, so she gave her one. "I'm giving thanks," she said. "I believe we're finally getting the house back to ourselves."

Her house that would suddenly seem empty. Oh, why had she insisted on making love? It was making everything so much worse.

With an impatient shake of her head, she stalked over to her desk. She had just addressed a note to Drake when the front door slammed and she heard raised voices that sounded suspiciously like Braxton and Chuffy.

"Give me some help with your master!" Kit bellowed.

Kate was up and running for the door. "Deuce take it," she snapped, wishing she didn't sound so frightened. "Now what?"

Chapter 22

By the time she could talk to anyone about her discovery, two hours had passed, and Mike O'Roarke was back in Harry's bedroom.

"What do you mean he fell off his horse?" Kate demanded of Kit. "Harry rides better than Grace."

It was Harry who answered, his voice faint as Mike prodded his chest. "It's nothing. Something spooked Beau."

Kit snorted. "That horse went mad, right in the middle of Hyde Park. Knocked Harry against a tree."

Kate took to rubbing her forehead. From the looks of Harry when he'd been carried him up the stairs, he was going to be confined to that room for a good few days. Which meant that she didn't dare tell him about her discovery. If it turned out that the only copy left of *Virtue's Grave* was locked in that priest hole, she was the only one left who knew how to find it. And Harry would climb back on that blasted horse and ride for Hampshire before he'd let her go.

Just the idea terrified her.

An hour later, Mike verified her conclusion. "He's broken at least two ribs, besides undoing all my good work, and he has a concussion for himself. He's to go nowhere for at least a week."

Kate's only option was to send for Drake, who arrived far too quickly.

"Explain," he said when she walked into her Chinese salon to find him pacing.

"Which?" she said. "Harry's continuing bad luck, or my inspiration?"

"I already found out about Harry. Someone inserted a large needle beneath his saddle, probably in the park. What about the verse?"

But Kate was distracted by the idea that someone had sabotaged Harry's horse. "Why him?" she demanded, already headed for the door. "I'm the one they're after!"

Drake caught her and redirected her to the couch. "And Harry is protecting you. Divide and conquer was old before the Romans. Now please. Tell me of the verse."

She sat down, still distracted. What a good idea that she had decided to distance herself from Harry, she thought sourly. Otherwise she'd be frantic over his continuing danger. She would be preoccupied and panicky and plagued with a racing heart.

"Kate?"

She looked up, startled, to find her hand pressing against her racing heart. "Oh. Yes." Quickly she explained about *Virtue's Grave*. Drake listened without expression, his eyes focused on the fireplace until she'd finished.

"You're sure this is where the verses have come from."

She nodded. "I can't believe I didn't recognize them right away. The line was misspoken on the flask, you know. There it says, 'Is not the fruit sweet, my first love?' The real poem reads, 'Is not the *first* fruit sweet, my love?' I'd think it was a mistake, but the second quote is wrong, too. 'Not all of me shall die' is actually 'Not a bit of me shall die.' I can't remember the reference." She grinned. "Only the more suggestive couplets. The flask quote, by the way, is taken from one of my favorite couplets. 'Is not the first fruit sweet, my love, when plucked by my own hand.'"

"And you think your uncle the bishop had been using it to come up with these signals."

Kate shrugged. "Seems awfully coincidental otherwise. The book was in his childhood home, and I sincerely doubt many other people know about it."

Drake sighed. "I'll tell Diccan to look. You didn't see it, obviously, in the things you went through."

Kate shook her head. "Trust me. I would have remembered."

"I don't suppose it could still be at Moorhaven. If Diccan doesn't find it with his father's things..."

"Unless Glynis redecorated the priest hole, I'd say it's a good chance." Kate did her best to seem unaffected. "I get to attend my niece's engagement weekend at Moorhaven Castle after all. Glynis will be so pleased."

Drake reached for her hand. "We'll do everything we can to protect you, Kate."

She looked up with a smile. He couldn't protect her from her own nightmares. "Don't worry. I'll manage. Just keep Harry out of it. He isn't up to it right now."

Drake squeezed her fingers. "We'll do our best." He'd just stood to leave when he smiled. "One bit of good news for you. Lady Riordan is safe."

Kate's head snapped up. "Where?"

He shook his head. "Safe. She thanks you with all her heart. We do, too."

"How did you get her out without them knowing?"

He looked far less sanguine. "Someone took her place."

Kate felt her heart slide into her shoes. She had a terrible feeling she knew who it was. Lady Riordan was buxom and blond. "Then we must be quick about recovering that book. Were any of the other wives there? The ones assumed dead?"

For a second, he looked off, his expression flat. "One. All perfectly legal. The administrator says that the Tudor rose they use comes from the family who first owned the house. It means nothing."

"You don't believe that."

"No. But powerful people are involved in that place. We have to step carefully."

Kate's laugh was hollow. "How nice that they have a place to hide their inconvenient women. Cowards."

In the end, Kate was glad she'd spent so much of her life dissembling. It helped protect her new secret from Harry, and mask her renewed fear at his injuries.

"You have fallen into some bad habits, Harry," she said as she considered the fresh bruising on his scowling face. "Am I going to have to provide you a nanny?"

"I've been trying to tell these *women* to give me my pants back," he snarled, his focus on Chuffy and Kit, who lounged by the window sharing Harry's brandy.

"Be happy to," Chuffy assured him. "Soon as you can stand up to put them on."

Kate ended the argument by retrieving the pants from where they were slung over an Adam chair. "No, it's back to being a man of leisure for you, my lad."

At least Dr. O'Roarke prescribed beefsteaks to eat, although even they didn't improve Harry's mood. Undoubtedly, Kate thought, because he was still incarcerated in his own home, where he couldn't avoid his wife.

How could she allow that to hurt so much? She was

stronger than that. She had survived too much to let a fleeting bit of happiness bring her low. So she pretended she was unaffected, and chatted with Harry's friends until Mudge returned with a meal.

How could he tolerate it, she wondered, being so close to Harry all the time and knowing that it was pointless? How could he torment himself like that, day after day, year after year, knowing how hopeless it was?

She couldn't do it. She *wouldn't*. And yet when Harry offered a reluctant invitation to dine, she accepted and spent the next hour torturing herself with his company.

The irony became unbearable when later she stopped by to make sure he was settled for the night. He caught hold of her hand, his expression regretful.

"You didn't sign on to be my batman," he said. "I'm sorry."

"I signed on to be your wife," she answered, "which includes all manner of jobs."

"You're all right?"

She couldn't help it: She looked into his eyes for some hidden meaning. But he seemed to be merely considerate. "A bit tired of starts and alarms," she admitted, shrugging. "But that isn't something I anticipate lasting overlong. Get some sleep."

Still he seemed unable to let go of her hand. Again she held her breath, wondering if he would make a declaration. He made a declaration; just not the one she'd hoped for.

"I sold my commission today," he said.

She blinked. *Here it comes*, she thought. *He's about to tell me that as soon as he's able, off to Istanbul he goes.* "What about Mudge? Isn't he still in the army as well?"

Harry's smile was gentle. "I've arranged for him to do whatever he wishes. He's certainly earned it, don't you think?"

She could see now the mistake she'd made. She had hoped that Harry had been so generous and devoted to her because he might be coming to love her. The truth was that he was just a generous man. She felt like weeping.

"I don't think he belongs in the army," she said instead.

"I agree with you. Men like Mudge don't fare well among the troops."

She quirked an eyebrow. "You know, of course."

But did he know that he was the one Mudge loved?

"It's why I brought him off the line. Mudge is a good lad. Not his fault he..."

"Loves a man."

Harry cocked his head, his expression complacent. He didn't know, then. Poor Mudge. Poor both of them, waiting for signs from Harry that would never come.

"Harry," she said, looking down to where his square, callused hand held hers with such gentleness. "Drake thinks he's found the poem. He'll fill us in soon. You know what that means."

She looked up, but he didn't answer. His eyes were so vastly dark, she thought. So uncertain, which was unrecognizable on Harry.

She took a steadying breath. "I know you're itching to get out on the road. The minute Drake has his evidence, you and I need to sit down and decide what *we're* going to do."

"What do you—?"

She shook her head. "Not now. We're both exhausted. But I do want you to know that you really did set me free last night. The least I can do is the same for you." Reclaiming her hand, she bent over and kissed him good night.

"Kate—"

But she couldn't bear to turn around. She didn't want him to see her tears.

*   *   *

Harry stared after Kate's departing back, trying to under-stand what had just happened. Had she really told him to leave?

Unable to take his gaze off the connecting door, he thought back over the last few days. He remembered the de-licious hours spent teaching Kate the wonders of her own body, and his own battered body ached with need. He wanted her again. He wanted her constantly. He wanted to help her remember the joys of lovemaking.

But he wasn't just considering lovemaking. If he stayed, he would be resigning himself to his own prison. He would be tying himself to Kate, to Bea and family and Eastcourt and England until he forgot how to dream.

Just the thought sent his stomach lurching. He felt the weight of his future dragging him down, responsibilities set-tling like rocks in his chest. He'd carried those rocks for years, men he'd commanded, enemies he'd killed, lies he'd told, and letters he'd sent to grieving parents. He was so tired of carrying the burden of others.

But Kate would be so much worse. He thought of Lady Bea's analogy about Kate. "Bone fine china." A strong woman with surprising vulnerabilities. A woman just on the threshold of discovery. Did he want that responsibility, too? Bringing her step by step past the violence and neglect that had shaped her? Cushioning her inevitable hurts and protect-ing her from disappointments?

The weight of her was so different: sweeter, sharper, more deadly. She was the weight, not of simple duty, but of need. Of want. She had already begun to settle into his soul. If he let her bind him to her, he would never again be able to ignore her or forget her or put her down like a half-finished book. He would never be his own person again.

But did it have to be like that? Would he really be a prisoner? Couldn't he find real purpose and freedom by her side? He couldn't mistake the fact that Eastcourt was special. When he sat down to study the estate books, he could almost feel the vitality that infused the place. Kate hadn't just recovered it. She had resurrected it and the people. Surely there was a way for him to make his own mark.

Construction. Additions. He could see a series of connected greenhouses in his head, open and airy and impervious to weather. He could see...

Dusty roads. Silence. Peace.

Kate.

She would certainly steal the silence. She had already shattered his peace. But what if he asked her to walk those lonely roads with him?

Why hadn't he thought of it before? Would she want to go to India? Or Greece or Ceylon or, maybe one day, Japan, where he'd heard houses were made of paper? Would she give up the home she'd worked so hard to build just to gad about with him? He knew he should have already asked her. He should have answered her declaration of love with the question, "How much?"

She was right, he thought as he closed his eyes. They needed to sit down together and negotiate a future. Give her a couple more days, he thought, settling into sleep. Then he could begin his campaign to find the compromise that could sustain this marriage of two disparate people. He would seduce her, as surely as he had in bed, into dreaming of sailing ships and exotic lands.

*   *   *

Drake returned two days later. Kate made sure Harry was still in bed when he arrived. The last thing she needed was for Harry to find out what she was up to. He would try to follow, and he wasn't physically ready for it yet.

"Breakfast?" she asked as Finney showed Drake in. "I was just about to sit down with Bea."

His eye on Bea, Drake hesitated, his uncertainty easily telegraphed.

"Marcus," Kate admonished. "If you can't trust Bea, you might as well keep secrets from yourself."

With a wry grin, Drake took his seat. Kate waited until he'd made inroads into his shirred eggs before speaking. "Diccan hasn't found the book, has he?"

Drake poured cream into his tea. "He's still looking. If his father had it, he hid it. Not quite the thing to share with one's wife, especially if you're a bishop."

Kate smiled. "The bishop was ever protective of his reputation. Which makes me wonder why he picked that particular book to use as a code."

Drake shrugged. "The rarity, I imagine. He could be fairly certain no one else had a copy but himself."

"There *were* two other copies," Kate reminded him.

"Which makes us more hopeful there is one left for you to retrieve."

She looked down at the eggs and gammon she had automatically piled on her plate and realized that her appetite had fled. She was going to do what she'd once sworn never to do again: She was going to Moorhaven. Ah, how soon vows are forgotten.

"Well," she said, setting her napkin on the table. "I'd better tell Bivens to pack. Isn't it serendipitous that this is the exact weekend Elspeth is to have her party."

Bea mimicked her action. "Duet," she said, her voice flat with intent.

"Oh, no," Kate protested. "I will not ask you to come." She turned to Drake. "Bea makes Glynis uncomfortable. Glynis can't get over the fact that even though Bea is 'unfit for social discourse,' as Glynis puts it, Bea is still sister of a duke. Not to be dismissed lightly in Glynis's very rigid world."

"Come where?" she heard from the doorway, and her heart dropped like a stone.

Harry stood there, tidily dressed in a bottle-green jacket and buff inexpressibles, his newly shaven face folded into angles of protest.

"Good morning, my dear," Kate said. "Finney, another plate, please."

"Damn another plate," Harry retorted, limping in. "You are not going to Moorhaven. I won't allow it."

Bea let go an inelegant snort. Drake focused on his cup. Kate battled a surge of resentment at Harry's presumptive tone. "We're merely discussing options. Let Marcus tell you about it. In the meantime, Bea and I have some work that needs finishing."

"You're not going to get around me this way, Kate. The answer is no."

"I'm the logical one to retrieve it," she said. "Especially if it's in the priest hole."

"No. I'll be the one breaking into Moorhaven." His argument might have carried more weight if he didn't still look as if he were breathing through ground glass.

"And if you're caught in the library at midnight, what will your excuse be?"

"I won't be caught."

She kept her opinion to herself. "How will you find the priest hole?"

"You'll tell me where it is, of course."

"It's on the wall that backs the rose salon. You press a piece of bookshelf."

"Which one? And which wall is against the rose salon?"

She shrugged. "I'm not perfectly sure. I was never good with directions, especially for a place I didn't want to go. I hope Glynis hasn't redecorated since I was last there."

"And you were planning to just keep searching until someone caught you?"

"At least I have a reason to be sneaking around the castle at odd hours. I used to live there. I can wax nostalgic."

*   *   *

In the end, Kate resorted to lies and laudanum. She drove out in the phaeton with Bea, ostensibly to look at stoves for the orphanage. What Harry didn't know was that George waited around the block to transfer them to the traveling coach. With the laudanum Finney was to slip into Harry's lunch tea, Kate hoped that it would be four o'clock before Harry wondered where she was, and by then she would be well on her way to Moorhaven. She even left a note.

Harry—You know you shouldn't be risking further injury. The worst injury I can suffer is to my pride, and it's survived far worse than Glynis. George, Thrasher, and Bea will be with me, and Drake follows to wait close by. I'll be home in three days at the latest. Please. Rest.

P.S. Don't sack Finney. It was my idea.

Chapter 23

It was precisely teatime the next afternoon when Kate and Bea pulled through the Moorhaven gates to see the castle rise stark and square-fingered from the chalk downs near Old Winchester Hill. Kate had always wondered at the Hilliards who'd named the place, since there wasn't a moor within a hundred miles. It certainly looked like it belonged on a moor in one of Mrs. Radcliffe's gothic novels, though, gray and square and unpretty. The Hilliards had ever been less interested in garnering their neighbors' envy than their fear.

Inside was another matter, of course. The family tended to fling an inordinate amount of blunt at whatever decorator was in vogue. The last effort Kate remembered was by Robert Adam, with his neoclassical swags and medallions transforming plain square rooms into jewelry boxes. She had no confidence that Glynis had stayed true to the eighteenth-century master, though, which meant that it would be harder to uncover the priest hole. She hadn't lied to Harry. She was abysmal at directions; she could remember a decor, though, and the library wall she wanted had backed the rose room.

Well, Kate thought, gathering her reticule and muff. If nothing else, this little travesty would tell the tale in her marriage. Harry would either be waiting at the house for her to return with the book, or he'd already be on a boat for Ceylon.

"Pull on through to the stables, George," she ordered through the trap as they topped the drive. "I believe I shall make an entrance."

Kate felt all the old pain and regret rise around her like fetid smoke as she looked on the grim face of her old home. She almost expected her father to step out of the great oak door, his white hair gleaming in the afternoon light, his brown eyes soft as sadness.

"You'll never leave me, will you, Bea?" Kate asked on impulse, her gaze on the site of so much grief.

She'd wanted comfort, not honesty. But Bea was honest. "Inevitable."

Kate swung around on her. "Not you, too."

Bea lifted a papery hand to cup Kate's cheek. "Love Harry."

For a second, Kate couldn't speak at all. She could only nod, tears crowding the back of her throat. "Ah, but will he love me?"

Then, before Bea could answer, George opened the door and set down the steps. Gathering her skirts, Kate descended. "The Ladies' Parlor, I think. At this hour, the guests will most certainly be gathered for tea."

Bea chuckled, straightening her elegant cream Cumberland bonnet. "Yoiks and away!" she cried, her favorite expression of engagement. Kate laughed back and squeezed her hand, hoping her voice didn't sound as panicky to Bea as it did to her.

Just as she'd hoped, the day had stayed unseasonably

warm, and the French doors into the salon had been thrown open, the women's voices spilling through making it sound like an aviary. Kate guessed there to be in excess of twenty women in the wide, long room that had always been decorated in hand-painted red poppy wallpaper. Today the sun seemed to reflect off walls of unrelieved gold. As Kate drew closer, she saw that everything was gold: dark gold, light gold, gold brocade, as if the salon had been taken by King Midas. Good heavens. What had Glynis done to the once cheerful haven?

Kate focused on finding her sister-in-law and Elspeth, the only two people whose reactions she cared about. She hoped for happiness from Elspeth, and that Glynis didn't summarily toss her back out on the lawn. From the militant expression on Bea's face, it was obviously a suspicion shared by her friend.

"Ah," Kate caroled as she stepped over the threshold to peel off her gloves, "there she is. Darling Elspeth, I have come, just as requested."

Her arrival was met with stark silence, then cacophony.

"Aunt Kate!" Elspeth squealed, running for her full-tilt. "You came!"

Before the girl cast herself into her arms, Kate had time to take in overdressed blond curls and an overfussy pink dress, obviously chosen by Elspeth's mother.

"Of course I did," she answered, hugging her niece tight. "How could I refuse one of my favorite girls in the world? Good heavens," she said, holding Elspeth back. "Who dressed you, Princess Caroline? Darling girl, you are made for clean lines and elegant colors, especially now that you are to be married. You look like a demented baby doll."

Elspeth giggled. Beyond her, Glynis looked as if she'd turned to stone. "You will not use that vile diminutive when addressing your aunt, Elspeth," she snapped, her jaw clamped tight. "It makes her sound like an Irish washerwoman. She is Your Grace."

Kate grinned. "Actually, no, Glynis. Remember? I've rectified that mistake."

"Really, Dolores Catherine," Glynis protested. "In front of your husband's sister."

Unbuttoning her scarlet pelisse, Kate laughed. "Don't be silly. Bea knows better than anyone what a paragon her brother was. Don't you, Bea?"

Bea made a rude noise, which delighted Elspeth even more than Kate. "Sodom and Gomorrah," Bea pronounced.

"Actually," Kate mused, "that might have been the only vice Murther failed to practice."

"Innocent ears," Glynis snapped.

"Don't be silly," Kate said. "Elspeth is getting married. She should be prepared."

"That is for her father and me to teach her."

"Let me have Wiggins prepare some rooms," Elspeth begged.

Kate looked up from where she was helping Bea. "Let's see how things go, sweets. I know Bea would love some tea, though. Wouldn't you, my dear?"

Since Elspeth was far more the lady than her mother, she immediately saw Kate and Bea to chairs, making introductions as she went around. Kate could tell which friends belonged to Elspeth and which to her mother just by the reactions, which varied from delighted to frigid.

"My, Glynis," Kate said, accepting her Spode cup. "You've redecorated."

"I have redone all the rooms," Glynis informed her. "They were sadly out of date."

"Yes, Harry did tell me that Livingston House is now

all over crocodiles. Harry has a particular loathing for the things, as one bit off the leg of a friend."

Kate had cornered Elspeth and was reimagining her wardrobe when Bea suddenly set down her cup. "River Jordan."

As they'd planned, Kate followed suit and stood. "Of course, dear. I'll show you."

"To the River Jordan?" the pinch-faced Lady Bromwell asked, eyebrows raised.

Kate smiled. "The necessity. Bea never wastes her breath on the obvious."

"I had heard she was an idiot," Lady Bromwell whispered to the next matron.

Slowly turning, Kate leveled quite her most glacial duchess stare on the woman and was pleased to see her pale. "No, dear, I would have to say that the only idiot in this room is the one who finds herself unable to control a viperish tongue."

"Indeed," Elspeth said, jumping to her feet to her mother's obvious dismay. "I've heard the story of how Lady Bea suffered her injury. She is a *heroine*. Isn't she, Aunt Kate?"

Kate silently apologized to Bea, who loathed such notoriety. "Indeed she is. Unfortunately, that has left her prey to the snubs from all manner of ill-bred persons. Being the daughter of a duke, she is far too high-minded to retaliate. Being the daughter *and* wife of a duke myself, though," Kate continued, "I have no qualms at all about chastising the mere daughter of a…what are you, dear? Oh, that's right. A jumped-up shopkeeper. Come, Bea," she said, taking her friend's hand. "I need a bit of fresh air. Glynis, you haven't turned the necessity into a billiards room or anything, have you?"

The plan was for Kate to use the time Bea took in the necessity to scour the library for the book. When she found it, she was to leave it tucked beneath the great Bellange desk, where Bea would retrieve it. No one would ever suspect Bea of theft, especially a book full of badly written erotic poetry. But Kate wasn't at all convinced that Glynis wouldn't search her luggage for stolen bibelots.

In the end, all that effort was for naught. For the first time in Kate's life, somebody was actually using the library. She stumbled over Elspeth's fiancé, Adam, sitting in a leather chair with his nose in a book. As much as Kate resented it, she would have to stay overnight.

                    *   *   *

The stay at Moorhaven was as nightmarish as Kate had feared. When Edwin discovered her in his parlor, he looked as if he might suffer an apoplexy. Just as Kate had known, though, there was nothing he and Glynis could do but include Kate and Bea in the festivities, which consisted of a paralyzingly formal dinner followed by three painful hours of musical offerings by various daughters in the party.

Just when Kate thought she would have to resort to throwing vases to bring an end to the evening, Elspeth did it much more tactfully by begging the chance to accompany Bea on the piano. Jaws dropped just at the suggestion. They didn't close for a good hour after Bea's spectacular rendition of "Dido's Lament" by Purcell. Since it was impossible to follow, the party broke up.

Bea went to bed, exhausted by her performance. It was just as well. It would have been difficult to explain the old woman's presence downstairs in the wee hours of the morning. Changed into a royal blue kerseymere dress for warmth,

Kate waited in her grim, pea-green guest room for the men to retire. The house settled. When the old long-case clock at the bottom of the staircase chimed twice, Kate stepped out of her bedroom door.

The house was deeply dark, the shadows held off by a few well-spaced night lanterns. Kate really didn't need light to know her way. She'd snuck through these corridors time out of mind. The library was only three doors past the great staircase on the ground floor. And inside it, the priest hole, waiting her return.

Her very own windowless hell. Would the phantoms that had populated it in her youth still lurk, or would she be able to see how puny those nightmares were compared with real ones?

Of course Glynis had redecorated the adjoining rooms out of recognition. Even the Adam ceilings, so elegant, had been painted to resemble an Egyptian sky. Kate scowled. Couldn't her brother have at least married someone with a modicum of taste?

At least the library was unchanged, four identical walls stacked with books nobody read. She stood in the doorway, her candle holding off the encompassing gloom, struck by the well-remembered scent of leather and paper and glue she had loved and hated so much. Her penance and her salvation all at the same time. If she looked closely enough, she swore she would be able to see a painfully neat little girl bent over a book in some dim corner, her store of half-burnt candles still secreted behind the travel section.

Taking a steadying breath, Kate oriented herself. Then, before her courage failed, she made for the rolling ladder and positioned it, praying that an extra copy still lurked behind the *Epicurus*. Setting down her candle, she climbed.

The *Epicurus* was where she remembered, second shelf

from the top, halfway down the wall. But the space behind it was empty. Uncle Hilliard must have made off with it.

Ah well, she thought, resting her head on the ladder. She'd have to see if the copy she'd snuck away was still in the priest hole.

It took her almost an hour to find the hidden door. By then her palms were sweating and her heart racing. How did one search for hell without resenting it?

And then, *click!*, and the wall parted. A fog of dust and damp wafted out, turning her stomach. God, she hated that smell. Praying that she wouldn't actually become ill, she pulled open the door and bent to pass through, her candle leaping erratically. Light licked along the wall, a sluggish pale snake slithering over uneven stone. Kate wiped perspiration from her brow. She held her breath. It was better than inhaling a decade of must and memories.

Setting down her candle, she ran her hands over the cool stone until one felt familiar. She pulled. It rasped, but moved. Her poor heart was battering at her ribs, ready to fly faster than she. This was too familiar, each action calling up a host of memories.

Finally, though, it slid free. And there, tucked behind the stone, a little tin box that held candle stubs and a flint, and next to it, a small stack of books. *Tom Jones*, Pliny's *Natural History*, and there, *Virtue's Grave*. She smiled. She'd forgotten the subtitle: *Worshiping at the Altar of Hymen*. She hadn't even understood most of the allusions; she'd just known they had to be sinful.

Flipping open the book, she smiled.

> *Now I laye me on my back,*
> *She sits upon my fayce . . .*

So it really had been that bad. She wished she'd had the chance to challenge her morally rigid uncle with his ownership of it. Grinning at the thought, she nipped out and slid the book beneath the desk for Bea to find. Then she bent back into the hole to retrieve her candle. She was just backing out when a draft of air alerted her.

"Well, well, well, so the rumors were true."

Kate spun around to find Glynis standing just outside the priest hole's door, still dressed for the evening in an ice-blue silk dress, a candle in her hand.

"Good Lord, Glynis," Kate, breathed, hand on chest. "You startled me. If I've upset you, I'm sorry. I was just reacquainting myself with old ghosts."

"I always knew you were unnatural. But I admit I am all wonder at finding you sneaking about my house in the dead of night. Although I thank you for finding the priest hole. We weren't able to."

Kate shrugged, praying Glynis hadn't seen her secure the little book. "I wasn't sure I would be able to, either."

Glynis set her candle on a table. "You've become quite a sneaking creature. I suppose I shouldn't be surprised. Your father warned me years ago how it would be."

The air seemed to disappear. "My father?"

"Of course. I was to marry Edwin. I needed to understand about you."

Kate felt even more confused. Understand *what* about her? "How nice for you. Now if you'll excuse me, I'm going to take my little stash of books to bed for some light reading."

"Did you find it?"

Kate felt the hair rise on the back of her neck. "What?"

"Please don't try my patience. *Virtue's Grave*. You're here because you've recognized the verse."

Suddenly there was a pocket pistol in Glynis's hand. Kate stared at it as if it had just spoken.

Glynis had a gun. *Glynis*. And she wasn't laughing, as if this were all a joke. In fact, she was looking impatient and cold, one eyebrow imperiously quirked.

"You look surprised."

Kate let go a breathy laugh. "I imagine I am." She could understand the bishop participating in a cabal of traitors. But *Glynis*? "Is Edwin…"

"Don't be ridiculous. Edwin sees only what's under his nose. Now, don't waste my time. If you have the book, give it to me." She lifted the pistol until it pointed at Kate's forehead. "The alternative is that I shoot you, take it, and leave you here to rot."

Breathe, Kate, she thought. *Bea will get the book.*

"It seems we're both out of luck," she said, lifting the other two books so Glynis could see the titles. "The book wasn't here."

Glynis frowned. "I don't believe you. If you give it up now, the worst that will happen is a bit of time spent in a well-run asylum. Just until the government is changed and you are no longer a threat. Uncle Hilliard made us promise that unless there was no other alternative, that was how we would control loose tongues."

Like Lady Riordan. Well, this was just an evening for surprises. Evidently Uncle Hilliard followed a few Christian principles after all.

Kate forced a laugh. "You can't just make a duchess disappear. Certainly not the daughter of one of the most beloved dukes in England."

Oddly, Glynis began to smile. "Well, you see, there's the interesting thing. I can. Even better, when I tell them why you disappeared so suddenly, I can tell the truth."

A cold chill snaked down Kate's back. Glynis's eyes were triumphant, as if this were a moment she'd waited years for.

"What truth? That I was trying to stop you from assassinating Wellington?"

Glynis smiled, delighted. "You really don't know? I swore you did. After all, your siblings do. I do. Edwin's father broke a solemn vow so he could warn me."

"You still aren't telling me anything, Glynis."

Glynis was still smiling, and Kate had the most awful feeling the woman was dragging this all out for the sheer pleasure of it. "He gave you to Murther," Glynis said, "because Murther said he could keep you away from the family. But Murther died. So it is now up to Edwin and me."

Glynis was gloating. Kate suddenly feared that gloat more than the gun. She knew she shouldn't ask. She couldn't help it. "You really expect me to believe that my father wanted his own daughter to stay away? There was nothing more important to Father than Hilliard loyalty."

"Now we come to the meat of the matter, don't we?" Glynis asked. "And after all these years of putting up with your condescension, I get to tell you the truth. The truth your mother made your father keep from everyone, even you." Her expression grew smug. "You aren't a Hilliard at all. You're nothing but a bastard."

Kate was stunned. "You would accuse my mother of cuckolding her husband? How dare you!" Instinctively she stepped forward.

Glynis lifted the gun. "I accuse her of nothing, except protecting you, which was a waste of her good heart. You may have been a duke's wife, but you were never a duke's daughter. You are nothing but the spawn of sin, a bastard born of violence and filth."

Kate shook her head, the words incomprehensible."What do you mean?" She could barely hear her own voice.

"Your mother was raped. That is what I mean. A stranger violated her and got her with child. The child that killed her. Your father hated you from the moment of your conception until the day he died. "

Kate was sure she was freezing. A vast emptiness yawned in her, a tipping, sliding realigning of the world. Of course. Everything made sense now. The distance, the silences, the insults. The eternal sadness in her father's eyes that only seemed to grow on seeing her.

It wasn't that he hadn't noticed her. It was that he'd wished she had never existed.

She couldn't seem to think. She couldn't move. Glynis slammed the door shut. The feeble candle flame shuddered to death. Darkness rushed in and Kate stood alone, with no company but the truth.

Chapter 24

Harry was furious. What the hell had Kate been thinking, walking back into that snake pit she called a family? And without him? By the time he woke early in the evening, she was long gone, and he was left with a growing sense of unease. Something wasn't right, and he couldn't put a finger on it. He was an old enough campaigner, though, to trust his instincts. He had to get down to Hampshire as fast as he could.

The only concession he made to his battered body was to commandeer Chuffy's chaise. With Chuffy and Kit Braxton along for support, he traveled straight through the night. They played game after game of cards. He stared out the window, that feeling of dread growing with each passing mile.

By the time the coach pulled into the Olde George Inn at East Meon fifteen hours later, he was almost frantic. It wasn't that his body felt as if he'd taken another spill; he expected that. But he couldn't overcome the growing sense that he was running out of time. He would have gone right up to the castle to confront Kate, but Chuffy and Kit convinced him to see Drake first while they changed out the exhausted team. Considering the fact that Harry felt like shoving Drake's teeth down his throat for encouraging this mad start, he considered it the perfect solution.

He knew he'd made the wrong decision when he stiffly climbed down from the coach to hear shouting coming from inside the whitewashed old coaching inn. One of the voices was definitely Drake's. Harry was afraid that another was Thrasher's.

"You know bloody well my lady didn't go nowheres!" the boy was all but howling. "'Specially not with jus' George. Somefin's bad wrong, I tell ya."

Harry began to run.

"Not…not…*not!*"

Bloody hell. That was Lady Bea.

"Harry, slow down," Kit begged, hot on his heels. Harry found Drake in a parlor, faced off with Bea, Thrasher, and Bivens, one more red-faced than the next.

"I can't…" Drake was protesting, hands in the air, looking unusually flustered. That might have been because Bea had him by the arm and was shaking him like a rat.

"Not!" she all but screeched, tears in her eyes. She had a little leather-bound book in her hand that Drake was trying to grab without success.

"Where's Kate?" Harry demanded, trying to catch his breath past protesting ribs.

Everybody turned on him. "Gone!" Thrasher cried, advancing. "Just…gone! When we woke up this mornin', that old trout says as 'ow Lady Kate took off with George in the middle of the night. Bollocks she did! They done somefin to 'er, that's what!"

Harry took hold of his perilously frayed temper. "Drake?"

Drake frowned. "Harry, you're not up for this yet. Sit down and we'll talk."

Harry almost throttled him. "Where. Is. She?"

Drake sighed. "I don't know. The last she was seen was last night when she retired. After this lot came to report her missing, I went up to the castle to inquire. If we could all sit down, I'll tell you what I learned."

The publican, a tidy barrel of a man wearing an old bag-wig, came in to offer refreshments, only to be sent running by Lady Bea. It only served to make Harry feel more unnerved. Breathing carefully to control the pain, he helped Bea into a chair.

"Bea," he said, easing down next to her. "Do you know where she is?"

She scrunched up her eyes. "Not...not..."

"Get the book from her," Drake suggested sotto voce.

Leveling a glare on the suave Drake that should have dropped him stone dead, Bea dropped the book right down her bodice. It almost made Harry laugh. Almost.

"The story," he demanded of his superior.

Drake ran a hand through his hair. "I would have questioned the story if Bea hadn't come out with the book. But the plan Kate devised worked perfectly. She found the book, left it beneath the desk in the library for Bea to retrieve. And then, sometime in the middle of the night, evidently she had George drive her away."

"Gobshite," Thrasher sputtered. "Pure gobshite. She wouldn't go nowhere without me 'n Lady Bea."

"She might," Drake retorted, looking regretful. "If she learned something that overset her. The story has already begun to circulate up at the house." He briefly looked down at his hands. "It seems Kate is not the daughter of the Duke of Livingston."

Harry was on his feet. "Who said so? I'll kill them. The duchess was the most honorable woman in Hampshire. She would *never*—"

Drake looked, if possible, worse. "It was rape. A passing soldier, they think, who caught her out in the orchard. The present duke said that the whole family knew of it, but that the duchess had begged the duke not to tell anyone, especially Kate. That it wasn't Kate's fault, and she didn't want her child blamed."

Harry heard an odd roaring in his ears. Something seemed to be blocking his throat, and he felt oddly dizzy. "Kate found out."

Drake nodded. "Last night. The duchess said she feels terrible about it, but she admits she blurted out the truth during an argument. The next thing she knew, Kate's coach was bowling down the drive with George at the reins and Kate inside."

Bea actually spit on the ground. "*Chien.*"

Harry sympathized. "What does the head groom say?"

Drake shrugged. "He was asleep. Woke when he heard the coach leave."

He may not have liked me, but he can never take away the fact that I am the daughter of a duke. Harry couldn't get Kate's voice out of his head. It was what she'd pinned her pride on. No matter how she'd been treated in her life, she'd known who she was. In one fell swoop, even that had been stripped from her.

A bastard. Daughter of a rapist. He thought he would be sick. "They're lying."

"No," Drake admitted. "They had a letter from the duchess." He rubbed at his forehead. "I should have figured a way to get in up there instead of waiting here."

Next to Harry, Bea had begun to sob. Thrasher stood, hands clenched, tears running down his face, and Bivens sat ashen-cheeked. Drake just looked stricken.

"Why don't you think Kate left on her own?" Harry asked Thrasher.

"'Cause she wouldn't!" Thrasher insisted, swiping his cheeks with his sleeves. "She promised. An' d' ya fink she'd leave Lady Bea behind with that bitch?"

That question stuck in Harry's gut. Thrasher was right. No matter what had happened to Kate in the last weeks, her first thoughts had been for Bea. It didn't matter how devastated she was, how upended, she would never have frightened Bea this way. Slipping off his chair, Harry went on his knees before the old woman. She had aged suddenly, her skin sagging and her hands trembling. Harry was afraid for her.

"Bea," he said as gently as he could when he wanted to crush something with his hands. "Do you know anything?"

Her breath still catching in little hiccuping sobs, she nodded. "Not…she…" Another sob escaped, her face screwed up in frustration.

"Sssssh," Harry soothed. "It's all right. Tell it however you can."

He got another frantic nod, and Bea squeezed her eyes shut, holding on to him as if she would fall. Harry tried so hard to be patient and wait her out, but he was suddenly sure Kate's staff were correct. She was in trouble, and only Bea knew what had happened.

Suddenly the old woman's eyes opened and she straightened, meeting Harry's gaze with determined gray eyes. And she began to sing. The tune, strangely enough, was "I Know My Redeemer Liveth."

"I know that they kidnapped my Kate, in the dark, during the night,
    When all did sleep, they forced her out into a coach and drove away.
    I know they took her to an asylum, and also George, since he would drive,

But not this time did he drive, I saw, I saw the coachman, not George.

That monster Glynis and her butler, not the duke, he was asleep.

Passed by my window in the dark."

Harry actually laughed. "Did they know you were watching?"

Bea nodded. "They said, that I was too dumb to tell it…"

Harry gave her a smacking kiss. "We'll name our first girl after you," he promised. "Drake? I'm going to the castle."

Drake blinked. "But Bea just said she wasn't there."

"Bea saw the coach. Not Kate. Besides, Glynis has some questions to answer."

"I think we'd save time just to go to the asylum."

"It will be my next stop."

"Lady Glynis," Chuffy said, shaking his head as they all got up to leave. "Dark horse. Who knew?"

"May I have the book now?" Drake asked Bea.

Bea glared, but in the end she reached back into her bodice, drew out the book, and handed it over. Drake began to leaf through it.

"Here it is," he said. "Kate was right. The verse is transposed. I wonder why."

"It probably changes the position of the code words," Harry said, helping Bea to her feet and giving her a hug.

She was shaking her head again. "Hierarchy."

They all stared at her.

"Good God," Drake breathed, his focus on the book. "It might just be. The next couplet reads, 'Second to none is your artistry, a woman's darkest skill.' The numbers continue. And…yes. 'Not a bit of me shall die.' The bishop's pin says 'Not *all* of me will die.' What if each member of the central team has a verse to identify himself to those he sends out. And they have icons, like the rose." He looked up, his posture suddenly taut. "My God. Kate was right. We have *two* verses. I have to get this back."

"To Thirsk?" Chuffy shook his head. "Not wise. Still don't know about Ian."

Drake was still paging through the little book. "I have someone else in mind."

"After we get Kate," Harry said.

Ten minutes later when he stepped through the great oak castle door, Harry knew he would have no luck. He didn't feel Kate anywhere here. Funny how it had never occurred to him before that he could always tell where she was, that odd energy of theirs connecting them as surely as a tether. He wasn't able to feel it now; all he felt was a vast emptiness. To make it worse, his arrival cemented the rumors that had circulated among the party. Kate, finding out she was worse than nobody, had fled rather than face society's scorn. The fact that her husband was looking for her made all the matrons nod.

The only one who seemed upset by Kate's distress seemed to be her niece Elspeth, who kept glaring at her mother as if she'd personally orchestrated Kate's downfall. It made Harry hopeful. It also made him realize that Kate had an unerring judgment in people.

By the time they reached the asylum in Richmond, Harry felt as if he were shaking apart. Only his desperation for Kate kept him going.

But Kate wasn't there. They went through the building like Visigoths sacking Rome, leaving screaming, frightened patients and outraged staff in their wake, but there was no sign of her. Harry had never felt so frantic in his life.

"I'm going back to have a talk with the duchess," he promised grimly.

Drake caught him by the arm. "You are not. There is another way."

Kate's little family took Bea back to London. Harry followed Drake and Kit Braxton to a tidy house near Harrow where they were greeted by a too-pale, nervous blond woman dressed in mourning whom Drake introduced as Lady Riordan.

"Is there another asylum?" Harry asked her before they'd even sat down.

She flinched as if he'd struck her. "I don't...I can't speak against my husband. He has my children."

Drake took her hand. "You don't have to say a word against him. But the lady who helped you has been taken, and we don't know where she is."

If possible, Lady Riordan grew paler. "I don't know," she said, straining Harry's patience. "I think so. They said the one I was at was a...reward."

He fought for patience. "Do you know its name? Where it is?"

She shook her head. "It's south. Near the sea. That's all I know."

Harry wanted to howl in frustration. Every moment they wasted Kate spent in the dark, with no company but the terrible revelation about her father. Even Kate couldn't hope to survive that with her soul intact.

His poor girl. She'd suffered so much, and he'd failed her again. He had to find her and make it up to her.

*   *   *

Kate didn't know where she was. One of Glynis's staff had poured laudanum down her throat before binding her hands and throwing her onto the floor of her own carriage, right next to poor George. They had driven all night.

By the time they locked her in the room where no one could hear her, she felt battered and confused and sick. She heard the lock turn and opened her eyes to a dark so deep that she couldn't even make out the outline of a door. The room was cold and damp and rank; Kate thought it might have been underground, maybe on a river.

"George?" she called, struggling to her feet.

The world dipped and swayed, now that it wasn't held down by horizons and direction. Kate's stomach lurched sickeningly. She needed to find a chamber pot. First, she had to find George. It was bad enough she was locked in here. George wouldn't understand at all.

"George, are you there!"

But nobody answered. No matter how much she called, or pounded on the solid door, no one came. She heard no sound at all, saw nothing, and wondered if she'd been mistaken. Could this be, not an asylum, but a tomb? Was she to be left here until the last person who knew her was dead? Would anyone really care?

She had to get out. She had to protect George. She had to get to Bea.

She had to find Harry. She needed to feel his arms around her; she needed to see the warmth in his sky-blue eyes. She had to thank him for bringing her back from the brink of madness. Even if he didn't want to know, she had to tell him that she loved him.

Please, Harry, she thought. *Find me. I was wrong. I should never have tried to keep away from you. There aren't enough hours, and I love you so much. I need your strength, your pragmatism, your exquisite patience. It isn't enough to survive. I want to live, and if I can, I want to do it with you.*

Chapter 25

Harry couldn't find her. He didn't sleep, he forgot how to eat, he lost the patience to wait. After five days of fruitless searching, he was visited by Baron Thirsk, who asked Harry what he knew about the book. Harry booted the officious little bureaucrat back out the door. Harry could give a cold damn about that book. He didn't care if it led to the assassination of every statesman in Britain. He couldn't find Kate, and the baron refused to put a gun to the head of the Duchess of Livingston to find out where she was.

Bea was inconsolable. Truly afraid for her, Harry wrote to Grace and begged her to come back to care for the old woman. Thrasher spent all his waking hours trolling the stews for information, and the Rakes searched the countryside. Diccan's household army polled servants, and Mudge watched the asylum for suspicious activity.

As for Harry, he followed every trail he could, his desperation increasing every hour Kate remained missing. His temper shortened, his anger grew, and his weight dropped. But even Kate's chef Marcel wasn't eating his own food. Instead he wandered the markets tracking large purchases for a clue to where a hidden asylum might be.

Harry's patience finally snapped on the tenth day, and he stormed the doors of Livingston House. But the family was away from home. Ignoring the jarring protest from his ribs and his head, he climbed on Beau and headed back for Moorhaven. He was halfway across Hounslow Heath before he heard the hoofbeats closing in from behind. But when he turned, gun in hand to shoot whoever was trying to stop him, it was to discover his household staff tracking him, every one as armed as he.

It didn't help. The Livingstons had left Moorhaven for an unknown destination, leaving behind a skeleton staff who blamed Lady Kate for shaming the family with her sordid revelations. They couldn't stop Harry from searching, and he did, all but tearing the library apart in an effort to find the priest hole.

When the door finally clicked open to reveal that square of darkness, though, it made everything immeasurably worse. He thought of young Kate trapped in the stony silence of that little hole, all the while wondering why her father couldn't love her, and he knelt on the floor and sobbed.

Come back to me, he begged, his head in his hands. *The darkness is a nightmare for me, now, too. The days are no better. I hear your voice and catch your scent on the air. But you're not there, and I can't bear it.*

When Harry finally emerged from that cold, empty house, Thrasher and Finney were waiting for him. They didn't say a word as Thrasher helped Harry back onto his horse and followed him down the drive. And when he felt compelled to ride to every private asylum within fifty miles, they followed silently along.

He didn't allow them to follow any farther, though. He

sent them home. And then, because he couldn't seem to help himself, he went to Eastcourt.

The minute he saw it he knew he'd made a mistake. It only made everything worse. The house was everything Kate had said: solid and homey and sweet, a tumbled, gabled old hodgepodge of a house, with a cottage garden so large it almost blocked out the buttery-yellow facade. But what froze Harry as he sat on his horse on the front drive was that he knew it.

Except for the color of the stone, Eastcourt could have been taken for his own home. If he walked through that front door, he suspected he would walk into those mad, chaotic, familiar rooms where Kate had once argued Greek philosophers and cadged cookies from his mother. He remembered how she'd said that the minute she saw Eastcourt, she'd known it was home. He was afraid he knew why, and it shattered the last of his reserve.

She could break your heart, that woman, he thought, desperately trying not to break down in the driveway. How could a man keep from falling in love with her? How could he not see how foolish he was to think that silence was better than challenge and humor, faith and strength. Christ, what strength.

It was only now, looking on the home she'd constructed from memory and determination, that he recognized how indomitable her spirit was. Beaten, branded, abandoned, locked in the dark, and yet she still worked to create a world that included every misfit and rogue who happened her way.

And one miserable ex-army major.

He loved her so much. Why hadn't he admitted it? Why hadn't he had as much courage as Kate and told her?

He would. As soon as he got her back, he would tell her. And keep telling her for the rest of their lives, no matter where they lived them. It didn't matter anymore. As long as he could spend his life with Kate.

He returned to London to find it in the midst of the greatest scandal of the decade. If Glynis had done nothing else, she'd made sure the story circulated about Kate's alleged disappearance. Kate's nemesis finally had her revenge.

It went on this way for two interminable weeks. Harry stopped sleeping. If he tried, all he did was dream of Kate. Young Kate with all the hope in the world in her eyes, even though she'd known the priest hole always waited; mature Kate, bright steel forged in the fire of pain. Kate who had soothed her own nightmares by easing others'.

Day after day he was visited by the widows and slum rats and veterans she had saved from despair with her deceptively casual assistance. And when visitors were forbidden the front door, Harry needed look no farther than Kate's own staff. She'd made that outrageous, notorious home of hers a haven, even for a tired Rifleman who'd once thought he'd have to wander the world alone to recover his peace of mind.

He had almost recovered it right here in this noisy, surprisingly whimsical, amazingly down-to-earth house in the middle of Mayfair. And then, because Kate saw the need to protect even him, he'd had it taken away.

He spent the majority of the day in his relentless search. The few hours that remained, he lay in her bed seeking her scent. Burrowed into her pillow, he replayed the moments of his marriage over and over in his mind. And inevitably, every night, he returned to that moment she had discovered that lovemaking could be a joy.

The image was sharp as etched glass: Kate, her skin pearlescent in the candlelight, her breasts proud and high, gently bobbing as she moved over him, her body sleek as a seal, all sweeping lines and lush curves. Her exquisite face alight with wonder, with nascent joy, with the laughter of surprise as she'd felt him fill her, as she'd tortured him, riding him like a mad hussar over the fences, spurs and heels and hands.

And every time he replayed those moments, night after night, he fought harder to believe that enough of her would come back to him, that they could rediscover the wonder they created together. That they could remember how to anticipate the future. And every time he lay there till the dawn, eyes open, tears tracking down his temples, the weight of trying grew heavier and heavier.

I love you, Katie, he repeated over and over again. *Come back to me.*

*　　*　　*

Kate had been gone a total of twenty-one days when Elspeth Hilliard appeared on Harry's doorstep. He had just come in from another sweep of the stews to have a grim Finney greet him at the door.

"Got a visitor. Lady Elspeth, she says."

Harry had sent her innumerable messages. He'd assumed they'd either been intercepted or ignored. Feeling the first hint of hope in days, he strode into the Chinese Drawing Room. There she sat, still clad in a hooded cape, as if afraid his staff would know her.

"Aunt Kate has the most exquisite taste, don't you think?" she asked, looking brittle enough to crumble. Harry had forgotten how young she was.

"I can't find her," he said baldly.

She nodded. "I know. I heard my mama say that it was what she deserved. But it isn't!" Suddenly she was on her feet, hands clenched. "She wouldn't run away from anything. And it wasn't her fault anyway."

"No," Harry agreed, easing her back into her chair. "It wasn't."

Elspeth sat very still, hands clutched in her lap, tears welling in large green eyes that looked so much like Kate's. Across from her, Harry waited. Kate loved this girl, which meant she had bottom. Harry prayed she would have enough to see this through. It would be a hard thing to go against her family.

"What did you come to tell me?" Harry gently asked.

Her head snapped up, and he saw a full range of emotions skim across her expressive little face. Poor girl. Caught between loyalty to her parents and the need to do the right thing for her aunt.

Her head went back down. When she spoke, her voice was so low Harry had to lean closer to hear it. "Aunt Kate wasn't the only one gone missing that morning," she said. "Thom the coachman was gone, too. When he met us in Dover last week, he said something about a quick trip to Chatham."

Her eyes painfully young, she looked up. "No one at our party was from Chatham."

"You've been thinking about it, though. What troubles you about Chatham?"

Her eyes huge, she shook her head, her curls bobbing.

Reaching over, Harry took her hand. "Did you know that your father had your aunt Kate committed a few weeks back?"

She pulled her hand back. "Don't be silly. Why would he do that?"

"I think you know," Harry said, and then went still, giving her the chance to think.

"Her birth embarrasses them. And she won't disappear."

She sat there for so long, Harry wanted to shake her. But

he knew what this visit would cost her. She had already proven her mettle just in showing up. In the end, it was her aunt who had gained her loyalty. "Our great-aunt Agnes was sent away to Chatham years ago," the girl said. "She killed Uncle Charles."

Harry could hardly hold still. "Do you know the name of the facility?"

"My parents wouldn't do that," she insisted. "They *wouldn't*."

But Harry had no answer, even as tears spilled down her cheeks. "If I help you," she whispered, "they'll never forgive me."

He wrapped his arm around her and held on. "Do you know, Elspeth?"

Still it took a moment. "The Rose," she finally whispered miserably. "They called it Tudor Rose."

It was Harry's turn to shake his head. God. How had he missed it? Gently he forced the girl to look up at him. "She's probably not even there. I'll let you know."

"As soon as you can."

It was the first real hope he had. He didn't like leaving the girl with her disillusionment, so he handed her over to Grace and Bea. And then, hardly daring to hope, he collected Kit Braxton and Alex Knight, and he rode for Chatham. It had been three weeks. He couldn't bear the thought that he would be too late.

Chapter 26

They reached Chatham about teatime. The weather was gray and damp, with a nasty little wind that dropped the temperature. It didn't help make the facility look any more inviting, a gray stone building just near the river that looked to have been modified from a warehouse. But it wasn't an asylum. The sign on the wall said ROSE WORKHOUSE.

Harry saw it and quailed. Worse than most asylums. Infested with disease, packed with the destitute, the pitifully mad, the villainous. Harry's heart rate tripled and his stomach soured. She couldn't be locked in this place. But if she wasn't, he had no idea where to look.

Inside was worse. They hadn't even made the pretense of painting. The walls were as gray as the inhabitants who shuffled through the overcrowded wards. Light barely forced its way through high, grimy windows, and the air was permeated with the stench of boiled cabbage. Babies cried, high, pitiful sounds of despair. Someone was weeping, and an oversize man in a frock coat was taking a slattern against a wall.

Harry didn't bother with being polite. He shoved a pistol under the chin of one of the matrons and demanded she lead him to Kate. She cooperated quickly enough with a whine and a wink, but swore no knowledge of the name. So Harry locked the entire staff in a closet and led his team on a thorough search.

"Kate! Kate, damn it! Answer me!"

Every minute in this place was stripping away his composure. Where was she? Why didn't she answer when he called?

He had just about given up when Kit Braxton gave a shout. Locked in a small back room was George. Thinner, dirty, lost looking. It even took a minute for the big man to recognize Thrasher, who hadn't stopped cursing since recognizing him.

"Where's the duchess, George?" Thrasher demanded. "George, you gotta tell us!"

For a long time, George just stared at the boy, as if trying to remember how to speak. When he started shaking his head, Harry all but crumbled.

But then, like a miracle, George smiled. "Hey, Thrasher. You come to get us, me and Katie."

Everyone froze. "Where is she, George?"

But George shrugged. "Dunno. Barnes says she's in a special place where nobody'll find her. Keep her safe, he says. That's good, huh? But I want to go home, Thrasher. I want Katie to go home with us."

Harry was already out the door. He knew who Barnes was, a slick, snake-eyed man with nervous hands who was waiting to be let out with the rest of the staff. Harry wasted no time. He threw open the door to the room they were locked in, so that it crashed against the wall. Then he stalked up to Barnes and shoved his pistol up his nose.

"Take me to her," was all he said. "Now."

Harry had only felt this out of control once before, and

that was when he'd realized what the British army was doing to the women of Badajoz after the siege. He'd killed men from his own army that day without compunction. Barnes must have seen that he would do the same today. Even so, he shook his head, the whites of his eyes showing.

"She ain't here," he insisted. "We kep' the big guy, 'cause he's a hard worker. She were a right pain in the ass."

Harry thought he would choke on the fear. "Where did they take her?"

"I don't know and that's the truth! Nobody does!"

No. Please, no. He couldn't fail. Not again. Not when she needed him. He searched that building like an enemy emplacement. He terrorized the staff and inmates. If Chuffy hadn't kept hold of him, he suspected he might have tried to shake information out of the children. He couldn't bear it.

"Where is she?"

They were standing outside in the hard gravel yard, nothing visible except weeds all the way to the river. There was nothing else to search.

"Maybe we should go back," Kit suggested. "Get help."

"No. She's here. She has to be here."

"She's here all right," a sharp, grating voice said behind him.

Harry spun around to see a scarecrow standing not ten feet away.

"Where? Where is she?" Harry demanded, advancing on him.

The man hopped back, hands out. "She said you'd pay me. I want my money."

Harry grabbed him by the throat. "You'll get a hangman's noose unless you take us to her."

The little man pushed at Harry. "You want her, you got her. I've had enough. Woman never shuts up. 'Get Harry.

Get Harry. Tell him I'm here,'" he mimicked in cruel tones. "Drive a man to drink, she does."

Harry just tossed him to the ground. "Get moving."

They never would have found her. The door was hidden in the larder, a sliding wall of shelves. Harry pulled it open and then, for a long moment, could do no more than look down into the darkness.

He had to go in. He cleared his throat, wiped his wet hands on his slacks. Took in a strident breath. *Please, God. Please. Let there still be light in those magnificent eyes. Let her be in there.*

Behind him, Kit laid a hand on his shoulder. "Harry?"

It was the hardest thing he'd ever had to do, but he walked into the darkness.

There were steps going down. Passing lanterns around, Harry led the way. One flight and then a half, all the while the air becoming colder, damper, thick with mold and refuse. Harry wished he had the Duchess of Livingston's throat in his hands. He'd choke her like a chicken. God, how could Kate survive it again?

He had just opened his mouth to call to her when he heard it. A woman's voice, rising, falling, echoing off the dank walls.

"I told you, Bert, if you would just get help for me, I'll pay you enough that you never have to work for these vile people again. In fact, I'm sure Harry will give you a government stipend. You have vital information about the Lions the government would love to have. Bert?...Bert? Fine. Deserted by another man. I might have known. They're all alike. They stay around as long as there are low-cut dresses and champagne. Give them a job to do, though, and off they go..."

Even before Harry turned the lock on the door everyone was grinning. He wanted to laugh, to shout. "Kate?" he called, hearing the strain in his own voice.

The key scraped and the lock clattered and then popped open. For a moment there was silence inside. "Harry?" Her voice was unpardonably small. Oh, how he would hurt people for doing this to her. "Harry, if you're just in my head, I wish you'd go away. Better yet, go get the real Harry. I'm running out of patience in here."

His hands had begun to shake. He opened his mouth, but suddenly he couldn't seem to get the words out. He yanked on the door.

She was sitting on a chair, like before. This time, though, she looked nothing like a proper miss. She was leaning forward, hands on knees, feet planted apart, as if poised to spring. Her hair was tangled and dull, but she'd done her best to keep it tidy.

Harry felt tears fill his eyes and course down his cheeks. Her eyes were open, alert and amazed.

"I'm here, Kate," he said, stepping in and opening his arms.

She sprang after all, right into his arms. "You really are!" she cried, burrowing her face in his neck. "Oh, Harry, you're here!" Harry had the most overwhelming feeling that he'd just come home.

"You smell so good," she crowed. "But I think anything smells better than my room." Pulling back, she flashed him a shy smile. "I did try and keep it neat. You would be appalled at how rare a good bar of soap is in this establishment. Hello, Kit, Chuffy. Thrasher, I think you're growing out of your uniform again. "

She'd lost weight. He could probably count her ribs. Her hair was a rat's nest, and one couldn't help but notice that she hadn't bathed. Harry didn't care. He had never held anything so precious in his life.

He cupped her face in his hands. "Tell me you're all right."

She smiled, then, and Harry didn't think he'd ever seen a more incandescent sight. "I found something out, Harry. You were right. I do much better if I stay alert." She hesitated, her eyes growing wide. "Harry, you're crying."

He pulled her into his arms and almost squeezed the breath out of her. He had to feel her heart. He had to hear her voice. "Kate. Remember when you told me you loved me?"

She froze where she was, as if afraid of missing something. "Yes, in fact, I do."

Behind him, Harry heard shuffling feet. "We'll…uh, be outside," Chuffy called.

He didn't really pay attention. He was consumed by the feeling of Kate in his arms. All of the fear, the uncertainty, the indecision disappeared. This was exactly where she should be. No matter where they lived, or what they did, it only mattered that they did it together. "I was a fool, Kate. I was afraid. I'd lived so long with nightmares I didn't realize when I was presented with a dream. I love you. I will always love you. I'll sell my traveling gear and dig tulips. I'll sign Eastcourt over to you and leave. I'll do whatever you want me to do, if you'll only love me back."

He heard the oddest snuffling and didn't know if she was laughing or crying.

It turned out, she was doing both. Tilting her head back, she smiled up at him as if he were the morning light. And lifting her hand, she wiped away his tears. "I spent a lot of time recently thinking about the benefits of travel. I would like to see India. And Venice and America and Portugal. But I can't simply wander off from my responsibilities."

"Would you like to consider working out something together?"

A pain of pure anguish ripped through him as he waited

for her answer. He knew, in the end, he'd agree to whatever she wanted. He needed to be with her. He needed her strength, her humor, her outrageous sensibility to leaven the nightmares. But she needed *his* strength, his steadiness, his eye. Didn't she?

In the end, he couldn't bear her hesitation. "I'm so sorry," he said. "I tried so hard to find you."

"I know you did. I never thought you wouldn't." She sounded hesitant, suddenly. "No matter what I am, I know you would never break your word to me again."

"What do you mean?" he countered, furious. "You're my wife. My love. My hero."

Her voice, when it came, was uncertain, her posture defiant. "I'm a bastard, Harry."

He wanted to weep again for her. He knew, though, that it was the worst response he could give her. So he kissed her forehead, her eyes, her nose. "You're the woman who recovered Eastcourt and started an orphanage and gave homes to some of the most disreputable rabble I've ever met. Has any of that changed?"

Not taking her gaze from his, she shook her head, her eyes wide and glistening in the uncertain light.

"Well, that is who I fell in love with," he said. "Not your lineage. I know it will be difficult with society, Kate. But I'll be right there with you."

Her laughter was abrupt. "Damn society. I consider this a very efficient way of determining my real friends."

He leaned his forehead against hers. "Did I pass?"

Her smile was soft and honest. "Oh, yes. Take me home, Harry."

*   *   *

Later that night, when the rest of the house had wandered to bed, Harry and Kate lay exhausted in each other's arms.

"Snuff the candles, Harry," she begged, running her hand up his chest. "It's time for a new experiment."

Harry kissed her forehead. She smelled like frangipani. "What experiment?"

She ran her fingers down his chest, leaving a delicious trail of fire. "If I tell you that I can't think of anything I'd rather do than travel with you—except maybe raise our children at Eastcourt—will you make love to me? Here in the dark."

Just the suggestion did terrible things to his cock. Rubbing his cheek against hers, he stretched up to extinguish the lone candelabra, leaving the room in profound darkness. "You're sure you want to do this?"

He could feel her smile against his skin. "You banish the nightmares, Harry. You replace them with something beautiful. I need that."

Pulling her close, he rubbed his cheek against hers. "Never let it be said that you're predictable, Kate."

She chuckled. "Heaven forfend. I might as well be dead."

Harry couldn't see a thing, but he could feel Kate; he heard her racing heart and felt the heat begin to glow from her skin. He knew she was smiling in his arms; he wanted to make her laugh. To make her sigh and chuckle and moan, her body weeping in anticipation and her climax shattering. He lifted a hand and captured her breast and thought that it was even more mysterious in the dark.

"I think we should make a practice of this," he murmured, bending down to kiss her. "There is something very seductive about making love in the dark."

She arched into his hand. "I think that's a brilliant idea. Now, does Ovid prescribe any other interesting positions?"

Epilogue

Kate wasn't sure she would ever become tired of Italy. It was October, and yet the breeze that ruffled the muslin curtains was still deliciously warm. The air was redolent with the scents of the sea, flowers, spices. Outside her open window she could hear the splash and slide of polemen as they propelled their gondolas. Occasionally, one would sing, his smooth voice a rich color in the soft night air.

As for her, she lay in a tester bed in an opulent suite papered in green and gold, a Murano chandelier dripping pink and green and white glass over her head. Clad in a night rail that would scandalize her husband, she was reading Byron and waiting for Harry to return from his meeting with the doge's architect.

She didn't think she would ever get used to the beauty of this country, or how friendly the people were. As for Venice, it was a fantasy out of time, as it dreamed on the water like a faded wedding cake. Corrupt, decadent, slowly sinking into the sea, it was still the most romantic city she'd ever seen.

She smiled, thinking of the compromise she and Diccan had made. Eastcourt was their home, where Harry was even now designing greenhouses for their flowers. But without these trips, Harry would shrivel. He needed this bouquet of sights and sounds as much as she needed the Eastcourt earth. His eyes lit in an unholy way when he spotted an interesting building. The Blue Mosque in Constantinople had almost given him the vapors.

Even so, they would have to spend the summer in England. Brand-new babies didn't travel well. They would also be going home for Elspeth's wedding. The poor girl had had to put it off to mourn her mother, who had met with an unfortunate accident while hunting. Kate knew she should be saddened. No one should die so young. But the truth was, she was relieved. She couldn't bear the idea that her family would suffer the kind of notoriety a trial would bring. Even Edwin, as disagreeable as he was, shouldn't have to face having a traitor for a wife.

Kate was glad she was well out of it, her only lingering nightmare waking up in a cold sweat afraid she was still in that cellar. Thankfully, it was Harry's arms she felt each time she woke, his voice soothing her.

Kate had been surprised by how much she loved to travel. Europe and the Levant and the slow, sun-drenched isles of the Caribbean. Most, though, she would cherish their time in India. Not only had she fallen in love with the country, but she'd been able to celebrate something far more dear to her heart. Her lovely Grace and her favorite cousin Diccan had found their way back together, and Kate and Harry had gone to help them settle into their new diplomatic post in Calcutta.

Kate missed them already, but she knew she would be back. Diccan insisted his children know their cousins. Kate had tried to remind him that they weren't cousins at all, but it hadn't flown. So cousins they still were, and expected back with bratlings in hand.

As for Bea, that dignified lady had grown quite bold in the last two years. How could anyone have known how happy she would be swaying on the back of a camel in Cairo or twirling through the crowded streets of Calcutta at Diwali? She threatened to become more notorious than Kate.

There was a scratching on the door. Kate sat up. "Enter!"

She couldn't help but smile. Mudge walked in, clad in the white embroidered kurta pajamas he had adopted in India, shadowed by a tall, painfully thin Italian man with liquid black eyes and a pockmarked face. Both wore the kind of stunned, fatuous expression Kate had seen on Elspeth's face when she'd looked on her fiancé.

Mudge had already asked if his new friend Tony could come along with them when they left. Kate had readily agreed. It was a relief to see Mudge find his own happiness. She wanted him to find someone who could love him back.

"Signora," the young Italian greeted her with a courtly bow. "You have all you need for the night?"

"Except my husband. Have you two seen him?"

"He's right here," Harry called behind them. "Call our gondola for nine, Mudge," he said, stepping into the room. "We are off for Sienna."

Seeing her husband, attired only in slacks and loose linen shirt, Kate stretched back on her pillows. "Do we have to go? I like it here."

Harry grinned. "Bea wants to buy a winery."

Kate laughed. "Of course she does. Well, at least she can't bring it back to Eastcourt. The staff are still trying to acclimate to the panther."

His smile changing, Harry approached over the echoing

marble floor. Kate thought the young men slipped out of the room. She wasn't really certain. She was too preoccupied with seeing reflected light shimmer over Harry. Since their time away, his hair had lightened to an almost white-blond, and his skin darkened.

"You must be overly warm, Harry," she said, slipping her hands behind her head. "I think you should seek some relief."

It took no imagination to guess Harry's answer. His eyes grew dark; his slacks strained. Thinking about just what would happen in their garden of pillows, Kate shared a sensuous smile.

"Happy to," he said, bending over her. "As soon as I greet the piglet." And placing his hands on her belly, he put his mouth against the gentle swell of her belly and crooned. "Take care of yourself in there, lad. You know how your mother is."

Kate swatted him on the head. "My child loves me."

Harry kissed her. "So do I." Standing, he pulled up his shirt. "You can't tell me that *you're* too cold," he said.

Kate blatantly watched. It was her right, after all. Harry was hers; he told her often enough, and she believed him. She trusted him. She wanted him.

As sensuous as a cobra rising to the sound of a flute, she rose up on her knees and took hold of her gown, soft gold silk, and began to pull it up. She heard Harry's breath catch. She didn't take her eyes from his appearing body. Belly, chest, arms, throat. God, how she loved his throat. She could spend days tracing his pulse with her tongue.

She couldn't resist watching the play of candlelight along his muscles as he lifted his arms over his head and tossed the shirt in the corner. She couldn't keep from watching his erection strain against the slacks. She never got tired of seeing how much he wanted her. She never tired of seducing him into wanting her. Ever since that first night when Harry had taken her in the dark, whispering endearments as he'd spread her thighs and driven into her, she had forgotten how to be afraid. The darkness had grown placid, and her scars had become marks of pride. She had survived. They both had. And as reward, they had been given each other to cherish and protect and love.

"No, no," she teased, up on her knees now. "I don't think you're cool enough yet, Harry. Those slacks must be constricting."

Harry was breathing faster. He had his hands on the placket at his waist. Kate's heart picked up speed and sent blood spilling through her. She spread her legs enough to feel the air brush the juice that had begun to gather between her legs.

"Come here," he growled.

Before she'd gotten to know Harry again, she would have stormed off. No one told Kate Hilliard what to do anymore. But that had been before Harry taught her the pleasure of give-and-take. Of temptation and challenge. Slowly, she rose to her feet. She approached silently across the marble floor. She walked right up to him, close enough that her breasts brushed against his chest. And reaching between them, she finished unbuttoning the placket and slid her thumbs inside Harry's pants.

She felt flushed and anxious, shivery with impatience. She knew her hands were trembling. With a smile as old as sin, she bent over and laid a pillow at Harry's feet. Then, sliding his pants down, she slid down with them until she knelt before him.

She inhaled. There was something so primal about the scent of an aroused male; especially Harry. Salt and musk, power and grace. She leaned right up to his penis and rubbed her cheek against it. He jerked, gasped. She chuckled.

"Don't you want me to do this?" she asked.

It was why she loved doing it. Because Harry never expected it. He was grateful.

"Only if you'll let me reciprocate."

She swore she melted inside. She swore she could already feel the rasp of Harry's tongue against her most tender flesh, the nip of his teeth, the delicious satin of his lips. Reaching down, she cupped his sac in her hands. Then, licking her lips in anticipation, she bent and took him in her mouth. All of him, deep; heat and steel and velvet, pulsing with power and taut with need. She sucked, she licked, she nibbled, a hot treat for a naughty girl. She delighted in the rising pitch of his groans, in the way his body bucked against her mouth, in the pull of his hands in her hair as he pulled her more tightly to him.

"You'll kill me . . . yet," he groaned, his head back.

She looked up the length of him, muscle and sinew and bone, to see that his eyes were closed, his mouth thin, his skin stretched in agony. She relished the sense of dominance she felt all while kneeling before him. What she loved even more was reaching the point where he could take no more. Suddenly, he pulled away. Lifting her up, he threw her onto the bed so hard she bounced. And with a guttural cry of need, he climbed over her, pushed her knees apart, and drove into her.

She felt split, pummeled, invaded. She looked up to see the desperate need on Harry's face, and she battled him. She refused to simply be taken. She took back. She wrapped her hands around his buttocks and pulled. She planted her feet flat on the bed and lifted up, slamming into him as hard as he did into her, until her body became slick, her voice thin and frantic, her neck bowed so far it should have snapped. When he bent to take her breast in his mouth and suckle, she screamed with pleasure. And when he slipped his hand between them to tease her, she flew apart; lightning and whirlwind and thunder, color and wonder and light, Harry's fierce yells the music of madness.

"Oh, God, I love you," he moaned into her hair.

She laid her head against his heart. "I love you, too."

She smiled, replete. He needed her. He loved her. He wanted her. And she, resurrected from her darkness, wanted him just as fiercely. Just as tenderly. Just as fully. As the dusk settled over them, she wrapped herself around Harry and looked forward to the night. She'd been right all those years ago, she thought.

Sic itur ad astra.

So *was* the path to the stars.

Olivia Grace has every reason to despise Jack Wyndham, Earl of Gracechurch, who scandalously married and then divorced her. Yet when she finds an injured Jack on a battlefield wearing the enemy's uniform, she can't resist saving him...

Barely a Lady

Please turn this page for an excerpt.

Chapter 1

All prey understands the need for concealment. Sitting at the edge of a crowded ballroom, Olivia Grace knew this better than most and kept her attention on the room like a gazelle sidling up to a watering hole.

Olivia couldn't help smiling. *Watering holes.* She'd been reading too many naturalists' journals. Not that there weren't predators here, of course. It would have been impossible to miss them, with their bright plumage, sharp claws, and aggressive posturing. And those were just the mamas.

Olivia was safely tucked away from their notice, though. Camouflaged in serviceable gray bombazine, she occupied a chair along the trellis-papered wall, just another anonymous paid chaperone watching on as her charges danced.

The ballroom, a converted carriage house at the side of the Duke of Richmond's rented home, was full to bursting. Scarlet-clad soldiers whirled by with laughing girls in white. Sharp-eyed dowagers in puce and aubergine committed wholesale slaughter of each others' reputations. Civilian gentlemen in evening black clustered at the edge of the dance floor to argue about the coming battle. Olivia had even had the privilege of seeing the Duke of Wellington himself sweep into the room, his braying laugh lifting over the swell of the orchestra.

It seemed all of London had moved to Brussels these last months. Certainly the well-born military men had come in response to Napoleon's renewed threat. Olivia had already had the Lennox boys, the Duke of Richmond's sons, pointed out to her, and handsome young Lord Hay in his scarlet Guards jacket. Sturdy William Ponsonby was in dragoon green, and the exquisite Diccan Hilliard wore diplomat's black.

With all those eligible young men afoot, it would have been absurd to think that families would have kept their hopeful daughters at home.

Tonight Olivia's employer had insisted on shepherding her own chicks, which left Olivia with nothing to do but watch. And watch she did, storing up every bit of color and pageantry to record for her dear Georgie back in England.

"Oh, there's that devil Uxbridge," the lady next to her whispered in salacious tones. "How he can show his face after eloping with Wellington's sister-in-law…"

Olivia had heard that Uxbridge had been recalled from exile to lead the cavalry in the upcoming fight. She'd also heard he was brilliant and charismatic. Catching sight of him as he sauntered across the room in his flashy hussar's blue and silver, his fur-lined pelisse thrown over his shoulder, she thought that the reports had been woefully inadequate. He was breathtaking.

She was so intent on the sight of him, in fact, that she failed her primary duty. She forgot to watch for danger. She'd just leaned a bit to see whose hand Uxbridge was bending over, when her view was suddenly blocked by a field of gold.

"You don't mind if I sit here, do you?" someone asked.

Olivia looked up to find one of the most beautiful women she'd ever seen standing before her. Even sitting against the wall, Olivia fought the urge to look over her shoulder to see who else the newcomer could be addressing. Women like this never sought her out.

For a second, she flirted with old panic. She'd spent so many years trying to evade exposure that the instinct died hard. But this woman didn't look outraged. In fact, she was smiling.

"It's quite all right," the beauty said with a conspiratorial grin. "Contrary to popular opinion, I rarely bite. In fact, in some circles I'm considered fairly charming."

"I do bite," Olivia found herself answering. "But only when provoked."

She should bite her *tongue*. She knew better.

The woman didn't seem to notice, though, as with a hush of silk, she eased onto the chair to Olivia's left. "Well, let's see who we can get to provoke you, then," she said. "I think what this ball needs is some excitement—more than Jane Lennox making cow-eyes at Wellington over dinner, at any rate."

Olivia actually laughed. "I think you might get some argument from all those men in red."

Her companion took a moment to observe the room through a grotesquely bejeweled lorgnette. "It never occurred to me. This is the perfect place to watch absolutely everything, isn't it?"

"Absolutely."

"I wish I'd been sitting here when those magnificent Highlanders did their reels. I don't suppose you caught a glimpse of what they wore under those kilts."

"Sadly, no. Not for lack of trying, though."

Olivia wondered why this peacock would choose to sit among the house wrens—especially since several of the wrens in question had taken umbrage. One or two sidled away. Olivia even heard the whisper of "harlot." Again she fought the old urge to hide, but the attention was definitely on the newcomer.

As for that petite beauty, she appeared to take no notice. A Pocket Venus, she looked to be no older than Olivia's four and twenty years. As fine-skinned as a porcelain doll, she had thick, curly mahogany hair woven through with diamonds and a heart-shaped face that might have looked innocent but for her slyly amused cat-green eyes. Her dress had been crafted by an artist. Draped in layers of filmy gold tissue, it seemed to flow like water from a barely respectable bodice that exposed quite an expanse of diamond-wrapped throat and high, white breasts.

"I noticed the way you watch everyone," the beauty now said, lazily waving an intricately painted chicken-skin fan under her nose. "And I've been dying to hear what you're thinking."

"Thinking?" Olivia said instinctively. "But I think nothing. Companions aren't paid enough to think."

The lady gave a delighted laugh. "If you only did what you were paid for, my dear, I sincerely doubt you'd ever move farther afield than your front parlor."

"The back parlor, actually. Closer to the servants' stairs."

Olivia knew perfectly well she was being reckless. Exposure was still possible, after all, and one gasp of recognition would destroy her. But it felt so good to smile.

Her new acquaintance laughed. "I *knew* I'd like you. Who is it who benefits from your companionship, might I ask?"

"Mrs. Bottomly and her three daughters." Olivia gestured

toward a group on the dance floor. "They felt that passing the season in Brussels might be . . . advantageous."

The beauty turned to observe the short, knife-lean matron in pea green and peacock feathers smacking a rigid Mr. Hilliard on the arm with her fan as three younger copies of her looked on.

"You mean that flock of underfed crows pecking at my poor Diccan? Good Lord, how did she ever manage to acquire an invitation?"

"Ah, well," Olivia said, "that would involve a well-timed walk along the Allee Verde, an even better-timed ankle twist that obliged the Duchess of Richmond to take Mrs. Bottomly up in her carriage, and Mrs. Bottomly's tenacious confusion as to the nature of the invitations to tonight's event."

Her new acquaintance shook her head in awe. "Why ever has the creature wasted her time with a mere ball? Let's introduce her to Nosey, and she can help him rout Napoleon."

Olivia wryly considered her employer. "Not unless he has three eligible officers who might be offered in compensation."

Just then, Mrs. Bottomly let off a shrill titter that should have shattered Mr. Hilliard's eardrums. Olivia's companion flinched. "Not something I'd want on my conscience. I'm afraid Wellington will simply have to rely on his own wits."

"Indeed."

"But what of you?" the beauty demanded of Olivia. "Surely you deserve better than service to an overweening mushroom."

Olivia smiled. "I've found that life rarely takes what we deserve into consideration."

For just a moment, her companion's expression grew oddly reflective. Then, abruptly, she brightened. "Well, there are small mercies," she said with a tap of her fan on Olivia's arm. "If that dreadful woman had decamped from Brussels like everyone else who anticipated battle, I never would have met you."

"Indeed you would not. For it is certain we couldn't have met in London. Not even Mrs. Bottomly would dare to aspire so high."

The woman turned her bright eyes on Olivia. "And how do you know that?"

Olivia's smile was placid. "Your gems are real."

Her friend gave a surprisingly full-throated laugh that turned heads. Olivia saw the attention and instinctively ducked.

Her companion suddenly straightened. "Grace!" she called with a wave of her fan. "Over here!"

Olivia looked up to see a tall, almost colorless redhead turn and smile. She was in the same serviceable gray as Olivia, although the cloth was better. A sarcenet, possibly, that did nothing but wash out whatever color the young woman had in her plain features.

Then she began walking toward them, and Olivia realized that she limped badly. Must have danced with the wrong clod, Olivia thought, and moved to offer her seat.

Her companion quietly held her in place. "Grace, my love," she caroled, her hand still on Olivia's arm. "What have you heard?"

The tall redhead lurched to a halt right in front of them and dipped a very fine curtsy. "Word has come, Your Grace. Fighting has commenced in Quatre Bras, south of us."

Your Grace? Oh, sweet God, Olivia thought, feeling the blood drain from her face. What had she done?

Unobtrusively, she searched the room for Mrs. Bottomly and her daughters, but suddenly it seemed the entire crowd was in her way. Many of the officers now milled about uncertainly. Young girls wrung their hands and chattered in high, anxious tones. Wellington himself was speaking to the Duke of Richmond, and both looked worried.

It had begun, then. The great battle they had all been expecting for weeks was upon them. Awfully, Olivia felt a measure of relief. She would be invisible again.

"Ah well, then," the duchess said, climbing to her feet. "It seems our time for frivolity is over. *Noblesse oblige* and all that. Before we go, Grace, come meet my new friend."

Olivia stood and was surprised to see that the duchess came only to her shoulder. And Olivia was only of medium height.

"I'm sorry we didn't have time to share more observations," the petite beauty said to her with a gamine smile. "I think we could have thoroughly skewered this lot."

Olivia dipped a curtsy. "It has been a pleasure, Your Grace."

The duchess lifted a wickedly amused eyebrow. "Of course it has. Although by morning you will be notorious for speaking with me. 'Oh, my dear,' they'll all whisper in outrage, 'did you hear about that nice companion, Miss...' "

The little duchess suddenly looked almost ludicrously surprised. "Good God. I can't introduce you after all."

Olivia froze. Had she finally recognized her?

"We never exchanged names," the duchess said, laughing. "I shall begin. I, for my sins, am Dolores Catherine Anne Hilliard Seaton, Dowager Duchess of Murther." She wafted a lofty hand. "You may respond with proper gravity."

Olivia found herself wondering at such a young dowager as she dipped a curtsy of impeccable depth. "Mrs. Olivia Grace, Your Grace."

"Good Lord," the duchess said, her eyes wide. "I'm a

grace, you're a grace, and, of course, Grace is a grace. A *real* grace, mind you, in all ways." She patted the tall girl halfway up her arm. "Introduce yourself and make the irony complete, my love."

With a smile that softened her long face, the redhead dipped a bow. "Miss Grace Fairchild, ma'am."

"Grace is the daughter of that grossly bemedaled Guards general over there with the magnificent white mustache," the duchess said. "General Sir Hillary Fairchild. Grace is one of those indomitable females who has spent her life following the drum. She knows more about foraging for food and creating a billet from a cow byre than I know about Debrett's."

Olivia exchanged curtsies. She liked this plain young woman, who had the kindest gray eyes she'd ever seen. "A pleasure, Miss Fairchild."

"Please," the young woman said. "Call me Grace."

"And I am Kate," the young duchess said. "Lady Kate, if the familiarity sticks in your craw. But never duchess or my lady or Your Grace"—she shot a glare at Grace Fairchild—"for how would we tell each other apart? Which would be unconscionable among friends. And we are friends, are we not?"

Olivia knew better than to agree. "It would please me immensely," she said anyway. "Please call me Olivia."

"Shall we see you later at Madame de Rebaucour's, Olivia?" Grace Fairchild asked. "She is organizing the ladies of the city to help prepare for the anticipated wounded."

"Never let it be said that I am completely without useful skills," Lady Kate boasted. "I've become absolutely mad for rolling lint."

"If my employer gives me leave, you can expect me there," Olivia said, casting an eye out for that lady among the crowd.

Lady Kate gave her a wicked smile. "Oh, I can assure you she will. Simply tell her you accompany a duchess." Flinging her zephyr shawl around her shoulders, she made to go. "We shall all help, like the heroines we are."

"And sully those exquisite white hands?" a man's voice demanded from behind Olivia.

Olivia froze. Shock skittered across her skin like sleet.

"Since these are the only pair of hands I own," Lady Kate was saying lightly, "I imagine they will just have to adapt."

Olivia couldn't move. Sound suddenly echoed oddly, and movement seemed to slow. Lady Kate was looking just past her to where the man who had addressed her obviously stood, and Olivia knew she should turn.

It wasn't him. It *couldn't* be. She had escaped him. She'd hidden herself so thoroughly that she'd closed even the memory of him away.

"A generation of young exquisites would go into mourning if you suffered so much as a scratch," he was telling the duchess in his charmingly boyish voice.

Still behind her, out of sight. Still possibly someone who only sounded terrifyingly familiar. Olivia desperately wanted to close her eyes, as if it could keep him at bay. *If I don't see him, he won't be there.*

She knew better. Even if she refused the truth, her body recognized him. Her heart sped up. Her hands went clammy. She couldn't seem to get enough air.

And there was no escape. So she did what cornered animals do. She turned to face the threat.

And there he was, one of the most beautiful men God had ever created. A true aristocrat with his butter-blond hair, clear blue eyes, and hawkish Armiston nose, he stood a slim inch below six feet. His corbeau coat and oyster silk smalls were only a bit dandified, with a silver marcella waistcoat, half a dozen fobs, and a ruby glinting from his finger. He was bestowing an impish smile on the duchess, who seemed delighted by it.

Olivia had once thought that his handsome looks reflected a kind soul. She would never make that mistake again.

"Dear Gervaise." Lady Kate was laughing up at him. "How thoughtful to persist in your delusion that I am a fragile flower."

His grin was disarming, his laugh like music. "Been thoroughly put in my place, haven't I? Daresay you'll ignore my heartfelt wish to safeguard your looks, and then where will you be when they're gone?"

Lady Kate laughed again and held out her hand to him. "Doing it up much too brown, Gervaise. You know full well that I'm content simply being outrageous. I'll leave you to hold the torch for natural perfection."

Gervaise bent over Lady Kate's hand, but suddenly he wasn't looking at her. He had just caught sight of Olivia.

She was probably the only one who caught the quickly shuttered surprise in his eyes. The glint of triumph. She wanted to laugh. Here she'd been hiding herself from judgmental mamas, when there had been a viper in the room all along.

"It seems I arrived just in time," he said, straightening with a delighted smile as he shot his cuffs. "As quickly as this place is emptying, I might have missed you all. I know Miss Fairchild, of course, Kate, but who is this?"

"Make your bows to Mrs. Olivia Grace, Gervaise," Lady Kate said. "Olivia, this is Mr. Gervaise Armiston. He is about to take me over to the door so I can see off our brave soldiers. I have no brave soldiers of my own. Only Gervaise."

Gervaise chuckled good-naturedly and extended an arm. "I also live to serve, Kate," he protested. "It's just that I only serve you." Giving Olivia a quick bow, he nodded. "Mrs. Grace."

Olivia swallowed against rising bile. "Mr. Armiston."

Lady Kate rested a slim white hand on his midnight sleeve. "Excellent. Come, Gervaise. Let us now go and remind our soldiers what they fight for. Grace, Olivia...tomorrow."

The duchess had barely turned away before Olivia's legs gave out from under her, and she sat down hard.

"Olivia?" Grace Fairchild asked, her face creased in concern. "Are you all right?"

Olivia looked up, trying desperately to quell her nausea. Suddenly, from the streets below, military drums shattered the night. Trumpets blared, and the Duchess of Richmond rushed about the ballroom, urging the men not to leave until after dinner had been served.

"Just another hour!" she pleaded.

Officers lined up at the doors to get a farewell kiss from the lovely Duchess of Murther. Some girls wept, while others swept off to dinner with the remaining men. And in the corner where the chaperones sat, Olivia's world collapsed.

Her hands wouldn't stop shaking. She had to warn Georgie. She had to warn them all.

She couldn't. Any contact with them would lead Gervaise right back to them, and that would prove fatal.

Just as it had before.

Oh, Jamie.

Grace touched her shoulder. "Olivia?"

Olivia jumped. "Oh...," she said, trying so hard to smile as she climbed to still-unsteady legs. "I'm fine. I suppose it's time to go."

"You're sure you're all right? You're pale."

"Just the news." Gathering her shawl, she avoided Grace's sharp gaze. Pasting on a false smile, she turned. "I wish I were more like Lady Kate. Look how she's making all the men laugh."

Grace looked to where the duchess was lifting on her toes to kiss a hotly blushing boy in rifleman green. "Lady Kate is amazing, isn't she?"

"She's a *disgrace,*" one of the nearby women hissed.

Several other heads nodded enthusiastically.

"Glass houses," snapped a regal older woman at the end of the row.

Everyone looked over at her, but the woman ignored them. Reticule and shawl in hand, she rose imperiously to her feet. She was a tall woman, with exceptional posture and a proud face beneath thick, snowy hair. She'd taken only two steps, though, before she caught her toe and pitched forward, almost landing on her nose. Olivia jumped to help, but Grace was already there.

"Dear Lady Bea," she said, steadying the elegant woman. "Do have a care."

The older woman patted her cheek. "Ah, for the last Samaritan, my child. For the last Samaritan."

"That's *good,* Lady Bea."

"Indeed it is," the older woman agreed. Grace smiled as if she knew what the woman meant and ushered her on her way.

"Lady Kate's companion," Grace confided as they passed.

"Mrs. Grace!" Mrs. Bottomly screeched. She was bearing down on them like a particularly skinny elephant with her calves in tow. "We are leaving."

Peacock feathers bobbing, Mrs. Bottomly herded her hopefuls toward the door. Olivia had no choice but to follow. Lady Kate waved as Olivia passed and then hugged a burly dragoon. Olivia saw that Gervaise wasn't with the duchess anymore and instinctively knew where he would be. She almost turned back for the safety of the ballroom.

He was waiting for her, of course. Olivia had made it only a few steps into the hot night when he stepped out of the crowd.

"I've missed you, Livvie," he said, reaching out a hand. "You'll see me, won't you?"

Not a request. An order wrapped in etiquette. Olivia couldn't prevent the sick cold or trembling that beset her.

She could hold her ground, though. She could face him eye-to-eye. The days of downcast eyes and prayed-for escape were long over. "Why, no, Gervaise," she said just as amiably. "I won't."

And before he could respond, she swept down the steps and into the chaotic night.

THE DISH

Where authors give you the inside scoop!

♥ ♥

From the desk of Bella Riley

Dear Reader,

The first time I ever saw an Adirondack lake I was twenty-three years old and madly in love. My boyfriend's grandparents had built their "camp" in the 1940s, and he'd often told me that it was his favorite place in the world. ("Camp" is Adirondack lingo for a house on a lake. If it's really big, like the Vanderbilts' summer home on Raquette Lake, people sometimes throw the word "great" in front of it.)

I can still remember my first glimpse of the blue lake, the sandy beach, the wooden docks jutting into it, the colorful sails of the boats that floated by. It was love at first sight. My mind was blown by the beauty all around me.

Of course, since I'm a writer, my brain immediately began spinning off into storyland. What if two kids grew up together in this small lake town and were high-school sweethearts? What if one of them left the other behind for bright lights/big city? And what would their reunion look like ten years later?

Fast-forward fifteen years from that first sight of an Adirondack lake, and I couldn't be more thrilled to introduce my Emerald Lake series to you! After thinking she had left the small town—and the girl she had once been—behind forever, Andi Powell must return to help run Lake Yarns, her family's knitting store on Main Street. Of course everyone in town gets involved in a love story that she's convinced herself is better left forgotten. But with the help of the Monday Night Knitting Group, Nate's sister, Andi's mother and grandmother, and an old circus carousel in the middle of the town green, Andi just might find the love she's always deserved in the arms of the one man who has waited his entire life for her.

I hope you fall as much in love with the beauty and people of Emerald Lake as I did.

Happy reading,

Bella Riley

www.BellaRiley.com

P.S. That boyfriend is now my husband (Guess where we honeymooned? Yes, the lake!), and four years ago we bit the bullet and became the proud owners of our very own Adirondack camp. Now, just in case you're tempted to throw the word "great" around, you should know that our log cabin is a hundred years old...and pretty much original. Except for the plumbing. Thankfully, we have that!

♥ ♥

From the desk of Jane Graves

Dear Reader,

In HEARTSTRINGS AND DIAMOND RINGS (on sale now), Alison Carter has been stuck in the dating world for years, and she's getting a little disillusioned. In personal ads, she's discovered that "athletic" means the guy has a highly developed right biceps from opening and closing the refrigerator door; and that a man is "tall, dark, and handsome" only in a room full of ugly albino dwarves. But what about those other descriptions in personal ads? What do they *really* mean?

"Aspiring actor": Uses Aussie accent to pick up chicks

"Educated": Watches *Jeopardy!*

"Emotionally sound": Or so his latest psychiatrist says

"Enjoys fine dining": Goes inside instead of using the drive-through

"Friendship first": As long as "friendship" includes sex

"Good listener": Has nothing intelligent to say

"Likes to cuddle": Mommy issues

"Looking for soulmate": Or just someone to have sex with

"Loyal": Stalker

"Old fashioned": Wants you barefoot and pregnant

"Passionate": About beer, football, and Hooters waitresses

"Romantic": Isn't nearly as ugly by candlelight

"Spiritual": Drives by a church on his way to happy hour

"Stable": Heavily medicated

"Young at heart": And one foot in the grave
"Witty": Quotes dialogue from *Animal House*

Alison finally decides enough is enough. She's going to hire a matchmaker, who will find out the truth about a man *before* she goes out with him. What she doesn't expect to find is a matchmaking *man*—one who really *is* tall, dark, and handsome! And suddenly Mr. Right just might be right under her nose...

I hope you'll enjoy HEARTSTRINGS AND DIAMOND RINGS!

Happy reading!

Jane Graves

www.janegraves.com

♥ ♥

From the desk of Eileen Dreyer

Dear Reader,

I love to write the love story of two people who have known each other a long time. I love it even more when they're now enemies. First of all, I don't have to spend time introducing them to each other. They already have a history, and common experiences. They speak in a kind of shorthand that sets them apart from the people around them. Emotions are already more complex. And then I get to mix in the added spice that comes from two people who spit and claw each time they see each other. Well, if you've read the first two books in my Drake's Rakes series, you know that Lady Kate Seaton and Major Sir Harry Lidge are definitely spitting and clawing. In ALWAYS A TEMPTRESS, we finally find out why. And we get to see if they will ever resolve their differences and finally admit that they still passionately love each other.

Happy Reading!

Eileen Dreyer

www.eileendreyer.com

♥ ♥

From the desk of Amanda Scott

Dear Reader,

St. Andrews University, alma mater of Prince William and Princess Kate, was Scotland's first university, and it figures significantly in HIGHLAND HERO, the second book in my Scottish Knights trilogy, as well as in its predecessor, HIGHLAND MASTER (Forever, February 2011). The heroes of all three books in the trilogy met as students of Walter Traill, Bishop of St. Andrews, in the late fourteenth century. All three are skilled warriors and knights of the realm.

Sir Ivor Mackintosh of HIGHLAND HERO—besides being handsome, daring, and a man of legendary temper—is Scotland's finest archer, just as Fin Cameron of

HIGHLAND MASTER is one of the country's finest swordsmen. Both men are also survivors of the Great Clan Battle of Perth, in which the Mackintoshes of Clan Chattan fought champions of Clan Cameron. In other words, these two heroes fought on opposing sides of that great trial by combat.

Nevertheless, thanks to Bishop Traill, they are closer than most brothers.

Because Traill's students came from noble families all over Scotland, any number of whom might be feuding or actively engaged in clan warfare, the peace-loving Traill insisted that his students keep their identities secret and use simple names within the St. Andrews community. They were on their honor to not probe into each other's antecedents, so they knew little if anything about their friends' backgrounds while studying academics and knightly skills together. Despite that constraint, Traill also taught them the value of trust and close friendships.

The St. Andrews Brotherhood in my Scottish Knights series is fictional but plausible, in that the historic Bishop Traill strongly supported King Robert III and Queen Annabella Drummond while the King's younger brother, the Duke of Albany, was actively trying to seize control of the country. Traill also provided protection at St. Andrews for the King's younger son, James (later James I of Scotland), conveyed him there in secrecy, and wielded sufficient power to curb Albany when necessary.

We don't know how Traill and the King arranged for the prince, age seven in 1402, to travel across Scotland from the west coast to St. Andrews Castle. But that sort of mystery stimulates any author's gray cells.

So, in HIGHLAND HERO, when the villainous Albany makes clear his determination to rule Scotland no matter what, Traill sends for Sir Ivor to transport young Jamie to St. Andrews. Sir Ivor's able if sometimes trying assistant in this endeavor is the Queen's niece, Lady Marsaili Drummond-Cargill, who has reasons of her own to elude Albany's clutches but does not approve of temperamental men or men who assume she will do their bidding without at least *some* discussion.

Traill's successor, Bishop Henry Wardlaw (also in HIGHLAND HERO), founded William's and Kate's university in 1410, expanding on Traill's long tradition of education, believing as Traill had that education was one of the Church's primary duties. Besides being Scotland's first university, St. Andrews was also the first university in Scotland to admit women (1892)—and it admitted them on exactly the same terms as men. Lady Marsaili would have approved of that!

Suas Alba!

Amanda Scott

www.amandascottauthor.com